Life's Fortune

A Novel

SUSAN AMOND TODD

ISBN: 978-1-954614-92-5

Todd. Susan Amond.
Life's Fortune

Edited by: Amy Ashby

Published by Warren Publishing
Charlotte, NC
www.warrenpublishing.net
Printed in the United States

*This book is dedicated
to my husband, Bill.*

Acknowledgments

Due to several life events, this book has taken me longer to get to readers than I had ever anticipated. It feels so good and gives me a sense of accomplishment to at last be getting this book to print. I have to first thank Amy Ashby, my editor, for all her work and help, and Mindy Kuhn, my publisher. These two ladies make my dream come true with each book.

I've dedicated this book to my husband, Bill, for being dragged along this journey with me. Thank you, Bill, for putting up with all the days I hole myself in my writing room, still in my nightgown at four o'clock in the afternoon, drinking endless cups of tea; the weekend book signings; evening book clubs; research I need to do; and all the other stuff that comes along with being an author. I remember the day I told you I was writing a book and you said, "Oh, okay," and continued what you were doing. Surprise! Just one of many.

I have many other people I want to thank. As always, my local Barnes & Noble stores for support I've received from them as a local author, my daughters Elizabeth and Julianne who never waiver in the love and support they have given me, my Aunt Lois for telling me how proud she is of me and how proud my mom would be, my brothers Drew and David who are always there for me, Sue Dresser Marshall for being my friend and cheerleader for fifty-two years, Brian Kramp and Lynda Shuler for being sources of information for this book, and all of you who read my books and reach out to me. You make me want to write more. A special thank you to Claudia Leeflang for sharing her lemon pie recipe. It is Bill Todd tested and approved.

Life's Fortune is the first in a series of four books, followed by *Life's Surprises*, *Life's Blessings*, and *Life's Journey*. Also check out my other books, *White Lake* and its sequel, *Return Home*.

Please visit my website susanamondtodd.com for more information and sign up for my newsletter.

Follow me on Facebook (susanamondtodd) and Instagram (susanamondtodd).

Email me at info@susanamondtodd.com for programs and book clubs—I can meet virtually or in person—or just to contact me. I love hearing from my readers!

Most importantly, thank you for reading this book.

Chapter 1

'Tis the gift to be simple, 'tis the gift to be free,
'tis the gift to come down where we ought to be.
And when we find ourselves in the place just right,
'twill be in the valley of love and delight.

"Simple Gifts" was one of Rebekah's favorite hymns. She closed her eyes as the words of the song beckoned to her. In her imagination, she saw herself skip, sway, and twirl as the music filtered through her body. Led by her heart, she pictured herself moving ever so poetically down the aisle of the church where she sat at this moment.

She covered a spontaneous giggle with a cough as she thought about what the congregation's shock might be at her unconventional behavior if she did jump up and start dancing. *I'm sure people danced in Jesus' time,* she thought. In fact, *they even drank wine.* She had never had an alcoholic beverage in her life but always thought she might like to try one.

This thought, along with the many others that occasionally popped into her head, could only get her in trouble. Years ago, when she was rather young, she had overheard some of the church people talking rather passionately about the free thinkers out in the world who drank, gambled, danced, lived in sin, and did other unchristian things, sending them directly down a path to burn in hell. After hearing that conversation, she decided it best from now on to keep the thoughts that went through her head to herself.

Rebekah had been born into this small religious community and only mingled with free thinkers when she worked or had to conduct other business. She remembered many times she'd heard her father say how it was a shame the rest of the world wouldn't be saved by God like they had been. Rebekah was puzzled by this. Did her family really have a more direct line to God than anyone else? Didn't God love everyone? Of course, she'd never asked, for fear of being chastised like she'd seen happen to other people from their congregation who had voiced this and similar questions.

She would never forget how one day, as a curious young girl, she had asked her mom whether Jesus and Mary Magdalene ever married and had children. After she had been spanked till she cried, her mom got out the Bible so Rebekah could copy verses as a punishment. But that wasn't the end of it. She was scolded verbally by her dad when he came home as he expounded on her obvious "heathenism." She did not know what that word meant at the time, other than being sure it implied that she was a bad person.

When true simplicity is gained,
to bow and to bend we shan't be ashamed.
To turn, turn will be our delight,
till by turning, turning we come 'round right.

Rebekah came back to the present as the congregation sang the hymn's chorus. She briefly looked over at her parents on the other side of the church and then at the pulpit where her husband of almost eighteen years, Ethan Hayward— the pastor of the Faithful Shepherd Church—stood, leading the song with his strong tenor voice. He was handsome and charismatic—tall and lean, sandy brown hair with a very slight touch of gray at his temples, and his chocolate brown eyes contained a warm look of caring in them. What more could you want in a pastor or husband?

> *'Tis the gift to be simple, 'tis the gift to be free,*
> *'tis the gift to come down where we ought to be.*
> *And when we find ourselves in the place just right,*
> *be in the valley of love and delight.*

Soon they had reached the end of the song, which culminated with the singing of the first verse again. Oh, how she wished the Sunday church services were filled with just singing songs. *Now that's uplifting.* Not that Ethan's sermons weren't, it's just that, well sometimes he was a little self-righteous. Of course she didn't tell him that. She always made sure to tell him it was good if he asked after the service.

She took a deep breath and let it slowly out while she turned her attention to the congregation in the sanctuary. Those present in the pews, all of them more than ready to hear what message their pastor would bestow on them this week, looked to Ethan with admiration as he stood tall and smiling from high up in the pulpit.

Ethan would usually start writing his sermon for the upcoming Sunday on Wednesday mornings. He occasionally asked Rebekah to read what he wrote when he was finished, just to see what she thought. She always told him it was great no matter what she *really* thought, having learned from experience that he didn't actually want to know her opinion unless it was one of praise. He took any suggestion she made so personally, and he would always ask her if she had any idea how hard he had worked on it.

He was so insecure sometimes.

She looked at Ethan from her seat in the sanctuary with admiration and a smile on her face, where in reality, the melody of the hymn they had just sung was running through her head as if on a continuous loop—her mind miles away. She envisioned herself barefoot on the side of a mountain in the middle of a field of flowers displayed in every color of the rainbow, wearing a pink cotton sundress with dainty white polka dots, feeling the warmth of the sun on her. Her tanned face was turned upward as she moved freely to the rhythm of the music, twirling about through the flowers. Her vision was a stark contrast from the present. In reality, it was late January, and she lived in northeastern Wisconsin on the edge of the Nicolet National Forest, where there was so much cold and snow around her, she thought summer couldn't come fast enough.

A clang got her attention as the brass collection plates began making their way across the pews, and she realized the sermon was over. Rebekah didn't enjoy the next hymn they sang as much as the first one, which was still running through her head, but she joined the singing anyway and placed her envelope with her tithe in the plate that passed in front of her. It seemed kind of strange for her to put money in the plate when the congregation used that very money to help pay Ethan's salary, but it's what was expected of her.

Soon the service was over, and they all headed to the fellowship hall for lunch, a church tradition the third Sunday of the month in the winter. Rebekah looked forward to this because it gave her a chance to visit with people she had known since she was a little girl.

She would always hang back in the sanctuary on Sunday after the service was over so Ethan could have his moment to shine. He had grumbled that too many people always wanted to talk to her, providing less opportunity for him to connect with the congregation; so, to keep the peace *and* keep her husband happy, she made sure she was always the last soul to leave the sanctuary into the narthex. He lived for the moment after the service where he was able to interact with the congregation and hear how much they enjoyed his sermon and how fortunate it was to have such a talented minister.

As she sat alone in the pew waiting for her time to leave, a voice came from behind. "We haven't seen much of you other than at church, Rebekah."

"Come sit with me, Mom." Rebekah turned to her mother Ruth standing in the aisle and patted the spot next to her. Rebekah seemed to never do anything right when it came to her mother, resulting in a so-so relationship between the two.

"Dad and I were just talking last night about how we never see you around home," her mom said as she maneuvered down the pew. "Your brothers are around all the time."

Rebekah had four brothers—Thomas, Jacob, Benjamin, and Stephen—who worked with her dad at Boulanger &

Sons Auto Repair, the family business that bore their name. The boys were older than Rebekah, ranging in age from five to ten years her senior. She also had a sister three years older than her, Dorcas, whom she loved dearly. Rebekah called her Dee. Sadly, their parents had forbidden them to bring up Dee's name after Dee had disappeared one night, almost twenty years ago, following an argument with their mom and dad. A day never went by without Rebekah wondering where Dee was and why she had left, praying she would come home to them one day.

"I'm just busy with work and home life. Business has been good at the store," she said.

Rebekah and Ethan couldn't survive on just what the church provided, so she continued to work full-time in the bakery of a local gourmet grocery store to help supplement their income. She had started working at the store as a cashier when she was sixteen years old, moving to the bakery after she and Ethan had married, and eventually became the bakery manager.

Rebekah was talented and creative when it came to baking. The owner of the store, Fred, encouraged her to experiment, and as a result, when word had gotten out about the unique cakes, pastries, and baked goods she created, business had picked up in the store. Her secret dream was to one day have a bakery of her own.

"I don't understand why Ethan allows you to continue to work there," Ruth said, shaking her head slightly as she quickly inhaled then exhaled. "Why would you even want to work there when your dad would give you a job at his place? I can't imagine some of the people you have to deal with. We need to stick together."

Rebekah had heard this from her mom regularly for years, especially after she had taken over managing the store bakery. The last thing she wanted to do was work at her dad's auto shop. She needed some space. The bakery was her other life—an escape. She couldn't live without it.

"They pay me well, and I love what I do, Mom. I've told you this before. It's not a matter of Ethan allowing me to work there; I *want* to work there, and it's a source of income we need for our family."

When Rebekah had married Ethan, he already had two boys from a previous marriage. His wife had died in a car accident when the boys were very young—so young they didn't remember her. Though they'd tried to have a child together, Rebekah was never able to conceive one. So Ethan's motherless boys became her own. She was proud of the young men they had become and felt it a blessing that she was their mother.

Rebekah looked to the back of the church and saw the last two people in line waiting to talk with Ethan. "Come on, Mom. Let's go downstairs to help in the kitchen." And with that, mother and daughter headed to the door.

Below the sanctuary and the church office was a large basement area with several rooms sectioned off along one side to be used for classes. The other side held a small kitchen and several bathrooms, leaving the center area for the fellowship hall. The church was old, and none of it was fancy, but it all worked well for their needs. By now, most everyone had migrated to the fellowship hall, where a long table held paper plates, utensils, cups, and napkins on one end, with salads, casserole dishes, and desserts—made with love by the congregation—filling the rest. Several smaller round tables covered in white cloths were set up around the room so the church's members could sit and eat.

The group waited patiently for Ethan to bless the food so they could start filling their plates. Finally, Ethan appeared and stood at one end of the table with his hands out and his eyes closed. Everyone in the room closed their eyes and bowed their heads as the pastor began to speak.

"Lord, we are grateful for this time of fellowship and this fine group of people you have brought together. We ask that you bless us, especially those who have lovingly prepared the sustenance we are about to partake in. You are a mighty God who has favored this group of people with Your Approval. Be with us as we celebrate Your Glory in this time we are together. In Your Name, Amen."

Everyone echoed the "amen" as they moved smoothly into a line where they patiently waited to peruse the table, hoping the dish that held their favorite wasn't empty when their turn came.

Rebekah enjoyed watching everyone as they filled their plates and sat down. As she waited her turn in line, she gazed around the room, noticing a great-grandmother holding the newest baby in their family who had just been baptized the Sunday before, a grandmother entertaining her three young grandchildren while their mother fixed them a plate, and a table filled with teenagers much too cool to sit with their families. The scene warmed her heart and gave her a feeling of well-being.

She always sat with her parents, brothers, and their families—the lot of them taking up two or three tables, depending on how many of them were there on any given Sunday. Ethan didn't sit with her; he enjoyed taking turns sitting with a different family in the church each month so he could get to know them better and find out what was going on in their lives.

She scanned the room, seeing her father Darrell, and brother Stephen and his family with full plates, enjoying each other's company. Steve was her favorite brother, probably because he was the closest to her age. Steve, Dee, and Rebekah had always played together until he outgrew the girls, preferring to hang out with *his* friends instead. He had always kept a special interest in Rebekah though, especially after Dee left.

"Hi, Dad," she said as she arrived at the table. "Got a seat for me? Looks like you found something to your liking," she said, observing the mound of food on his plate. She sat down next to Steve, facing her dad.

"Oh, don't ya know I love these church potlucks, Rebekah. Best food ever." He shoveled in a fork of what looked like macaroni and cheese. "I like to get a little of everything on my plate," he muttered, his mouth full as he spoke.

Rebekah observed his plate, seeing more than a "little" of everything—and he hadn't even gotten to dessert yet. She turned to look at Steve, who rolled his eyes before they both turned their heads so their dad couldn't see them laugh.

"How's it going at the store, Rebekah?" Steve asked with a smile. He was always interested in her work.

"Good. I'm going to start doing wedding cakes this year. Kind of excited about that. They're going to send me to a class in Green Bay this spring so I can learn the new special techniques and get some tips."

"I'm proud of you, sis. People have been talking about your creations. I think you should consider yourself an artist from what I hear. Hey, how about making your poor old brother here a birthday cake for my next one?" Steve laughed and put an arm around Rebekah's shoulder.

"I promise," she said, raising her right hand. She was grateful to have him as a brother.

Church events were the only times she really ever saw her whole family since everyone was busy with their own lives. Times like this when they were together, she often wondered what it would be like if Dee were still there. They had been so close. Why wouldn't their parents talk about her? If anyone knew anything about why Dee left and what had happened the night she did, they never said it. But surely someone did know. Maybe one day Rebekah would get up the nerve and press her mom about the situation. How could a mother not know where her daughter was?

When they finished eating, the men sat around talking while the kids played and the women cleaned up. Doing the cleanup together helped make the work fun and quick. Most of the women would see each other at the Tuesday morning Bible studies Ethan led for those ladies who didn't work outside the home. But on the first Sunday evening of each month, all the women of the church would get together for Women's Group in the church fellowship hall to eat, sing, and talk. Rebekah looked forward to those Sunday nights and tried to never miss a meeting.

After everything was all cleaned up, Rebekah said her goodbyes to everyone and bundled up for the snowy drive home. Ethan would stick around to lock up the church after the last person left. The last hanger-on usually departed midafternoon, which meant she would have the house to herself for a couple of hours. This gave her a little time to read some of a book her coworker Tammy had lent her. It was written by a favorite author of hers who wrote Victorian murder mysteries. She usually was only able to read at work and some afternoons when Ethan wasn't home since Ethan felt reading anything other than the Bible—or related books—to be a waste of time. She didn't agree and figured he didn't have to know.

When she got home, she turned the heat up to get the chill out of the air, then changed into some comfy, warm clothes and made a cup of tea. She would sit in the front room, curled up in a chair with her book and a soft, cuddly blanket so she could see Ethan pull into the driveway. This would allow her enough time to make her getaway and stash the book back into the bottom of the canvas bag she brought to work with her every day. She knew he would never look in there.

As she sat down in an overstuffed chair, getting cozy with the book, tea, and blanket, she smiled, took in a deep breath, and let it out. After several sips of her tea, she eased into relaxation, then closed her eyes and thought prayerfully—*It truly is the little things in life that make one happy.*

Chapter 2

Alight snow was falling as Rebekah drove down the empty highway that was bordered on either side by forest. The clock in her car said 3:45 a.m., and by the look of it, she was the only human on the road as she started her day.

Being a baker meant you worked early mornings to get your goods ready and available for customers. She did this every day except Wednesdays—and Sundays, of course. Her staff consisted of an assistant manager, an afternoon manager, and four other bakers she scheduled as needed throughout the week. She also managed six people who waited on bakery customers.

Ethan insisted she not work on Sundays because it would set a bad example for others. She was a minister's wife, after all, and he needed her for support at church on Sundays. She'd worked it out so she had the day off, but if one of her assistants were ever on vacation or sick, she would have to fill in. Ethan agreed to this compromise—reluctantly—saying she was putting him in an "uncomfortable position." Rebekah knew, although Ethan would never admit it, that the extra money had won out.

One time at church, she overheard him explain to someone the reason she hadn't been at church the Sunday before was because a poor coworker of hers had a family crisis. He told the woman Rebekah's heart compelled her to work that day in an effort to relieve the woman's suffering. Rebekah rolled her eyes when she heard him. Whatever he felt he had to say, she didn't care.

The store she worked for, Fred's Market and Café, was open 6:30 a.m. to 9:00 p.m. and had, over the years, evolved from a local grocery store to more of a gourmet market with specialty grocery items, a bakery, deli, café, and coffee bar. She managed the bakery, and Fred's son Michael, who Fred was grooming to one day run the store, had managed the deli ever since he finished college.

In the morning, as she got ready for work, Rebekah would only have a cup of coffee, saving room for all the taste testing that had to be done once the freshly baked items started coming out of the ovens. She should have been overweight but was still the same size she had been in her early twenties. *Must be good genes*, she figured.

The drive from her house to where she worked took about forty-five minutes—sometimes less, sometimes more—depending on the time of year. Before she left during the winter months, she always pulled out her phone and checked the weather to make sure there weren't any surprise snow flurries up ahead. Her parents criticized her and Ethan—not to Ethan's face of course—because of the electronic devices they used. Her mom and dad thought electronics the work of the devil. Ethan insisted that she and their college-aged sons, James and Andrew, have cell phones for "security and safety," but it was clear he really liked using them himself.

Each day as she drove down the highway at this time of the morning, Rebekah was able to appreciate the things a person normally didn't see once the sunshine penetrated the dark forest on either side of the road. Day by day, the route she drove every morning provided her with a different picture as the seasons changed. She loved the sight of a doe guiding its newborn fawn through the trees for the first time or the sight of birds as they frantically prepared for their day. These simple glimpses of nature put a smile on her face and a warm feeling in her heart. One time she had seen a bear in the middle of the highway, at a distance, lumbering straight toward her. Uncertain of what to do, she pulled over, honked her horn, and flashed her lights. Startled by her actions, the bear opened its mouth wide, showing its teeth as it proceeded forward. When just a hundred feet away, it jumped about a foot off the ground and did an about-face into the forest as it howled in fear. She laughed in relief, doubting he would come near the road again.

This morning's drive was uneventful, and when she arrived at work, the store parking lot contained only a few cars belonging to several of her fellow coworkers who also started early.

Rhinelander, where she worked, was the largest city close to where she lived. She liked working there because it was far enough away from home that no one knew her as the preacher's wife, only as the woman who ran the store bakery. Rhinelander was still considered small with a population of about 7,500 people, but it seemed big to Rebekah, who had never even left the state of Wisconsin. True, she'd been to the Upper Peninsula of Michigan, or the "UP" as it was called by people in the area, but didn't feel that counted since it really seemed like an extension of Wisconsin.

Her life had been uneventful and sheltered, having been homeschooled with other kids from their church ever since she was small, all the moms taking their turn as teacher. As a result, she didn't meet many other kids. This was the life she had known until, at age sixteen, she took a job at Fred's Market and discovered a whole new world.

Her best friend, Tammy Jankowski, was her assistant manager. Rebekah had first met Tammy when she started working at Fred's as a cashier. Tammy had been five years older, already an adult, whereas Rebekah was just a teenager. Rebekah believed she gravitated toward the woman because Tammy helped fill the void inside after Dee had left just one year prior. Dee and Tammy were nothing alike, but Rebekah had always felt the same kind of sisterly love toward Tammy.

Tammy loved to tell the story of how she had met her husband, Spencer, on day one of an annual event in Milwaukee called Summerfest. She and several girlfriends were excited to hear Alabama—one of their favorite country bands—and noticed a group of guys who always seemed to be in the same place they were. One guy kept looking at Tammy, and when their eyes at last locked, he raised his beer can and smiled at her as if he could read her mind. He was the cutest-looking guy she had ever laid eyes on, so after she'd had a few beers herself, she got up enough nerve to go over and ask him why he kept staring at her. At this point in the story, Tammy would always put both hands over her heart, pause, and close her eyes for a moment before looking back at whomever she was telling the story to. Spencer replied that he had never seen a woman as beautiful as her before. She had been just eighteen at the time, and now, each time she told the story, she would always make it clear to her audience that she had met Spencer *before* Wisconsin raised the drinking age to twenty-one.

Spencer was from Rhinelander. He and his buddies stayed at a local hotel for three days of the fest. Fortunately, he and Tammy had all three of those days to fall in love. On the last day, Spencer asked her to marry him and she said yes. Tammy's parents were beside themselves and insisted they have a church wedding, preceded by a respectable engagement time, of course. The couple agreed. What her parents didn't know, however, was that when Tammy later went up for a five-day trip to Rhinelander to meet Spencer's family, she spent the first two days rendezvoused with Spencer at a motel in Appleton. Spencer had told his parents he needed to go to Appleton to help out a buddy of his.

When Tammy turned up pregnant, the respectable engagement time went out the window. They were then married—still in a church—but within four months of meeting each other. Their first child was born before their first anniversary, and another child followed every two years thereafter until baby number four, at which point Tammy said "enough" and got her tubes tied. She had said there was no way she could give up sex and, to this day, still thanked God in her prayers every night and morning for the doctor who had performed the procedure so she would never again need worry about getting pregnant.

As Rebekah walked into the store and toward the bakery, she thought about Tammy and what it must be like to have given birth to that many kids. That's when she heard the familiar, friendly voice.

"Good morning, sunshine," said the positive, enthusiastic voice. Sitting at a table was the always smiling Tammy, with her curly, blonde, highlighted hair, a blue mug in one hand and her phone in the other. The mug's large, rainbow-colored lettering read Life's a Beach. "I got the coffee started first, and then I turned on the ovens and the fryers," she informed Rebekah. Tammy took a slow drink from her mug and set down her phone. "I was just checking the lottery numbers from last night."

"Great. Did you win? What time is it? Am I late?" Rebekah asked one question after another, not waiting for an answer as she peeled off her knit hat and stuck it, along with her gloves, into the pockets of her heavy winter jacket. Next, she unwrapped the scarf around her neck and pulled it through her right sleeve enough for it to stay there as she began to take off the jacket.

"No, I didn't win," Tammy said with a tone of disappointment in her voice, "and I'm just early today. Hey, yesterday was really busy for a Sunday. I'm thinking we may need to schedule another person to help just on the weekends when summer rolls around. I mentioned it to Fred yesterday, and he said he would talk to you today about it. Just giving you a heads-up," Tammy said as Rebekah passed her.

Rebekah went in the back to hang up her coat. She grabbed her apron and her pastel floral mug with All Is Possible Through Love emblazoned across it in bright pink letters. She filled the mug with freshly brewed coffee and a little flavored creamer. They had roughly two hours until the bakery opened.

Over time, the success of the bakery had prompted Fred, the owner of the store, to allocate a section between the bakery and deli for a little café with wrought iron tables and chairs that connected the two areas to bring in more business. In the summer, there was an area outside where people could sit as well. Customers could buy deli and bakery items to take home, or they could have a sandwich made to order and pick out a dessert as they relaxed in the café.

Fred had given Rebekah free rein in the bakery to create whatever she wanted. Over time, she had evolved the bakery's offerings from take and bake, and frozen and ready for the oven items to one-of-a-kind specialty baked goods, custom decorated cakes, and other experiments she came up with. It was Fred's plan for the bakery to branch out into wedding cakes that upcoming year, having seen the opportunity to use Rebekah's talents even more.

It was exciting for Rebekah to feel not only the confidence but also the freedom to do something she loved every day. Her family knew she was good at baking but had never fully understood the passion she had for it. Her work at the store made her feel special. *Everyone needs to feel like there is something special about them.* She had read that in a book once and never forgotten it.

"Hello … Rebekah?" Tammy said and waved her hand to get her friend's attention.

Rebekah realized she had been somewhere else and hadn't heard a word Tammy said. She laughed and replied, "I'm sorry. Lost in my thoughts. What did you say?"

"I said, did you buy any lottery tickets for the drawing tonight? It's a big one."

"Yes, I did. How great would it be to win that?" Tammy had her attention now.

"Well, it sure would," Tammy said, taking a big drink from her mug and gazing out into the store. "First thing I would do is quit my Friday night bartender job at the tavern and then buy a bigger house, a fancy new car for me, and some big-ass, black truck with shiny chrome and huge, fancy wheels for Spencer. Oh my God, I can see the look on his face. Good thing I got my tubes tied because if I win, I might not come out of the bedroom for a week while he shows me his gratitude." Tammy's infectious laugh soon had Rebekah giggling with tears in her eyes as Ann and Betty, two of the three bakers she had scheduled for the morning, walked in.

Tammy's laughter subsided at the sight of them, prompting her to pull a napkin out of the table dispenser to wipe her eyes. "Fun time's over. I guess we better get to work," she said.

Tammy turned to the two young women, who looked not quite awake yet, as she and Rebekah stood up to get to work. "The ovens should be ready for the bread by now, so how about one of you come with me to pop the loaves in and the other go to help Rebekah," Tammy said, motioning to Betty to come with her.

"Okay, I think it sounds good," Rebekah said, slipping her apron around her neck and tying it around her waist. "Then, when you two get the bread in the ovens and set the timers, come help us get the rest in."

As Rebekah put the bread pans into the oven, she started thinking about the lottery. One day, after Rebekah had been married for several years, Tammy told her she should try buying a lottery ticket because "you never know." Rebekah had objected, telling Tammy if her husband ever found out about the tickets, she knew he would not understand or approve.

"Really? Why would he care?" Tammy had responded, quite puzzled. What Tammy didn't understand was that buying lottery tickets was unacceptable to a minister who preached against gambling and other sins. But Tammy always had a solution to a problem. "You just don't tell him," she said with a chuckle.

"But what if I win?" Rebekah asked, not sure how she would pull it off.

"Trust me, if you win it big, he'll retire, and you guys will live happily ever after." Tammy flashed a big smile.

That, Rebekah knew, would not happen—especially the happily-ever-after part. Tammy had no idea about the dynamics of Rebekah's life away from the store. Tammy thought everyone had a life like her own—one where you always had fun, your husband and family went out to eat or drink at a bar, and you hung out with friends. Rebekah envied Tammy at times.

One day, Rebekah had indeed bought a lottery ticket and some scratch offs—and then she did it again. And to her surprise and pleasure, she started winning regularly. Tammy said she had never seen anything like it before.

And then Rebekah panicked. The only place she had to keep her money was her work locker.

Tammy again had an answer. "We need to open you a little account over here at the credit union," she told her, "to keep your money safe. You can use my address on the account so no one's the wiser about it. Now the other problem you will have is tax time. You have to claim what you win … and then your husband will know."

"Oh, Ethan and I do our taxes separate, not together," she informed Tammy.

Trancelike, Tammy gazed off as she thought a moment or two. "Really?" she looked back at Rebekah, puzzled. "That's just odd. Why would you do that?"

"I'm not sure. Ethan said it was better for us financially. It might have to do with him being a minister. I don't know much about that kind of stuff, so I go along with it," Rebekah said. They had always done it that way, and she didn't think it unusual.

Tammy now furrowed her brow and pursed her lips before she spoke. "I wonder if he's up to something?" She paused a good while before she continued. "You don't think he's secretly playing the lottery too, do you? Boy that would be a good one." She shook her head and laughed. "Or has a secret life. You know, like one of those movies on the Lifetime channel. I love watching those."

Rebekah didn't know about the Lifetime channel. *Ethan? Secret life? Never.* He was about as straight as they come—to the point of boredom. "No, he wouldn't do that. He's so pious and good. He'll go straight to heaven; I'll be the one in hell." Rebekah chuckled, thinking of when she was a kid: Every time she did something her parents didn't approve of, they told her to be a good girl so she wouldn't burn in hell.

Tammy raised her eyebrows as she spoke in an even tone. "I don't ever want to hear you say that again. You are one of the most beautiful people I have met in my whole life. And sweetheart … there is no hell. Preachers like your husband use it to control us and make us feel guilty. I believe in a God with every cell in my body, and I know there is a power that loves me. I also know that same power would never burn me up in hell, no matter what. We just go on to another place better than this one."

"Okay, okay. I won't ever say that again."

"That's not enough, Rebekah! You have to believe it," Tammy said with conviction as she shook her head. "It's a good thing you met me." A finality lingered in her voice.

"I believe it. I promise," said Rebecca.

And at that moment, she did.

So Rebekah opened a checking account and, without fail, deposited her winnings—whether two dollars or *a lot* more. Nobody knew how much money she had but herself. But Rebekah knew Tammy would be shocked if her friend ever learned how much she had acquired. It turned out that Rebekah was *very* lucky.

Just how lucky, however, was Rebekah's secret.

***

Rebekah and Tammy would always leave work between 12:30 and 1:30 p.m. This had been helpful when James and Andrew were school-age. Before they started school, Rebekah's mother kept them until after nap time, and once they were in school, Rebekah was always home well before the bus came. Eventually, the boys were able to drive themselves to and from school. Both schedules had allowed her to take a little nap before they got home, a real treat since she was up so early every day.

James and Andrew were not homeschooled like Rebekah had been but went to public school instead. When the boys were young, she had noticed there was no longer a large enough concentration of children and mothers willing to teach in their community. And Rebekah was fine with that;

she didn't want the pressure of having to give up her job at the bakery to teach.

After the boys graduated from high school, both had gone away to college in Milwaukee as fast as they could to get out of the small-town environment—and the watchful eye of their father. Even though Rebekah was not their birth mother, she was the only mother they had ever known. Both boys loved her dearly for providing a buffer between themselves and Ethan and, in her opinion, his strict and unrealistic guidelines for the boys. This had created a special bond between them, and she was proud of her boys and their accomplishments.

Ever since they had been married, Ethan worked from home on some mornings, but would always head to the church in the afternoon. Now, with both James and Andrew away at school, Rebekah would come home from work to an empty house. She'd use the time to get caught up with household chores, make supper for she and Ethan, or go for an afternoon or sometimes an evening walk, as there were often programs going on at the church well after supper. Then she'd get to bed early so she could start it all over again the next day. Not too exciting, but it was her life.

***

The bakery cases were once again full for customers stopping in on their way to work, school, or elsewhere; those meeting with friends for business or lunch; or the few enjoying a moment to themselves in the café.

Sitting in the back office, Rebekah looked at the clock on the wall and saw her work day was coming to an end. As Rebekah was locking up her desk, Tammy came in.

"Hey, you ready to go?" Tammy asked.

"Yes, I guess so. Elizabeth and Julianne are here for the second shift, so we can take off," Rebekah answered. "I need to pick up a few groceries first, though. How about you?"

"I just have to get another ticket for tonight's lottery. I'm feeling *really* lucky," Tammy said with a chuckle as she rubbed her palms together and raised her eyebrows.

"You say that every time, Tammy." Rebekah patted Tammy on the arm as they both laughed.

The two women walked side by side out of the café, Tammy turning to the ticket counter and Rebekah grabbing a grocery cart to get what she needed.

That Tammy, she thought. How Rebekah loved her.

After Rebekah had checked out with her groceries, she swung by customer service and—thinking, *Why not?*—bought another random lottery number for that evening's draw. If she won anything, it would go into the checking account with her other money.

What was she going to do with all that money anyway? She sighed and swept the thought away as she headed out of the store. She had an idea what she wanted to do, but that was her own secret to keep.

She placed her grocery bags in the car and returned her cart to the cart corral. There, she noticed that all the snow piled up from plowing loomed like a mountain on one side of the parking lot. Even though the sun was shining strong in the cloudless sky, she knew there would be several more months of the snow pile, maybe more. Someday, she told herself, she was going to get away from here on a trip to somewhere warm but, as she traveled down the highway through the snow-covered landscape, her mind began to fill with her immediate life. She planned to wash the kitchen floor when she got home and had to figure out what to make for supper. As these thoughts invaded her mind, any idea she had of a warmer place began to fade away, totally forgotten by the time she pulled in her driveway.

Chapter 3

Rebekah Louisa Boulanger had been born on a warm July day—the sixth child in the Boulanger family and, hopefully, the last as far as her mother was concerned. She weighed a fairly average seven pounds, five ounces, with blue eyes and a full head of dark brown hair. From the moment Rebekah arrived in this world, if she wasn't sleeping, her big blue eyes were wide open and alert, taking everything in.

Her only sister, Dorcas, just three years old at the time, thought Rebekah was her personal baby doll and mothered the child constantly. Rebekah loved the attention from her big sister, making the girls inseparable as they grew up. It was, therefore, no surprise when Rebekah's first word wasn't "Mama" but "Dee," for Dorcas, since it was hard to say her big sister's name. This made Dorcas happy because she disliked her name. She felt it was old fashioned and had been teased by kids who shortened it to Dork. Darrell and Ruth Boulanger's intention had been to give all their children names from the Bible, but Dorcas never understood why they couldn't have picked a pretty name like Sarah or Naomi for her. Their four brothers, Tom, Jake, Ben, and Steve, also started using Dee, and soon, so had most everyone else.

Ruth, though, refused to go along with the rest of the family in calling her daughter Dee. Afterall, Ruth had been the one who picked the name Dorcas. Over and over, Ruth had told Dee how Dorcas in the Bible had been known for her good works and acts of love toward the poor and how, when Dorcas died, the Apostle Peter had come and raised her from the dead.

One time when they were older, Rebekah had said to Dee, "Just be happy they didn't name you Jezebel!"

Yes, that would have been worse.

***

Rebekah's father, Darrell, owned Boulanger's Auto Repair, a business that had been in the family for decades. Her grandfather had been the one to open the business, passing it on to her father, who intended to pass it to his sons. The family felt blessed by God to have had a successful business that would be a source of income for generations of Boulangers.

The Boulanger family had been long-time members of Faithful Shepherd Church since Darrell was a child. Because of this, most of the people Rebekah had interacted with while growing up were either relatives or members of the congregation—or both. Since the area they lived in wasn't heavily populated, the parents of their church decided to start a home school, which Rebekah and her siblings attended from kindergarten to twelfth grade. Like all the parents whose kids attended, her mother helped teach.

Growing up close to the Nicolet National Forest in Wisconsin was like living in God's country. The winters were freezing and harsh but still beautiful, and though the Boulangers enjoyed participating in cold-weather sports, there was nothing like summer. Summer activities were endless—swimming, fishing, camping, riding bikes on the trails—and the longer days were a kid's dream. They would get on their bikes in the morning and ride all day. Often their mom would pack them lunches, and they wouldn't be home until just before dinner.

Those were the days.

Darrell Boulanger and his four brothers had been born in the Upper Peninsula of Michigan. When his parents, Rebekah's grandparents, were newly married, they decided to relocate to Upper Michigan from the town of Châteauguay in Quebec, Canada, to start a new life, bringing their own parents, Darrell's grandparents, with them. He remembered his grandparents, who lived with them, speaking French when he was a little boy, but when he was elementary school age, he, his mom, dad, and brothers left the UP and moved down to Wisconsin, where everyone found it easier to just speak English. The only French words Darrell could recall from when he was a boy were *merci*, *oui*, and *s'il vous plaît*.

Many years before this, Rebekah's great-great grandparents on her father's side had immigrated to Châteauguay after leaving France, where their family had been in the bakery business for generations, making pastries, bagels, breads, and cakes. In France, the last name "Boulanger" meant you were a baker. So it was natural for them to do the same when they migrated to Châteauguay, where the family had remained in the bakery business until her grandfather's generation came along. Her grandfather and his siblings had not been interested in baking but wanted to do other things, resulting in Rebekah's grandfather moving to the UP and eventually moving to Wisconsin to make his own way. Her grandfather, whom Rebekah called Père, bought a big piece of property bordering the forest, where they all lived now, and started an auto repair garage. Père's other brothers went their way, also pursuing different professions and putting an end to the family baking tradition.

Rebekah's love of baking, therefore, had originated with her grandmother Marie Claudine, also known as Mère. When Rebekah was a child, they had always been in the kitchen, baking something together.

"Mère," she had asked her grandmother one day when they were making some madeleines, "why didn't you start a bakery on your own? You're so good at it, and you enjoy baking."

"A woman wasn't encouraged to go out on her own to do such a thing in my day. Only men opened businesses. So Père would have not allowed me to do so. I told him once I wanted to open a bakery myself, and he said no," she said rather sadly.

"I don't understand," Rebekah replied. Only eight years old and still quite innocent, this information puzzled her.

Mère smiled and took Rebekah's chin in her hand so their eyes would connect and not waver. "I like the way you think, *mon cheri*. Don't ever let anyone take your dreams away from you. You are my hope. The rest of the family are all the same, but you and Dee will make me proud someday. I'll be smiling down at you from heaven."

She kissed the top of Rebekah's head and let go of her chin but not before Rebekah saw tears pooling in her eyes.

At that moment, Rebekah felt as if there were endless possibilities ahead of her and she couldn't fail.

"I'll do it, Mère," she assured her grandmother. "I promise."

Mère contemplated for a good while, in silence, before giving Rebekah another kiss and a hug. Then she smiled and said, "Let's get back to our madeleines. I want to make sure you know how to make them perfect."

Mère had definitely favored Rebekah and Dee more than their brothers since their own mother seemed more interested in the boys than the two girls. So she took the two of them under her wing. When Rebekah was fourteen years old, Mère died, which created a big hole in Rebekah's life. Then Dee left home the next year, leaving Rebekah to fend for herself, and the hole grew even bigger.

***

Dee had left the month after her graduation from high school, just before Rebekah's fifteenth birthday. Late at night, after an argument with their parents, Dee had gone upstairs, packed a bag, and left, never to be seen again. She didn't even say goodbye to Rebekah. When Rebekah asked about what had happened, her mother first yelled something that Rebekah couldn't understand, then proceeded to cry. That was when her dad pointed a finger at Rebekah, telling her to never again mention Dorcas in his home.

And that was it.

Her parents may have put an end to her talking about Dee, but they couldn't control Rebekah's thoughts. She thought about Dee every day and prayed for her well-being—wherever she was.

***

It was around that same time that Rebekah had begun working at Fred's. Up until she met Tammy, she had led a sheltered life. With Tammy in her life, Rebekah's view of the world began to change.

Tammy was already twenty-one, married with children, and living a life so foreign to Rebekah, it was as if they lived in two different worlds. When asked by her parents if any of the people she worked with at the grocery store were heathens, Rebekah was smart enough to give the right answer: "I'm not really sure because I keep to myself and don't talk to them." This was just what her parents wanted to hear, though far from the truth.

Because her parents were so strict, Rebekah had never had a boyfriend growing up, which didn't bother her. With four brothers at home, she had no interest in bringing another male into her life. Other mothers who taught at the church told her all the time that she was very smart. And it was true; she did well in every subject never causing any problems. A "good girl," she enjoyed reading, but was never allowed to read anything but the Bible or novels that were deemed "appropriate" books for young women. Her family owned one TV, only used on special occasions and not for everyday watching.

When Tammy had found out Rebekah enjoyed reading, she began to share the paperbacks she read during breaks. These were not the type of books that would be on the approved-novels list at her school or permitted by her parents, so Rebekah kept them safe in her locker at work. Thus began her education about the interaction between men and women. She had seen animals procreating in the forest, but that was nothing like the men and women in these books. She wasn't sure she could ever do those things herself, but then again—maybe she could. The people seemed to enjoy themselves immensely, and something stirred inside her when she read them.

Rebekah had also been friends with Fred's third and youngest son, Michael, who also worked at the grocery store. He was a year older than Rebekah and possibly "had a thing for her," according to Tammy. Michael was tall and blond—not bad looking—and was hardworking as far as Rebekah could tell. Tammy told her he would take over the store one day. Rebekah found she enjoyed talking to Michael, who seemed to be very interested in talking with her also. She knew better than to think she could be anything more than a friend with him, though. Her parents would probably have made her quit her job at the store if she ever mentioned his name.

***

Rebekah had ended up graduating at the top of her class of ten students. She was seventeen and would turn eighteen that July. At that time, her future plans were to continue working at Fred's store while living at home. No one suggested that since she was so smart, maybe she should sign up for classes at the technical college or even consider a real four-year college. Nobody suggested it, of course, except Tammy.

For graduation, Tammy gave her a card with ten dollars in it and told her to do something crazy with it. Rebekah kept the card and money in her work locker, waiting for the "something crazy" to materialize. It was around this time that Tammy had also told her "to hell with your family." She said there were ways for people like Rebekah to go to college and that she would help her figure out what she could do. Rebekah wasn't sure what she wanted to do or if she wanted to do anything at all, but then she remembered her promise to make Mère proud. She told Tammy she needed some time to figure things out and that Tammy would be the first to know when she knew what she wanted to do.

***

One Sunday night in September of that same year, Rebekah's parents had said they wanted to talk with her about something. The previous winter, Reverend Pegram, the minister of their church, had fallen severely ill, so the congregation was forced to find someone else to lead them. They ended up hiring a twenty-four-year- old widower with two small boys ages three and five. The new minister had recently approached Ruth and Darrell about interest in Rebekah. Evidently, her father told her, the young pastor had been taken by her intelligence and maturity and, as a result, wanted to marry her.

Rebekah was in shock. In the few months he had been with their church, she had spoken very little with the man, if for no reason other than to be polite and welcoming. She thought he had been simply trying to get to know her as a member of the congregation. Now she realized he had been trying to get to know *her*. But how could she have known this, having no experience in these matters? There was nothing in the books Tammy had shared with her that would've given any guidance on someone she barely knew wanting to marry her. The characters in the books knew each other well—in the biblical sense.

"Your mother and I want you to accept," her father had stated firmly.

"I don't want to marry him," Rebekah responded, just as firmly.

Darrell stood up, walked a few feet away, and stopped with his back to Rebekah while Ruth spoke.

"Rebekah, it is an honor to have a man of God choose you to be his wife. This is a privilege and a blessing bestowed upon you and our family. Now it's not as if you have any prospects knocking your door down. You need to jump on this before his eye catches one of the other girls."

"Mom, I'm only just eighteen! I want to see some of life first. Have you considered that I might want to go to college? I'm not a dummy; in fact, I'm smart," Rebekah responded, not having ever said any of this before. She struggled to control the tears that she could feel wanted out.

"Where have you gotten these ridiculous ideas?" asked Ruth. "Nobody in our family has ever gone to college, so what makes you think you will? There is no money for college. If we could afford it, we would have sent one of your brothers."

"But, Mom—"

"*There is no money for college!*" her mother repeated. "Do you get it? This is the best deal you're going to get."

Then Darrell turned around. "Listen, young lady, you're going to marry him and live happily ever after, or you can get out like your sister, that ungrateful little whore."

Rebekah was stunned at her father's words but knew this might be her chance to find out what had happened. She stood in silence for a moment as she steeled herself for the question. She could feel herself begin to shake. "Why did

Dee leave?" she asked, her voice quaking slightly. "Why haven't you ever told me or any of us?"

Her father was motionless and stared at her for what felt like hours before he finally responded. "Don't ever say her name in this house again. You can ask *her* why she left, but first, you'll have to find her." With that, he left and slammed the door.

Her mother took a deep breath, then spoke as calmly as she could. "Rebekah, Reverend Hayward is a good man, and those two little boys are so sweet. You would be such a good wife and a good mother to those boys. Consider it and try to get to know Reverend Hayward a little more, then you'll see. It's not like he's a stranger. He's the preacher of our church. How much better can that be to have for a husband?"

Rebekah looked down, thinking about what had just been dropped at her feet, before she spoke. "You and Dad have thrown a lot at me, Mom. Despite what you say, I'm still just a kid. I need some time to process what you've said. I have dreams for myself, you know, to—"

"You have *dreams*? Well, forget them. It doesn't happen for folks like us. Go ahead and process all you want, but your dad means what he said. I would marry Reverend Hayward if I were you. There's no one else around here for you to marry, so grab him up, Rebekah." Then, with a sigh, she turned and left Rebekah alone in the room.

Rebekah had never expected that this would be what her parents wanted to talk to her about. She thought they were going to tell her they wanted her to quit her job at the store and take part in the family business or something similar, but not to marry somebody—especially their own preacher.

For the next several days, her dad wouldn't speak to or even look at her. Her mother acted like nothing was wrong, offering no guidance or support. Rebekah wished Dee were there, but she was beginning to realize that making wishes and believing in dreams were for kids. She thought about Michael from work. He was in college. Maybe she could find out from him more about what it would take to go to college herself. His dad was probably paying for it, but he might know what to do to get financial assistance. She thought she might also talk to Tammy, but then she thought better of it—feeling a little embarrassed about the whole thing—and decided it was best to keep it to herself.

Finally, it was the end of the week, and her boss, Fred, said he wanted to talk to her. *Oh no*, she thought. But unlike her parents' news, it turned out to be something good. He told her he wanted her to work a day or two in the bakery and asked if she was interested. She would even get a raise. She didn't hesitate in telling him yes and felt encouraged as she drove home. That's when a plan began to form in her mind.

The next morning, she paid Reverend Hayward a visit at his home. He answered the door with his two little preschool-aged boys at his side. She was used to seeing him in a suit and minister robes on Sunday mornings, but he was shoeless, dressed in jeans and a T-shirt, with uncombed hair, which made him look like an ordinary person. He didn't speak for a few moments, probably from the surprise of seeing her.

"Come in, Rebekah," he said and led the way to his living room. On one end was a devoted play area for James and Andrew, scattered haphazardly with trucks, cars, blocks, and books. Rebekah felt tenderness in her heart when the boys each grabbed a toy car, then came over to show and tell her about what they had. She didn't have much experience with kids, being the youngest in her family. Her mom did most of the babysitting for her nieces and nephews, so this gesture by the boys melted her heart. She couldn't help but love them.

"I came by to tell you my parents shared your proposal with me. I don't understand why you had to go through them and not speak to me, though." She was to the point, sitting straight and tall in her chair, and not about to dance around the matter at hand. She wanted him to know she made her own decisions, not her parents.

"Well, I guess I'm old fashioned and felt I needed to talk to your parents first," he responded, blushing slightly and looking down at his stocking feet.

"I think the person you're interested in should have some awareness of your interest. Reverend Hayward, nothing you have done or said since I met you has led me to believe there was anything between us. I'm in total shock and, quite frankly, *insulted* that you went behind my back." *There*, she thought, *that should show him I'm not some little girl who's going to be pushed around.*

The reverend drew in a deep breath. "I'm sorry, but that's why I've spent every chance I've had to speak with you. I want to get to know you—and you me."

She was totally puzzled now. How could she have been so naïve that she didn't realize he'd been trying to get to know her personally?

"I had no idea," she said and turned away, feeling a warmth flooding her face, afraid that he may notice her cheeks had reddened. Maybe it wasn't a good idea for her to have come over there after all.

"Rebekah, I'm so sorry. I'm really not very good at these things. Can we start over and do this the right way? I would like to take you out to lunch one day next week—somewhere not around here—so we can talk. No one has to know but us. You work in Rhinelander, right? I'll drive over any day you say, and we can talk."

She turned back toward him and could tell by his words and the look on his face he probaby wasn't very good at these things. Well, neither was she. Maybe she should give him a chance. The mere thought of marrying one of the few boys she had gone to school with made her shudder. Then, she looked over at the two little boys who were sitting on the floor, playing with their toy cars. She did want to get married someday and have children. What would it hurt to meet with Reverend Hayward? *It's just lunch,* she thought. That would work.

"Okay, Reverend, how about Monday afternoon at twelve-thirty? Say at JJ's Diner? It's down the road from where I work."

"Works for me. But I insist you call me Ethan,"

She felt a slight smile creep across her face. "Okay, Ethan."

***

Monday came, and she told Fred she had to run an errand around lunch time and needed to take an hour. When 12:30 rolled around, she met Ethan at the diner. He was sitting in a booth, facing her as she walked in. A huge smile spread across his face when he saw her, and he stood up to make sure she saw him. He then waited for her to sit down before he did.

"Hi," she said.

"Hi," he said, matching her tone. "Having a good day at work today?" he asked, the words coming out rather awkwardly.

"Um," she said, having never met a man for lunch before, "yes, it's been okay." She needed to get over this.

Before they could say anything else, the waitress arrived to take their order. After the woman had walked away, Rebekah spoke. They couldn't continue like this since she had to get back to work.

"I'm happy we could meet like this, and I'm not going to waste time because I only have an hour." She hesitated, collecting her nerves. "I'm not going to lie, I am interested in getting to know you better ... but I feel awkward," she said, briefly gazing at him once or twice as she mostly stared at the table.

"Can we maybe date and see where this goes?" he asked.

This was what she had been hoping for. He really was nice looking and had a manner about him she could appreciate. He wasn't from around the area, so it made him of more interest to her also. He was someone different, from the outside, someone who had maybe seen the world and would take her places.

"Yes, I think that would be good," she said as she looked into his brown eyes and smiled.

They had a little time to talk about themselves—he telling her about how much he enjoyed being a minister and a father, she sharing about her family and her job at the bakery—and soon it was time for her to get back to work.

"We'll do this again," he said, "but first I'd like to have you come to dinner at our house. I'll cook, of course," he added.

"That would be nice," she said. The men in her family had never cooked.

"This Friday night would be good. Nothing's ever going on at the church Friday nights, so I'm free to do what I want. Come by, let's say, about five thirty? It may seem early, but the boys need to eat early. I start heading them to bed at around seven or seven thirty. I would love it if you hung around after they go to bed—some adult conversation maybe," he said and chuckled.

"Sure. I love to bake. Could I bring dessert?" she asked.

"I never say no to that request," he said with a smile. "So I'll see you then?"

"Yes," she replied simply.

On her drive back to work, she thought, *This is going to be interesting.* She had never been on a date before or had a man invite her to his home to cook *her* dinner. *This is rather exciting*, she thought as she put her car in park and got out to go back into the store. She saw her reflection in the glass store window as she entered and thought she had a little glow on her face. She better get that under control before Tammy got a look at her. Tammy saw everything. Rebekah wasn't ready to share this secret yet.

On Friday night, Ethan made hamburgers and hotdogs on the grill for dinner—a favorite of the boys, he told her, but she guessed it was also easier for him—along with baked beans and potato chips. James, five years old, sat at the table and Andrew three years old, in a high chair. They were both pretty messy when they ate, but were well-behaved.

Her dessert was pretty fancy for the meal but something she enjoyed making: a four-layered, raspberry swirl cake, with raspberry jam and almond buttercream, decorated with more raspberries on top.

It was a big hit.

"Do you always bake like this?" Ethan questioned, almost in disbelief as he stared at the cake.

"Usually, though I can do better. My grandmother taught me everything I know. I come from a family of French bakers, so I guess I got the baking gene. I guess that's why I work in a bakery," she said, smiling with a glint of pride in her eyes.

She helped Ethan get the boys ready for bed and read their bedtime story before tucking them in. She had never done anything like this before and found she enjoyed it. James was in a big boy bed in his room, while Andrew slept in a crib in his own room. Rebekah and Ethan had gone to sit down alone in the living room when Andrew started crying and calling for Daddy.

"I'll be right back," Ethan said. "He probably threw his blanket or his favorite stuffed bunny out of the crib. It's a little game he plays sometimes, but yet he can't get to sleep without either." He excused himself, then left her alone.

She looked around the room. This would be her life and her home if she decided to marry Ethan.

They spent the rest of the evening getting to know each other. Ethan had come from upstate New York originally, not far from the Canadian border. The boys' mother had died in a car accident, and Ethan still had a hard time talking about it. He had been working at a church as an assistant minister at the time and felt he couldn't stay there anymore; everything reminded him of his wife. So he began looking for another church. He saw the ad for Rebekah's church, Faithful

Shepherd, in a church newspaper he received monthly and thought, *Why not?* So he sent his resume, interviewed, and was hired. He was very happy to serve their church.

Rebekah told him about the simple life she led and her family, a little about what she did at work, and before they knew it, the clock read 10:00 p.m.

"I have to work in the morning," Rebekah told him, "bright and early to start baking, so I better get home. It was nice having dinner with you and the boys. Thank you for inviting me."

"It was our pleasure. Maybe we can do it again?" Ethan asked.

"Yes, let's do it again," she replied.

When they reached the door, Ethan took the light jacket she had over her arm and held it open for her. She slipped her arms into the jacket, then turned to say thank you. But before she could utter a word, he leaned in and placed his hands on her shoulders, pulling her toward him before softly kissing her. *Her first kiss.* A warmth traveled through her body, and a flush entered her face. She hoped the dim light of the entryway would conceal any redness she could feel blossoming in her cheeks. His hands lingered on her shoulders after the kiss, and when she finally looked into his face, she found he wore a simple smile and a look of amusement in his eyes. What should she do next? What should she say?

"Good night" tumbled out of her mouth as she swiftly ran to her car, not giving Ethan a chance to say a word. On her drive home, she came to a stop sign. Since it was late and no one would be crossing her path, she sat at the sign for about five minutes, savoring what had just happened. She'd been kissed by a man, not a boy. She liked the way it made her feel … kind of special and grown up. She understood now what Tammy and the other girls at work were talking about when they shared the details of their relationships.

She continued on her way, and as soon as she got home, she scurried to her room and flopped into bed. She didn't want to face anyone with questions tonight. The house was quiet, so her parents must have been asleep. *Thank goodness.* Tomorrow would be here soon enough, and she would be bombarded by their probing interrogation.

As she lay in bed, she went over the evening in her head. It was fun. She did like Ethan's company—and he was rather handsome. Plus, his little boys were so sweet. She already loved them.

And then she thought of Michael from work. He did pay her a lot of attention. The other day he had told her that he and his friends went out to some place on the weekend for a couple of beers and to play pool. Maybe she would like to come also and meet all of them? She told him she was under the drinking age, but he said it didn't matter at the place they went to. *Oh, wouldn't that go over well at home*, she thought. She *would* have liked to get to know him better but knew her parents would never allow it. She could only marry someone they approved of.

Someone like Ethan.

She closed her eyes, taking a deep breath and slowly letting it out. Soon her mind stopped swirling as she fell asleep.

***

The wedding took place, of course, at Faithful Shepherd Church during the last week of December. Reverend Pegram rallied and said it was an honor to be able to marry them, this probably being the last wedding ceremony he would ever perform. They had no attendants—other than James and Andrew as ring bearers. The small wedding reception was held at the fellowship hall in the basement of the church. Rebekah's mom and several other family members provided food, but the cake was made by Rebekah herself. She wouldn't have trusted it to anyone else—except maybe Mère if she had still been alive. She was now Rebekah Hayward, barely eighteen-and-a-half, a married woman and an instant mother of two of the sweetest little boys on the planet.

Chapter 4

Nowadays, every day seemed the same as the day before. Another week of work was done, and here Rebekah was at church again, about to start the next week and all it would bring before her. On this particular Sunday, Ethan's postchurch meeting was with the church elders, so as always, she drove herself home, knowing it would be late afternoon before she would see him again.

Today was a cold but sunny day for the end of January, so after Rebekah had lunch, she decided to bundle up and brave the cold for a walk in the woods. She knew once she got moving, she wouldn't even notice that the temperature was not much above freezing.

The house and property they lived on backed up to the Nicolet National Forest, just like the home she'd grown up in and where her parents still lived. She was a real country girl and loved being out in nature, never having known anything else. Rebekah found that a walk through the forest on a day like this could regenerate her internal battery for days.

Down the road about a quarter of a mile, wide trails used by snowmobilers snaked through the woods. She always took advantage of these trails during this time of the year since the continual treading of snowmobiles prevented the snow from getting too high and allowed for good traction as she trekked along. As she got into a steady walking rhythm, she felt the cold, crisp air fill her lungs, eventually feeling as if it were stimulating every cell in her body.

The majority of the trees on the path were missing their foliage, allowing the sun to shine through the branches, which produced a pretty dapple effect on the snow at her feet. The sun's rays weren't strong enough to warm her body, but the bright light that rained down from the cloudless sky warmed her in a different way—it renewed her spirit and energized her soul.

About a mile down the trail was a lake where they would fish in the summer and winter. Fishing adventures always consisted of just James, Andrew, and herself. Rebekah found it odd how Ethan never liked to do things like that with his sons. She had been used to her brothers and dad going hunting and fishing together. That was where "men could be men," as her dad would say.

Then there were the Green Bay Packers. Her parents may not have allowed much TV watching when she was a kid, but they always tuned in for Sunday Packers games—no questions asked. And yet Ethan didn't care for the Packers at all—or any team or sport as far as she knew. She once overheard her brother Ben say to the others, "Something's wrong with that guy not being a Packers fan. I'm not sure we can trust him. He's probably a Bears or Vikings fan and afraid of the knowledge becoming public. You know, people might leave the church, and then he's out of a job! Everybody knows God's a fan of the Pack." They all laughed. Thankfully Rebekah's brothers and dad had taken her boys under their wings and made sure they had an appreciation for sports, including hunting, fishing, and the Green Bay Packers.

One thing was certain, Ethan loved his religion, and he spent most of his free time reading on the subject and writing in his study. He had been working on a book since before they were married, or so he said, although she was not exactly sure what it was about. When asked, he would say he wanted to keep it private until it was done and ready to be published. He did tell her the book would change the face of Christianity. *Okay*, she thought and didn't ask him anymore about it.

Having been lost in her thoughts, it felt like no time passed before she arrived at the frozen lake. There were several ice shanties off in the distance, and Rebekah noticed a few cars driving out to them. Once the ice was eight to twelve inches thick, people could drive on it, allowing them to haul their shanties out onto the lake. They then would pull them back in before the spring thaw started.

She went over to the big tree stump she liked to sit on whenever she came down to the lake. After brushing off the small amount of snow that had accumulated on the stump, she pulled her jacket down to cover herself before she sat. "Brrr," she said aloud. At times like this she found it helpful to think about something warm, like a bonfire or a stove top or, in this case, the seat warmers in her car.

She took a deep breath of the cold air into her lungs. The lake was always so pretty in the winter, though it never disappointed at any time of the year. Today it was frozen in time with its blanket of snow that would hang around till the spring, when it came alive again. Because the lake was in the National Forest, there were no permanent houses built around the body of water, leaving it untouched and natural. She pulled her cell phone out and took a picture so she could send it to the boys and maybe share it with Tammy at work tomorrow.

Next weekend, she decided, if it were sunny again, she would come prepared with warmer clothes and her boots with better traction to walk the whole perimeter of the lake on the ice. She always enjoyed that.

She had started some braised short ribs in her slow cooker before she left and planned on making the lemon meringue pie Ethan loved once she arrived home. *A nice spring dessert for a cold winter day*, she thought, and chuckled.

All of a sudden, a strong breeze blew past, sending a chill through her and she knew it was time to get going again. She would feel warmer once she started walking and her blood began pumping through her body.

She gave the lake one more look before she stood and headed home. "Hope to see you next week," she said aloud, then laughed at herself before heading back home along the wide-open trail.

Chapter 5

Because Rebekah didn't want anyone she worked with—including Tammy—to know about her luck when it came to the lottery, she had thought it better if she stopped at different grocery stores and gas stations around the Rhinelander area to buy her tickets and have them run through the ticket machine to find out what she won. The most she had ever won was $50,000, and she'd won $25,000 more than once. She eventually stopped counting the times she'd won between $5 to $10,000. Rebekah thought she was doing well.

Over time as she began to win, she started to feel uncomfortable when she went into the savings and loan Tammy had originally taken her to, so she only kept a small percentage of her money there. The people who worked there knew she and Tammy were friends, and Rebekah was afraid someone might make a comment about her luck—or worse—begin to question it. Hoping not to draw too much attention to herself, she decided to open accounts at two other banks and eventually started to deposit most of her checks and winnings at an ATM. That way, she didn't have to go into the bank at all. She decided it was better to stay as anonymous as she possibly could. The debit cards were kept in her locker at work and only removed when needed—in fear Ethan would find out.

She'd also had to open a P.O. Box when she started to win big amounts because anything over $500 had to be mailed to her. The whole thing had been quite complicated, but once she found a system that worked well for her, the process became easier.

On one rare occasion when Rebekah had decided to go into the bank to make a deposit, a young man approached her and said he could help her make even *more* money with what she already had in her account. This sounded appealing to her, so she let him start investing some of her winnings, and the money she won started making her more money.

She began to form a plan for the money. Her dream was to use it to open a bakery one day. How this would actually happen, she wasn't sure, but she knew if she kept the dream in her heart and believed, it would materialize. She knew in her heart this was to happen as sure as the sun would rise every morning.

She often wondered what Ethan would say if she told him about wanting to open a bakery. She figured he would say the same thing Père had told Mère: "No!" And if she told him, as she had often dreamed she would someday, well … a phrase came to mind that Tammy used all the time: "The shit would hit the fan!"

Then there was consideration of what would happen with the money if she were to die before she opened a bakery. She wanted the boys to have it all. She found out after overhearing a conversation between two of her coworkers that it was possible to designate James and Andrew as beneficiaries for all her accounts. There was no doubt in her mind as to whether this was the right decision and planned on taking care of adding them the next time she was at the bank.

At the end of this year, she and Ethan would be married eighteen years, which sounded like a long time—and yet it had flown by. Recently, she often thought, *I will have been married half my life. It's strange to think of it that way.* And then her heart warmed as she thought, *The best part of being married to Ethan is being a mother to James and Andrew.*

Rebekah loved those two boys as if they had been born from her own womb. They were both so different from their dad and always sensitive to her feelings. Ethan was hard on them; as a minister, he had always said he couldn't have his own sons setting bad examples. Whenever she challenged him on this and said they should be allowed to be normal kids he said that ministers' kids were always held to a higher standard, and he was not going to change his mind, so it would be best she not bring the subject up again.

She remembered the time when, as a teenager, Andrew said he was going to a school football game but really was on a date with a girl. Wouldn't you know he got a flat tire? And, since the family owned an auto repair shop, he naturally called one of his uncles to help him out with changing the tire, not thinking that the next time the whole family was together, his uncle would tease him about the girl. It was clear that Ethan was angry.

When they got home, Ethan took Andrew into his office, and although she could hear the raised voices, mostly Ethan's, she couldn't make out the words being said. Andrew went to his room, and Ethan stayed in his office the rest of the evening.

The next day she asked Andrew about it. He put his hand on Rebekah's shoulder and smiled at her. "Don't worry, Mom. I'll be going to college soon. He won't have any idea what I do then. It's just not worth it now. I can bide my time," he said, and he gave her a hug before heading off to soccer practice. Such a mature young man.

In reality, what Ethan's behavior had done was create a stronger bond between Rebekah and the boys. It bothered her how he expected the boys to be perfect and would criticize them all the time. Whenever they were fussed at by their dad, they would look to Rebekah, knowing some extra loving was on the way. Rebekah's relationship with the boys was so different. She could accept them as they were.

To Rebekah, the best times spent with James and Andrew were when they baked in the kitchen together. Andrew had a gift for baking and James, a gift for *eating*. It was not unusual to find Andrew whipping up a batch of cookies or a cake after school, with James as his sous chef.

Those moments spent baking with the boys always took her back to the days when she had spent long mornings and afternoons with Mère, doing the same. Many times, she swore she could feel her grandmother's presence in the kitchen, looking over her shoulder as she took something out of the oven.

***

Rebekah would never forget the first lottery ticket she had bought. Tammy had been going on and on about a big jackpot and how she knew she had the winning ticket. Both women had just gotten off work and were getting their belongings out of their lockers, and Rebekah laughed to herself about

Tammy's optimism. Tammy had said the exact same thing about her tickets every week, always claiming that she could just *feel* she'd win that time. The two women said goodbye, and as Rebekah continued to rearrange her locker to accommodate several of the latest romance novels Tammy had given her, she realized that something on the top shelf was preventing her from sliding them in.

She put her hand way in the back to see if she could find the obstruction, and her fingers felt some papers. With a firm tug, she pulled out an envelope. Inside it was the card Tammy had given her three years earlier when Rebekah graduated from high school. She pulled the card out of the envelope, and a ten-dollar bill fell to the floor. Rebekah picked it up and remembered how Tammy had said to do something crazy with it. That's when the idea came to her: *What could be crazier than buying a lottery ticket?*

So Rebekah went straight to customer service at the grocery store and found Michael manning the desk. Seeing him made her hesitate for a moment. Things had been awkward between them ever since she married Ethan, but now they seemed to be falling back into a normal friendship. Michael was still in school getting his master's in business, so she only saw him in the summer during school breaks and occasionally when he came home for a short visit. When Michael was around, Tammy always brought up how she thought he still had feelings for Rebekah. Rebekah didn't like to hear Tammy say that, so she would remind her of how Michael had always been just a friend and how she should stop bringing it up.

Setting her awkwardness aside, Rebekah boldly walked up to the counter.

"Hi, Michael. Home for the weekend? How's school going?"

"Yeah, I was in the mood for some home cooking," he said. "School's going great. How's it going for you? Dad told me what a great job you're doing in the bakery. You should be proud of yourself."

"Thanks. Your dad kind of gives me free rein. Who wouldn't love that?" said Rebekah, and they both smiled. "Anyway, I want to get two numbers for tonight's lottery and the rest in scratch offs," she said and laid her ten-dollar bill on the counter.

"Really? I've never seen you buy tickets before, Rebekah," Michael said with a surprised look and a smile on his face.

Rebekah chuckled nervously. She had a hard time looking him in the eyes, feeling the guilt build inside her. "I guess Tammy's rubbing off on me" was all she could say.

Michael gave her the tickets, and she went directly to her car, where she quickly closed and locked the door, making her feel more secure. After grabbing her wallet out of her purse, she fumbled for a quarter in its coin pouch, her hands shaking.

After reading the directions on the first ticket, she used the quarter to scratch the designated area. *Twelve dollars!* Wow, she had already recouped her ten. She proceeded to scratch the others with excitement, her heart pounding a bit. The next scratch off revealed nothing, but the third won her two dollars and the last fifty dollars! *Sixty-four dollars? And that easily? This is fun*, she thought. *Now what?* She had seen Tammy cash in tickets and scratch offs at the customer service desk. Rebekah didn't want to take the chance of Ethan—or anyone else for that matter—finding the tickets, so she immediately went back into the store. Thank goodness Michael was gone, and now Fred was alone at the desk.

Fred looked up with a smile. "You forget something, Rebekah?" Fred asked.

"No—cash these in," she spoke softly. Her nerves had caused her throat to close up a little, making her talk with a slight rasp.

Fred laughed as he ran the rectangular cards under a scanning device. "Whoa, sixty-four bucks! Wait till Tammy gets word of this. Don't you know she's going to be jealous?"

"I'd like to keep this between you and me Fred, if that's okay?" Rebekah responded. "I mean, I want to be the one to surprise her."

"Oh, heck ya! I understand," Fred said as he counted out three twenties and four ones. "Is this okay, or do you want me to break one of those twenties?"

"No, it's fine," she said and then quickly added with surprise, "You know what? I did leave something in my locker, Fred. So, I better go get it." And without another word, she took off, hearing Fred's laughing behind her.

When she got to her locker, the room was empty—*thank God*. Rebekah did the combination on her lock and found the envelope the ten dollars had been in. Inside it, she tucked the sixty-four dollars and the two lottery tickets. *This will do for now*, she thought as she closed and relocked the locker.

She remembered how Tammy had mentioned that the lottery drawing was tomorrow evening, so the tickets would be safe in her locker in the meantime. *Maybe I could put the cash in the collection plate on Sunday*, she thought, but then again, maybe someone would see her put the money in and wonder where it came from. And maybe they'd even ask her about it. She knew she was overthinking all of this due to the guilt she felt—but why *should* she feel guilty? She knew Ethan considered the lottery gambling, but who was he to dictate what others should do? *We all have a right to make our own choices,* she thought. She wasn't going to hell for a few scratch offs and a lottery ticket. She wasn't hurting anybody, so why was it wrong?

Get a grip, she told herself as she started her car and left the parking lot. What if she *did* win the "big one"? During her forty-five-minute drive home, she began to daydream about the wonderful things she could do with all that money. A content smile crept across her face as the guilt evaporated, and an excitement unlike anything she had felt before began to take over.

***

The lottery drawing came and went. Rebekah had not won the big jackpot, but she did win one of the lesser prizes—$500, in fact. Tammy was so excited when she told her and wanted to know what her friend was going to do with it. Rebekah wasn't sure and said she would decide once the shock wore off.

After she retrieved the $500 cash, she put it in the graduation card envelope where the sixty-four dollars still remained—but not before taking twenty dollars out to buy some more tickets and scratch offs. *This is* really *fun*, she thought, knowing she could do it again and win.

And she did win—again and again and again.

Chapter 6

"Hey, Mom, it's me," Rebekah called out as she walked through the front door and into the living room of her childhood home. She looked around the room that hadn't changed much in the past twenty-plus years. The same couch and chairs were now covered with slipcovers in an attempt to update the look, but nothing had been done to help the outdated octagonal end tables and wagon-wheel coffee table that all showed the wear and tear of the six kids who had grown up there.

Ruth came through the kitchen door donning a floral apron upon which she wiped her hands.

"Rebekah? What are you doing here? Usually we only see you at church on Sunday. Why aren't you working?" Ruth responded in her usual no-nonsense voice and placed her hands on her hips—never a hug or a kiss on the cheek from her.

"That's not true, Mom. I came for supper just a little over a week ago," Rebekah said, trying to keep an even tone. It seemed she could never please her mother with anything. Truth be told, Rebekah only visited now and then out of *obligation*, not because she enjoyed her mother's company. "I have today off, so I thought I would come by."

"I would think you'd have to clean your house on your day off and not be bumming around," her mother responded. She was always putting a negative twist on things.

"Actually, Ethan and I don't mess things up much. Now when the boys were home, that was another story. Where's Dad?" she asked in an effort to change the subject. "Is he at the shop?" Darrell was semiretired now, letting his sons run things at the auto repair shop the past few years but still keeping a foot in the door and an eye on the business.

"Yes, he decided to go in today to help your brothers out. Seems a lot of people have had more than the usual amount of car problems recently, so they appreciate the extra hand. I was in the kitchen getting a roast ready to put in the oven. We don't all have the luxury of a day off with nothing to do." Her mother looked her up and down before she turned and headed back to the kitchen with Rebekah following behind.

Ruth was as good a cook as Rebekah was a baker. On the counter was a large roast, potatoes, onions, carrots, and a big pot to put them in.

"That's a pretty big roast, Mom. Are you expecting company?"

"If you came around more, you would know what's going on. Ben is having some trouble at home, so he's staying with us for a while. I'm surprised Ethan hasn't told you. He's been counseling Ben and Rene."

"Ethan doesn't share stuff like that with me," Rebekah said, surprised to hear of her brother's apparent marital struggles. "He keeps everything confidential, but I'm sorry to hear that they're having issues. Ben must be upset. How long's he been here?" she inquired.

"About four weeks. Rene says she doesn't think she loves him anymore," Ruth said, turning back to her roast. "Too bad I say. It doesn't work like that. When the Lord brings you together that means forever. It's the way it is. Why decide all of a sudden at this point in their life? At least their kids are grown," Ruth said with finality as she started vigorously cutting a potato as if it were Rene on the cutting board.

Rebekah thought about her and Ethan for a moment. Did she still love him? Of course she did. In the beginning of their marriage, she got to know him better and then grew to love him over the years. She was sure many relationships were like that. Then she thought about Tammy and the other girls at work and their talk about relationships with boyfriends and husbands and about being in love before they were married. It had never really been that way for her.

When Rebekah had agreed to marry Ethan, she stepped into a role as wife and mother of an instant family. But now that James and Andrew were gone on their way in the world, she felt she didn't have a definite role anymore. It did seem that the boys' departure had weakened the glue that held her and Ethan together, and she wondered sometimes if her love for the boys and their well-being had been the only reason she agreed to their marriage. The boys and their activities had given Ethan and Rebekah something in common. They had tried to have their own child, but it seemed that after several years with no baby, Ethan lost interest. She suggested they have some tests done, but Ethan said if the Lord wanted them to have more children, they would have them. He wasn't going to be subjected to tests. It hurt at first when he said that to her, but as time went on, she told herself to be thankful for James and Andrew. She truly felt they were hers.

Rebekah had done the right thing by telling Ethan before she accepted his marriage proposal that she wanted to keep her job at the grocery store. She didn't want to give it up and was so glad she hadn't. It had come as a pleasant surprise when her mother agreed to take care of James and Andrew till they were school age. Rebekah was appreciative for this because it made keeping her job easier with her ready-made family.

She had been right in keeping her job. After all, it was not long after she and Ethan were married when the manager of the bakery quit, and Fred offered her the vacated position. She was afraid at first to tell Ethan for fear of him saying no, but shockingly, he said the increase in pay would be helpful, and that he was okay with it—as long as she didn't have to work on Sundays. For Rebekah, the job gave her a sense of independence from the parts of her life she found confining, and it allowed her to do something she loved.

To some, a bakery manager position may not have seemed like that big of an accomplishment, but to Rebekah, it made her feel like a professional and legitimate baker. She remembered the day she told her mom about the job and her mom's discouraging words about her "biting off more than she could chew." One would have thought her mom would be a big supporter of her daughter's promotion but, sadly, no. From then on, Rebekah kept any of her work-related successes to herself so she could enjoy them. And she'd given up trying to figure out her mom long ago. It just made life easier.

Even though Ruth never encouraged or complemented Rebekah on her creativity and success at work, she never hesitated to ask her daughter to bake a cake or other treats when needed for church and family events. It didn't matter; Rebekah didn't need her mother's praise. She received appreciation from her customers and people at work, and that was enough. She knew she was talented, and more than that, she was proud of herself.

"Would you and Ethan like to come have supper with us tonight? You're right about it being a big roast," Ruth said and let out a little chuckle. "I've never gotten used to cooking for just a few people." She paused and looked at Rebekah a moment with a smile on her face. "I bet you don't remember all the cooking I did when you kids were young. At one point when you all were still home, I felt I might as well put a bed in the kitchen and live there." Ruth shook her head, still smiling at the memory. Then, going back to the roast, she continued, "Why your brothers could eat their weight in food while you and Dorcas ..." Her mother looked up, a white shock spreading across her face. She threw her hand over her mouth as if to stop any more words coming out.

Dorcas? Her mother never mentioned her sister's name. Here, Rebekah saw an opening, a ray of light, hoping to discover more about her sister's disappearance. "What about Dee, Mom?" Rebekah asked, and put a hand on her mother's arm. Then, she looked into Ruth's eyes, hoping her mother would sense her question without her having to ask it.

Ruth's hand shook as she put down the knife she'd been using. Slowly, she walked to the sink. "I can't believe I just said that. I haven't said her name in years. Oh my God, if your father heard that ..." Tears streamed down her face as she washed her hands, never looking up. "I don't know what made me say that."

"Why, Mom? Why? Tell me what happened. I miss her so much."

"You need to go," Ruth said. Then, turning toward Rebekah, she added, "If you want to come to dinner, fine, but do not utter a word about this to anyone! Do you hear me?" There was threat in her voice as she pointed a finger at Rebekah. Her mom's flushed face showed distress from the mention of Dee's name.

Rebekah walked forward and wrapped her arms around her mom. Ruth's body fell slightly limp, and as she leaned against Rebekah's chest, clinging to her, she released an uncharacteristic sob.

It took Rebekah a moment to find her words. Her mother had never before shown this kind of distress over Dee's absence. "I won't say a word, Mom, but maybe we can talk about Dee one day … just the two of us?" Rebekah asked as sweetly as she could muster.

Ruth's stance became rigid once more—a posture with which Rebekah was all too familiar—as she withdrew from Rebekah's arms. "I'll look forward to seeing you and Ethan later, say at about five thirty or so," she said, quickly looking down before returning to her vegetables. She was done talking.

Rebekah watched her mother, a sense of pity welling up inside her unlike any she'd ever felt before. What must it feel like to not know where her child had been all these years? Now that Rebekah knew her mom still had a soft spot for Dee, she would wait for another chance to find out what had happened. Silently, she turned and walked out of the room, not stopping as she reached the front door, leaving Ruth to her own thoughts.

***

"Ruth, you make the best roast of anyone I've ever known," Ethan said as they sat around the Boulanger's dinner table later that evening. "It melts in your mouth."

"Why thank you, Ethan," Ruth said. She was always a different person when Ethan was around; after all, he was a preacher and "man of God," as she always put it. "I even made green beans the way you like them. I thought after Rebekah was here this afternoon and I invited you both, she might have made a dessert—I mean, she was off all day."

"You should have said you wanted me to make dessert, Mom," Rebekah said with a bite in her voice as her eyes widened. "I didn't know you were expecting me to bring one, otherwise I would have." *Why did it always have to be this way?*

Ignoring her daughter, Ruth smiled and asked her son to pass the green beans.

"This is the kind of meal we need after the day we had at the shop, ain't it, Ben?" Darrell asked his son. "I mean, I've never seen so many people with car problems," Darrell addressed them all. "Nothing worse than car trouble in the winter for them, but it's great for us. In the summer, they might try to fix things themselves, but in the winter, they bring them into the shop to see us since it's just so cold! I love days like today."

"It's also our reputation, Dad," Ben said. "We're known for gettin'er done and doin'er right. Pass the rolls, Ethan, will you?" he added.

Ethan passed the rolls and talk went from the family business to the weather, opinions on why the Packers didn't make it into the Super Bowl this year, what the team should do next year, and, finally, how James and Andrew were doing.

"I hate thinking about those two boys out there in the world," Ruth said. "Why they couldn't stay at home and go to Nicolet College, I'll never understand. God only knows what kind of riffraff they have to put up with. You too, Rebekah—at that store."

"I can assure you, Mom, there's no riffraff at the store, and the boys are both smart and well-grounded. Why, if Ethan hadn't gone to college, he wouldn't be here with us right now either." Rebekah looked at Ethan and smiled as she tried to reason with her mom.

"Ruth, the boys are fine," Ethan assured her. "Rebekah and I raised them right. They're good examples for the rest of the world. I couldn't be prouder of them."

"If you say so, Ethan," Ruth said, and that was the end of it.

After dinner, Rebekah helped her mom clean up in the kitchen, and just as they were finishing, Ethan walked in.

"Rebekah, I just got a call on my phone that Eddie Johnson was taken to the hospital in Rhinelander, and the family needs me. I'm going to take off for there now, and I'm not sure when I'll be back. Ben offered to take you home."

"Okay, of course. Did they say what happened?"

"It sounded like a heart attack. Eddie's had one before—a few years ago. I'll see you at home whenever."

"Yes. Give them my best and tell them Eddie's in my prayers."

Rebekah was used to this. Her husband was always on call for all the congregation's tragedies. Ethan threw on his coat and was out the door.

The kitchen was clean, and Ben came in to see when she might want to go home.

"I think now sounds good." She sighed. "Got to get to bed since I work tomorrow."

So after saying goodbye and thanking her parents for supper, she and Ben headed out the door.

They rode along silently for most of the two-mile drive to Rebekah's house until, at last, her brother spoke. "I guess you heard about me and Rene?"

"Not till this afternoon when Mom told me," she responded.

"It's all such a big mess," he said as he pulled into Rebekah's driveway. "Can I come in and talk with you? I've got so many people telling me what to do, and you've always been someone who knows how to listen. I won't keep you too long so you can get to bed."

The car's headlights reflected off the snow, casting a shadow across Ben's troubled face. The desperation in his voice touched Rebekah's heart as she felt a slight twinge in her chest.

"Why sure, Ben. We can talk as long as you want," Rebekah said, taking his gloved hand in hers.

Ben turned the car off and followed Rebekah in, where she made them both a cup of tea and put some snickerdoodle cookies she'd made a couple of days ago on a plate.

"I don't know where to begin," Ben said once they were seated at the kitchen table. "You know, since Paige is married, and Jeff is on his own, Rene and I have kind of drifted apart.

We've really been like strangers and haven't been happy for years, and I think the kids being gone has made it more obvious. We got married so young that I'm not sure we knew what we were getting into—and now we both want out."

He paused a moment, rubbing a hand along his brow before he continued. "I'm not proud of this, but I've found I love someone else—and so has Rene. I know it sounds crazy, but we both want a divorce so we can go our separate ways and be happy. Is that too much to ask?"

Rebekah nodded, processing what Ben had just shared with her. No one in their world ever got divorced. It was like her mom had said: "When the Lord brings you together, that's forever."

"What has Ethan told you?" Rebekah asked.

"He said we had to work it out. But there's nothing to work out because there's nothing between us. Rene and I have already started divorce proceedings. That's why I moved in with Mom and Dad; they just don't know it yet. Nobody knows except you. I'm looking for a place to rent, and then, once we get our divorce finalized, I'm moving somewhere far away from here and starting a new life with the woman I love."

"How did you meet this woman?" Rebekah asked.

"She works at the bank I go to. Her kids are grown also. Her husband died when the kids were young, and she never remarried. Said she never wanted to get married again till she met me." He looked down for a moment before fixing his eyes on his sister's. "I love her, Rebekah."

"Ben, I'm not going to lie—I'm surprised by what you've told me." Rebekah felt tears sting her eyes. "Surely you don't have to move away, though. We love you, and we can learn to live and adjust to this."

"Your husband told me I would have to leave the church if I divorced. A divorce can't be tolerated."

"No, I can't believe he would say that. You misunderstood."

"Ask him," Ben said, once again looking his sister in the eye. "Listen, Rebekah, I didn't mean to upset you. I just wanted you to know what was going on. I knew you would be understanding." He stood up and scratched at the back of his head. "Anyway, you have to get to bed. I don't want you to be tired at work tomorrow because your sorry brother unburdened himself on you."

"I'm so happy you told me. I do understand, and I want you to be happy." And she meant it. She held her arms out for a hug.

"I love you, little sister," Ben said as he folded his arms around Rebekah, and they stood for a while, a quiet moment between brother and sister. When Ben pulled away, he had a few tears trailing down his cheeks. "I'll keep you posted," he said as he wiped his eyes on his sleeve and put his coat on.

Rebekah threw her jacket on as well and walked Ben to his car. He got in and then rolled the window down.

"I guess when Mom and Dad find out, I'll have to disappear like Dee did," he said.

Before Rebekah could respond, he closed the window and began to back out. Rebekah started toward the car, wanting to ask if he knew something about Dee, but his head was turned to watch behind the car, and he didn't see her. *What could he know about Dee?* she thought, her heart pounding as she stood at the end of her driveway and watched her brother's headlights disappear into the night.

Chapter 7

Ethan came home from the hospital not long after Rebekah got up Thursday morning for work. He'd left her a voicemail during the night, telling her he was certain he'd be at the hospital until morning, probably home after she left for work so she shouldn't be concerned. He felt his presence there was a help to the family. Just as she was fixing her morning coffee, he walked in the back door. His hair was a mess, and his eyelids drooped.

"You look like you've been up all night," she said, making a slight joke, and then gave him a kiss, hoping to make him smile and lighten the gloom that spread across his face. "I didn't think you'd be back before I left for work." She turned away to finish fixing her coffee.

"Eddie died," Ethan said flatly with no feeling.

Rebekah put her cup down and turned back to face Ethan, never having expected the news he gave her. She took a minute to process before she spoke. "I'm so sorry. How's Nancy doing? I'll maybe take her a cake after I finish work today."

Ethan took off his coat and hung it on the back of a kitchen chair, where he then flopped down, placing his elbows on the table and his head in his hands.

"Are you okay?" Rebekah asked.

After a long moment, he looked over at her and spoke in a loud, angry tone. "No, I'm not okay. And how do you think Nancy's doing? She just lost her husband! Do you really believe a cake is going to help her?"

She jumped, stunned by the way he talked to her. Thinking she could make things better, she walked over to him and put her hand lovingly on her husband's shoulder. "Ethan, what's the matter?"

He shook his shoulder, and she pulled her hand back. She had never seen him act this way before and felt fearful. What had happened at the hospital?

"Do you have any idea of the constant pressure on me?" he said, scanning the room for a few seconds before returning his gaze to the table. He waved an arm as if trying to swat a fly. "These people look at me like they expect me to perform a miracle with my prayers, and then when I don't come through for them, it's like I'm a failure. I have to stand there and tell distraught family members that it's all in God's plan. They ask me stuff like, What did they do to deserve this? How do you answer that?" He shook his head and raised his hands slightly. "Do you know Eddie was just a year older than me? I don't think I can do this anymore."

He placed his face in his hands again for a minute or two then suddenly stood up and started pacing the floor. After a moment, he went toward the doorway leading to the hall where Rebekah now stood. "Get out of my way," he said and then pushed her with such force, she fell to the floor.

Still on the floor, dazed by what had just happened, she listened as his footsteps traveled down the hallway, and then the door to his office slammed. She lay there, stunned.

Then she heard the lock on the door click.

After she'd found her bearings, Rebekah brushed herself off and went to the bedroom to finish getting ready, glad she was working that day.

Her thoughts raced like a freight car. *He didn't mean to do it.* She knew that. *He was just upset.* She started to rationalize all that had just happened, thinking about how she could make things better. *Poor Ethan*, she thought. A minister is always at work, responding to the needs of his congregation—never his own. Even Rebekah, as a minister's wife, had dealt with this neediness, though on a smaller scale. But she had her job in Rhinelander, and she could escape for a while when needed; Ethan had nowhere.

Suddenly, it became obvious: Ethan needed to get away. In the entire time they'd been married, they had never taken a vacation, and it was long overdue. She had heard people at work talk about visiting Door County, the little peninsula of Wisconsin that looked like a thumb over on the east side of the state. It sounded so charming, with its cottages on the water, restaurants, and little shops, and it wasn't too far away. She was sure she could convince him to go there. They would go during the week so he would be back for Sunday. Excitement welled up inside her.

She would wait, and once he had cooled down, she would suggest they go on a vacation—just the two of them. There was no real reason Ethan couldn't get away every now and then, but she had to ask at the right time. Timing was everything. So she'd have to find the perfect moment to convince him that getting away could only make him a better minister. Her dad and two of her brothers were deacons at the church, so she would talk to them and ask for help if she needed some backup convincing him. After all, that's why they had deacons: to pick up the slack for the minister when needed.

It was decided.

Having made a plan, she felt better starting out her day and even knocked on Ethan's office door before she left.

"I'm going to work, Ethan. I love you very much. Let's talk later today when I get home and you've had time to rest and feel better." She waited a few seconds, but there was no response. *Maybe he's fallen asleep on the couch*, she thought. If he got a good sleep, she knew things would be better by the time she returned.

***

Thoughts of Ethan and what had transpired before she left that morning filled Rebekah's mind on the drive to work, but once she got there, it was down to bakery business. Just like every morning, Rebekah and Tammy got the ovens started, and before long, the baking was underway, and the incident with Ethan free from her thoughts. Rebekah felt excited as she started her two-day process of making a wedding cake for the upcoming Saturday. Fred had said if that side of the business continued to pick up, he was thinking of adding on a special cake room just for couples and other people who wanted customized cakes for their special day.

As she began work on the wedding cake, she thought about the cake-decorating class in Green Bay that she was looking forward to attending this spring. She began to daydream about the class and how nice it was going to be to get away all by herself. She had never done that before. Maybe she'd even make friends with some of the other individuals taking the class—people who were as passionate about baking as she was. Some of them may even own their own bakeries, and Rebekah could ask them about their businesses. They could exchange phone numbers and email addresses to stay in touch. And to think of the beautiful cakes she'd be able to make after taking the class ... She was still deep in thought when Tammy came into the kitchen.

"There's a woman out here who wants to ask you a question. Says she needs to talk to a manager. I told her I was the assistant manager, but it didn't fly with her. Sorry, I know you're busy."

"It's okay. I'll be there in a minute," Rebekah said, hoping today wasn't going to be one of *those* days. She washed the cake flour from her hands and went out to the counter. The woman had brown hair and blue eyes and was about her height and size. When she looked straight at Rebekah, for a moment, there was something familiar about her that she couldn't place, though surely she hadn't seen this woman before.

"Hi, I'm Rebekah, the bakery manager. What can I help you with?" she asked with as genuine a smile as she could put forth.

"My name is Emily Hayes," the woman said, sounding nervous. "A guy over in the deli said he wasn't hiring but thought I should talk to you about the bakery. I'm new in the area and need a job. I have experience in retail sales, and I've worked in a restaurant. I learn really fast."

"It's nice to meet you," said Rebekah. Then she frowned slightly as she shook her head. "I'm sorry, though; we aren't hiring in the bakery right now either. But if you want to fill out an application, you're welcome to do so, and I can keep you in mind if something becomes available."

For a second, Emily looked like she might cry, but she quickly collected herself. "Okay, thank you. I'd like to fill one out."

"Sure, go ahead, Emily. Sit over there, and I'll bring you an application and pen," Rebekah replied. She wasn't sure why she said the next words that fell from her mouth, other than the fact that she felt sorry for the woman. "I'll bring you a cup of coffee and something from the bakery also." The woman glanced at her sideways, and there it was again, something familiar in her face—no it was her eyes—the way they looked at you.

"Oh, you don't have to, but thank you," the woman replied. Then, she shook her head and laughed, her nerves still clearly visible. "Actually … I'm really kind of hungry."

After a few minutes, Rebekah came back with the application, a cup of coffee, and a bear claw. She was curious to read the woman's application.

"Well, I have to get back to work. So when you get done, give it to the woman you first talked to. She's my assistant manager, Tammy, who will make sure I get the application."

"Thank you, Rebekah. I appreciate you taking the time to talk to me. Oh, and thanks for the coffee and donut."

Donut, Rebekah thought. Emily obviously didn't know the difference between a donut and a pastry, but then again, neither had many of the other girls when they first started. She nodded, then returned to the kitchen.

***

Rebekah's work day was finally coming to an end. She had made major strides to get as much done on the wedding cake as she could. Everything was baked and trimmed; tomorrow she would do some assembly and icing, then she'd finish the decorations on Saturday before she delivered the cake later that morning.

She sat at her desk, looking at her calendar. February was right around the corner, and it would soon be Valentine's Day. Rebekah had watched some shows on the baking and food channels that had inspired some new ideas for the romantic holiday. Her thoughts included puff pastry, miniature heart-shaped cakes with a mirror glaze, and decadent raspberry brownies.

"Hey, Rebekah. Here's that woman's job application," Tammy said as she walked in the office with her coat on, ready to go home.

Rebekah's focus snapped back to the present.

"I guess you should keep it in case we need someone," Tammy continued. "I looked it over. She's from Canada originally and worked at two big retail stores in Buffalo, New York, then a restaurant in Michigan. She's nice ... but seemed kind of desperate, didn't you think?"

Rebekah scanned the paper and, without looking at Tammy, said, "Yes, I felt the same way. She said a guy in the deli passed her over here to me, which could only be Michael. Maybe he sensed her desperation and didn't want to deal with it. I wonder if she has kids to support or something? Anyway, we don't need anyone right now, so I'll put it in the file. She has no bakery experience, but we can train anyone." She looked up at her friend with a big smile.

"Indeed, *you* can," said Tammy. She walked over to Rebekah and gave her a hug. "Just look at how you trained me when I started in the bakery. I knew nothing." She started to leave, then turned back around. "Oh, I almost forgot to tell you! I won one thousand dollars on that last bunch of lottery tickets I bought," she added, raising her eyebrows and giving Rebekah a big smile. "Too bad you didn't buy any. You gotta get some the next time."

"Okay," Rebekah said, not sharing that she had won $1,000 herself.

She looked more closely at the application from Emily Hayes, then unlocked her file cabinet, placing Emily's application behind the four others already there. Rebekah hoped the woman would find a job somewhere because the people who worked for her usually stayed a long time. It had been two years since she'd hired anyone.

***

After checking in with her staff, Rebekah was heading to her car when she remembered what had happened that morning with Ethan. She was so busy all day, she had forgotten the whole mess. The drive home was long enough that it allowed her to go over a plan to convince Ethan he needed to go on a vacation, and she decided not to wait. When he got home from the church today, she was going to tell her husband they were going on a vacation as soon as the weather was warm enough. And if he said he didn't want to go, she would say she was going by herself ... and she meant it. That should get his attention.

To her surprise, Ethan's car was still in the driveway when she got home, so she figured he must have decided not to go in and work on Sunday's sermon. He didn't like to be disturbed when writing the sermon, so she knew she may have to talk to him later about the trip. When she opened the back door, however, he was there to greet her with a hug and kiss.

"I'm sorry about my behavior this morning, Rebekah. You're a wonderful wife and mother. What would I have done without you?" he said and kissed her again.

She kissed him back. "It's because I love all of you. We're a family."

"I love you so much," he said, his kisses becoming more passionate until, soon, he led her to the bedroom.

It had been such a long time since they had made love. As she lay there, naked and content, she remembered Tammy talking about "makeup sex" and how great it could be. She was now a believer and understood what Tammy had been talking about. Now that Ethan's mood had drastically improved, it seemed like as good a time as any to bring up the vacation idea.

"Ethan, I was very concerned about you this morning before I went to work."

His eyes closed as he grunted something unintelligible from his side of the bed.

"You work so hard and give so much to everyone." She paused, getting up her nerve. "I think we need to take a vacation … not far, mind you. I've heard so many people talk about going to Door County and how relaxing and fun it is. I want us to go there this spring once it gets warmer. What do you say?" *She'd said that well,* she thought.

"Sure, why not," Ethan said and, after a very long pause, added, "I don't deserve you."

"What are you talking about?" She held him in her arms, kissing his forehead.

"You know, Eddie was my age. Last night at the hospital, I thought about his life and then thought about mine." He paused again for a moment and sighed. "There was a time in my life that wasn't good. And there are things about me you don't know."

Rebekah nodded as she thought, *And there are things about me you don't know.* Maybe it was time to tell him about the money she had been amassing through the lottery. Once she told him, though, she could never take it back. Her instinct told her she should wait.

"I don't want to hear anymore," Rebekah said. "Let's get dressed, and you take me out for dinner in Crandon." She rolled out of bed and headed toward the bathroom.

"What's that bruise on your hip?" he asked as he watched her cross the room.

She looked down, and there it was: a bruise the size of an egg. At first, she wasn't sure how it got there, then she remembered how she'd fallen that morning after Ethan pushed her. It happened so fast; he must not have realized she had fallen. Things were going so good for the moment; why make him feel guilty?

"Oh, I must have bumped something at work. You know, I don't even remember. I'm so busy all day. It doesn't hurt, so I'm fine," she said, rather convincingly.

He sat up and slid to the edge of the bed before pausing. "You know, I really have to finish my sermon. Maybe we can go out another time." And he lay back down.

When Rebekah came out of the bathroom, he was asleep. She didn't care; he must still be tired from last night, but she didn't feel like cooking. A can of soup sounded like a good option to her.

When Ethan woke from his little nap, he said he felt refreshed and went to work on his sermon until dinner.

***

At around six thirty, as they enjoyed the grilled cheese sandwiches Rebekah had made to go along with their soup, Rebekah asked, "How's the sermon coming along?"

"Oh, it's coming along okay. I almost forgot—did you know Eddie was into gambling? Not only was he into lottery tickets and these things called scratch offs, but he went over to that Mole Lake Casino fairly often. Made me decide to do my sermon on the sins of gambling this Sunday. Can you believe that about him?"

Rebekah gasped, causing her to choke on her grilled cheese.

"Are you okay?" Ethan asked.

"Yes, I'm fine," she said matter-of-factly and coughed. "I had no idea he gambled. Well, it's his business if he wanted to do that. He must have enjoyed it. Everyone has a right to decide to do what they want."

"Not if they plan on spending the afterlife in heaven," Ethan replied and took a bite of his sandwich. He looked down into his soup and shook his head. "Eddie's burning in hell right now," he said, then looked back up at her after placing judgement on Eddie. "You know … I can't do the funeral at our church, now that I know all this."

"What do you mean you can't do the funeral?" Rebekah was outraged. "His family has been a part of our church for years."

"I have an example to uphold for others. It's my responsibility. How can I stand in the pulpit on Sunday and look into the eyes of the people who turn to me for guidance?"

"You're passing judgment, Ethan. What gives you the right?"

"I think you need to spend some time with your Bible, Rebekah," he said, focusing his eyes on her.

She was annoyed with him at the moment, glad she had gone with her gut feeling to keep her own gambling activities to herself, and decided a change of subject to something more positive was needed quickly.

"I'm so happy we're going on a vacation finally. You know they call Door County the 'Cape Cod of the Midwest.' There's a restaurant on the peninsula that has a grass roof with live goats roaming on it. I've seen pictures of the place from some of the girls I work with. They also serve great food, I've heard, and then there's something called a fish boil that several restaurants do where they cook in a big cauldron over a fire on the beach. It's very dramatic," she continued, trying to sound as animated as possible.

Ethan was quiet and clearly uninterested.

Rebekah put her spoon down and looked intently at him. "You haven't changed your mind already, have you?" she asked.

"Don't get yourself too excited yet. I have to run it by the church. They depend on me."

Rebekah continued to look at him, not blinking as she said, "Ethan, everyone takes a vacation. You have never taken one, and it's time. We have deacons in the church for that exact reason! It's just the end of January, so we have several months to work this out. After what I saw this morning with you, I'm going to have to insist you take a break. It's for your own good. You're my husband, and I have to watch out for you."

Ethan didn't speak much the rest of the evening. He went back to his office to work on his sermon, she guessed. Eddie's death had clearly upset him. The funeral would probably be that weekend. She would go by to see his wife and take a cake—no matter what Ethan decided. Eddie had done nothing wrong in her eyes.

But she felt there *was* something wrong with Ethan. She had wondered before if they were on the same page, but today her concerns were brought front and center. It was becoming clear that the God she knew was not the same one Ethan knew. *Her* God was one who fluttered in her chest more often than not. Maybe Ethan had lost his flutter. That's exactly why she had to get him away for a while. Maybe a trip would help bring it back.

Chapter 8

Eddie Johnson's memorial service would be held at the funeral home in Crandon the following weekend. On her day off, Rebekah went by the house with a cake to see Eddie's wife, Nancy, and express her condolences. Nancy was not as warm and friendly as she had been in the past, though Rebekah attributed it to Ethan's refusal to hold the funeral at the church or even officiate.

Rebekah still disagreed with Ethan. He was placing judgment on Eddie just like her parents had always done with her. But judging someone wasn't their job. Who did they think they were? She couldn't imagine what any of them would do or say if they ever found out about her "sin." Especially Ethan, Mr. Perfect, who never seemed to step out of line or harbor any secrets.

True to his word, Ethan's sermon that Sunday was about the sins of gambling. Rebekah didn't want to hear it and decided instead to think about other things while Ethan expounded his opinions at the pulpit. She occupied her mind with the cakes she was to make that week, the latest romance novel she was reading, James and Andrew and when she might see them again, and, last but not least, the lottery ticket she had bought the day before at a Rhinelander gas station.

***

The following week, on her day off, Rebekah planned to meet Ben for lunch in Townsend, where Ben's lawyer was located. They both figured they could talk there without the worry of bumping into any family who might want to join them, thus disallowing their conversation.

Rebekah had decided she would take this opportunity to ask Ben what he knew about Dee. His comment after he'd driven her home the previous week had her wondering if he knew something she didn't. Since he had been older when it happened—around twenty-two or twenty-three—she figured he *must* know more than she did.

Rebekah walked into the diner and, looking to her left, spotted Ben, who gave her a quick wave. He stood up when she reached the table and planted a peck on her cheek.

"So happy to see you, Rebekah. You're the only one in the family I feel comfortable with talking about this."

"How was your visit with your lawyer? Any complications?" Rebekah asked, though inside, she was dying to ask about Dee.

"It's all fine. We're going through with it. Last week I had an interview and job offer from a company in Green Bay looking for someone to do auto parts sales. What I would do is call on shops to get their parts business. They want me to start as soon as I can. I really think I will love the job, Rebekah. I want to leave the area, move away from family, get a new start. Otherwise, I'll hear about this divorce every single day of my life. You know how our family is. It's going to be better in the long run."

Rebekah felt a touch of sadness at Ben's news. She loved having all her brothers around, but she knew he was right about moving away. Ethan would frown upon her seeing him after the divorce anyway, so he might as well be in Green Bay.

"I think it sounds great. Tom, Jake, and Steve should be able to run the auto shop just fine." She chuckled "It'll give Dad an excuse to come out of semiretirement, as if he were ever really there."

Ben laughed too. "Dad does need to start taking it easy," he said. "He's not in good shape, Rebekah. He eats junk all day, gets no exercise, and he huffs and puffs just walking across the shop sometimes. I have to say, watching him has made me take better care of myself. Mom makes these big heavy meals, and he puts them away. She gets mad at me because I eat sparingly and not like Dad. I can't wait to get out of there and be on my own. Soon."

"I think I would prefer to pitch a tent in the forest than to move back to Mom and Dad's house," Rebekah responded, and they both laughed more.

"Don't worry though. I'll still be home plenty," he assured her.

They ordered their food, and Ben shared more of his plans. The woman he'd fallen in love with was named Mary Lou. She would follow and find a job at another bank. Ben figured she shouldn't have a hard time finding one with all the experience she had.

"I want you to meet her sometime, Rebekah. She kind of reminds me of you."

Rebekah was touched by Ben's remark. "I would love to meet her and maybe even drive over and visit you in Green Bay for the day." Without his saying so, she knew Ben was thinking the same thing she was: if she visited with him, she couldn't tell anyone.

They continued to talk about nothing in general when she got up the courage to ask Ben about Dee. "Ben ... I was wondering what you know about Dee leaving? The other night, just before you backed out of my driveway, you said you would have to disappear like Dee did. What did you mean by that?"

There. She had said it.

"I meant it was like she dropped off the face of the earth, like she'd never been a part of our family. I've asked Mom and Dad about it a dozen times, and so have the rest of us. All that does is make Mom cry and Dad angry."

Rebekah nodded.

"I stopped asking years ago," Ben continued, "but have always kept hope Dee would come back here one day. She was a great sister—just like you. I wonder if we would even recognize her if she did come home again. I can't remember how many years ago it was, do you?"

"Twenty. It's been twenty," Rebekah said without hesitation.

"I did meet some girls one time who knew Dee. They worked with her at a restaurant here in Townsend before she left. They said she was dating a guy and heard they ran off together. I don't think they really knew, though, but were just guessing. If it was true, I'm sure the guy wasn't suitable for Mom and Dad. You know when Rene and I wanted to get married, Mom and Dad would only except Rene into the family if she joined our church. Rene said okay just so we could get married. It's ridiculous. And now look—we're getting divorced."

"But why would Mom and Dad not liking her boyfriend cause her to run off, and why would all of us be forbidden to talk about her? There must be more to it." Rebekah was sure of it.

"I don't know, but if Dee wanted to come back, I think she would have by now. She must have found a much better life to make her never want to come back here."

Rebekah hoped it was so; she just wanted to know it for sure.

"I guess you're right," she said reluctantly. Then she smiled. "It sure was nice getting together like this. I'll be going to a cake-decorating class this spring in Green Bay, so I'll come see you then."

"That would be great." He took her hands in his. "I worry about you. Are you happy with Ethan?"

She cocked her head, taken aback by his question. "Why do you ask?"

"I don't know. Going through this marriage counseling with him has made me wonder about your happiness. He's a nice enough guy, but there's something about him that bothers me. You're my little sister. Is he good to you? Are you happy?"

Suddenly, she wanted to cry. No one in her family had ever been concerned or asked about her happiness before. Funny, but it wasn't something she'd ever thought about either. She just lived her life. Didn't everyone?

"Well, of course I am," she responded, as happily as she could manage.

"Are you sure?" Ben asked. "You haven't got me convinced. I love you, Rebekah, and if you ever need a place to get away to, I'll be there for you."

One single tear rolled down her cheek that she quickly brushed away. "I'll remember that, Ben. And I love you too."

Rebekah said goodbye to her brother and headed back to her car. On the way home, she stopped at a popular candy store in Townsend to get some treats for the care packages she was sending to James and Andrew. Even though they were grown, she still liked to do little things like that so they knew she was thinking about them.

As she drove home, she had plenty of time to think about Ben's question. *Was* she happy? She lived in a nice house and had a job she enjoyed, two kids she loved, a husband dedicated to his profession, friends, and a lot of money saved. *Happy?* She paused ... happy. Why wouldn't she be happy? *Stop*, she told herself. She wasn't going to spend another minute worrying. Yes, of course she was happy.

What Ben had told her about Dee was another crumb of information that swirled through her mind. She would keep her ears open for other crumbs, and maybe, one day, she'd put it all together and find Dee.

Then, and only then, could she say, "Yes, I'm happy," without any doubt.

***

The next day was Valentine's Day. The bakery was always busiest when there was a holiday, so Rebekah had scheduled an extra person to help handle the demand.

The first bakery rush had passed, and Michael needed some help in the deli, so he borrowed Abby—one of

Rebekah's most dependable employees—to lend a hand. Rebekah and Michael worked well together and occasionally helped each other out as needed now and then during the day.

When Abby came back to the bakery, she asked Rebekah if she could talk with her. They went to Rebekah's office.

"So what's up Abby?" Rebekah asked. "Is everything okay with you?"

"Well, it's okay but, well … I don't want you to think I haven't appreciated everything you've done and taught me. But when I was over in the deli, I was thinking how much I liked it, you know something new and different from the bakery, and so I talked to Michael about a job over there," Abby said, her nerves clearly the cause of her rambling. "He has a position he's trying to fill that's afternoons and evenings. I've never been a fan of coming in so early like I do now … so I've decided I'm going to move over to the deli. I hope you're not mad at me," she said and took a breath.

Rebekah was shocked. Abby had been with her for eight years. She was well trained and dependable.

"But Abby, I thought you loved the bakery. We have such a great group. The deli has a lot of turnover with its employees. Are you sure? Maybe you should think about it." Rebekah sounded as if she were pleading—and, well, she was.

"No, I've thought about it, and I'm moving over there. Michael said I could give you two weeks' notice—or as soon as you hire someone else," Abby said with a tone of finality as she looked at Rebekah and folded her arms.

Wait till I talk to Michael, Rebekah thought.

And she did speak with him as soon as her conversation with Abby had ended.

"Hey, what's the big idea stealing one of my best employees?" she asked when they were out of earshot of the customers. "I can't believe you're that underhanded."

"I did no such thing. She asked me if I had any positions, and I do, so I told her I did. For all I knew, she was asking for a friend," Michael responded.

Then Rebekah remembered the woman who had come in the other day interested in a job. Michael had told that woman he had nothing and to go see Rebekah.

"What about the woman the other day? Why don't you hire that girl?" Rebekah came back at him.

Michael hesitated long enough for her to know he was making this up as he went along.

"I talked to my dad last night about adding some help, and when Abby asked me about working here, it seemed like the perfect situation to me. Why don't *you* hire the woman from the other day? She's available."

Rebekah said nothing; she was furious. He had stolen her employee. Still, she would talk to Fred to see if Michael actually was telling the truth.

She went back to her office and shut the door. Yes, Michael was the owner's son and heir apparent, so she guessed Fred would let him do whatever he wanted. Still, he shouldn't go around taking good employees from her.

Rebekah took a deep breath, knowing she needed to calm down. After all, Abby had said she didn't like coming in so early, so maybe she had been looking for a different job elsewhere anyway. The girl had been a good employee, and who was Rebekah to stop her from doing something she wanted to do? Tomorrow morning Rebekah would tell Abby she wished her the best in the deli and ask if she could stay on until Rebekah found a replacement.

Still feeling somewhat annoyed, Rebekah went to her cabinet and pulled out the file where she kept applications from prospective employees. She reminded herself that a new employee could be a good thing and bring in new ideas. She would begin her search tomorrow. If the five applications she had didn't work out, maybe she could steal one of Michael's employees as fair turn around. That would fix him.

***

"Hello, is this Michelle? Hi, it's Rebekah Hayward from Fred's Market & Café. You filled out a job application with us for a position in the bakery about six months ago, and I have one open now. I'd love to have you come in for an interview if you're still interested." Rebekah said, hoping she didn't sound too eager. The woman on the phone was the fourth application in her file. If this person wasn't interested, she would call the woman from the other day, hoping she hadn't found a job yet.

"Oh, you did? Well, okay. Yes, it was a while ago you filled out the application. Happy you found something. Thanks! Bye."

Emily Hayes's application lay before her. She punched in her number and heard the ring. The call went straight to voicemail.

"Hi, Emily. This is Rebekah Hayward from Fred's Market & Café. It's funny how these things happen, but someone just let me know they will no longer be working in the bakery! So I have an opening and wondered if you might still be interested in interviewing. You can get in touch with me at this number. Hope to hear from you soon," she said and hung up. All she could do now was wait and hope Emily Hayes would be a good fit.

Around twelve thirty, Michael found her in the kitchen. "That woman is here—you know the one who was interested in a job. This may be your chance."

She gave him a sideways glance. "I called her earlier and left a message. Didn't expect her to just come by, but that's fine. Let me go out to get her."

She found Emily by the bakery case, looking at the contents. "Looks good doesn't it?"

Emily jumped a bit.

"I'm sorry, I didn't mean to startle you," Rebekah said. "Come on back to my office, and we'll chat," she added and led the way.

Once they were seated, Rebekah dove right into the interview. "So tell me about yourself. It says here you're originally from Canada? What brought you to the states?"

"Just wanting something different. You know, a fresh start. Oh, and I have my green card and social security number," Emily informed her.

"Well, that's good. And how about your previous jobs?"

"I have cash-register experience, and the last place I worked was in Michigan, at a restaurant. I began as a hostess, then worked as a server, and then they started training me to cook. I found out a longtime friend of mine used to live in this area and loved it, so I decided to give it a try." She then handed Rebekah a piece of paper. "Here are my references. Feel free to call any of them."

"Working here in a bakery is different than a restaurant, starting with our hours. You would have to be here by 4:30 a.m., but that can be a benefit if you have a family—"

"I don't have one." Emily interrupted. "I don't have anyone. It's just me," she said flatly.

Rebekah didn't know what to say and then started, "Well then—it's still nice because you get off early."

They talked more about the bakery business and about the area before Rebekah thanked Emily for coming in.

"I'll give your references a call and get back to you." Rebekah got up and shook her hand. "I have a few other people to talk to also."

Emily stood up and gave Rebekah a big smile, and there it was again. Something familiar.

"Emily, this may sound odd, but … have we ever met before? There's something familiar about you."

Emily stopped smiling and looked at her straight on. "No, Rebekah, not that I'm aware of. Maybe it was in another life," she said. Then she laughed.

Rebekah gave an awkward half laugh also and walked her to the door. There was no way she knew Emily; it must be just a coincidence. Unless something crazy turned up after Rebekah talked to Emily's references, she would offer her the job.

Chapter 9

Although Rebekah wasn't happy at first about having to hire Emily Hayes to replace Abby, she soon got over her displeasure. Emily was not only a hard worker but also a quick learner. Rebekah had definitely gotten the better end of the deal and would be certain to keep Emily away from Michael, lest he get any notions about enticing her to the deli. It seemed as if Emily had been working with them for months, though she was just finishing her first two weeks.

Things were working out well for Rebekah, not only at the bakery but also at home. Something had changed in Ethan after Eddie died. Rebekah figured it was because Ethan was so close in age to Eddie; Eddie's death had prompted Ethan to think of his own mortality. Ethan wasn't old in Rebekah's eyes—only forty-two—but whatever had put the spark in him, she didn't mind. He was happier and had begun spending more time with Rebekah, even coming home early so they could go for a walk before dark. He had more interest in making love on a regular basis also. The combination of it all made Rebekah a happy woman.

***

One day after Emily had been working in the bakery for about three weeks, she and Rebekah were alone, chitchatting while putting the finishing touches on some cupcakes. In addition to being a quick learner, Emily had some decorating talent, much to Rebekah's pleasure. Perhaps in the future, Emily could be trusted to do decorating on her own.

"I was wondering about your family, Rebekah. You're married, right?" Emily asked.

"Yes, I'm married. In fact, it will be eighteen years in December. I have two boys who have kept me busy."

"Have you always lived here?"

"I don't live here in Rhinelander but just east of here, between Crandon and Laona," said Rebekah. "I've lived there my whole life. Never even been out of the state of Wisconsin—well except for the UP, but I don't count that."

Emily became silent and turned away so Rebekah couldn't see her face. Had Rebekah said something wrong? Maybe Emily was divorced, had lost a child, or wasn't able to have children herself just like Rebekah, but who knew?

After a while Rebekah decided to ask, "How about you, Emily?"

"I think I remember telling you when you interviewed me, I have no one. It's just me," Emily reminded her.

"Oh yes, you did tell me that. I'm sorry … I forgot." *Geez.* She truly *had* forgotten and was only trying to get to know Emily better by asking. She hoped Emily realized that. Now what could Rebekah say?

They finished the cupcakes in silence. *There's more to this woman than meets the eye,* she thought. It seemed Emily didn't want anyone to know about her history, so Rebekah would respect her privacy. Someday, when Emily got to know Rebekah better, she would possibly feel comfortable enough to share whatever was burdening her.

***

Later, when Rebekah and Tammy were alone and getting ready to leave for the day, Rebekah asked her about Emily.

"Tammy, I was wondering what you thought about Emily. I think she's working out well, in fact, better than I thought she would."

"She's sure a hard worker and smart too. I almost feel like she went to college or something. She's friendly enough, though she hasn't shared much about herself. It's like she's interested in our conversations and participates but never puts her two cents worth in about what she thinks or what she's been through. You know me, though. I can always feel that dark energy, and I feel it around her. A secret. You can be as sweet as pie, but don't *ever* try to hide your dark energy from me. No way. I'm like radar when it comes to hunting it down."

Funny thing about Tammy and her dark energy—she *was* always right. Rebekah was unsure whether it was Tammy's theory on dark energy or something else.

"You may think this crazy," Rebekah said, "but I feel like I've met her before. When I interviewed her, I asked her about it and she said no. Sometimes when I talk with her, though, there's just something. I can't put my finger on it."

"Huh, maybe you knew her in another life," Tammy said, shrugging. She then took a few deep breaths before continuing. "I did invite her to The Dome a few weeks ago— you know the tavern where I bartend on Friday nights—

thinking she might enjoy the fish dinner. Today she told me she was going to come tonight and check it out," Tammy informed Rebekah. "Hey, maybe I can get her drunk and find out a few things," Tammy said excitedly.

Rebekah knew she wasn't kidding. "No, don't do that, Tammy. She has to work here tomorrow. We don't want her coming in with a hangover," said Rebekah.

They both laughed.

"I guess she's one of those guarded people we'll get to know over time," Rebekah continued. "I do like her and want her to stay working with us, so we need to mind our own business." Then she looked at Tammy, raised her eyebrows, and in her sternest voice added, "And that means no getting anyone drunk."

"Yeah, yeah, okay ... unless she gets herself drunk. She might spill her guts then. You know me, I'm easy to talk to. I can't help it, people love me," Tammy said.

It was true.

"In that case, find out all you can," Rebekah said, and they both laughed once more as they headed out the door.

***

Ethan told Rebekah he was going to take a Tuesday off toward the end of March or beginning of April. Could she possibly change her usual Wednesday off to a Tuesday? He wanted to go down to the Appleton area, which was south of them, and maybe go to the mall and to lunch somewhere fun.

And, there was also a church he wanted to visit. He might be interested in a job there. This was the first she had heard of him wanting to change jobs. He had always seemed quite content where he was. A big fish in a little pond.

"Ethan, you've taken me by surprise. Why didn't you tell me you want to change jobs?"

"I don't know if I will or not," he said. "I feel I need to look and see what's out there while I'm young enough for someplace else to want me. You can't blame me for wanting to better myself, right? The kids are grown and on their way. Seems like, why not?"

Yes. Why not? she thought.

"What's the name of the church?" she asked.

"Elevate Life Church."

"Huh. That's a nice name. I would love to go down there and look around. How about we plan on the last Tuesday of the month? I'm actually a little excited about this, Ethan."

"Well, I think we need to keep it to ourselves," he said. "I don't want anyone from the church knowing—including your family."

"You don't have to worry. My lips are sealed," she said and kissed him.

Rebekah had heard about Appleton from other people. It was part of a small metropolitan area called the Fox Valley. She could only imagine the opportunities that may lay there. She would love to move to a new place. Perhaps she'd even get to open the bakery she dreamed of. She wouldn't breathe a word about this.

"And you know how you wanted to go on a trip for a few days?" Ethan added. "Let's do it. You plan it for the end of June. You're right. I do need to get away."

Rebekah was speechless, looking at him for several seconds before she smiled and spoke. "Who are you, and where is my husband, Ethan?"

He laughed, leaned in, and kissed her.

Rebekah couldn't believe the change in Ethan. She guessed it must be an early midlife crisis. A year ago, he never would have brought up wanting to move, and she wouldn't have been as receptive to the idea either. But now she saw how James and Andrew were thriving away from home, and the news of Ben moving away to start a new life encouraged her that she and Ethan could do the same and be happy.

***

Ethan and Rebekah left early on the decided Tuesday morning for their trip to Appleton. Ethan had told the church he had things to do at home and couldn't be bothered. Everyone probably assumed he was working on a fabulous Easter Sunday sermon.

The trip took just a little over two hours. Ethan dropped Rebekah off at the mall before he went over to meet the people at Elevate Life Church. He said he would call her when he was finished, which should be around lunchtime. She felt she had died and gone to heaven as she started at one end of the mall and worked her way down to the other.

At about eleven thirty, Ethan called and said he was going to lunch with some of the staff and church members, so she should grab something to eat at the mall. She didn't want to eat a big lunch, anyway, since Ethan had promised he would take her out for dinner somewhere before they went home, so she found a place where she could get a small salad.

He showed up at the mall around one thirty and was all excited. He liked the church and felt it would be a nice move for his career if she were on board.

"I am if that's what you want," she said.

"Why don't you finish up here, and then we can ride around and see the area before we go to dinner?" he suggested. "I'll tell you all about my interview then."

***

Since Appleton was farther south than where they lived, some of the snow had already started melting in the area, allowing them to get a good look at the surroundings. They started in Appleton then drove through Menasha, Neenah, and all the way to Oshkosh before they turned around and came back to the mall area for dinner at an Italian restaurant called Carmella's.

"I love Italian food," Ethan said when they had been seated for a few minutes.

"I didn't know that," Rebekah replied.

"I do, but we don't really have many places that serve it by us—you know, legit Italian restaurants. I'm going to have one of my favorites tonight, chicken parmigiana," he said and set down his menu.

Rebekah made a note to herself about finding a recipe to make chicken parmigiana for him in the future. "I think I'll have the same," she said.

"So tell me how everything went," she asked once they had placed their order.

"It's very different than our church since they have several staff members; at our church, I *am* the staff," he said, pointing a finger at himself. "The position is for associate pastor, which is fine with me. It's a good opportunity to learn about working with a little bigger church. They're interviewing several people and may not get back with a decision until closer to summer, but they loved me—I could tell. Even though I'm sure they want to hire me, I've decided that if this doesn't work out, I'm going to keep looking. I think now's a good time in our lives to do this."

"Well then, I hope they call you back for another interview. If they do, I'll come back with you. I'll check online before we come to find out about the bakeries in the area and maybe drive around to check them out." And then Rebekah decided to test the waters. "It's always been my dream to open up my own bakery—not like the old-fashioned kind but something different, more cakes and some catering, I think. This could be my big chance. Maybe I could open my own place," she said with a slight excitement in her voice.

Ethan looked at her as if a horn had sprouted from her forehead. "What are you talking about? *Your own bakery?* Are you serious? We don't have money to do something like that. I figured you could get a job working in any old bakery like you do now." He locked eyes with her and shook his head.

"Well, what if I could get the money?" she replied, attempting to hide the defensive feelings inside her.

Now Ethan laughed. "You would have to win the lottery or rob a bank to do that!" He continued to laugh and looked away. "And we know that won't happen because both are sins, and *you* are a God-fearing woman who would never do such a thing."

"Right," she said and took a long sip from her water glass.

***

Rebekah was very quiet on the trip home. Fortunately, Ethan talked nonstop about the job at the Elevate Life Church, so her silence wasn't even noticed. It was evident he had given no thought or concern to what she might do if he took the job. All she could think about now was where *she* was going to fit in to all this. She also needed some fulfillment in her life. She was going to be thirty-six soon, with a whole lot of life yet before her. He was only thinking about himself and not about what kind of job *she* could get. After all, he hadn't even told her before he started looking for a new job to see if she was okay with it. Now that she thought more about it, the whole situation began to bother her.

It was dark when they arrived home. She needed to go to bed soon since she worked the next day, so she went into the closet to hang up a few new things she had bought at the mall that day. *It's always nice to have something new to wear*, she thought. When she came out, Ethan was sitting on the bed, waiting for her, with nothing on.

His eyes locked on hers as he came closer, pulled her shirt off, and then guided her smoothly onto the bed, kissing around her neck and chest as he ran his hands up and down her body and tugged at the rest of her clothing.

She really wasn't in the mood. "Ethan, I'm tired. I've got to work tomorrow," she protested.

"Don't spoil my mood, Rebekah. Today was a good day for me, and making love to you is the perfect ending," he said, pressing his forehead against hers. "I love you so much. I couldn't ask for a more perfect wife."

Soon, they were entwined in each other's bodies.

***

When they had finished, Ethan uncharacteristically wanted to talk. "I know they really liked me today. The church isn't going to make a decision till May or later, though, and then I'll have to give Faithful Shepherd notice to find a new pastor, which means it will be longer than that before I can start," he said. He paused a moment before asking, "Are you okay with that, Rebekah? How much notice do you have to give the bakery?"

She hadn't given much thought that she would be quitting her job. She began to feel sad but knew moving to a bigger area could be good for her. Not ready to provide an answer, she pretended to have fallen asleep, hoping Ethan would stop talking.

He did.

Rebekah's mind was swimming. It dawned on her—what was she going to do without Tammy in her life? Ethan didn't have the job yet, so she shouldn't speculate; it might not work out for him. Still, it sounded like he was determined to find a new job no matter what. She wanted to go to sleep, so she thought about the cake class she would be going to soon. She couldn't wait to go somewhere alone. Then she wondered if it was fair to have Fred pay for her to go to the class if she would be quitting? Maybe the class could be postponed until they found out if Ethan got the job or not. She heard Ethan start talking again, a distant jabbering as she drifted off to sleep.

***

The next day at work, Rebekah received a text from Ethan. Elevate Life Church in Appleton had thanked him for coming in to interview. They still had two other individuals to speak with but were so impressed with him, he was on their short list of potential candidates. There would be no decision made until after the Easter holiday since everyone was so busy.

That would be May then, Rebekah thought. *It's a long time off.* She wondered if Ethan might decide to apply at some other churches now that he felt it was time for him to make a career move. Much could happen between now and May. Ethan might change his mind and decide not to except the offer. That was, of course, assuming they offered him the job. Then she thought about how Ethan might handle it if he *didn't* get the job. He always took everything so hard. She would have to be strong and support him, though she couldn't imagine them not choosing him.

Chapter 10

The snow had just started melting in the forest around her house by the time April arrived. This meant Rebekah still wore her boots when she went for her afternoon walk, since it could be quite muddy on the trails this time of year. The trails were now transitioning from snowmobile use to the popular all-terrain vehicles (ATVs) used by so many people from spring to late fall. There were trails for the ATVs that led all the way to Canada, with hotels and restaurants along the way.

Soon the forest would come alive with lush greenery, baby animals, and wildflowers. If Ethan got the job in Appleton, she knew she could find similar areas and parks to visit.

Today was Sunday, and this morning, she'd felt like she couldn't get out of church fast enough, wanting to take in as much of the fresh spring air as she could. This was the best way to rid herself of those last remnants of cabin fever that still hung around after a long winter.

She set out at a brisk pace and was soon warm enough to take off her sweatshirt and tie it around her waist. The small trail that ran off the main path to the lake was still very muddy, so, disappointed, Rebekah turned around and headed back home, knowing it wouldn't be wise to trek down to the lake unless she wanted to get stuck. Now that the days were getting longer, she may try the path later in the week to see if it had dried out more.

As she walked, she again pondered the idea of moving to Appleton. Ever since Ethan had interviewed at the church there, it was all he talked about, and she had to admit, she was getting tired of hearing it. She had a reprieve the mornings she worked since he didn't get up as early as she did. Any time she was with him, however, he expounded nonstop on what he would do once he started at Elevate Life and how it would be a boost to his career. He didn't know exactly what his job would be as an associate pastor, but that didn't stop him from speculation. She wasn't looking forward to the inevitable disappointment if he didn't get the job.

On a whim, she'd bought a fifty-dollar scratch-off ticket that Friday before she left work and won another prize. She would deposit the check in her investment account when it arrived in her P.O. Box and add it to the rest of her money. She knew what she wanted to do with the money, but exactly how she would get there was another question.

When she went for her walks, she would imagine the bakery she would open with her money. She saw the beautiful shop with its big glass windows, inviting customers inside to satisfy their deepest, most decadent sweet desires. Tables and chairs in an eclectic mishmash of different styles, shapes, and sizes would sit to the left of the door. A crystal chandelier would hang in the middle of the ceiling—not really for the light it would give off but for effect and ambiance— low enough for everyone to see and admire it like a piece of art as they entered. To the right, you'd find her display cases containing baked goods of beautiful and imaginative patisserie items so artistic that folks would almost not want to eat them. In the back, she would have a private room for meeting with people interested in cakes and pastries for events. On the desk would be a thick book full of pictures of all the unbelievable delicacies she had concocted in the past, and more pictures of the mind-blowing fruits of her imagination would line the wall. Lastly, next to the private room would be the kitchen, where all the baking magic would take place.

Appleton could very well be the place to make her dream come true. She smiled to herself, feeling a warmness inside. She wasn't sure how, when, or even where, only that her dream would come true someday.

***

"Rebekah, are you back here?" It was Emily calling to her, sounding slightly panicked.

"Yes, just doing some paperwork. What do you need?" Rebekah called back.

Emily entered the office. "There are two couples out here wanting to talk to you about wedding cakes. What should I do?"

Rebekah laughed and looked up from her papers. "Well, I'll come out and get the couple who arrived first, and you tell the other couple if they could wait thirty minutes, I'll be happy to talk to them after I'm done with a previous appointment. Get the second couple a cup of coffee, tell them to pick something out of the bakery case they might enjoy while they wait, then seat them at one of the café tables."

"You're so smart, Rebekah. Why didn't I think of that?" Emily responded.

Rebekah laughed again and shook her head, then quickly met with the first couple. They were having a June wedding and wanted a one-of a-kind cake to express their love of camping. The bride had some pictures of their favorite places to visit to help inspire Rebekah. The couple thought two tiers was enough and wanted each layer to be a different flavor. Rebekah got an idea of what they had in mind, then made an appointment for them to come back to taste some different cake flavors and look at some sketches she would do. Twenty minutes later, she did the same thing with the second couple.

When she was finished, Emily came over. "You did that so well. Have you ever thought of opening your own place? I mean, you're a real business woman."

"Well, thank you, Emily. I've been doing this for a long time, so I have lots of practice."

"You need to give yourself more credit. I'm serious about opening your own place. Hey, how about trying out for one of those baking competitions on a food channel?"

Hmm. Rebekah had never thought about that. "I'll put that into my five-year plan," she said and added with a chuckle, "Actually, if I had a camera in front of me, I think I might use salt instead of sugar or forget how to turn the oven on."

Emily laughed. There it was again in Emily's laughing face. Something familiar.

Rebekah went back to her paperwork, the part of her job she most disliked. Today, she was working on the schedule for the next month. Her and Tammy's schedules stayed the same, but those of the other employees were always changing because of the needs that arose in their lives.

Tammy walked into the office. "There's a guy out here who says he's your brother Tom, and he needs to see you right away."

Rebekah looked up at Tammy with a blank, puzzled look. No one from her family ever came to the café.

"Show him back here," she said.

A minute later, Tom walked in, his head down, and Rebekah knew something was wrong. "Tom, what is it?"

"We've been trying to get ahold of you, but you haven't answered your phone."

"I've been really busy today, so I haven't checked it. There must be something wrong for you to come all the way here. Did something happen to Ethan?" she asked, clearing her throat in an attempt to release the knot that had quickly formed there.

"No, it's not Ethan. He's fine. It's Dad. This morning he went into the auto shop early before the rest of us—for what reason, I don't know. When Jake and I showed up, we found him on the floor next to one of the cars, unconscious. Naturally we called 911 right away, but he had already passed. They believe he had a heart attack."

She was stunned. Her dad had only been in his sixties. That was too young to die. Still sitting at her desk, she looked up at Tom, feeling numb and not knowing what to say or ask.

"I … can't believe it." What else could she say? "How's Mom doing?" The knot tightened.

"Not good," Tom said and shook his head. "She's a basket case. I'm worried about her."

"Let me find my assistant, to tell her what's going on, and then I'll get my things from my locker." She braced herself as she pushed up from the desk, her head spinning and her mind trying to wrap itself around what she had just found out.

Rebekah found Tammy in the kitchen. When Rebekah told her what had happened, Tammy wrapped her arms around her and held her for a long minute.

"Are you going to be okay here by yourself?" Rebekah asked her.

"You know I am, sweetheart. Go with your brother and don't think twice about us. I'll tell Fred and Michael what's going on. We're fine. Give me a call later. I'm sure your mom could use you right now."

Her mom. Rebekah didn't want to think about what her mom might be like given what Tom had said.

"Does Ethan know yet, Tom?" she asked her brother when she returned to the office.

"Yes, Mom called him right away. He's at the house. Why don't you leave your car here, and I'll drive you home? I know you're upset; maybe you shouldn't drive. We can figure out how to get your car later. What do you think?" he asked.

"Well, I guess." She hesitated. "On second thought, I want to take my car. I'll be fine following you," she said. She wanted to be alone.

Before she got in her car, her brother gave her a hug, holding on like he didn't want to let go.

"You're my baby sister, and I want to look out for you. Just get behind me and follow me, okay? I'll see you at home."

She was right to drive her own car. It was good for her to have a little alone time to let the news settle in.

Her dad was dead.

How could it be?

When she arrived at her parents' home, cars filled the driveway, and some parked on the grass. She saw Ethan's car and parked next to it.

All her brothers were there along with their wives—except Ben's wife, Rene. Rebekah wanted to find Ethan, so she briefly scanned the room before Steve, Jake, and Ben came to her wanting to know if she was okay. She assured them she was, but they wanted to replay the story of how their dad had died. The repeated details overwhelmed her, but if she had been at the shop when they first found him, maybe she would have needed to talk about it as well.

Finally, she saw Ethan in the kitchen, and their eyes met. He excused himself from one of her sisters-in-law and headed her way.

"Oh, Rebekah," he took her in his arms. "I'm so sorry we couldn't get ahold of you sooner. I was going to come get you, but Tom insisted I stay here with the family and let him go. Did he tell you all about it on the way?"

"He did before I left work, but I decided to drive my own car home. It gave me time to think."

"You never cease to amaze me—such a strong woman," he said and kissed her. "Your mom's been waiting for you. It's all she kept asking: 'Where's my girl, Rebekah?' She's so distraught."

Rebekah dreaded seeing her mom, uncertain of how her mom would react. Ethan led the way to the family room, where her mom was sitting with a tissue in her hand. Rebekah waited a minute or two and observed her. Ruth was talking to some people from church who must have come by to see what they could do to help; then she saw Rebekah. For a moment she looked blankly at her daughter, then broke down in tears and put her arms out. Rebekah went to her side, instantly forgetting the dread and the years of distance and criticism Ruth had dumped on her. Now her mother was hurting. She needed some love.

"Oh, Mom," she said and began to sob as well.

The two women held each other while the magnitude of her dad's death hit Rebekah like a brick wall. Life would never be the same again, would it? Her mom continued to cry, not saying a word.

When at last she turned away, Ethan embraced her, whispering, "I'm so sorry, Rebekah. I love you."

They stayed late into the evening. Tom and his wife decided to spend the night so her mom wouldn't be alone. The next day, plans would need to be made for the funeral. Rebekah was exhausted, as was everyone else.

When she finally arrived home—tired, worn-out, and ready to fall into bed—she managed to gather enough strength to call Tammy and let her know she wasn't sure when she'd be back to work. Tammy, of course, told Rebekah to not worry a bit. They would all pitch in. After Rebekah hung up, she found Ethan in the kitchen.

"I called James and Andrew this afternoon to give them the news," Ethan told her. "Both of them will be home on Wednesday. They said to give you their love and that they might give you a call tomorrow."

"That's good. I'm glad you told them, and I didn't have to," she replied flatly. "What about school and work for them?"

"Not a problem for either one, they said. They want to be here for you. After all, you're their mother."

The boys had both loved Rebekah's dad. He had always taken them hunting and fishing, built things with them, worked on cars, gone camping, and so many other things boys love to do.

She went into the closet, took her clothes off, and slipped her nightgown over her head before she went into the bathroom to get washed up.

When she came out of the bathroom, she saw how Ethan had thoughtfully pulled back the covers on the bed so she could just slide in. Once she made herself comfortable, she felt her body sink into the mattress and let go of some of its tension as her bed embraced her in a soft hug. Ethan came back in, silently, and sat down next to her, running his fingers through her hair and massaging the back of her neck lightly. She replayed the day in her head, not yet fully believing her dad was gone. Ethan continued to massage her neck until she finally let go and drifted off to sleep.

***

The next morning when Rebekah awoke, she felt panicked, thinking she had overslept and missed work. Then the events of yesterday came forward, and she lay back down, pulling the covers up to her chin. *What do we do next?* she wondered. She was sure Ethan knew and could guide her family through this. Ethan walked into their bedroom as if he knew what she had been thinking.

"I'm glad you're awake," he said. "I decided to sleep in James's room so you could get a good night's sleep. The next several days will be tiring for you and your family, so you need your rest. Your mom is going to be leaning on you a lot."

He came over to her side of the bed, bent over, and kissed her forehead.

"Where do we start?" she responded.

"Your brothers and I talked about that some yesterday. I'm going with your mom, Ben, and Jake to the funeral home this morning to help them with the plans."

"Do I need to go also?" Rebekah asked.

"No, you stay home. I'm meeting them in thirty minutes, so I'm leaving soon. I find the more family members involved in funeral arrangements, the more complicated and difficult they become."

"We're so fortunate we have you to help." She smiled faintly. "I feel a little guilty though."

"Not to worry—there will be plenty to do," Ethan assured her. "I'll see you later," he said and kissed her forehead again before leaving.

The back door shut and then, a moment later, his car's engine revved as he backed out of the driveway. She listened until the sound of his motor drifted to silence. The house was so quiet. This is what it would be like for her mother from now on.

After a few minutes, she headed to the kitchen to make a cup of coffee.

In the family room was a big picture window that looked out on the backyard and a tree house the boys had played in when they were little. Next to it sat a swing set that had seen better days. Her dad had built them both for James and Andrew not long after she married Ethan. Darrell had assumed Ethan would be a big help building the structures but soon found out his son-in-law didn't know a hammer from a screwdriver. Her brother Steve had "randomly" shown up that day like he was just stopping by, but Rebekah knew her dad had probably called him in for reinforcement.

Her dad had always liked doing things with her brothers and usually ignored her and Dee, almost as if they hadn't existed sometimes—unless, of course, they had done something wrong. *Then* they got a lot of attention from him. Their mom had always seemed to like the boys better as well. It could've been that after already having four boys, adding two girls had made Ruth's life more complicated. Rebekah and Dee had different needs than the boys: Ruth helped fix their hair in the morning and eased their concerns about what to wear each day. Their mom wasn't interested in dealing with all that, so Rebekah and Dee always stuck together and supported each other. That's why, after Dee left, Rebekah was so lost. She wondered how different things would have been if her sister were around—especially during a life event like this one.

Rebekah began to cry, not for her father this time but out of longing for her sister's company. All the old questions about what had happened and where Dee was came flooding in like a broken record she'd listened to way too many times. She remembered when Dee's name had slipped out of Ruth's mouth and how concerned her mother had been about her dad finding out. Ruth's reaction that day had led Rebekah to believe her mom might not have shared in Darrell's shunning of Dee. *That's okay*, Rebekah thought. She would wait for the right moment to bring Dee up again and hope her mother would tell all. She'd give all the money in the world to find her sister, if only she knew where to look.

Chapter 11

On Friday, the whole family was in the basement of the church, waiting for Ethan to give them the word to enter the sanctuary. Rebekah looked around at her brothers and their families. This was the first time in years this many of them had been together in a group, causing her to realize how large the family had become. What a shame it had taken a funeral to make this happen. She didn't even recognize many of her nieces and nephews since they had all gone off elsewhere to make their own lives and families. Why, look at her own two boys who had left for Milwaukee as soon as they could.

Ruth sat off to the side with a group of relatives. She guessed they must be her dad's brothers and their wives. Darrell had been the youngest of five boys and the first of them to die, so they had all come home to say goodbye. Rebekah thought it strange that they would come now as they had never kept any contact with her dad while he was alive. She wasn't even sure of their names since her dad had never talked of them.

The only other family funeral Rebekah could remember attending was Mère's when she was fourteen. Before Mère died, she had told Rebekah she knew the time was coming when she wouldn't be around anymore. She wanted Rebekah to be happy after she was gone; Mère had lived a wonderful life and, by that time, felt like she was just wearing out. She couldn't do the things she enjoyed in the same way anymore, and to her, that wasn't life.

About a month later, Mère went to sleep one night and didn't wake up. Mère lived with them, so Ruth went to Mère's room to see why she hadn't gotten up yet and made the discovery. Rebekah, wanting to see for herself, went into the room as well and found her grandmother lying in bed as if she were just peacefully asleep, a gentle smile spread across her lips—one Rebekah was all too familiar with. She took the old woman's hand, and although she didn't say it out loud, she sent an "I love you" to the sweet woman who had molded Rebekah into who she was.

"We're ready to begin," Ethan said, having just come downstairs to the fellowship hall.

"Ruth, your children and their families are first, and then the rest of you can assemble after, please. We have the first fifteen pews on the left in front of the pulpit reserved for family. There's not an empty seat in the church," Ethan said in a take-charge voice.

They congregated with minimal talking. Tom and his wife had taken responsibility of their mom, for which Rebekah was grateful. Tom was Ruth's favorite child, after all, and could get her to do pretty much anything.

Rebekah looked to either side of her, where James and Andrew now stood, both taking one of her hands. She loved each of her children exactly the same. Such handsome, smart, kind young men they were.

"Are you doing okay, Mom?" James asked.

"Yes, sweetheart, just thinking about how I've missed you and your brother," Rebekah said. She squeezed their hands and smiled as best she could.

Andrew put his arm around her.

"I love you both so much," she added as her eyes briefly began to water.

The moment was soon interrupted by the procession to the sanctuary. A hymn was playing as they walked in, and Rebekah felt awkward as everyone turned to stare at them while they paraded to the front of the church. Ruth began to sob as she settled into the pew with Tom, and the noise echoed throughout the room. There were so many family members present, Rebekah and her boys ended up two pews behind her mother.

A spray of white roses and carnations rested on top of her dad's casket, which sat on the altar. Pots of white lilies flanked either side of the casket. Rebekah knew they were there even before she saw the lilies; their smell carried throughout the church. They were not a favorite flower of hers because of that strong fragrance.

Ethan officiated a nice service for his father-in-law, sharing the way Darrell had welcomed Ethan into their family when he married Rebekah and how much he had loved spending time with his grandchildren, especially outdoors. Rebekah's brother Jake spoke next, telling some funny stories Rebekah had never heard before. Like the time they had been ice fishing, and their dad's car keys fell out of his pocket, slid across the ice, and fell straight into the hole they were fishing in. Steve felt a tug on his line, and when he pulled it out, there were Dad's keys dangling on his hook. This made everyone laugh.

When all was done, everybody who had attended the service went to the church basement so people could give their condolences and visit with the family. The ladies of the church had put together a little luncheon, as was tradition whenever there was a funeral. Rebekah was surprised at how the service gave a bit of closure and made her feel better—better than she thought she would—and she even saw a smile or two on her mom's face. It was a celebration of her dad's life.

Later, when the family finally left the church, they took the leftovers from the luncheon to Tom's house and invited the extended family to join them. This included her dad's brothers, Dan, Mike, Will, and Chuck, along with their wives. Everything went fine until one of them asked a question.

"So the rest of us were wondering if you're going to sell the auto shop, or buy the four of us out?" asked Dan, the oldest-looking of her dad's brothers. The other three nodded their heads.

Steve was the first to respond. "I don't know what you're talking about. Your father, our grandfather, left the business to Dad. He was the only one who stuck around to build the business while the rest of you went off to make your fortunes. It belongs to us now." Steve was surprisingly calm, matter-of-fact, and to the point.

Chuck, the tallest of the brothers, stood up, his massive frame more than a little intimidating. "I never heard any such thing. Our father left it to all of us; you should either buy us out or sell it all together. It's our legacy."

Tom then stood. "It was left to our dad in Père's will when he died. He and our dad worked side by side, and Père knew who deserved it. You all left here and never came back; you deserted Père and Mère. Is that the only reason you came here today? Is this all about money to you?"

Will now spoke. "We're only asking for what's rightfully ours. We've talked with a lawyer, and he's looked at Père's will. It was never left to Darrell."

"That's not the way I heard it. Père always said it was our dad's because he stayed to help him," Tom said. He went to the front door and opened it. "You know, I think you should all leave. We just buried our dad today, and I find bringing this up at this time not only cruel but also in very bad taste." His voice was much firmer this time.

"This isn't going to be the last you hear from us," Dan said as he looked Tom straight in the eyes, and the brothers and their families filed out of the house in silence.

Rebekah was speechless and proud of Steve and Tom for standing up the way they had.

"Who do they think they are walking in here like this?" Ruth had been silent till this point, her tone now heavy and almost frantic. "Your father and you boys built that business. It wasn't much of anything when Père was alive. You all put our money and hard work into it. I remember times your dad came home wondering if the shop would make it into the next week. It wasn't till you boys came on board that we started making money and a better life for all of us. And now your uncles waltz in here like they own the place."

Ben attempted to put his arm around Ruth, but she stood up, waving her arms as she paced the room, working herself up more and more with each breath. "Who do they think they are? *Who do they think they are?*" she repeated, her anger apparent in both her voice and her cheeks that grew increasingly crimson.

"Mom, calm down." Jake went to is mom, trying to get her to sit back down.

"We will work something out, Mom. Right Tom?" Rebekah said, concerned her mom was going to give herself a stroke.

"Yes, Mom, don't you worry," Tom said. "They don't have a leg to stand on. We'll have our own lawyer look things over. The fact that they have never taken any interest till now must be taken into account. If anything, I would think the most they can ask for is what the business was worth the day Père died, but we'll have to talk to a lawyer to be certain. I don't think they should have any claim over what we've built it into," he assured his mom.

Tom was the one who kept the books and handled the business aspect of the garage. Ruth finally sat down, relaxing into her chair, Tom's words seeming to have calmed her down some.

"I want you to stay here tonight," Tom said to Ruth, then looked to his wife. "Deb can let you use one of her nightgowns. In fact, you can stay as long as you want. We can go by your house tomorrow, and you can get a few of your things. How does that sound?"

"That's a good idea, Mom," Rebekah encouraged.

"Well, okay," Ruth said. "I think for tonight."

Rebekah knew her mom would be better off staying with Tom that night after the long, emotional day.

The siblings then decided it was best for all of them to go and let Mom get some rest.

Rebekah took Tom aside before they left. "Do you really think they can force you to sell the company?" she asked.

"I don't know, Rebekah. I'm trying to stay positive, but until I talk to a lawyer, I'm not sure. Monday morning I'm going to call one—a woman who's also our customer. I feel I can trust her to tell me straight. Then we'll have to decide what route we take. We're going to end up in a legal battle no matter what, I think. It could ruin us."

***

Ethan had kept unusually quiet at Tom's house, but when they got home and were alone, he gave his opinion. "Rebekah, I'm afraid your brothers are in for a long fight. It shocks me—the greed of your uncles to bring this up the day of your dad's funeral. As a minister, I'm exposed to a lot. Yet, so much of the time, I'm still surprised at what people hold in their hearts and the double standards that many of them live by. How will your mom live now? I'm thinking you and your brothers will have to support her. Tom and I spoke about it a while back and said your parents would be good into retirement because of the business. But this could change things for your mom and everyone else. You plan for your future, and with a snap of someone's fingers, it's gone."

Rebekah felt sick to her stomach thinking of how hard her dad and brothers had worked to make the shop a success. And now this had happened.

Ethan changed the subject. "Hey, the kids are leaving Sunday morning right after church. How about tomorrow we drive down to Appleton and look around. I'd like to share with them my news about the job I interviewed for."

Rebekah was taken aback. "I think it might be nice to stick around here," she said. "And besides, I know you feel very confident, and I'm happy you are, but it's possible you may not get the job." She couldn't believe he would suggest this when her dad had been laid to rest that very day. "It's better to surprise everyone than have to explain not getting the position."

"Oh, I suppose you're right. I just hate the waiting." He laughed. "In my mind, I already have the job."

"There's nothing wrong with that. Intentional thinking goes a long way." Rebekah took a deep breath and exhaled slowly. Now that they were home, she suddenly felt exhausted from the day. "I'm tired. Let's go to bed. Today was draining, so I think it's best to just spend the day here tomorrow. I'll make a big breakfast, and then maybe we can walk down to the lake. The kids will like that. We can even bring some fishing poles with us, and if we catch anything, I'll cook it up for supper. How does that sound? Besides, I want to go by Tom's and check up on Mom also."

Ethan put his arms around her and held her tight. "I was blessed the day you agreed to be my wife," he said as he pulled back to look at her, still holding her in his arms. "I love you, Rebekah," he added and then kissed her gently.

"I love you too, Ethan," Rebekah said. She laid her head on his chest, but she was still thinking about what had happened with her dad's brothers and wondered what the outcome would be. She would talk to Tom tomorrow when she checked on Mom and tell him to call after he got information from the lawyer on Monday.

***

Although she hated the circumstances, Rebekah was happy to have James and Andrew at home. To have both her children under one roof with her was the best medicine she could ask for. Unfortunately, however, both boys were happy away from the small-town area they'd grown up in. She didn't blame them. There was much more excitement going on in Milwaukee.

They did go fishing the next day—minus Ethan. He said he had to brush up on his sermon for Sunday, and they didn't push him. They had fun, even though they didn't catch any fish for supper. Fortunately, Rebekah had a backup plan of hamburgers to throw on the grill. James was the grill master, so she had very little to do the rest of the day.

Later in the afternoon, Rebekah went over to Tom's house. She found her mom, Ben, Tom, and Deb on the back patio, enjoying the beautiful day.

"Hi," she said as she came around the corner of the house. "How's everyone today?"

"I'm better today," her mom said, her voice unusually pleasant. "Tom says everything is all worked out and will be okay. Right, Tom?" She looked over at him with a smile. "Ben's going back to Green Bay soon so he came to say goodbye." She offered Ben the same smile she'd given Tom.

"Yes, Mom, all is fine. I've taken care of it." Tom smiled back.

Rebekah was confused. She'd never seen her mom like this before. With a slight furrow of her brow, she looked at Tom from the corner of her eye as if to say, *What's going on?*

"Rebekah, come with me. I want to show you something. Mom, you sit here with Deb, and we'll be back," he said and nodded to his wife.

"What do you want to show me?" Rebekah asked as they walked into the house.

"I really want to talk to you about a couple of things. After everyone left, Mom got so worked up over all this stuff with the business, I contacted the doctor, and they called in a prescription to help calm her down. That's why she's so happy. I was afraid she was going to have a stroke or heart attack herself," he said, running his hand through his hair then resting it on the back of his neck as he looked Rebekah in the eyes.

"That explains a lot. I don't think she's ever been that pleasant toward me before." Rebekah chuckled and shook her head. "So what else?"

"Last night I went over to Mom and Dad's house and found Père's will. Since Père died before Mère, everything was left to her—including the business. Her will specifies that everything passes equally to the five brothers. I don't need to pay a lawyer to tell me what that means. After the funeral, I called Dan and asked him what the brothers wanted. They feel that at the time of Mère's death, the business was probably worth $100,000, which they would divide five ways, making it $20,000 for each brother, and Dad's portion would go to us. We've built the business up considerably since then, so he's not being greedy. The thing is, most of the money today is tied up in the equipment and building we use to run the business. I can't sell the equipment because then we wouldn't have a business. We could somehow come up with $80,000, but it would impact our cash flow. If we don't give them the money, they could sue us. Damned if I do, damned if I don't."

"Tom, you've done a great job keeping the books and the company going but ...." Rebekah hesitated for a moment, then an idea popped into her head.

She had Tom's attention. "What is it? Do you know something I don't?"

"Can you put Dan and the rest of them off for a short while?" she asked.

"I suppose. What are you up to, Rebekah? You're making me uncomfortable," he said with his hands on his hips and a confused look on his face.

"I'm not up to anything—trust me. Can we meet Tuesday in Rhinelander right after I get off work?" she asked. "You still need to see a lawyer Monday and get some kind of legal agreement for Dad's brothers to sign and release their interest on the business. That way they can't come back on us, right?"

"Sure, but are you going to tell me more?"

"No. I have one more thing we will need. Get their full names and text them to me before you go to the lawyer's office on Monday. Everything is going to be okay," Rebekah assured him.

Tom stared at his little sister for a good while before he answered. "I sure wish you'd tell me what you're up to, Rebekah. I don't want any trouble."

"Neither do I, Tom. Neither do I." She gave her brother a peck on the cheek. "Tell Mom goodbye for me."

***

Most Sundays, Ethan stayed after church, but today he came home so he could have lunch with his family and say goodbye to the boys. They both needed to get back to Milwaukee that afternoon—James to work and Andrew to school.

Rebekah had made some bread the day before and picked up some deli meat on her way home from Tom's so they could make sandwiches. Ethan and the kids were talking and laughing at the table while Rebekah sat back in her chair, thinking about how she had missed this so much. The three most important people in her life were right in front of her. She was in heaven.

"You haven't said much, Mom," Andrew said. "Why are you so quiet?"

"It's been a long week, son. Life isn't going to be the same," she said with a slight smile. "As long as I have the three of you, though, I'll be just fine."

By 1:30 p.m., both kids were packed and ready to head back to Milwaukee and their life there, leaving Rebekah and Ethan alone again.

The rest of the day, Rebekah stayed busy so she could keep her mind off all the events of the past week. She thought it might be a good idea to make some meals and freeze them for her mom to have when she eventually came back home from Tom's. So she looked through some of her cookbooks and made a grocery list of things she needed to pick up.

Ethan was in his office working on something. She asked him if he wanted to go for a walk and, to her surprise, he said yes.

They didn't go to the trail but stayed on the road. Ethan took her hand in his.

After a long, companionable silence, Ethan spoke. "Have you ever wanted to live somewhere else?"

She was confused by his question. "Does this have anything to do with you looking for a new job? If so, I'm okay with us moving away from here. You know there's no great bond between my mother and me. She won't miss me if we move—other than not having someone to criticize. I'll go anywhere you take me, Ethan." After their visit to Appleton, she thought it might be good for them to move. Something new and different in their life.

He stopped, turned her toward him, and looked at her, keeping his eyes on her face a long time before speaking. "The day you said yes to marrying me was one of the most blessed days of my life. I couldn't have asked for a better mother for my boys or a better woman to support me. I don't deserve you." As he spoke, his breathing became irregular, and his eyes welled with tears.

"Ethan, what's wrong?" She put her arms around him. Maybe he had changed his mind and didn't want to move after all. "Don't you want to move? We can stay here forever if that's what you want. Is all this death getting to you? Eddie and now my dad. It is close to home, but you're fine."

He kissed her and took her hand again. "I'm okay as long as I have you," he said, and they walked home in silence.

After dinner, when she was alone in the kitchen cleaning up, Rebekah thought about her conversation with Tom from the day before. The solution was simple: she'd give him the $80,000 to pay off her dad's brothers. She had the money, so how could she not? But how would she explain where the money had come from? She would need to come up with something—and soon.

When she finished in the kitchen, she checked her phone to see if the boys had called or messaged; a mother always worries when her children travel. There was a text from Tom.

> I talked with Dan. Here's the full names
> of the other brothers. Sure wish I knew
> what you were up to, little sister.

She responded with a thumbs-up.

Tomorrow after work she would go to the bank and have four $20,000 cashiers' checks written for each of the four brothers. On Tuesday, she would meet with Tom and give him the checks so the business could continue. It was done. Now the only thing they'd have to deal with was learning to cope in with a world without their dad.

Chapter 12

All Rebekah had on her mind when she drove to work on Monday was the interaction with her dad's brothers. She was so happy she could do something to help out and was relieved her dad didn't have to experience this. After all, he had put so much hard work into building the business. She knew that after they paid the brothers, the full impact of her father's death would hit her family. There was no doubt this would be a tough year for them all.

Rebekah had decided to come into work earlier than usual so she could have some alone time. Tammy had done a great job keeping things running while she was gone. Rebekah was glad Tammy had been able to show her ability to take charge. If Ethan got the job in Appleton, Rebekah thought Fred would probably offer her vacated position to Tammy, and she was certain Tammy could handle it.

She walked into her office, where she found a bouquet of beautiful flowers sitting on her desk. The card that rested against the vase was signed by everyone in the store, extending their sympathies to Rebekah and her family. *So sweet of them*, she thought. The flowers were an eclectic combination and reminded her of a field of wildflowers. *What a great way to start the week.*

Rebekah settled into her desk chair and had begun looking over her never-ending paperwork and emails when she heard activity out in the bakery, followed by Tammy's friendly voice.

"I knew I would find you here. Come and give me a hug," Tammy said as she entered the office. She extended her arms out like two wings, ready to enfold Rebekah.

Rebekah accepted her warm hug and, almost immediately, began to sob.

"There, there," Tammy said. She held her friend tight and patted her back.

Rebekah felt her feelings flood out onto Tammy. Her friend made her feel so safe; what would she do if she and Ethan moved?

"I'm sorry, Tammy. I'm not sure what came over me."

"Oh, hon. It's just how it is when people die. You break down at the most inopportune times. The craziest little things will trigger you, and you think you're going nuts, but you're perfectly normal. That's just grieving," Tammy replied, looking fully into Rebekah's eyes as she stroked her hair. "You're going to be just fine, my friend. Now tell me all about it."

They spent about fifteen minutes talking about the family and funeral before remembering they needed to start the ovens. Rebekah decided to omit the drama from her dad's brothers, even though she knew the story was one Tammy would enjoy. Tammy loved family drama, and Rebekah was certain she would want to share her opinion as to what they should do.

"So the staff did well last week? How about Emily? Hey, I forgot to ask you if she showed up that Friday night at the tavern." Rebekah asked.

"Nope. Never showed. Had some excuse about having some things to take care of. I like her, but like I said, she's kind of secretive, and I feel some dark energy. I guess I can be intimidating, though, so it's probably just me." Tammy laughed.

Rebekah looked at Tammy. "You? Never!" Then both women laughed.

The day went on like any regular Monday. When Michael came in, he made sure to find Rebekah and give her his sympathies.

"Dad wanted me to tell you that if you need any time off to take care of things, don't hesitate," he told her.

"Well thank you, Michael. Your family has always been so good to me," she replied.

Michael's face flushed, and for the moment, things were awkward between them once more.

"Back to work," she said, breaking the discomfort, and Michael returned to the deli.

It was good to be back to normal life … for now. She would still have to stop at the bank after work to have the checks made out for each of the four brothers, which, she had to admit, felt far from normal.

Fortunately, obtaining the checks was much easier than Rebekah had imagined. She filled out and signed a form, ran her debit card through the terminal, showed the teller her ID and a paper on which she had written the four names, and was done.

She didn't want to take her debit card or the checks home with her, so she went to the back room in the store to visit her locker, hoping to avoid any notice.

"Hey, what are you doing back here? Any problems I need to know about?" It was Michael, who walked up behind her just as she was approaching the lockers.

"Ah, no, ah … just forgot something," she said, turning to get away from him.

"I thought you would be home by now. You didn't get home and have to come back, did you?" Michael persisted.

Why couldn't he mind his own business? "Oh. No. I did a little shopping in town and realized I needed to get something from my locker before I headed home," she said and turned away from him, continuing toward the lockers.

Michael followed her, rambling about some idea he had for the deli. Rebekah paid no attention as she arrived at her locker and waited for him to leave. He stood, waiting for her response.

"Michael, I have to get home. Can we discuss this tomorrow? I'm in a bit of a hurry." Finally, he took the hint and walked off.

As soon as Michael was out of sight, she put the four envelopes under the latest stack of romance novels Tammy had given her. Then she remembered the excuse she had given Michael and realized she better have something from her locker in case she ran into him. She grabbed the romance novel on the top. Good thing she had because there was Michael again.

"So you forgot your book," he said. "I'm the same way when I get reading. Just can't put it down. Well, enjoy. See you tomorrow."

"Bye," she said and headed straight for the door.

When she got home, she put the novel in the canvas bag she took to work every day and left it in the car, shoved under one of the seats. After changing her clothes and making herself a cup of tea, she called Tom.

"Hi, Tom. I wanted to check in with you. Did you get to the lawyer's office today?"

"I did. She's going to have some documents for me on Wednesday," Tom informed her, then quickly changed the subject. "I'm still trying to figure out what you have up your sleeve."

"Don't worry about it. Just meet with me tomorrow like we talked about," she said.

"That's the other thing. I was wondering if I could meet you about halfway instead. When you get to Highway 45 on your way home, take the exit and turn right. Continue down that road till you see a place on the left called The Boondocks. We won't see anyone we know in there. I'll be waiting for you."

"Okay," she told him. "You've been there before?"

"You might say so," he said, then laughed. "Can't wait till I see you tomorrow."

"Everything is going to be fine; trust me. See you then," she said, and they said their goodbyes.

Now what was she going to tell Tom about the money? A shade of the truth would probably be best. She decided that after she saw how their conversation went, she would know what to say to him. She'd go on faith.

***

Even with giving Tom the $80,000, Rebekah would still have enough money to open a bakery and more. Her secret would be out at that point—and then what? The money didn't seem real to her and felt more like a bunch of numbers. She had to admit, though, it gave her a rush every time she added more and saw her balance. The investment guy she worked with handled everything for her. Sure, he made money off her, but she considered it well worth it for the excellent job he did managing her funds. She guessed she might be one of his wealthiest clients. He also took care of her taxes since she had to pay quarterly. Ethan thought she went to one of those storefront places every year. Unbelievably, it worked out well that they had decided to file their taxes separately.

By midday on Tuesday, Rebekah felt caught up with emails and paperwork and was able to spend more time actually baking and talking with her staff. They were all genuinely concerned about her family. It was so nice to work with people like that.

Later in the morning, she and Emily were putting some finishing touches on some small fruit tarts for an order to be picked up soon thereafter.

"Are things going okay here for you, Emily? You're coming up on two months, but it seems as if you've been here longer. You really do a good job."

"Thanks, Rebekah," Emily said. "I like being here. I'm surprised, but I find a lot of satisfaction in baking. Kind of weird."

Rebekah placed her hand on Emily's shoulder. "Not weird at all. It's the same thing I feel. I love to bake for my family or friends, and while they taste what I made, they go on about how wonderful it is. That always feels good."

They both smiled.

"Where did you get your love of baking?" Emily asked.

"My grandmother lived with us and taught me everything she knew about baking. Our family history was in baking—for centuries, I've been told—going back to when my ancestors lived in France. My maiden name is Boulanger, which meant you were a baker back in the old days. It's in my genes," she shared.

"That's nice," Emily said. "Maybe it's in my genes also because I sure do enjoy it. I especially like making pâte á choux for eclairs and crème puffs. I love what the batter transforms into. You can make it into whatever shape you decide to create with your piping bag."

Rebekah smiled again. "Go ahead and experiment with it and see what new creation you come up with. I have some cookbooks at home with ideas you might want to look at. I'll bring those in. Over the years, I've found that our customers love when we sell something new and different. You can even make savory fillings for the puffs if you'd like. That would be nice to offer close to the holidays," Rebekah suggested.

"Okay," Emily said. "Thanks, Rebekah." She seemed excited.

"I'm just curious, Emily. What do you do with yourself when you're not working?" Rebekah ventured.

"Not much. I've been riding around, becoming familiar with the area. I visited a church this past Sunday. Thought it might be a good place to make friends."

Rebekah had an idea. "I'd love to have you visit my church. We're outside of Rhinelander to the east, not too far. I'll give you the address, and you can come this Sunday if you would like. No pressure. If you come, make sure you look for me, and we can sit together. Like I said, only if you want to."

"I'll think about it," Emily said.

Rebekah wrote down the address for her, then decided she wouldn't bring it up again. After all, Emily hadn't visited the tavern when she told Tammy she would come by. Maybe she didn't like mixing work with her private life. That was okay.

"Now let's get these tarts in a box for pickup," Rebekah said, ending the church conversation. Emily may have been different, but she sure was a good worker. And a hard worker like her was exactly what Rebekah needed, so she would leave it at that. Besides, she had her upcoming meeting with Tom to concentrate on.

***

As Rebekah was walking out of work, she called Tom to tell him she was on her way.

A little less than halfway home, she came upon the exit for Highway 45. She took the exit and, after a while, came to a red building on the left-hand side of the road. As she pulled in to the gravel parking lot, she saw Tom's car and parked next to it.

The large sign on the building read The Boondocks. Below it was smaller sign that said Home of Ugly Bartenders, Warm Beer, Lousy Food, Slow Service. *Okay*, Rebekah thought. *I don't think I have to worry about seeing anybody I know.* She went through the door, and before her eyes could adjust to the darkness, she heard Tom's voice coming from the bar area.

"Rebekah," Tom called and walked over to her. "Let's sit over here," he said and pointed to a table off in the corner. She went to it, not noticing the beer he had in his hand until they sat down. She looked at him with surprise.

He raised his glass. "I like beer," he said and took a long gulp before asking, "Do you want one?"

"No, I'll take a pop," she responded, still a little stunned to see Tom with a beer. "Did Dad know you drank? Or does Mom?"

He chuckled and shook his head. "Nope. We all drink, Rebekah. Heck, any one of our siblings could walk in right now. We come here because there's no chance of bumping into Mom, Dad, or your husband—no offense." He took another drink. "We play poker on Thursday nights. We would rather play on Wednesday, but we're usually at church," he said with another laugh.

"No offense taken," she responded, thinking about the sermon Ethan would come up with if he knew about this. It was good to know she wasn't the only one with a secret. "I thought you picked this place because we wouldn't see anyone we knew, not because you're a regular."

"Let's just say," Tom responded, "we won't see anyone who could make things difficult for us here. What happens here stays here. So, little sister, what do you have up your sleeve? You have me totally in the dark about what's going on."

Rebekah opened up her purse and pulled out the four envelopes and handed them to Tom. He opened them up one by one and then looked at her not similarly to the way she had looked at him when she saw the beer in his hand.

"What have you done?" he asked. He looked up to meet her gaze, his eyes wide with disbelief. "Where did this come from?"

"It's to pay off Dad's brothers," she said, trying to sound casual.

"Well, I figured that out but—I mean—it's a lot of money. I had no idea you and Ethan had that kind of money."

"*Ethan* and I don't." She paused a long time before proceeding.

Tom stared at her, waiting.

"It's my money. Ethan doesn't know anything about it."

She could see Tom look away slightly and squint his eyes as he tried to make sense of what she had just said. This prompted her to come clean with him ... but not to the full extent. Partial honesty was the best line of defense for her. She was a wealthy woman, but that was nobody's business but her own.

She took a deep breath and began. "A long time ago, I started buying lottery tickets and scratch offs. I was lucky. Everyone at work was buying them so I thought, *Why not?* You know what would have happened if Ethan had known. Well, I won several times, so I opened a savings account for my winnings—$80,000. So when you said that's what you needed, I thought, *Wow, God has provided for our family!*"

Dang she was good.

"That's a lot of money. What about taxes? You know you have to claim that. I play the lottery also."

"You do? Did Dad know?"

"You think I'm crazy? No."

"Well, Ethan and I have always done our taxes separately. He told me we needed to do it that way, so it worked out well," she explained.

"What? That makes no sense, Rebekah—to do your taxes separately, I mean. I'm not a tax expert, but I think it's always better to file as married," Tom said.

"Right now, that's not important." She waved her hand in the air. "You've got your money, but no one can know where it came from. So what are you going to say?" Rebekah asked.

Tom thought for a while—a long while. He took another drink of his beer and then another before responding. "I don't know," he said.

Then Rebekah had an idea. She was on a roll. "How about you tell the family your lawyer found a loophole, and it turns out Dad's brothers have no claim on the business. Then, tell the brothers we'll pay the money, but they can never tell anyone else they received the funds. Have the lawyer indicate in the paper she's putting together that none of them can speak about the money to anyone. Honestly, I think they started at twenty thousand dollars, each knowing we would try to negotiate for less. So they should be happy about what they're getting and, hopefully, willing to keep quiet. Also put in the paper they sign that they may never contact anyone in our family as long as they live. I'm sure we'll never see them again anyway."

"I'll have to think about it," Tom said. "I told them they had to give us some time to put together the money anyway, so let's just take this slow, okay? Not go too fast and make a mistake."

"Okay. You're right. We don't want to make the wrong move."

"I want you to keep the checks till we need them," Tom said, handing them back to Rebekah.

"No, you keep them. I can't take a chance that Ethan will find them. Besides, as far as I'm concerned, you're taking care of it. My part is done."

"I have to say, it's good to know we have the money. I'm grateful, and your secret is safe. See? We all have secrets."

"I guess we do," she said and laughed.

***

On the ride home, she felt good knowing she wasn't the only imperfect one in the family. But were they really imperfect? Or was she just made to feel that way? Wasn't life about enjoying the journey and not constantly striving to behave in the way others wanted you to?

Her mom and Ethan came to mind. Rebekah only conformed to them so as not to make waves. She wanted to stop this but wasn't sure how. Maybe that's why Dee had left. Maybe Dee hadn't wanted to conform. Maybe Dee told their parents what they could do with themselves, like Rebekah wanted to sometimes. Maybe, in reality, the ones who thought themselves normal were really the abnormal ones, and the rest of them were actually perfect and normal just as they were.

Now that her dad was gone, she decided she was going to insist her mom tell her what happened with Dee. She wouldn't relent until she knew the truth. Rebekah would find the sister she had constantly wondered about since the day Dee left her behind.

Chapter 13

On Friday, Rebekah received a text from Tom. He had talked to Dan and told him they were still dealing with funeral things and would get back with him after Easter.

"Let them sit and wait," Tom told her. Rebekah just wanted the whole thing to be over.

Next week being the week before Easter meant there was a lot to do in the bakery. People were ordering a range of baked goods for their Easter weekend celebrations, meaning the days would get busier as the holiday drew closer. Rebekah was in the supply room, making a list of what she needed to order, when Emily came in.

"I was thinking about your invitation to come to your church, and I want to take you up on it if it's still okay," Emily said.

Rebekah put her clipboard down to give Emily her full attention. She'd actually forgotten she'd invited Emily with everything going on in her life.

"Well of course it's okay. I'm happy you want to come. Service starts at ten thirty. Do you still have the address I gave you the other day?" she asked.

"Yes."

"Listen, my order is due to be picked up in an hour, so I have to get back to this, but if you have any questions, let me know, okay?"

"Sure," Emily said.

Rebekah was happy Emily had decided to come. They didn't get a lot of visitors, so this would be nice. Soon her concentration was back to her order and the things that needed to be finished before she went home.

***

Palm Sunday was a joyful day at church. All the children were gathered at the back of the sanctuary, waiting to be given a palm frond just before the music started. If they were given one too far in advance, the boys would terrorize the girls with them and use them as weapons on anything walking by.

Rebekah kept an eye on the back of the church, watching for Emily to walk in. She was beginning to think Emily had decided not to come when she suddenly appeared, weaving her way through the sea of children. Rebekah gave a little wave to get her attention, and Emily headed her way.

"I'm sorry, but I took a wrong turn coming here. Such a cute, old-timey church," Emily said, looking around as she sat next to Rebekah.

"Well, no problem. You made it just in time. The service is about to start," Rebekah told her. As if on cue, the organ music began, and the children made their way down the aisle. Rebekah leaned over with the hymnal in her hands to share with Emily, who it turned out had a pretty singing voice.

Rebekah loved to watch the little ones as they processed. A few were eager, some looked overwhelmed, and the youngest of them followed the older ones with a look that said, "I don't know what's going on." All of them made sure to search for their parents in the congregation to get that reassuring smile that told them they were seen.

"I remember my boys doing this as if it were yesterday," Rebekah said to Emily with a little catch in her throat.

Ethan brought up the rear of the procession and sat on the side of the altar that she and Emily couldn't see. The children found their parents, and once everyone was settled, they began. Some prayers were said and scripture read before they sang another hymn while the collection plate was passed. Rebekah saw Emily drop some folded bills into the plate when it passed by. Several of the church deacons conducted this part of the service until it was time for the sermon.

As Ethan stepped up to the pulpit, Emily took in a sharp inhale that didn't go unnoticed by Rebekah.

"Who is that man?" Emily whispered, her voice panicked.

"The minister. He's my husband."

Emily looked at her blankly before she continued. "Your husband?"

Ethan's eyes scanned the congregation as he prepared to speak, but when he reached Emily, he fixed his gaze on her, not looking away. His smile faded as he stared without uttering a word, creating an awkward silence as everyone waited for him to begin. The color drained from his face, and his body wavered as if he might pass out.

What's wrong? thought Rebekah as she felt her chest tighten.

Sensing the situation, one of the deacons went to Ethan's side to speak to him, but Ethan waved him away as he kept his eyes on Emily. The deacon persisted and forced Ethan to sit down.

"I'm sorry, Rebekah," Emily said with tears in her eyes. "I didn't mean to hurt you. I've got to leave." Without hesitation, she stood and ran, slipping out of the church. Everyone's eyes were focused on Ethan.

Rebekah was so confused. She watched Emily leave, then went to where Ethan was sitting, his eyes rolling around and his breathing heavy. She looked to the deacon who had gone to Ethan's side.

"I think we need to call 911," the deacon said as Rebekah squatted next to Ethan.

But as soon as Ethan heard this, he screamed, "No! Let me alone. Where is she?"

"Rebekah's right here," the deacon said.

By then, Steve and Jake had run up to see if they could help.

Ethan said it again, wildly. "Where is she?"

"Rebekah's here, Ethan." This time it was Jake telling him.

"No, not her." Ethan looked around, his eyes wide and glassy. "I think I saw a ghost," he said.

"A ghost? Of who?" Jake asked, looking at Rebekah.

Rebekah felt sick. What was going on?

Ethan's head was bobbing, and he began to slide out of the chair. But after a moment, he seemed to rally and said he was fine. He stood up and staggered a few steps before falling forward and hitting his head on the altar. He was out cold.

"That's it," the deacon said as he pulled out his phone and dialed 911.

Tom stepped down from the altar to tell the congregation who had gathered at the front of the church that it appeared Reverend Hayward needed to go to the hospital, and they should go home and pray for him. Many of them still hung around outside, but the sanctuary was cleared by the time the paramedics arrived.

Two paramedics hustled down the center aisle, wheeling in a gurney and some equipment. They asked Rebekah questions about his medical history, medications, and the like as they hooked him up to monitors, took his blood pressure, and, ever so gingerly, guided him onto the gurney. Because of the head injury, not to mention Ethan's strange behavior prior to the fall, the best thing was to get him ready and stable for transport as quickly as possible. They would monitor him in the ambulance and maybe have some answers by the time they arrived at the hospital in Rhinelander. Rebekah could ride in the front with their driver.

It all happened fast. Tom sent Deb home with their mother and told the rest of the family Rebekah didn't need a bunch of people at the hospital. He would follow in his car to be with her and let everyone else know what was going on when he found out.

Rebekah was sitting alone in the waiting room, dazed, when Tom found her.

"Rebekah!" he said, as he spotted her. He moved quickly to her side and embraced her. "What have you heard?"

"Not a thing. I'm so happy you're here, though," she said, her voice trembling. "I'm not sure what's going on, but I think there's more to it than meets the eye."

"What more could there be? Ethan had a heart attack or something, and he hit his head."

But Rebekah had seen the look on Ethan's face when he first spotted Emily. Emily's remarks—"I'm sorry, Rebekah. I didn't mean to hurt you"—echoed in her head. And Ethan had thought he saw a ghost. What was going on?

"I'm sure you're right," she said, but she didn't believe it.

It seemed like forever until a tall physician came to the waiting area and introduced himself as Dr. Clark. Ethan had not had a heart attack or stroke, but a panic attack. Sometimes, he explained, a panic attack could mimic a heart attack with its symptoms. Ethan did have a concussion from his fall, however, and had been so delirious and agitated, they had to sedate him. As a result, they wanted to observe him overnight. If all seemed well come morning, he would be allowed to go home late in the afternoon.

"Can we go in and see him?" Rebekah asked.

"Your husband said he didn't want to see anyone," the doctor told her. "I know he isn't himself right now, but we have to respect his wishes."

"Even though he's my husband?" she said with slight indignance.

"Yes, but he did ask about you, Emily, wanting to know if you were here," the doctor said reassuringly.

Tom was the first to respond. "Emily? Who's Emily?" He gestured toward his sister. "This is his wife, Rebekah."

The doctor coughed and raised his eyebrows. "Like I said, he was a bit delirious. It's not unusual for people to be confused after a head injury."

Rebekah felt her throat and chest tighten while her stomach churned.

"I'm also going to have one of our staff therapists stop by in the morning to talk with him. Something triggered the panic attack. We want to make sure he knows there's help for him if he has another one. If the attacks continue, there are some medications that can help. Since he has never had an attack before, I'm reluctant to put him on anything at this time, but if they become regular, he needs to pursue that route."

Rebekah stretched out her hand. "Thank you, Dr. Clark. I appreciate you taking care of my husband. I'm not sure why he doesn't want to see me other than he might be embarrassed. Would you mind going back to see if he has changed his mind?"

"Sure, I'll ask again," he said and left.

"Rebekah, it's odd that he doesn't want to see you," Tom said after the doctor was out of sight. "Maybe it's good he's going to talk to someone tomorrow."

"Yes, maybe so," she responded.

A nurse by the name of Jessie came out and kindly told Rebekah that Ethan just wanted to rest. "I'm caring for him myself, so if you want to call later, I'll give you an update, okay?" She handed Rebekah a slip of paper with her name and phone number. "Don't worry, sweetie. Men can be very difficult when something goes wrong. They think they're made of steel. A good night's sleep is best sometimes." She put her hand on Rebekah's back for a moment, and they said their goodbyes.

Tom drove Rebekah back to the church to get her car. It was late afternoon by then.

"Hey, why don't you come back to my house for dinner? No need to be alone right now. We're going to cook on the grill tonight. There's always room for another bratwurst," Tom suggested.

"No, I think I need some alone time. I'm going to give James and Andrew a call to let them know what's going on, and then I might sit out on my deck."

"How about a bottle of wine?" Tom suggested. He laughed and added, "I won't tell."

She tapped his arm, playfully. "Don't tempt me." And she laughed as well.

Tom wrapped his arms around her for a big bear hug that lifted her feet off the ground. Then he kissed the top of her head. "I love you, little sister. I'm always here for you. You know that, right? Our family has had a lot going on, but we have each other. Don't forget it."

"I won't," she said and gave him a peck on the cheek before getting in her car.

As much as she loved and appreciated Tom, the last thing she wanted was to have to make conversation with anyone—especially her mom. They would all want to talk about what had happened to Ethan, and God only knew what her mom might have to say. No doubt Ruth would find some way to blame it on her. No, Rebekah didn't want to have to relive what had happened that morning. She was better off alone for now.

Once inside, Rebekah changed her clothes, made a cup of tea, and went out on the deck with her phone to call the kids. She tried James first, but he didn't answer, so she called Andrew.

"Hey, sweetheart. How's your day been?" she asked, trying to sound positive and upbeat.

"It's been good, Mom. The afternoon warmed up enough that I went biking."

"Did James go also? I called him, but he didn't answer."

"Ah, no, he had other things to do," Andrew responded.

"It's nice the two of you live together. Makes a mom feel good knowing you guys watch out for each other. I know I usually call you later on Sundays, but I wanted you to know Dad had to go to the hospital today—nothing serious." She wasn't going to tell them it was a panic attack. "He got dizzy just as he was getting ready to give his sermon this morning, and he fell and hit his head. We were worried that it came on so fast, so he went to the hospital to get checked out. The doctor felt it wasn't really anything major, but they're keeping him until tomorrow afternoon just as a precaution to make sure. Dad just wants to rest, so I came home," she said and sighed.

"Gee, Mom. That's kind of scary after what happened to Grandpa."

"I know, but your dad is a young guy. He's going to be fine."

"Are you okay?" he asked.

How sweet of him to be worried, she thought. Both boys were always so protective of her. "I'm fine, son. I'm a rock."

"You are the rock of our family, that's for sure. Should I give Dad a call tonight? James can also if you think it's a good idea," he suggested.

"Actually, I think it best to let your dad rest. You can maybe call him tomorrow night, after he's back home."

"Okay, sounds good," he said.

Rebekah changed the subject and asked about what was going on in Andrew's life, how school was, and other general conversation.

"Tell your brother I love him and to call if he has any other questions about Dad. He's really okay and just needs to take a rest, I think. We've talked about going on a little vacation to Door County after Easter, and as far as I'm concerned, I'm not letting your dad talk me out of it after all this."

"I agree, and you can always come see us. Lots to do and good food in Milwaukee. You should come down and visit the bakeries, Mom. I'll be happy to go with you. Come by yourself sometime if Dad can't get away."

"You know what, I'm going to do it after Door County. Love you, Andrew."

"You too, Mom," he said and hung up.

A loneliness settled in Rebekah's heart. She missed the boys and the activity they brought to her world but understood why they would prefer to be in Milwaukee. The opportunities for smart, driven young men like them were so much greater there.

Next, her mind went to Emily. Although confusing by all indications, it appeared Emily and Ethan somehow knew each other. But Ethan never came over to Rhinelander, and Emily was new to the area. Maybe Emily hadn't been truthful to Rebekah. Could they have been having an affair? *When would Ethan even have time for that?* she wondered. Still, maybe an affair could have explained Ethan's previous lack of interest in her, though he had been more interested lately. That could also be the reason why he wanted to move. A fresh start for them. It was possible. But Emily appeared not to know Rebekah was married to Ethan or that he was the minister of a church. He could have lied. She was overthinking it all way too much.

She went in and made another cup of tea, then came back to the deck before deciding to call the nurse who was caring for Ethan. She was put on hold a few minutes before the nurse picked up.

"I'm happy you called," the nurse said. "Nothing has changed. He keeps saying he saw a ghost. Do you know what he means?" she asked.

"No, I have no idea," Rebekah answered.

"Maybe he was imagining things from the bump on the head," she rationalized.

But Rebekah remembered him saying that *before* he bumped his head. Had he thought Emily was a ghost? Emily appeared to recognize him, but maybe she just thought she did. It was all so confusing. The answers would come tomorrow.

"I really don't know," Rebekah repeated. "When should I come by tomorrow to get him?"

"Late morning, maybe after lunch, so we have time to review all the tests, and the therapist can talk with him. Give me a call in the morning, and I can tell you what time. He seems like a really nice man. I'm sure things will be fine for you."

"Yes, I'm sure you're right," Rebekah said. "I'll see you tomorrow."

The sun was beginning to sink behind the trees. Soon it would start to get chilly. Rebekah decided she would go into work at the usual time tomorrow. The week before Easter was busy, so she needed to be there, especially after all the time she had taken off when her dad died.

Plus, she wanted to talk to Emily.

Life can really pour it on, Rebekah thought. She was tired—two major life events within two weeks.

Tom called to check up on things and offered to accompany her to the hospital the next day, but she told him things would be fine. She was going into work and would call midmorning to see how Ethan was and what time she could bring him home. He said okay but not to hesitate if she needed him.

It had become dark, so she went inside. Somehow being outside with the trees and animal sounds had kept her mind distracted from the reality of life at the moment. She wished she could just sleep on the deck, but it was cold, not to mention the fact that her bed was more comfortable.

Tomorrow she would face Emily. It would be awkward, but it had to be done, even if she learned that Ethan and Emily had been involved with one another. Until she knew the truth, Rebekah wasn't sure how she would handle it. Then again, it could all be nothing. She would know soon, either way.

Chapter 14

Emily didn't show up for work the next day. No call, nothing. Tammy tried calling her but received no answer. This was not a good sign.

"I hope she's okay. Did she show up at your church yesterday?" Tammy asked.

"Yes, but ... well ... I don't know ..." Rebekah said, hesitating.

"What do you mean, *I don't know?*" Tammy's eyes widened with anticipation as she waited to hear something juicy. "Okay, so what happened?"

"I'm not really sure," Rebekah responded. "Emily came to church yesterday, but ...." She shrugged, uncertain of what to say next.

"Hey, let's go to your office so you can tell me everything, uninterrupted," Tammy said and led the way.

Rebekah sat in her desk chair, with Tammy across from her.

"Start from the beginning," Tammy said, raising her eyebrows.

Rebekah proceeded to tell her everything she knew. She really did need a friend like Tammy right now.

When Rebekah finished, Tammy was speechless for a few seconds and then finally spoke. "Holy crap! You have got to be kidding. Holy crap!" She stood up and paced in the small office, her mouth hanging open in shock. "That sweet little Emily. Do you think they're having an affair?" She sat back down in her chair put her elbows on the desk and her chin in her hands as she waited for Rebekah's response.

It was hard for Rebekah to hear Tammy's question aloud, even though it was the same question she had been asking herself. She could only shrug her shoulders.

"So what's your plan?" Tammy asked.

"Well, I'd planned to talk to Emily when she came into work today, but otherwise, I have none."

"Oh, please, you've got to have a better plan than that. It's a good thing you know me. I say let's confront her. I'll be right by your side. I bet she seduced him. She's so cute and sweet—in fact, she kind of reminds me of you. He fell for it. Men can be so weak …." Tammy went on and on, shaking her head from side to side before letting out a loud, exaggerated sigh.

"Tammy, stop. I'm picking Ethan up from the hospital after lunch, and then I'll get the answers. I'm sure it's nothing, and I have too much work to do here to let any speculation interfere today. Don't bring it up again, okay?" Rebekah said, on the verge of tears.

Tammy breathed in and out with a sigh before answering. "Okay."

***

Later in the morning, Rebekah called the hospital and talked to Jessie, the same nurse from the day before, to ask about Ethan and when to pick him up.

"Well," she hesitated, "he checked himself out this morning against our wishes. We can't forcibly keep anyone," she told Rebekah.

"Where did he go? Who picked him up?" Rebekah asked, her questions falling from her mouth in a deluge.

"We have no idea," the nurse responded.

The moment she was off the phone, Rebekah found Tammy and told her.

"Time for a plan, Rebekah," Tammy said, her voice filled with determination. "Let's finish up here and then give Emily a visit. We have her address. I'm going with you for moral support, so don't even try to talk me out of it. After all, he may be at her place," Tammy said with a sly tone.

Rebekah thought for a good while and then said, "Okay, but let me do the talking when we get there."

Tammy went to a locked file cabinet and, after finding Emily's employee folder, wrote her address down on a piece of paper. "I know right where this is," she said as she relocked the cabinet. "In a few hours, you'll have your answers."

***

Emily lived on the left side of a duplex. Even though her car wasn't parked in the driveway, they still knocked on the door. Tammy was expecting Ethan to answer, but he didn't. In fact, nobody did.

"Well, darn," Tammy said as they walked back to the car. "What should we do now?"

"I guess go home," Rebekah responded as she climbed into the passenger side of Tammy's car.

Just as they started down the road, Tammy eyed Emily's car coming from the opposite direction. She executed a quick U-turn.

"Ha, ha! We're going to catch her before she gets in the house," she said, and they were in hot pursuit.

They arrived just as Emily was getting out of the car. She was preoccupied with a bag of groceries, allowing Tammy and Rebekah to approach the house unnoticed.

"We missed you at work today," Tammy said.

Emily jumped then quickly turned around.

"Please leave me alone," she said. She turned to Rebekah with a pleading, anguished look across her face. "I had no idea, Rebekah."

"Emily, please tell me. What's going on?" Rebekah moved closer to her. "How do you know Ethan? I need some answers."

"You really don't know?" Emily asked, looking as if she might cry. "I like you so much, Rebekah, and would never want to hurt you. You gave me a job and were so kind when I needed it. I don't know how to say this."

"Just tell me," Rebekah pleaded.

"You know him as Ethan, but his real name is Edwin. I don't know what he's told you but ..." Emily hesitated, staring down at her feet for a moment and then back up at Rebekah. "I'm married to him. He's my husband, Rebekah. Not yours." And with that, Emily stepped into her house and slammed the door.

Tammy turned to Rebekah, her mouth hanging open for a moment, before she finally spoke. "Wow. I sure did not see that coming. I've seen this stuff before on TV but never in real life. You really had no idea?"

Rebekah turned and, without a word, walked to Tammy's car. Tears flowed down her cheeks. "Take me back to the store so I can get my car," she said.

Rebekah was grateful Tammy knew her well enough not to speak. When they got to the store parking lot, Rebekah was more composed and finally spoke. "Tammy, I appreciate you going with me to find Emily. You have always been such a great friend. At this point, I don't know what's real or made up, but I'm going to get to the bottom of it. First, I have to figure out where Ethan is so I can get some straight answers. I'm going home for now, but I'll see you tomorrow." And before Tammy could say anything, she hopped out of the car and into her own to head home.

The ride home gave her time to go over what Emily had said. It made no sense. Emily must be delusional or have other mental issues.

To Rebekah's surprise, Ethan's car was parked in its usual spot in the driveway. How did it get there? Maybe one of her brothers had brought it home so it wouldn't sit at the church, adding to the congregation's curiosity about what had happened the day before. Her question was soon answered when she walked through the back door, for there was Ethan, sitting at the kitchen table. In his hand was a glass filled with ice and an amber-colored liquid, a tall, brown liquor bottle to his right. She took her eyes from the bottle and looked at him.

"Ethan, how did you get here?" she started. There were so many questions. "I called the hospital to see what time I could pick you up, and they said you had left against their wishes. How did you get home?"

Ethan was a mess, still wearing the same clothes from church the day before. His hair looked like it hadn't been combed in the last twenty-four hours, and an unfamiliar stubble had sprouted from his cheekbones down to his neck. He took a big drink and then exhaled with a quick sigh. He still hadn't looked at her or acknowledged her presence. She could see his eyes were glassed over and unsteady.

"Have you ever heard of these people you can just call to pick you up and take you wherever you want to go? For a fee, of course," he replied after several long seconds. He took another swig of liquor before speaking again. "They'll take you anywhere."

"So … that's how you got home?"

"No, that's how I got to the church to get my car. Then I came home—no wait, I didn't come straight home. I stopped at the liquor store to get this bottle of whiskey. I didn't buy the cheap stuff either," he said, his voice somewhat slurred. He raised his glass. "Do you want some too?" he asked, still avoiding eye contact.

"I'll pass," she said and sat down across from him. She decided she wasn't going to waste any time and went straight to it. "So what was that all about yesterday, and who's Emily?" She wasn't going to tell him about how she knew Emily. She wanted to hear his story first. He didn't respond, so she asked again. "So what was that all about yesterday?" she repeated.

"I heard you the first time. I just don't want to answer," he said, finally looking her in the eyes.

Now it was her turn to be silent. She stared at him without wavering.

Almost falling, Ethan got up from his chair and said, "I have to pee," before stumbling down the hallway to the bathroom.

He seemed to take forever, and she was getting ready to check on him when she heard the toilet flush, then water running. Another minute or two passed before the door clicked open, and he returned. He sat down, took another long drink of whiskey and then another before he began.

"I don't know where to start," he said, running his fingers through his disheveled hair.

She waited. It was a good five minutes before he spoke again, but as far as Rebekah was concerned, she could wait all day. She wasn't going anywhere until she had some answers.

"I met Emily in Canada. I was born in this country, but when I was a kid, my dad took a job in Canada, and we moved there. So that's really where I grew up. Somewhere along the way, I got a dual citizenship so my family could easily go back and forth between the countries and visit our relatives, but Canada was my home.

"My first day of college, I met Emily. We were in the same dorm and quickly fell in love. I had always wanted to be a minister, so after the first semester of my freshman year, an opportunity for me opened up at a college in the United States—in New York. I asked Emily to marry me and come to the US, but her family was strongly against it." He paused as he looked down into his almost empty glass and swirled the partially melted ice before drinking the rest of its contents. He then got up, filled his glass with more ice, sat back down, and poured several more fingers of whiskey over the cubes before taking a long drink.

"Her parents didn't like me—said I wasn't good enough. They had money and a different idea of who Emily should marry. Then we found out Emily was pregnant, so that was that. We were married and moved to New York, where I would finish college. That's where James was born and, two years later, Andrew," he said, both hands cupped around the glass, his eyes never leaving it as he spoke.

"We made a trip to Canada after Andrew was born—for a visit with Emily's family—in the late fall. About fifteen miles from her parent's house, we drove into some unexpected snow flurries, which made it hard to see. All of a sudden I saw headlights and then a truck in front of me." Tears had begun to stream down Ethan's cheeks as his steady voice continued. "We hit head on. I felt helpless as the truck hit our car, and we spun around and around. It seemed we would never stop. When we finally did, I first checked on the boys, who were both screaming in their car seats. I then turned to talk to Emily and saw she was slumped over. There was blood trickling through her hair from somewhere on her head.

Rebekah couldn't believe what he was telling her but kept silent, waiting for him to go on. After what seemed like an eternity, he continued.

"Everything that happened next is a blur. An ambulance came and took us all to the hospital. James, Andrew, and I didn't even have a scratch, but Emily, they told me, had hit her head. Badly. At first the doctors thought she might be brain dead, but after more tests, they said they needed to put her in a drug-induced coma so she could heal. I remember one of the doctors saying, 'Time will tell.'

"Of course, Emily's parents showed up and started accusing me of whatever they could think of. I was in shock, so I just stared at them, not speaking. It was the worst night of my life," he said, dropping his head into his hands for a few seconds.

"I called my sister since she lived in the same town. She came and got the boys so I could stay at the hospital." He looked up and finally made eye contact with Rebekah. "I never left that hospital for a whole week until, finally, it looked like Emily was getting better. So they brought her out of the coma, and day by day, she seemed to be coming back, ever so slightly." He paused and let out a sigh.

"Then, a couple of weeks later, she suddenly had a stroke. The doctors said they didn't know how much more she could take. Emily just lay there sleeping, hooked up to machines. They told me she would need to go to a place where she could get professional help, which I didn't want to hear because I didn't have the money to pay for it." He looked down at his glass again and swirled the ice, keeping his gaze there once more.

"Her parents said they would pay for everything—with the stipulation that they would decide how she was cared for. What could I say? I knew they would give Emily the best, so I agreed. They found a wonderful place for her, but nothing changed. She stayed the same. Of course, I had to drop out of school and was able to live with my sister while I figured things out."

He closed his eyes. "I'm so tired."

Rebekah didn't say a word.

"I've done a good job to forget this part of my life and haven't thought about it for years." He looked through her as if she weren't there before he dropped his head and sobbed into his hands.

It surprised Rebekah that she didn't care. She didn't comfort Ethan but waited patiently for him to lift his head and continue.

"Then, one day," he said, "I received a letter from a lawyer, informing me that my in-laws were taking me to court for custody of Andrew and James. How was I going to fight them? They had all the money and influence, so I panicked. I packed us up in the car and came back to the US. In fact, I drove all the way to Texas. I didn't want Emily's parents to find me and take the boys away, so I changed our names. My boys were all I had. I figured Texas would be the last place her parents would look for me. I decided to start a correspondence class to finish my ministerial coursework. To make it more difficult for Emily's parents to find me, I moved somewhere else every few months until I had my degree.

"At this point, I wasn't sure if Emily was alive or dead, but I had to convince myself that my previous life was gone— Emily was dead *to me*. It was the only way I could cope. I made no contact with anyone I previously knew." He looked at Rebekah, his eyes searching as if begging her to say she understood, but she kept silent. "I had to keep what was left of my family together," he said.

"So I got my degree to become a minister and had started looking for a job when I found the one advertised for Faithful Shepherd and thought it couldn't be more perfect. Who would ever look for me in small-town Wisconsin? I made up my references, applied, and was hired. Just like that, I was walking through a door to a new life and shutting a door on what had been, never looking back." He looked up at her.

"And then I found you. You reminded me so much of Emily that I was drawn to you the first time I saw you. I do love you, Rebekah," he said with tears in his eyes. "We've built a wonderful life together, haven't we?"

She didn't respond.

He continued. "So over time, I just figured Emily had probably died. Back in those days, we didn't have places on the internet to find things out as easily as we do now, and I wasn't going to contact anyone I knew and blow my cover—that would be risky. I just accepted she must have died and moved on with my new life as father, minister, and husband—never imagining she survived. After all, the doctors had told me they didn't think she would." He looked at her with a pleading in his eyes again.

Rebekah didn't know what she was thinking as she surveyed the man opposite her. She didn't know him at all. Maybe a glass of whatever Ethan was drinking wasn't too bad of an idea.

After a minute or two, she finally spoke. "Ethan, I can't even process this right now. I'm hoping this is a bad dream, and tomorrow I'll wake up from it. You lied to me, my family, the church, and—worst of all—our boys."

He drew in a long breath and then exhaled slowly.

"I know, I know. But I'm trying to figure out how Emily found me and just happened to be sitting next to you in church. I really thought I was seeing a ghost."

"Emily is alive and well and has been working for me in the bakery. I invited her to church yesterday because she was alone and new to town. Evidently she was just as surprised to see you as you were her, given her response yesterday—and today."

"You saw her today?" He looked up, interested.

"Yes." Rebekah got up from her chair. "I think I need to get out of here. Since Mom is staying with Tom indefinitely, I'm going to pack a bag and stay over at my parents' house. If all you have told me is true, then we're not actually married. We never have been. I don't want to stay in the same house with you for one night, even if it's in separate rooms. I'm not sure what's next. Please don't try to contact me. I'll let you know when I'm ready to talk."

Rebekah recognized she was on autopilot. That was the only thing keeping her together.

"Don't go, Rebekah," he pleaded.

She didn't say a word but got up and went to their bedroom to pack a bag. She moved mechanically, pulling some clothes together, then headed to the bathroom to gather the things she needed from there. Her life was on a disaster course right now, and she felt the flight was going to crash if she didn't get as far away from him as possible.

She came back to the kitchen and found Ethan resting his head on the table—the whiskey bottle and empty glass in front of him. He was sound asleep and snoring. She was tempted to just leave him there, but it was in her nature to care for others, even if this one had just destroyed her life.

"Ethan," she said, shaking him roughly, "go to bed." She guided him to the bed they had shared for eighteen years. Semiconscious, Ethan fell onto the mattress. Rebekah threw a blanket over him and left the room.

Back in the kitchen, she picked up the whiskey bottle, finding it to be half empty. She took a whiff and pulled back. *Why would someone drink this?* she thought and put the bottle back down before walking out the back door and locking it behind her.

***

It was early evening when she got to her parents' house. Even though it was still daylight, she found the house dark, cold, and unwelcoming. She headed straight upstairs to her old bedroom—the same room she had once shared with Dee—with the things she brought. Why did she have to think of her sister right now? Wasn't everything with Ethan enough? If Dee were there, she would have had a shoulder to rest her head on, someone to tell her all was okay and hold her hand through the mess she knew was yet to come.

Rebekah saw some missed calls from Tom and decided she should call him and let him know she was staying there. Tom had been a big help so far, and she knew she could lean on him if needed. Besides, he was probably waiting to hear from her.

"Hi, Tom. It's me," she said after he answered.

"I've been worried about you, Rebekah. I've called you twice." he replied. "What's going on with Ethan? Is he going to be okay?"

"Yes, he's out of the hospital and at home. I don't want to talk about it right now. I need to process a few things, and then we can talk. I wanted to let you know I'm staying at Mom and Dad's right now."

"At Mom and Dad's? What's going on, Rebekah?" Tom questioned.

She hesitated, took in a deep breath, and exhaled before she replied, "It's complicated."

"I'm coming right over," Tom insisted.

"No, please don't, Tom. I need to be alone. Please. I'm going for a walk before it gets dark—to clear my mind. I need a few days; you'll understand when I explain what's going on; trust me. By then I may have some more answers to my questions."

"Well, okay, but I'm still probably going to call you."

"Okay, but if I don't answer, don't worry. I'll call you back." She paused. "And Tom? Don't tell anyone else I'm here, okay? I need some space."

"I won't, but send me a text occasionally till you're ready to talk, just so I know you're okay. I'll come find you if you don't."

"I promise," she replied, grateful she had someone who cared so much about her.

She grabbed her sweatshirt and headed outside to the woods around her parents' house. Over the years, her dad had created trails throughout the twenty acres of land they owned. The trails connected to a small pond with a cleared picnic and camping area not too far from the house and the auto shop on the opposite side of the property, near the main road. She decided to go to her favorite place, the pond.

It had been years since she had walked down there, and she was surprised not much had changed. She needed somewhere to think, so she sat on one of the benches her father had built. As she looked out over the still pond, she began to calm, thinking about all the memories she had formed over the years in this spot. She went into a prayerful meditative state for a few minutes, opening her mind and heart and finally feeling safe and secure. Then suddenly, she broke down and cried.

She hadn't believed it when Emily told her Ethan— or Edwin—was *Emily's* husband. And *Edwin*? He didn't even look like an Edwin. But then Ethan had confirmed everything. He was, in fact, married to Emily and not to her. Their whole marriage had been a lie from the beginning.

She then thought of James and Andrew. What were their real names? And how were they going to take all of this? Emily may have given birth to them, but they were Rebekah's children. Would they turn their backs on Rebekah when they found out the truth? She couldn't bear the thought of it.

Now she understood why Emily had looked so familiar. It was so obvious. The boys. They had her eyes.

She got up from the bench and began to pace, growing angrier with each step, her breath coming faster and faster. She stopped, threw her arms with clenched fists in the air and screamed as loudly as she could as every muscle and cell in her body contracted and screamed with her. A flock of birds, frightened by her display, took flight above her head.

"*Why?*" she shrieked. Then, through her sobs, she continued, allowing her voice to travel through the trees and bushes and across the pond to the ends of the property. "What did I do to deserve this? I hate him. My life is ruined. How can I face anyone after this? I'm humiliated. People will pity me. I was a fool to marry him. I was just a girl. Everyone pushed me." Then she shouted once more, her voice echoing through the forest. "I hate him! I hate them all!" She picked up a handful of stones and, one after another, threw them as far and as hard as she could into the water until, at last, she fell back on the bench, exhausted.

She put her head in her hands for a moment until she heard a rustling to her side. She jumped as several deer flew past her, obviously curious about her wails. They stopped about ten feet away, then, meeting her gaze, took off once more into the woods.

Rebekah sat on the bench and continued to cry—for how long, she wasn't sure—until no more tears came. She noticed it was getting darker and knew she should head back. *I should just sleep on this bench*, she thought. *Maybe a bear will find me in the night and take me away. That should make Ethan feel bad.* She shook her head at such a childish thought.

The sun was setting just above the roof line of the house when she came in through the back door that led to the kitchen. Hungry, but not really, she looked through her mom's pantry and refrigerator to see if anything appealed to her before settling on a yogurt. She first checked the expiration date because her mom hadn't been back to the house since the funeral. It was current, so she got a spoon and went into the family room, where she felt a little more sadness, seeing her dad's recliner off in the corner of the room and knowing she would never see him sitting in it again.

She turned on the TV, hoping it might be good company, and flipped to one of the food channels, wanting to find a show on baking. The current show was about food trucks, but the next one was a baking competition. Rebekah loved watching those.

One of the competitors was making a rhubarb cake, triggering a memory of one her mom used to make. Her mom was always very secretive with her recipes and would never share with anyone, not even Rebekah, going as far as to hide her recipe box. Rebekah decided since Ruth wasn't there, she was going to look for the box, but not tonight. She was exhausted and had to get up early for work in the morning.

Normally Rebekah liked to pack a lunch; tomorrow she would buy one.

Her phone rang, and she saw it was James, probably wondering about his dad. She felt a little sick as she answered because she knew she would have to lie to him.

She took a deep breath. "Hi, son. What's new?" she asked as she forced a pleasant voice.

"Not much, Mom. I worked today, and Andrew went to class. I really want to know how Dad's doing. I tried calling him, but there was no answer. Is he around?"

"Ah, no, sweetheart. He's at the church, checking on some things. He's fine, though—no need to worry. I imagine he'll be tired when he gets home, so maybe try calling him tomorrow." She didn't know what else to say.

"Okay. Well, tell him I called and that I love him. I love you too, Mom," he said.

"And I love you and your brother also. You're the two most important things in my life," she said, swallowing a big lump in her throat and fighting back tears.

"I'll let Andrew know. Tell Dad to call us."

"Will do, son. Bye." Then she hung up before any more words slipped out of her mouth.

She watched a little more TV to distract herself, though she knew she needed to go to sleep. When she at last got into bed, her body felt numb as she crawled between the covers. Maybe tomorrow she would wake up in another time line, where life was perfect and none of this had happened. She began to cry again, softly this time, her head sinking into her pillow as the day's fatigue softened, soon helping her to fall asleep.

Chapter 15

Work had always felt like a separate place for Rebekah, but now Emily's presence had brought the two worlds together. Since Emily surely wouldn't be working with them anymore, the amount to be done for the upcoming Easter Sunday and the sheer fact she needed to keep busy helped Rebekah make the decision to work that Wednesday, her usual day off.

Ethan had called her Tuesday morning, but she didn't answer, not wanting to talk to him yet. His words from the day before were still sinking in. She didn't talk to anyone about what had happened, other than the texts she sent Tom to let him know she was okay. She knew Tammy was dying to know what was going on, but Rebekah kept herself business as usual.

Then midmorning on Thursday, Emily showed up at the bakery.

Tammy stepped into Rebekah's office, where she sat hunched over some paperwork. "Hey, listen, sweetheart," Tammy said.

Rebekah looked up.

"Ah, stay calm, but Emily's out there, and she wants to see you."

Rebekah lowered her eyes but didn't say anything.

"Now if you don't want to, you just say the word, and I'll tell her to leave, but you're going to have to talk to her eventually, so you might want to get it over with now. I know you haven't told me everything, but I know enough. And I know *you* enough to know you need to talk to Emily for some answers."

Rebekah continued to look at Tammy for a long time before she rose from her chair and turned her back while she thought. Was she ready for this? Would she ever be ready for this? Probably not; talking to Emily would propel the inevitability she was trying to avoid.

She turned back around and, with a sigh, said, "I guess you might as well bring her back here."

"Okay, I'll be close by. All you have to do is call me." Tammy gave her a big hug before leaving the room.

Rebekah sat down, waiting for what seemed like forever as she once again ran through all the what-ifs that had been going through her head since church several days ago. Her thoughts were interrupted as Emily finally walked through the door.

She had no makeup on, and her hair looked like it hadn't been washed in a while. Dark circles and sunken eyes signaled that the pressure had taken its toll. "Hi, Rebekah," she said.

Rebekah gestured toward a chair, and Emily sat down. Neither of them said anything, not knowing where to start. Then at last, Rebekah decided to get things going. "I've talked to Ethan—Edwin to you, I guess—and he's told me his side of the story. But I would like to hear yours."

"I don't know where to begin," she said.

Rebekah raised her eyebrows and exhaled before she responded. "Ethan said the same thing. I know all about meeting, marrying, and having the boys and the car accident. Just begin there."

"Okay," Emily said. Her mouth opened and closed in a few false starts before she began. "Well … I was hurt pretty badly. I don't remember a lot, but I have been told what happened. For a while, I was very confused, not remembering I was married or that I had children. My parents were in total control and only told me what they wanted me to know, even making up things and keeping me away from other people who might tell me otherwise. As I slowly recovered and became stronger, I began to remember things and started asking where my husband and children were. My parents told me Edwin—uh, Ethan—had deserted me. I couldn't believe it.

"I became severely depressed, wishing I would have died in that accident. There were a lot of times when I thought about taking my own life. Then, my dad died about six years ago, followed by my mom three years later. I was free. I began talking with family members and learned there was more to what had happened than what I was told. Then I found Edwin's sister, and she told me everything. Once I heard that, I knew I had to find my husband and my boys.

"At one time, my parents were quite wealthy, but their business failed, and they spent a lot on my care. I didn't inherit much from them but had enough that I was able to hire an investigator who spent almost two years looking for

Edwin. That led me here to northern Wisconsin. I took the job with you because I needed some money and wanted to fit in to the community, hoping that one day, I would find my family."

Rebekah couldn't believe what she was hearing. In fact, if she were not so deeply involved in this story, her instinct would have been to feel sorry for Emily.

Emily continued with tears in her eyes and a catch in her throat. "How are Ricky and Pete?"

It took Rebekah a second to realize she was talking about James and Andrew. She chose her words carefully. "They're fine young men. They go by Andrew and James, though." Starting to tear up as well, she rose from her chair and turned away, not wanting Emily to see. "Listen, Emily. I don't know what you want to do next. It's clear to me you are Ethan's wife. I'm so angry with him I don't know where to begin. I have spent ..." Her voice began to waver. "I have spent almost eighteen years with him, thinking I was his wife. What do I do next? We've built a life together. I've raised his children as their mother."

Emily stood up. "I don't care what you did together. It was wrong, Rebekah. He's my husband, they're my children, and I want them back. I want my life back," Emily said firmly. Her manner was so unlike the woman Rebekah had gotten to know.

She felt numb. Emily was wanting to take away her life, her identity, her purpose. But in the same moment, it dawned on her that all these things had dissolved the second Emily saw Ethan at church—and things could never be the same.

Rebekah drew in a shaky breath. Who was she now? She reached for a piece of paper and a pen. "Here's Ethan's phone number. Good luck. Now I have a lot of work to do because this Sunday is Easter and, as you know, I'm short an employee," she said, sitting down to return to the paperwork she had been working on.

Without a word, Emily walked out.

No sooner had Emily moved out of earshot than Rebekah broke down in sobs.

Shortly after, Tammy came in and put her arms around Rebekah. "I think it's time you tell me what's going on."

Rebekah continued to sob for a few more minutes and then, starting from the beginning, filled Tammy in on the details.

Tammy was in shock and never interrupted her once. She waited till Rebekah finished and, even then, sat for a few minutes before speaking. "I know I'm usually a wealth of support, knowledge, and opinion, but this one has me floored," Tammy said as she rose and started walking around the office. "I mean, what in the heck did that son of buck think he was doing? Messing with people's lives—and a minister to boot! I want to find him and give him what for right this minute. Spencer has some good-sized friends I could send over to scare the crap out of him—just rough him up a bit—let him know he can't hide anymore. They could go at night and really scare him."

"I appreciate the offer but don't think it's a good idea," Rebekah responded, her voice flat and defeated. "I have to find a way to move forward. Emily is his wife. There's no denying it." She stood up and walked over to Tammy, who instinctively opened her arms to comfort her friend as she cried.

"Well, if you change your mind, all I have to do is make a phone call." Tammy pulled away, holding both of Rebekah's shoulders so she could look her in the eyes. "You think I'm kidding, but I'm dead serious."

After a pause, both women laughed.

Thank goodness for Tammy, Rebekah thought and responded, "I love you, Tammy. Let's get back to work. We have so much to do, so I'm going to keep myself busy with it the rest of today. Rebekah wiped her eyes, blew her nose, and the two went out to the bakery side by side.

Chapter 16

Rebekah was grateful her mom was staying with Tom. Tom had said he wasn't sure when Ruth would be moving back, given she was taking their dad's death hard and didn't want to be back in the house yet. This allowed Rebekah somewhere to live and be alone while she worked things out. At the same time, she was sad about how her mom was responding. Now that Darrell was gone, it seemed as if Ruth felt she was no longer the person she had been. Rebekah understood. That's how Ethan's lies made her feel.

She had made it through the Easter weekend and was curious about what might have taken place yesterday at the Easter Sunday church service. A part of her wanted to know if Ethan had conducted a service or if one of the deacons had filled in. Surely, he hadn't shown up—or had he? If he hadn't done the service, what was his excuse? Or if he had, how did he explain his behavior on Palm Sunday? And what had he told everyone about Rebekah not being at church on Easter?

It had been strange for Rebekah to be alone on Easter. Normally she'd have been at church in the morning, then made a big dinner or gone to her parents' house. Instead, she made herself a sandwich that she could only manage to eat half of. To her, it felt like a day off and nothing special.

Both James and Andrew had been unable to get enough time off to travel home for the holiday this year. That was a relief given the circumstances, but the inevitable disclosure that their birth mother was still alive still loomed around the corner. Their dad would have to tell them—and then what? She refused to think about it. Oddly enough, they hadn't called on Easter, either, and she decided not to call them lest they ask any more questions about their father.

Did they possibly already know?

***

Midmorning on Monday, she received a phone call from Tom at work.

"Hi, Tom. I know I didn't answer your last text, but I'm fine," she told him before he could speak.

"Rebekah, I want to meet with you today and find out what the heck is going on. Ethan was at church yesterday, business as usual, and said you were terribly sick and couldn't attend. Now I know that's a bald-faced lie. I had to stand there and listen to his story all the while knowing you were not sick."

At that moment, Rebekah *did* feel sick.

"I'll be by there at Mom's around four this afternoon to see you and talk about all this," Tom said.

Rebekah knew she couldn't go on keeping this to herself. And Tom was so concerned; he was someone she could lean on. She really needed his love and support right now and owed him an explanation.

"I'll be there waiting for you," she said. "And thanks, Tom. I love you."

"Well, I love you too. But I need some answers, Rebekah."

"We'll talk at four," she said, and they hung up.

***

Tom arrived at 4:01 p.m. and Rebekah met him at the door.

"Rebekah," he said as he stepped inside, "I've been so worried about you and wanted to respect the fact you needed some space, but after church yesterday, I couldn't go any longer. What the heck is going on?"

"You better sit down for this," she said. "I don't know where to begin." There it was again. The same thing both Ethan and Emily had said to her.

After a long breath, she began sharing the whole story, beginning with when she'd first hired Emily and ending with how Emily, Ethan's real wife, now wanted him back.

"That SOB!" Tom exclaimed when she'd finished. "Sorry, Rebekah, but that's what he is. I'm going to call Steve and Jake, and we'll get Ben to come home from Green Bay so we can beat the crap out of him for doing this to you." Tom stood up, pulling his phone out as he paced the floor.

"You'll do no such thing. What's that going to prove? Put your phone away," Rebekah said, standing to face him. "Tom, I'm so confused right now that I'm not sure what to do. The last thing I need hanging over me is the four of you in jail. And what about Mom? She needs all of us right now. I'll never forgive any of you if you leave her in my hands. She doesn't even like me."

"Oh, you know that's not true. Mom loves us all."

"Okay, but she loves some of us more than others." Rebekah shook her head "Oh, that's the least of my worries right now. You take care of Mom and let me sort this out if you really want to help me."

"What are you going to do? I think he could go to jail when all this comes out. You need a lawyer to protect your interests. I mean, eighteen years of dedication, and you're thrown out on the street like you're nothing. *And* he's a minister! Actually …" Tom paused for a moment as a thought hit him. "We don't even know if that's true."

It hadn't occurred to Rebekah that Ethan could have been lying about being a minister. Regardless, she didn't care about getting money from him. She had more than enough to support herself.

"I have to ask you this, Rebekah. Do you still love him? What if he wants to stay together with you? I mean for cripes' sake, you raised his kids as if they were your own and made a darn good home for him. He couldn't ask for a more supportive woman than you," Tom said, looking her straight in the eyes.

All her brother had said was true. Rebekah wasn't the type of person who could turn her love on and off, but Ethan—the man she had loved since she was eighteen years old—was a lie. All she cared about right now was her relationship with Andrew and James—*her* children. Did she love Ethan? She didn't want to think about it. She was certain she'd mourn their life together like a death, but she also knew she never wanted to see him again.

"If I never saw him again, I would be fine, Tom," she said very calmy. "What he did to me is unforgivable, and I have no trust left. He and Emily can have each other. I'm done," she said. She had done a good job of holding it together until the wave of anxiety she thought she had contained bubbled up unexpectedly, and she broke down. Her brother put his arms around her as she leaned into them.

Tom stayed for an hour to provide some comfort, talking with Rebekah until her tears had subsided. Even though Rebekah hadn't felt much like eating, she invited Tom to have dinner with her. He declined, saying he had to get home.

"Listen," he told her, "I don't care what time it is. If you start feeling bad or upset, you call me. I'm going to tell the rest of our brothers what's going on"—he put his hand up, anticipating Rebekah's protest—"because they will also want to be here for you. Talk about never forgiving someone. They'll have a fit if they find out from someone else. It's better to tell them so we can all stick by you together." Tom paused. "And I'll make sure they keep their mouths shut and don't go find and kill Ethan." He gave her a little smile that she returned.

Rebekah hugged her brother like she would never let go. "I love you," she said, not knowing what else to say.

***

At the end of work on Tuesday, after much persuasion, Tammy convinced Rebekah she needed to take her usual Wednesday off to pamper herself with a massage and a mani-pedi. Even if Rebekah had wanted to take her advice, she would have to drive to Rhinelander to find a place to enjoy either luxury since there was nothing like that close to where she lived. *Maybe someday after work*, she thought, since her time was now hers to do with what she wanted.

On Wednesday morning, Rebekah lazily pulled the sheet up to block the sun that shined on her face as she woke. The house was so quiet. She turned her head to look at the clock and saw it was already nine. It had been years since she'd slept that late. She rolled over and lay there, content for another fifteen minutes, before she slid out of bed to head to the bathroom.

Still sleepy, she brushed her teeth and washed her face, then applied lotion and combed through her hair, assessing what she saw in the mirror. She knew she wasn't beautiful and thought herself fairly average-looking, which wasn't a bad thing.

As she studied herself, she couldn't stop the questions going through her head. *How is this all going to work out? Will I be alone for the rest of my life? Will anyone ever love me again?* She didn't want to spend the rest of her life alone. Right now, she felt hate for Ethan—and the hate felt good. She wanted him to hurt like he'd made her hurt. But then she thought about how it must have hurt for him to face Emily's injuries with no guarantee his wife would get better. Why did Rebekah have to be a nice person and think of this? Couldn't she just hate him? Still, even his past struggles were no excuse for how he'd lied to her.

After throwing on some yoga pants and a T-shirt, she went downstairs to make a cup of tea. While she waited for the water to boil, she searched through a white paper bag that contained a few pastries she'd brought home from the bakery yesterday. Finding a lemon scone under a bear claw, she placed it on a plate and then put it in the microwave to freshen it up a bit.

She plopped herself down on the couch with her tea and scone and pushed the power button on the remote. An old-time Fred Astaire and Ginger Rogers musical had already started, so she got comfy and settled in, allowing the movie to take her away to another era and time for a while. She loved these old movies and the polite atmosphere they lived in. The clothes the women wore were attractive and classy—and to learn to dance like they did? How fun would that be?

After the movie ended, she flipped to one of the only channels she watched on a regular basis: The Food Channel. The baking show she'd watched the other day was playing again, and she remembered something. Her mom's recipe box.

Rebekah spent the next twenty minutes rummaging through the kitchen cabinets with no success. Finally, she opened the last cupboard door, and there it was: the recipe box. Ruth had hidden the box behind a stack of pots and pans she didn't use regularly. Rebekah knew the box had originally belonged to Ruth's mother. Rebekah had never known her maternal grandmother because she had died just after Ruth and Darrell were married.

Looking the box over, Rebekah wondered how old it was. Made by hand out of maple, it was held together with tiny dovetail joints and still sturdy as ever after all these years. She was just about to start flipping through it when the front doorbell rang. Just in case, she put the box in an upper cupboard before she answered the door.

To her shock, Ethan was standing in front of her. It had been over a week since she'd seen him in his drunken condition. He was all cleaned up, looking like his usual self in a pair of jeans and a green sweatshirt. Her inner warning system told her to proceed with caution.

"Hi, Rebekah," Ethan said. He gazed through her then back down at the floor, over and over, not meeting her eyes. She'd never seen him look so guilty.

"What do you want?" she asked and placed a hand on each side of the doorframe as if to say, *You're not welcome here.*

"Can I come in? I want to talk to you, and I don't want to do it outside."

She didn't think she was ready for this, but would she ever be? They would have to talk sometime. She was in mental turmoil, still replaying the same questions over and over. Then she shook her head as she thought, *Just get it over with.* It was as good a time as any, and she was as ready as she would ever be to hear what he had to say.

Silently, Rebekah opened the door wider and cleared the way for Ethan to enter. She led the way to the family room and sat down, Ethan following suit. Then, she waited for him to start. She was not going to make this easy.

Just as Ethan looked like he was going to begin, he cleared his throat, cleared it again, and then waited another moment before speaking. "I first want to apologize." He looked down at his hands. "I never intended to hurt anyone— especially you." His eyes shifted again, and Rebekah sensed his discomfort.

Good, she thought, *suffer like you're making me suffer.*

"I only wanted the best for my boys," he continued. "I wanted to give them a normal life with a mother and family. When I met you, it was like God had sent me what I asked for. You were so much like Emily, I instantly fell in love with you. I didn't think Emily was alive when I married you. You have to believe me, Rebekah." He looked up at her once more, his eyes searching, pleading.

Rebekah stared at him. There was so much going through her head that wanted to work its way to the surface, but she was unable to express it. Of course Ethan would bring God into it. But God wouldn't do this; only a stupid, self-serving man like Ethan would.

She hated him.

Rebekah gathered herself together before speaking. "I believe you only think of yourself. Have you told Andrew and James, or should I say, Pete and Ricky?"

Ethan's eyes widened with surprise when she said the boys' birth names. It was as if he'd seen another ghost.

Rebekah waited a moment, letting it sink in before she continued. "When are you going to tell them, or do you have a new story made up?" she said with a sharpness in her voice she didn't even recognize.

"I've already told them," he said.

Now Rebekah was surprised.

"We went down to Milwaukee this past Saturday, and they met with their mom."

Rebekah felt a knife in her heart. How dare he call Emily their mom! Rebekah was their mom; she had loved and nurtured them into the men they were today. She had taken care of them when they were sick, helped with homework, and told them they could be whatever they wanted. She loved them more than life, and now Ethan was trying to take them away.

She stood up. "I've heard enough. You could go to jail for doing this. Did you know that? Playing around with people's lives. Who do you think you are? And a minister on top of it all! I should call the police right now."

"Yes, I know. Emily has pointed that out to me," Ethan said, rubbing his temples. "In fact, I'm leaving tomorrow to go back to Canada with her and will never darken your door again. She's pointed out we're still married—husband and wife. She feels I 'owe her' and will have me arrested if I don't make an attempt to give her the life she has been 'cheated out of.'" He looked down and wouldn't meet Rebekah's eyes. "I asked her for a divorce, and she refused."

He continued. "I'm only taking a few personal things from the house. Whatever's left, you can have. Much of it belongs to the church anyway." He took a few breaths before he went on. "Rebekah, I promise once I get a job, I'm going to send you some money every month to help out."

"Keep your money," Rebekah replied quickly. "I don't need or want it. I can take care of myself. I won't be bought off so you can make yourself feel better or bribed to not take you to court. I'll tear up any check you send me."

There was a long silence. How could she have lived with this man as long as she did and not seen how weak he was? Still, in her heart, there was a small ache. An ache of knowing he had loved her—and still did. She knew he wanted to be with her. Why wouldn't he? They had built a life and a family together.

At last, he spoke. "I hope you can forgive me—maybe not today, but someday." Ethan exhaled a long, shaky breath. "This is goodbye, I guess."

Misty-eyed, he stood and went to Rebekah, wrapping his arms around her tightly with the familiarity of their many years together. Then, with passion and longing, he kissed her—and she let him. Ethan continued to hold her like he'd done hundreds of times before, and she felt so comfortable and at home in the embrace of his arms. Rebekah placed her head on his chest, taking in the scent of his aftershave, memorizing the steady beat of his heart. She didn't move. She barely took a breath as she melted into him, surrounded by his warm and loving touch.

Finally, Ethan let go and walked toward the door. "You need to know this." He turned around; his face wet with tears. "The visit with the boys didn't go well. They'll need you." He put his hand on the doorknob to leave and wiped his face with the sleeve of his sweatshirt before he continued. "I love you, Rebekah. I always will. You brought life, happiness, and hope at a time in my life when I didn't think it would ever be full again. You're an amazing woman."

Ethan paused as a sob escaped.

"I'm sorry," he said and walked out the door. Rebekah stood, motionless, until she could no longer hear his car's engine and she was alone in the raging silence that surrounded her. She finally sat down, still staring at the door Ethan had just walked out of. Her throat had closed up, but she managed to whisper, "I don't want to be alone. Please come back. I want to pretend this didn't happen. I don't want to be alone. Please, please, please. Come back."

The tears began to flow as if a faucet had been turned on. She could barely catch a breath between the sobs. This was like nothing she ever felt before. Something must have broken inside her. The multitude of emotions seeping out was more than she could bear.

Once every tear was spent, she went upstairs to her room and slid between the covers.

***

Rebekah was still in bed the next afternoon when her brother Steve showed up. She hadn't answered any of Tom's phone calls, so Tom had called the bakery and was told she hadn't shown up for work or answered the bakery's calls either. So Tom asked Steve to go by and check on their little sister.

Still groggy, Rebekah could see him standing over her. She didn't care what he was saying; to her it sounded like "Blah, blah, blah." Steve brought her a bowl of soup and said she needed to eat it, so reluctantly, she did. When she finished, she went into the bathroom to wash her face and brush her teeth. When she came back to her room, some clean clothes were lying on the bed, so she changed into them and went downstairs.

"Hey, I have a great idea," Steve said enthusiastically once Rebekah was cleaned up and dressed. "Why don't you pack a bag and come stay at my place tonight? You might enjoy being around people, and we could cook out hamburgers and brats for supper and do some visiting."

"I don't want to," Rebekah told him flatly. She had no desire to see or talk to anyone and kind of wished he would leave. "I want to sleep. I'm too tired. Maybe another day." And with that, she went back to bed.

This went on for several days. Tammy came by and told her about what was going on in the bakery, thinking that would get her attention, but nothing could pull Rebekah out of the dark place she was slowly sinking into. Her family came in daily to make sure she ate and was okay, but she had no desire to do anything else. Normally she would have been taking advantage of the warm May day by going for a walk or spending time on the deck, but the desire had left her completely.

It had been a little over a week when, one afternoon, her sister-in-law Deb came over to have lunch with her. Ruth was still staying with Deb and Tom, so Deb updated her on Ruth's unchanging status. As Deb opened the cupboard for a glass, she discovered Ruth's recipe box.

"Hey, look at this old recipe box," she said. "Is this your mom's?"

"Yes," Rebekah said. She had forgotten about it but now strangely felt a desire to go through it. "Just leave it there on the counter, and I'll take care of it."

Setting the box back down, Deb said, "I heard James and Andrew are coming home this weekend. You must be happy."

"I am," Rebekah said and meant it, even if she didn't sound like it. She knew she was spiraling down a path of depression and didn't know what to do about it. Maybe seeing them would lift her spirits.

After Deb left, Rebekah decided to take the recipe box outside to the deck area and sit in the sun. She hadn't been outside the house since before Ethan had come by. It was a nice day, and she could see some crocuses had bloomed, and a few pink and yellow tulips were poking through the soil. Maybe Rebekah would get some pansies for the yard. She loved the happy little faces on the flowers. She would get yellow, purple, and white to plant at the door.

Once situated in a lounge chair, she set the box in front of her, opened its slanted top, and began fingering through the recipes, starting at the front. Her mom had the box organized nicely into sections. When Rebekah got to the back of the box, she found three envelopes addressed to her mom. She wondered why they were in there until she saw who they were from.

The letters were from Dee.

Rebekah blinked as she noticed the return address from Milwaukee. She looked at the mail dates stamped on the front of the envelopes and saw they had been sent after Dee left. Ruth must have been hiding them from Darrell, knowing he would never look in the recipe box.

As Rebekah read the first letter in her sister's familiar handwriting, the fog that had been surrounding her lifted ever so slightly. Her heart pounded in her chest. Slowly, a feeling of well-being came over her. Then, the same voice in her mind—the one that had said Get it over with when Ethan was there—began whispering over and over: All will be okay ....

Chapter 17

After finding Dee's letters, Rebekah had begun to feel more like herself. So on Friday morning, she left the house—for the first time since Ethan had paid her a visit—to go grocery shopping for Andrew and James's visit. It would be different having them at her parents' house instead of their home at the parsonage, so she planned to stock the fridge as if they were at home. She would eventually have to go back to the parsonage to get some of her things but not just yet. The house and the majority of the furniture in it belonged to the church anyway, not leaving her much to remove except her personal items. When the church found a minister to fill the spot Ethan had vacated, the new family would live there, as had Ethan and the minister before him.

Finding Dee's letters had given Rebekah a new hope, a purpose she desperately needed. She even stopped by a gas station on the way home from the store and bought ten lottery tickets. She never bought more than five at a time, but it had been over two weeks since she purchased her last ticket, and she figured she was due a win.

She couldn't believe she finally knew what had happened on that terrible night over twenty years ago.

Dee had been pregnant.

It all made sense now. Even the part where Darrell had insisted Rebekah marry Ethan. Her dad had wanted to make sure nothing like that ever happened again. Darrell had always been very strict on religion, looking down on people who didn't believe as he did. So Dee's being pregnant out of wedlock would absolutely have been enough to set him off.

Poor Dee. From her letters, Rebekah had learned that the baby was a girl named Rose and that Ruth had secretly sent some money to help Dee out. The father had disappeared before Rose was born. Dee had worked at a local restaurant in high school and became close with one of her coworkers, Jen, who later moved away from the area to Milwaukee. After Dee was kicked out, Jen kindly invited Dee to live with her until the baby was born. The third letter mentioned how Dee had found a job at a lawyer's office after Rose was born and gotten her own apartment. She wrote about how Rose was such a beautiful and sweet baby and expressed her hopes that maybe Ruth could come to see them and bring Rebekah.

And then Dee had written something that brought tears to Rebekah's eyes.

She reminds me so much of my sweet Rebekah. Please tell my sister I love and miss her.

Of course, Rebekah never got the message, and her mom never went to Milwaukee to see Dee or the baby. It occurred to Rebekah that Rose would be about twenty years old now—not much older than Dee had been when she went away.

James and Andrew were going to arrive before lunch Saturday morning. Rebekah's goal that weekend was to help them work through the events of the past two weeks, which, she hoped, may also help her do the same. The three of them would do it together.

She wondered what had happened when the boys found out Emily was alive—and then met her—especially after Ethan had said things hadn't gone well. Since then, they'd all had some time to let the news settle in, but Rebekah would allow them to tell her about it in their own time and not press the topic. What she really wanted was affirmation that *she* was who they considered to be their mom. Maybe this was selfish of her, but it was one more thing she needed right now to be able to go on.

Rebekah wasn't sure what the boys would want to do while they were home, but she knew they wouldn't go to the church on Sunday. Rebekah knew she would never attend Faithful Shepherd again after all this.

She would suggest that James and Andrew—if they were up to it—go to the parsonage and get some of their things to store in the garage at her mom's house.

But what *was* next? What was her future? She guessed that she'd continue her job at the bakery, and maybe she could travel. She had the money to do it, but who would go with her? She didn't think it would be much fun to go alone.

She thought again about the letters from Dee. It would be beyond her wildest dream to find her. Since the boys lived in Milwaukee, she was going to ask them if they could help her locate her sister. To find Dee, she would definitely need the boys' help. She thought if she gave them the address on the letters, they could check it out. It was unlikely Dee was still there after twenty years, but Rebekah figured, *You never know.* It was a place to start.

***

The boys arrived around eleven on Saturday morning and greeted her with the best hugs ever. Both seemed to be the same as always. That was a good sign.

"I have some deli meat and cheese to make sandwiches for lunch, and I thought we could go out to eat tonight at The Burger Barn. I haven't felt like cooking much lately," Rebekah said. She noticed the boys giving each other sideways looks but didn't say anything.

"Sure, Mom," James said and gave her another hug. Andrew followed suit, and Rebekah fell into full-blown tears.

"Now don't do that, Mom. I think we should talk before we do anything else and get this situation out in the open," Andrew said with authority and led the way to the family room, where they all sat down.

James took over. "Andrew and I were more than shocked when we met Emily. I think she thought we were going to except the news and embrace her as our mother. She may have given birth to us, but she's a stranger. Dad just stood there with a stupid look on his face. She said she wanted us to move to Canada with her and dad. Why doesn't Dad just divorce her? That's what I want to know."

"Yeah, we both told them immediately there was no way we would go to Canada," Andrew said. "I thought Emily was going to have a breakdown. She said, 'But I'm your mother. Why wouldn't you want to be with me?' We just looked at each other. We didn't know what to say. I told her we have lives established here in Wisconsin. We're not kids. We've gone to college, and we're ready to make our way in the world."

James continued. "She went on about how great Canada was and how we would be a family. I told her we appreciated her coming by to meet us, but there was nothing that could convince us to change our minds. After that, they left."

Ethan hadn't lied when he told Rebekah things didn't go well.

"Did they tell you the whole story?" Rebekah asked.

"What story? They didn't tell us anything other than the fact that Emily is our birth mom, and Dad is apparently still married to her. Emily started freaking out, and Dad got her out quickly. He kind of let her do all the talking, which is weird for him. We had no chance to even ask any questions," James said.

Rebekah told them what she knew about the whole situation, starting with how their dad and Emily met to when he left after the accident for fear of having the boys taken from him. When she was done, the boys sat silent for a minute.

"It's sad, and I feel bad for Emily, but we can't go back and change what happened. I want to stay here," Andrew said.

"Me too," agreed James. "But why didn't Dad stand up to her? He's never been one to hide his feelings."

Rebekah got herself together before she spoke.

"Because what your dad did—marrying me before confirming that Emily had died—is a felony. Emily threatened to turn him in to the authorities if he didn't go along with her. I don't want to be responsible for tarnishing your opinion of your father any further, but it's the truth and you're old enough to know."

"What a dumbass ... Sorry, Mom, but he is," James said, and Rebekah silently agreed, grateful that Ethan and Emily would not be staying around.

"I don't know how you're doing so well, Mom," Andrew said.

"I've been having my moments," Rebekah said, knowing it was an understatement. She had hit rock bottom, but Dee's letters had been a ladder, allowing her to begin climbing out from the hole she'd been in for the past week. The boys didn't need to know about her depression though. The wallowing was behind her, and she was not going to let something like that happen to her again. From now on, she would only look to the present and the future the best she could.

"This weekend I want us to have a good couple of days together. Let's go make our sandwiches and let me tell you some good news I have," Rebekah said and led the way to the kitchen.

Over their sandwiches, she told them the whole story about Dee—from the day Dee had left to Rebekah finding the letters in the recipe box. She had never really elaborated about Dee's departure in the past because there wasn't much to tell. The boys seemed interested in what she shared.

"Let me get my computer, and we can do a little research right now," Andrew suggested. He retrieved his laptop then sat back down. "Let's first search the address you have and look at what shows up on a satellite map," Andrew continued, "you'd be surprised how much you can see."

Rebekah held her breath as he typed in the address.

"Hmm ... looks like maybe the property was rezoned as commercial because this is an office building," Andrew said as he pointed to his computer screen. "And this parking lot is the address you gave me. I mean, she lived there twenty years ago. Milwaukee has changed a lot in that time."

Rebekah was disappointed, but really, what did she expect? Dee and Rose had probably moved several times during the years. Milwaukee wasn't like her area, where sometimes several generations occupied the same house over decades.

"Well, it was worth a try," she said with a smile.

Next, Andrew typed in variations of Dee's name with no luck. They thought maybe her given name, Dorcas, would have shown up since it wasn't common. *At least there were no obituaries* Rebekah thought. Most likely, Dee had gotten married at some point and changed her name.

"Thank you, Andrew," Rebekah said. "I'll have to come up with another idea. Who knows, maybe Grandma has more letters hidden somewhere in the house?"

They decided after lunch to go down to the pond, do a little fishing, and walk the trails. Although both the boys loved the big city, they also loved the land where they'd spent their childhood.

After they had cleaned the fish they caught, Rebekah put them in the freezer for the boys to take back to Milwaukee and fix another day. So far, the day had turned out better than Rebekah thought it would, and she was relieved.

They got to the burger place at about five thirty, hungry after their active afternoon and glad they only had to wait about five minutes to be seated. Rebekah scanned her menu before she looked up and noticed four people from the church at another table. They were looking right at her and turned away when she noticed them. *That was awkward,* Rebekah thought. She put her head down, looked out of the corner of her eye, and saw them looking at her again while talking and shaking their heads. *Am I paranoid?* She decided to ignore them and focus on the two most important people in her life while they enjoyed their dinner.

Before they left, Rebekah stopped in the ladies room. An older lady with a cane walked over and started to use the sink next to her. Rebekah smiled.

The woman, someone Rebekah had never seen before, looked at her and asked, "Aren't you the woman who thought she was married to that polygamist minister?"

Rebekah didn't know what to say. "I *was* married to him," she responded.

"That's impossible according to what I heard. He was married to a woman from another country, and so you moved in, thinking it didn't matter. Everybody's talking about it. I thought I had heard them all in my life, but this story takes the cake," the old woman said as she hobbled out the door.

Rebekah looked in the mirror. *I'm the subject of gossip?* she thought as her cheeks reddened. She had to get out of there and hurried back to the table.

"Come on. We've got to go," she said as she tried to catch her breath.

"But they haven't brought us our check," Andrew said with a confused look. "Are you okay?"

She got out her credit card and tapped it rapidly against the table.

Finally, the waitress came with the check. Rebekah gave her the credit card, quickly signed the receipt when she received it, and said, "Let's go," as she hurried to the door.

She felt sick to her stomach. People were talking about her.

Once in the car, James took the wheel and spoke. "What was that about, Mom? You were a different person when you came back from the bathroom."

"There was an old woman in there who asked if I was 'the woman who thought she was married to that polygamist minister' and that everyone is talking about it. She made it sound like I knew Emily was alive all along. How can they pass judgment on me like that?" Rebekah was in tears. She had been doing so well until this moment.

"That's the craziest thing I ever heard," Andrew said from the back seat. "Where the heck are they getting their information from?"

"From an unreliable source, that's for sure," James said. "People don't have enough in their own lives so they stick their nose in others'. You know I want to go back and have a talk with that old lady."

"No," Rebekah said. "Leave it. You'll only give them more to talk about, son." And then she had an idea. "Let's swing by your Uncle Tom's house, and you can say hi to Grandma. She's not been herself since Grandpa died, you know. Very depressed and disconnected from life. She might like seeing you."

"Okay," James said, "but are you sure you're up to talking to people right now?"

"Yes, I'm fine. I wanted to talk to Uncle Tom a minute."

So James turned down the road to Tom's house.

Her mother was still not accepting Darrell's death and was beyond sadness according to Tom. Rebekah guessed she was still heavily medicated by the smile and the glassy look on her face. She had never looked that happy in the past. The TV was on, and Ruth kept her eyes on the screen, a smile on her face, not saying a word other than "hi" when they walked in.

Rebekah was proud of the boys when they sat in a chair on either side of their grandmother and tried to make conversation. Ruth just smiled and nodded.

This gave Rebekah a chance to quietly ask Tom if she could talk to him a minute, and they walked into the kitchen.

"Rebekah, it's so good to see you back to your old self. I knew the boys could bring you out of your funk. I was really worried about you. I'm happy to have my sister back." Tom hugged her tightly and kissed the top of her head.

"I'm feeling better and taking it day by day," she said as she pulled away. "Tom, I think people are talking about me and this whole situation with Ethan. Have you heard anything? Why don't people mind their own business?"

Tom looked down and then up and waited a long while before he spoke. "I'd hoped you wouldn't hear about it. I'm not sure who leaked the information, but yes, they're talking, and I tell you, the church members are the worst ones. I mean how else would this all get out? None of us are setting foot in that church again. They should be supporting you, but instead, this is their entertainment," Tom said in a disgusted tone.

Rebekah felt like she might pass out and pulled out a chair to sit down. Was she foolish to have thought her life could go on as normal with nobody interested in what happened? At least she worked a distance away. She would have to focus on her life at work. Maybe even move to Rhinelander. Thank God she had this option.

"This will eventually pass, Rebekah, when they find something else to talk about. We have to band together as a family. We'll see how that church survives without the Boulanger family supporting them. At least everything was settled quietly with Dad's brothers and the business, or they would be adding that to the gossip too, I'm sure. I gave the lawyer the checks at the beginning of last week when you weren't quite yourself. According to our lawyer, they signed everything over and didn't complain at all, so that's over." Tom ran his fingers through his hair and shook his head.

"That is a relief." Rebekah hadn't thought about the situation with the auto shop since she'd been dealing with Ethan. Right now, she was preoccupied with the gossip. "But Tom, I can't handle people talking about me right now. Please don't say anything to James or Andrew. They've heard enough, and I want to have a good weekend with them. I go back to work on Monday. I think getting back to a normal routine is best for me right now, and then I can go forward," she said, mostly trying to convince herself.

"Well, there is one thing I want you to think about. It might be good for Mom to go back to her house, and since you've been staying there, you can just permanently live there with her. The rest of us can take turns checking up on her during the day while you're at work. The doctor said it might be good for her to live back in her home at this point, you know, so she can come to terms with Dad's death. We'll feel she's safe knowing you're there at night, and we can visit during the day. Just think about living there with her as a possibility, okay? No decision has to be made right now," Tom said with a pursed-lip smile before he put his hand on her shoulder. "We just want you to consider it as an option."

"Yeah, okay," Rebekah replied. Had she been more herself the past few weeks she probably would have seen it coming.

They were trying to dump Mom on her. This whole thing with Ethan had her off her game.

Shortly after they left Tom's house, Andrew asked about what Rebekah and Tom had talked about.

"Oh, he wants Grandma to move back home and thinks since I'm living there it should work out great. I don't know if I agree. Grandma has never really liked me that much, so I don't know."

"She must be taking some heavy-duty drugs because she was saying some odd stuff to us while you were talking with Uncle Tom," Andrew said.

"Yeah, she asked when we would start high school and if we were looking forward to learning how to drive," James chimed in.

"Then she started looking above our heads and said, 'I love that kind of bird.' So we both told her we did too."

They both started laughing.

"I mean, what else could we say?" Andrew said between laughs.

"You know, Mom, it might work out okay living with her if she stays like that," James added.

"I don't share your optimism," Rebekah responded, thinking, *What do I do now?*

***

The next morning, Rebekah made a big breakfast for the kids. They would be going back to Milwaukee midafternoon since they had work and school the next day. Having them home had been so helpful for her. She felt more confident than ever that they were *her* children, and no one could take them away. She'd never forget how she'd fallen in love with the boys that night Ethan had invited her over for dinner. They had both come to her, wanting to show and tell her about their cars. That was the moment they captured her heart forever.

Those memories would get her through the rough days to come, and in time, things would get better. After all, she was her own woman, able to take her life down whatever path she should choose. Now all she had to do was wait for a path to show up.

Chapter 18

Tammy had coffee waiting Monday morning when Rebekah walked into the bakery.

"I am so happy you're back! I'm not going to lie; I was worried about you last week when I came by to see you at your mom's house. I'd like to get my hands on that son of a beehive, Ethan. I kind of feel sorry for Emily, though—but only a little. I mean, geez Louise, what was going on in that man's mind? I'll never understand. Even still, all's going to be fine, Rebekah—mark my words," Tammy expounded, ending with a huge hug that smothered Rebekah.

Rebekah couldn't help but break down, knowing she was in a safe place with Tammy.

"Don't worry, hon. I'm here to lean on. You just say the word, and I'm there for you," Tammy said, patting her on the back. "Now, do you want me to find a hit man for Ethan?"

Rebekah's tears turned to laughter. Tammy always knew what to say.

"I'm not kidding," Tammy said, her tone and expression very serious for a few seconds before she waved her arm and laughed also.

Rebekah dried her eyes, filled her coffee mug, and sat down next to her friend. "Honestly, Tammy, I think Ethan might prefer a hit man to living with Emily. I don't think she's stable. He asked her for a divorce, and she said no, then threatened him with jail if he didn't go back to Canada with her to resume their married life. But it's a felony to do what he did. I guess you could say he's under house arrest now."

"Oh yah, what an idiot. 'Oh, what a tangled web we weave when first we practice to deceive.' My mother used to say that to me all the time," Tammy said as she chuckled. "I came early this morning and got everything going so we would have time together to chitchat. Now I want to hear everything."

So Rebekah obliged and, for the next forty-five minutes, filled her friend in on the details of the past few weeks.

"Man, this would make a great book or movie," Tammy said once Rebekah had finished. "I wouldn't be surprised if you heard from a talk show. I watch all those shows, and they *love* this stuff." She took a gulp of her coffee as she shook her head.

"Please, Tammy. I want to keep this as quiet as can be. I may have to move here to Rhinelander because the people in my area are gossiping like crazy about me. I can't stand it. I just want to start a new life and begin putting the old one behind me. I hope the anger I feel for Ethan will help me move on. Emily can keep him," Rebekah said with a sigh before adding, "Thank God I still have James and Andrew."

"Kids are everything," Tammy said, putting both hands to her heart while closing her eyes. "I would die for mine."

"Me too," said Rebekah. "Now, I have something else to tell you that's good news," she said, eager to switch to a more positive subject. "Remember my sister, Dee, I told you about? It turns out she wrote some letters to my mom after she left. Mom hid them in the back of her recipe box, which I found and was looking through this past Friday. Dee was pregnant! That's why no one talks about it. My dad couldn't handle it, so he threw her out and forbid my mom to ever say a word."

"Well, that was real Christian of your dad," Tammy said.

"I know. Poor Dee. She ended up going to Milwaukee and had a little girl named Rose. And that's all I know. I got an address from the envelopes. Andrew looked it up online, but it's a parking lot now. We searched various versions of her name, and there was nothing. It's still my dream to find her someday."

"And you should. Wow. I guess if Ethan hadn't pulled this monkey business, you may never have found out. You know, I believe everything happens for a reason. I say this is a sign, sweetie. You just never know," Tammy said, taking another long swig of coffee and shaking her head once more. She glanced at her watch. "Hey, we better get started," she said, and they returned to the kitchen to begin baking.

At the end of the work day, Rebekah felt better knowing she still had some small piece of normal life to grasp onto. The more she considered it, the more she was convinced that moving to Rhinelander would be for the best. She dreaded telling Tom she wouldn't be living with their mother and felt bad that he was stuck with her at the moment. Still, Rebekah's other brothers could help out and take their turns. Rebekah would still do her part, but right now she had to focus on herself and make the right choices for her future.

And she hadn't given up on her dream to go into business herself; in fact, she felt more determined than ever.

***

By Wednesday, Rebekah was feeling bold and decided she would take some empty boxes she had found in her mother's garage over to the parsonage to start packing some of her things. It was her day off, so she figured now was as good a time as any to begin the arduous task of moving out. She started in the kitchen with her baking tools and supplies. Soon, the boxes were filled. As she began loading them in the trunk, she noticed two men walking up the driveway. The sun was in her eyes, preventing her from seeing their faces, though she wondered if they might be from the church. As they came closer, she noticed one was holding a large video camera.

"Hi," said one of the men. "Are you Rebekah Hayward?"

Rebekah put a hand over her eyes to block the sun. "Who are you?" she responded.

"I'm Dan Deville from WRWI TV station in Rhinelander. I was wondering if you would tell us—you know, your side of the story—about Ethan Hayward. Kind of set the record straight in an exclusive interview? Let people know what really happened and what it was like living with a polygamist."

Rebekah couldn't believe her ears. What was wrong with these people? Taking entertainment in another person's troubles. "Please leave this property," she said firmly.

"Everyone wants their chance on TV," Dan said with smile.

"If I were you two, I'd be getting as far away from here as possible," Rebekah said as she pulled out her phone and typed in three numbers.

"Aww, come on. You want to set the story straight, don't you?" Dan persisted.

"You're trespassing and harassing me, and I just dialed 911. I feel like my life is in danger, and just so you know, I won't hesitate in pressing charges on you and your station," Rebekah said in a voice she didn't know she had. In actuality, she had dialed random numbers, not 911, but they didn't need to know that.

The cameraman shook his head, brushed Dan on the shoulder, and said, "I told you this wasn't a good idea, but you never listen, do you?" He huffed as he added, "You're an idiot. I'm getting out of here." With that, he headed back down the driveway.

Dan, though, wouldn't give up. "Here's my card. Just call me when you change your mind."

Rebekah backed away. "Take your card with you. I will never talk to you," she said, staring into his eyes.

Dan raised his eyebrows, then turned to leave.

Rebekah waited until she saw their car pull away before she went back inside. Once inside where no one could see her, she dropped into a kitchen chair and sobbed into her hands, the tough demeaner she'd just displayed gone. *What is wrong with people?* she thought. These men were from Rhinelander. How had they found out? She couldn't wait to get back to her parents' house, where she felt more certain nobody would know to look for her. From now on, she would have someone with her when she went to the parsonage.

***

Tammy and Rebekah pulled into the store parking lot at the same time the next day. Rebekah had just opened her mouth to wish Tammy a Good morning when Tammy said, "I have to talk to you before we get inside."

She motioned for Rebekah to get into the passenger seat of her car.

"There was some guy in the store yesterday looking for you. I recognized him as a reporter named Dan Deville from the TV station—"

"He found me yesterday," Rebekah said, waving a hand to cut her off. "I was finally feeling strong enough to go over to the parsonage and start collecting some of my things, and he and his cameraman walked up as I was putting boxes in my car. I told them they better leave because I had just called 911. I didn't really do it, but it made them take off. Must have been a slow news day to come find me."

"What a scumbag," Tammy said. "I'll never watch that station again."

"Why would anyone care about this?" The whole situation was so baffling.

"Well, I don't know, but it seems they do. We had a much busier Wednesday than usual yesterday. And it's not just Dan Deville. There were several ladies from women's organizations that came in wanting to talk with you, plus a couple of lawyers, a magazine, and just nosy folks wanting to get a glimpse of you. Looks like you've got those fifteen minutes of fame people talk about—just not the way you'd want it."

"I've never wanted it, Tammy," Rebekah said. "Why is anyone interested?"

"Well, it's no different than when people drive by an accident on the highway. They have to look, and that's what they're doing right now—looking because they're bored with their own lives, or it makes them validate what a good life they have, or maybe they're just plain mean and love to see others suffer. I've met all these kinds of people. In fact, some of them are in my own family. I have a big family, so it's inevitable we'd have some oddballs and … well let's just call the other ones jerks. I just avoid them as much as I can." Tammy paused and looked straight at her friend. "We're going to have to ride this thing out, Rebekah."

Rebekah was speechless. Was it going to be the same today—all these people coming in to look for her?

As if Tammy were reading her mind, she said, "I have a plan for today. You stay behind the scenes, get your paperwork caught up, read your emails, maybe work on the schedule, and let me run interference in the front, okay? And if any of those—ah what the heck, let's call them what they are—*a-holes* come in, I'll give them Tammy with both guns. How does that sound? I'll do the same tomorrow if I have to and the next day till they get bored with the story and move on to some other poor soul. What do you say?"

What *could* she say? "It sounds like the only way to handle it right now."

"Great," Tammy said. "We have to take it one day at a time."

And with that, the two women went in to start their day.

As Tammy had predicted, the curiosity seekers came in. Rebekah stayed in the back, hoping that by Monday, all of this would be old news and life would start to return to normal—though she wasn't really sure what normal was anymore.

***

Rebekah made it through the rest of the week without having to confront any people and their curiosity. Once home safe and sound on Saturday afternoon, she had just changed out of her work clothes with the intent of going for a walk when she heard a car come up the driveway. It was Tom and Steve, probably coming by to check up on her.

"Hey, sis," Steve said when she opened the door, and he gave her a hug.

Tom followed suit. "Have a good week at work?"

They sat down in the living room, and Rebekah told them about the past several days—the men from the news station and the other interest in her crisis.

"Kind of sick and pathetic," Steve said, rubbing his forehead. "I want to be honest with you, I'm hearing a lot also. I've had to tell several folks it's none of their damn business. I swear, the guys are worse than the women. I know this probably makes it harder for you, but one of the reasons we came by is to talk about your plans for the future. The church is looking for a new minister, who will be moving into the parsonage, and you'll need to get any of yours and the boys' personal stuff out. We just want to help you. You don't have to go this alone."

What would Rebekah do without her family? This was the help she so desperately needed. "Thanks, guys. I've already gone over and packed a few boxes, so we can start as early as this weekend on the rest of the stuff. How does that sound?"

"Great," Tom said. "I'm thinking we bring the packed boxes here and store them in the garage. But what about after that?"

Her mind was blank. She had no definite plans as to where she would live.

Tom didn't wait for an answer. "I think Mom is ready to come back home. I spoke to you about the possibility of the two of you living here. We'll give you a break now and then, so don't worry about having all the responsibility."

Rebekah may have been uncertain as to her plans, but it was clear she didn't want to live in Rhinelander with all the attention she was getting there, and she definitely didn't want to live with her mom. She needed freedom to do what she wanted and never have to report to anyone ever again. She doubted she would want to marry again. How could she ever trust another man? As a minister, Ethan was about as trustworthy as one would believe, and look what he had done. The only real plans she had were to find Dee and open her own bakery business, but she would keep both things to herself until the time was right.

"I don't know what I want anymore," she said, trying to find the right words. "I'm sorry. You need to give me more time to figure out my life. I won't live permanently with Mom—just temporarily. That's the only commitment I can give right now." *Yes*, she thought. *That's a good answer.*

The brothers looked at each other for a moment.

"That's okay," Steve said, "but we think staying with Mom is the best for you. Think about how easy it will be. You can live here, and we'll know Mom and you are safe. Mom might have to go into one of those retirement communities otherwise, and I don't think that would be good for her.

Besides, you have no other family commitments. It seems like the best answer," he finished.

Tom nodded his head in enthusiastic agreement.

"This sounds more like the best answer for all of you, not me," Rebekah said. "Look … I'm actually thinking of getting my own place."

There. She had said it.

"I have some things going through my head I'm not ready to talk about. I want to go over them with James and Andrew first. They're the most important people in my life. I may not have given birth to them, but I'm their mother, and *they* are my family."

"Okay," Tom said. "Fair enough. We still need to get your things out of the house, so what do you say we do it this Wednesday on your day off? You let us know what time you want to meet over at the parsonage, and we'll help you."

"I think it sounds good," she said. "Thank you for trying to understand."

Both men got up and hugged their little sister.

"We only want the best for you," Steve said. "I don't mean to push you, but a little push may help you start putting things back together. The rest of the world isn't going to stand still for you while you decide. Talk with James and Andrew," he added, and they left.

The house was silent now, and Rebekah looked around, taking it all in. None of these things were hers, nor did they appeal to her. She wanted her own place with things that were of her choosing, not all the things she had grown up with. No, she didn't want to live here. In her mind, it would be a step backward to live in the house where she'd grown up. Her mom would never let her be herself. She imagined herself having to explain her every move, day after day, and just waiting for the moments when Ruth would criticize her. Nope, she wasn't going to do it. Steve had been right—the world wasn't waiting for her.

It was time to jump back in. It was a beautiful May day, and Rebekah knew a walk would help clear her head. She grabbed a banana and headed out the door. Once outside, she decided instead to check if her old bike from when she was a teenager was still in the garage. She found it tucked away in the back behind an old car her dad had hoped to restore. The bike was a one-speed Schwinn, with a purple body and silver fenders. She'd never forget the day she had received it as her thirteenth birthday present. She was especially excited because Dee had gotten a similar one—a pretty robin's egg blue with the same silver fenders—for her birthday several months earlier.

The bike's tires were a little flat, and Rebekah hoped they were still in good shape. She found her dad's air compressor in the same place it had always been and soon had the tires pumped and, fortunately, holding air.

This was going to be fun.

Back when she was a young girl, nobody had worn helmets for any activities, be it bike riding or roller blading. So she headed out just like she had then, bareheaded, the wind blowing her hair and making her feel like a kid again.

It had been years since Rebekah had ridden a bike, and even though she still knew how to pedal, she found she had the balance of a five-year-old just learning to ride. She wouldn't be making any sharp turns or popping any wheelies today.

It was no surprise that she was the only one on the road; her family owned most of the property nearby that the roads bordered, and anyone driving down there would be coming to see one of them. She rode along at a leisurely pace, in no hurry to get to ... nowhere, really. It was so nice.

Her mind drifted to what she would do. The good thing was she had a lot of money—over $500,000—in the bank. It amazed her how Jeremy, the guy she entrusted to invest the money, had multiplied it. She could buy her own house and open a bakery too, for that matter. It was great having options.

First, though, she needed to find Dee. That was where her focus should be, and then she could go from there—but how? If she found Dee, Rebekah would want to be where her sister was to make up for all the time they had been separated. She would talk to James and Andrew tonight and get their opinion.

Although she still hurt over all that had happened with Ethan, she decided she would no longer think about him. Hard as it would be, that was her goal. Besides, Ethan didn't even exist; he was really Edwin. Ethan was dead, and focusing on him would only keep his actions alive, preventing her from moving on.

She took a deep breath and, pumping the bike's pedals as hard as she could, looked to the sky and said out loud, "Rest in peace, Ethan, and Godspeed, Rebekah."

Chapter 19

There were just as many curiosity seekers at the store the next week as the one before. Several more lawyers dropped their cards off, and then on Thursday, someone from the state district attorney's office stopped by. Unlike all the others, Rebekah knew she had to talk to him.

Information about Ethan had been brought to the attention of the state DA office, prompting an investigation and possible charges pressed on her behalf if she desired. *How in the world did they get wind of this?* she wondered. She told the attorney she had no intentions of pressing charges and had nothing to say on the matter. Ethan no longer lived in the United States, and as far as she was concerned, good riddance to him.

***

That evening, Rebekah had called the boys to talk about the decision to live with her mom when Andrew came up with a suggestion she hadn't thought about.

"Why don't you move to Milwaukee so you can be by us?" he asked. "It would be a brand-new start for you. Nobody knows anything about you here, and I think you'll love it. You can live with us while you see if you like it."

James piped in. "That's a great idea. Neither of us will probably ever move back up there, and you can stay with us while you adapt and get to know Milwaukee. We like it down here, and you can continue your search for Dee. She probably lives somewhere in Milwaukee or around it. What do you say?"

"I'll think about it," she answered.

Why hadn't Rebekah come up with that?

The more she thought about it all week, the more she came to like the idea. Milwaukee *would* be a clean slate. The idea of being close to the boys appealed to Rebekah, and no one would care a thing about her.

The following Sunday, James called. "Mom, we're wondering if you gave our suggestion any thought. We want to be close to you and take care of you. I think this is the best option," he said, sounding so much like an adult.

"I've given the idea a lot of thought and, well—I'm going to do it, son. I'll tell your uncles today and give my two weeks' notice at work tomorrow."

Wow! It was so good to make a decision and know she was headed in a positive direction. She felt lighter and, well, happier—like she was eighteen again and starting her life as an adult.

She called her brothers one by one and told them the news. They all sounded disappointed but were supportive. Jake said he planned on coming down to visit, as did Steve. Tom mentioned he would get someone to come in several times a week to keep an eye on Mom, and Ben told her to follow where her heart led.

The next morning, when she got to work, the first person she told was Tammy. Tammy's eyes filled with tears, though she kept a smile on her face as she told Rebekah how happy she was for her.

"You should be with your kids, Rebekah. Life is too short. They'll be getting married and giving you grandkids, and you want to be there for it."

After telling Tammy, Rebekah gave Fred her two weeks' notice and suggested he make Tammy bakery manager. Tammy had more than enough experience to step into the job, plus it would give her a nice pay raise that she could really use. Soon, the word spread through the store, and employees from various departments stopped by to wish her well. Rebekah was overwhelmed by everyone's kind words. She realized she had spent more than half her life working at this store, and although she would miss the people and her job, she would treasure all the good memories.

On Wednesday, Ruth moved back home. Tom thought it would be good to do it that way—let Mom spend some time with her daughter before Rebekah moved away, then transition to the woman who would come in to help and provide Ruth with a little company each week.

Things were moving fast. James and Andrew came up from Milwaukee that weekend to help pack up the rest of the family's belongings at the parsonage. Ethan had left a few things Rebekah told the boys to handle. She didn't want to touch anything that had belonged to him. They put everything in the garage at Ruth's house, where it would remain until the second Monday of June, when they would start loading the moving truck. Her last day at work would be on the Friday before she moved, and her coworkers had planned a big party for her.

The toughest part of her last day was saying goodbye to Tammy. It hit Rebekah when they were in the bakery office going over some things Tammy needed to know before she took over as manager.

"I'm going to miss you, Tammy." Rebekah looked at her friend and felt a little pang in her heart.

Tammy's head had been down, and when she looked up at Rebekah, her eyes were wet with tears. "Now don't get me going. I know you think I'm so tough. Everybody does. But I'm a softy inside—and if you breathe a word of this, I'll tell people you're a liar."

"Oh, Tammy." Rebekah stood, and the two wrapped their arms around each other, not needing to say a word because they shared the love of true sisters.

Rebekah spent the weekend before her move with her family—minus her boys since they weren't coming back up until Monday to help pack the truck. The weekend felt like old times with her brothers, reminding her of when they were kids. On Saturday, they went fishing and cooked what they caught for supper. On Sunday, the weather was beautiful, so they cooked on the grill and visited on the deck until the mosquitoes came out. Her brothers would be back on Monday and Tuesday to help pack up.

Sunday night, after everyone had left and she was alone with her mom, Rebekah wondered if she should dare ask her mom about Dee. Maybe Ruth had more information that she had kept to herself all these years. Rebekah had made copies of the envelopes and letters she found in the recipe box and put the originals back, not wanting her mom to know she had found them.

It was just the two of them in the kitchen. Rebekah was washing some dishes that didn't fit in the dishwasher, and her mom was sitting quietly in a chair at the table with a towel, drying them. She decided to take a chance.

"Mom, I was wondering if you would talk to me about Dee?"

Silence.

Rebekah was beginning to wonder if her mother had heard her when, after a good while, Ruth looked her straight in the eyes and replied, "Why do you ask?"

What the heck? Rebekah thought. "I know Dee left because she was pregnant. I want to find her, Mom. Do you have any information that could help me?"

Ruth turned away and appeared to have drifted off into the world she seemed to live in now. Then, after another long silence and to Rebekah's surprise, she spoke in a flat voice. "I saw the baby once. I had to sneak around and lie to your dad. It was on a day he was going to the UP with Ben and Steve to get a new piece of equipment for the shop. I met Dee at a park down by Pickerel Lake, where there was no chance of bumping into anyone we knew. No telling what your dad would have done if he found out.

"The baby looked just like her name—Rose. I held that sweet thing to my chest and smelled the top of her head, not wanting to ever let go." Her eyes became glassy as she recalled the moment. Then, closing her eyes as if to savor it, she said, "I'll never forget the smell of that baby's head; it was like heaven."

Ruth turned to Rebekah and smiled. "She looked just like you when you were a baby," she added, and her smile slowly disappeared. "It broke my heart to say goodbye to them that day. Dee said she would try to get together another time, but I never heard from or saw her again. I wish I could have stood up to your dad that night he threw her out. I'll never forgive myself for not doing so."

Rebekah had never felt such pity and love for her mom before. Looking at her now, she saw a shell of the woman Ruth had been when Rebekah was a child. She remembered her mom always in the kitchen, cooking and doing laundry— never having fun and always working. With six kids, she hadn't had a choice, Rebekah guessed. Ruth had never enjoyed life because she was always covered up by it. Maybe that's why she was taking Darrell's death so hard. She'd been in so deep, she'd never found the person she really was.

And then Rebekah realized she could have easily become like her mom herself. But not now.

"I also found out she moved to Milwaukee, Mom. Now that I'm moving there, I want to try and find her. Rose too. When I do, I'll bring them home to you."

"Would you really do that, Rebekah?" Ruth said with the pure hope of a child.

Rebekah saw a light twinkle in her mom's eyes.

"I want to tell her I'm sorry. I imagine Rose is a beautiful young woman just like you now," Ruth said.

Rebekah smiled. She had always felt that in her mother's opinion she must be plain and ordinary.

"You find her for us," Ruth continued with an eagerness in her voice, "so I can feel complete again, knowing where all my children are."

"I'm going to do it, Mom. I promise," Rebekah said.

Then mother and daughter held each other for a long time, something Rebekah had never before experienced.

***

It was nearly moving day. James would drive the rental truck with Rebekah's belongings to Milwaukee and thought it best that Rebekah follow him in her car with Andrew behind her to make sure they didn't get separated. *Those boys*, Rebekah thought.

The boys arrived around noon on Monday, and soon, along with Rebekah's brothers and their families, they had the truck and cars loaded for the move. Tuesday morning, Rebekah said her goodbyes before she took off for Milwaukee—and a new life. The farewells were not easy, leaving Rebekah full of emotion. This was where she had lived her whole life, where all her memories were. Still, she knew she was doing the right thing for herself; she could feel it in the excitement that kept welling up inside her.

Ruth was the last person she hugged.

"Find Dee and bring her to me," Ruth said after giving Rebekah a big hug and a kiss.

"I will, Mom," said Rebekah. "I love you." And at that moment, she had never meant it more.

With that, they were off.

The only stop they made during the four-hour trip was in Green Bay for lunch and gas—then it was straight to Milwaukee.

When they got to Milwaukee, Rebekah realized why James had wanted her car between himself and Andrew—the traffic! She had never seen traffic like this before. How in the world was she going to maneuver around this place? The last time she had been in Milwaukee was for James's graduation, but Ethan had done the driving.

The house the boys lived in was an older two-bedroom, two-bath house with an enclosed porch that could serve as a third bedroom. Rebekah figured they would put her there until she got her own place.

She was excited about buying her own house one day—mind you, nothing too big, but the perfect size for her. In her mind she could see the house: at least three bedrooms and two-and-a-half bathrooms. She wanted to be able to have room for company, hoping her brothers would come visit. A nice kitchen and family room were a must. Outside, she didn't want much yard other than a sunny spot in the back for a small garden and a deck. She would decorate the inside any way she wanted, in colors she picked—nothing like the boring, drab, beige and brown colors of the parsonage.

"So, Mom," Andrew said once they had arrived and moved some of Rebekah's things into the house. "I'm going to sleep in the porch bedroom, and you can have my room."

"No, Andrew," Rebekah said. "I won't take your room."

"It's already been decided," he said, placing a hand on her shoulder. "Now James has something to tell you."

The room became silent.

James hesitated. "Well," he said and cleared his throat as Rebekah's curiosity grew. "This is something you don't know, Mom … I have a girlfriend."

"A girlfriend? Son, why didn't you tell me?" Rebekah said with a smile that spread ear to ear. She always wondered why she had never heard about any girlfriends the boys may have had.

"One reason was because of Dad," James said. "He probably wouldn't have liked her at all. You know how he was about that stuff."

"Well, he's not here. So when do I get to meet her?" Rebekah was so happy. A girlfriend!

Andrew started laughing and left the room.

James was beet red. "Um, well, she lives here with us," he said, looking down at his shuffling feet.

"Oh," was all Rebekah said, and now she understood why Andrew had laughed. The girl lived with them. No, Ethan would never have approved of this arrangement. But how did Rebekah feel?

"I hope you're not disappointed in me, Mom. She's really nice and very smart. She's an accountant also," James continued. "We met in school and have been dating for about three years. It's not going to be a problem is it?"

This was not something Rebekah had thought she would have to deal with. She wasn't sure how she felt about it. But then her mind went to Dee and how, if their parents had been more loving and supportive, things might have been different.

She nodded and smiled at him. "James, I'm okay. I've no doubt she's a fine girl. You like her, and that's good enough for me." She saw the relief sweep across James's face, the red flush leaving.

"I don't like her, Mom. I love her," he responded with a little chuckle.

"Well, all the better. I can't wait to meet her," she said and gave him a big hug. "What's her name?"

"Her name is Violet. We're the same age," James shared, smiling.

"Violet. What a lovely name," Rebekah said. "Now let's unpack the truck."

***

At about five thirty, after Rebekah and the boys had finished unloading the rest of her things into the garage, Violet showed up. She was a very energetic young woman who obviously loved James as much as he loved her. On closer inspection, Rebekah noticed the tattoo on her ankle as well as ones on her wrist and the back of her neck. Rebekah's first reaction was that of judgment, but then she reminded herself that this was unimportant to the personality and disposition of the blonde-haired, blue-eyed young woman who stood before her. They hit it off just fine from the first word out of Violet's mouth—and could this girl ever talk.

"Mrs. Hayward, it's so nice to finally meet you. Both of your sons talk about how awesome you are and how everything you bake is out of this world. My mom never baked much, so I don't know how to do anything other than open a box, throw in a couple of eggs and water, and then stir. I can even ruin that and have on occasion." She let out a quick chuckle then continued before Rebekah could say anything. "Maybe you could teach me how to bake something simple. I'm clueless about it. Give me a bunch of numbers, though, and I'm in heaven. I love anything math."

Violet finally took a breath and Rebekah jumped in. "Violet, I'm so happy to meet you and, please, call me Rebekah. I'm not really a Mrs. anymore, so Rebekah is fine. And yes, I bake. While I'm here, I can certainly teach you something," Rebekah said, returning Violet's smile.

"Awesome, Rebekah," Violet said. "I enjoy reading also, do you? Give me the classics, I say. I love Jane Austen—and have you ever read Edith Wharton? OMG, I would have hated to be a young woman in those days, not being able to marry who you want. Have you watched Downton Abbey? If not, I have the DVDs you can borrow."

"I've read some of the classics but haven't seen Downton Abbey. If you think I would enjoy it, I would love to borrow your DVDs," Rebekah countered.

"Hey, we have to get the truck back," James interjected before Violet could respond. "Why don't you drive me back home after I drop it off, Violet, and let my mom settle in and relax."

"Okay," Violet said. "Bye, Rebekah."

And they left.

Andrew looked at his mom and laughed, shaking his head. "That's Violet. She's really great, but she talks a lot. Very smart, though—in fact, smarter than James and me put together."

"Yes, I can see she's friendly and … has great verbal skills. Well, she seems nice, and I look forward to getting to know her better." And Rebekah meant it.

"Oh, and by the way, in case you're wondering, I don't have a girlfriend right now, so no surprises from me. I'm just a boring college kid who can't wait to graduate," Andrew said. He would graduate in December of that year.

"Soon, sweetheart, soon," Rebekah said, laughing. "So let me check out your kitchen."

***

When James and Violet came back from dropping off the truck, they all went out for pizza and then dropped by the grocery store. Rebekah made a list of some things she thought they needed. What else was a mother for, right?

After putting the groceries away, she found the boys and Violet watching TV, so she joined them.

"So you two go to work, and you go to school tomorrow, right?" Rebekah asked, pointing first at James and Violet, who were cuddled up together on the couch, and then at Andrew, who was stretched out in a recliner. Andrew was taking some summer school classes on campus.

"Yep," Andrew responded, not turning his focus from the baseball game he was watching.

After about fifteen minutes, there was a commercial, so Rebekah knew she would have their attention. "I'm pretty tired, so I'm going to get in bed and maybe read. Andrew, I feel so bad kicking you out of your room."

"Mom, we all decided this is the way we would do it. I love that porch room, and besides, we're all going to be up early anyway, so you can sleep as late as you want. You deserve it after all those early mornings at the bakery."

"Thanks, son. I'll probably take you up on that." She laughed.

"What will you do, Rebekah? I mean what are your plans now that you're here?" Violet asked, leaning forward and looking over at her.

"Well," Rebekah said and then paused. "Right now, I think I'll explore Milwaukee. Then I'll eventually get a job. Discovering my new world is top on the list for now."

"That sounds great," Violet said and gave her a big smile.

"Mom also has a sister who was estranged from the family almost twenty years ago," James said. "We recently found out she came to Milwaukee after she left. She had a kid that none of us have ever seen. Our grandpa was really strict when my mom was young and threw her sister out because she was pregnant."

"How terrible," Violet said and furrowed her eyebrows. Her attention was on Rebekah now, and she was full of questions. "So was she older or younger than you?"

"She was my older sister by three years," Rebekah responded. "I also have four older brothers, but my sister, Dee, was my everything when I was a girl."

"Wow—and she had a baby. Things back then were really rough; I mean a baby shouldn't cause people to freak out like that, right? Your poor sister. So, where did she live in Milwaukee?"

"We already looked up the address Mom had, but there's a parking lot there now," Andrew shared. "Mom has no idea where she might be." He turned to his mom and smiled. "But we're going to find her, right Mom?"

"Right, Andrew." Rebekah loved that both kids were supportive of her quest.

"Rebekah," Violet said as Rebekah was leaving the room.

"Yes, Violet," she answered.

"One of my uncles was a Milwaukee police officer who retired and started his own private investigation business. I wonder if he could help you find your sister. I'll get his number from my mom if you want to talk to him. Could help you expedite your search."

"Thank you, Violet. I hadn't thought of that."

Rebekah felt a ray of hope.

"I mean, just talk with him and see what he might do for you. The way I see it, you've nothing to lose. and I know he's reputable. Might even give you a deal," she said.

"Yes, get his number from your mom. Thank you," Rebekah said and gave a hug to Violet and both of the boys. "Goodnight."

Rebekah went into the bedroom and sat on the bed. A private investigator. Why hadn't she thought of that? That's what Emily had done to find Ethan—and she was even in another country. Rebekah didn't care how much it cost—she would talk with Violet's uncle. She was excited now, knowing she could be days or weeks away from finding her sister.

***

Rebekah never heard the kids leave the next morning, and when she eventually rolled over to view the clock, she saw it was eight thirty. This was pure luxury. The leftover coffee was still warm in the carafe, so she poured a cup and reheated it in the microwave. She wanted a scone or something but settled on a piece of toast with homemade mixed-berry jelly, wondering where the jelly had come from. It was delicious.

Now, what to do today? She thought she might get in her car and explore, so she got out her laptop and typed in "bakeries near me." Seemed like a good place to start. There were several café bakeries around the university area where the boys' house was, but none were the old-timey type bakery she wanted to visit, so she broadened her search and found there were several not far away. She got dressed and was switching to a smaller purse when she found the ten lottery tickets she had bought on impulse several weeks ago.

She'd find somewhere to run them through today before she came home.

The day was beautiful. It seemed every tree and flower in the city had blooms on them. Rebekah first drove through the college campus. The only other time she had been there was for James's graduation. Ethan had moved the boys down to Milwaukee when they started college since she'd had to work and his schedule was more flexible. And the boys always preferred to come home, so she'd had no need to visit them at school.

What would her life have been like if she'd gone to college instead of marrying Ethan? Her high school teachers had told her all the time how smart she was. Then she remembered her mother's words when she brought up college after Ethan's proposal: "Where have you gotten these ridiculous ideas? Nobody in our family has ever gone to college, so what makes you think you will? There is no money for college, Rebekah. If we could afford it, we would have sent one of your brothers. Do you get it? There is no money for college! This is the best deal you're going to get."

She'd never forget those words as long as she lived. Had Rebekah known things like scholarships existed, she may have investigated the option more, but back then, she had been sheltered, trained to submit and go along.

Then time—and Tammy—had taught her differently.

Rebekah visited four bakeries she found nearby and bought something delicious to take home at each one. Wouldn't the kids love a treat after their hard days at work and school? She thought about driving down to Lake Park to get a good view of Lake Michigan and was headed that way when she saw a sign that said Tea House and pulled into the parking lot. Right next door was a gas station that prompted her to remember the lottery tickets. She would stop in the gas station before she left.

The Tea House was bright and colorful inside with big glass windows and several tables in different sizes. You could either get loose tea to take home, hot tea to go, or sit and enjoy a cup of tea with some pastries. The pastries appeared to be commercially made, not on the premises. Still, Rebekah liked the little place and thought she may come back again another time—maybe with Violet. This thought made her smile. She liked the girl and had to admit she was happy to have a little female companionship.

The line was long inside the gas station, but she had no place else to be at the moment, so she waited. The man ran her tickets through, then held one ticket by itself in one hand and the rest in his other hand.

"These had nothing, but this one says you have to go to the lottery office to claim it. Says it has to be the main office in Madison. Must be a big one," the man said with a smile and a little excitement in his voice. "Did you buy it here?"

"No, I bought it up north where I'm from. What do you mean go to Madison? Don't I just have to fill something out and send it in, and then they send a check? I've done that before."

"Like I said," the man repeated and lowered his voice, "it must be a big one." He tipped his head down, giving her a wink and then said even more quietly, "Congratulations. Go online to Wisconsin Lottery and check your numbers so you'll know how much. The site will tell you what to do. Might have to make an appointment at the lottery office."

Rebekah thanked him and had begun to leave when he motioned her to return to the counter.

"Oh! And make sure you sign the back as soon as possible. In fact, here's a pen. Go ahead and sign."

Rebekah signed the back and thanked him again before she turned around and walked outside, her mind racing as she moved to the car. How big could it be? After sitting in the car a few seconds to calm her head before she drove, she decided it best to skip the park and visit another day. For now, she was going home to check her ticket.

***

She couldn't park her car and get into the house fast enough, happy no one was there but herself. She went to her room, pulled her laptop out of its bag, powered it up, and waited. When it was ready to go, she typed in "Wisconsin lottery" and clicked on the site to look at the date of the drawing and compare the numbers. She found the right one, her hands clumsy and shaking. One by one she compared the numbers on the ticket and couldn't believe her eyes. She then looked to see what the prize was, and it took her breath away.

Three million dollars.

She checked the numbers again. Yes—three million dollars. She fell back in her chair, feeling as if time were standing still. After a moment, a small laugh escaped. This soon erupted into a fit where she laughed and cried at the same time, harder than she had ever laughed before. Thank God no one was home. Now what?

She did a search for what to do when you win the Wisconsin lottery and found a list. The first thing was to sign the back of your ticket—done. Then, the list said, put your ticket in a safe place until you're ready to turn it in. She would have to think about where to keep it.

The man at the store had said she needed to visit the office in person. Then a thought came to her. She decided to first call Jeremy, her investment guy in Rhinelander, before she did anything else. Surely, he had clients who had won the lottery. She dialed Jeremy's number, and he picked up on the third ring.

"Hello, Jeremy Dombrowski speaking."

"Jeremy, I'm so happy you answered. This is Rebekah Hayward. Could I have a few minutes of your time to talk? I have a situation, and I need to ask your advice," Rebekah told him.

"Of course, Rebekah. What can I do for you?" Jeremy asked.

"Well," Rebekah continued, "it appears I've won a bunch of money in the lottery—not the real big one, mind you, but big enough for me."

"Really, how much?"

She had Jeremy's attention. "Looks like three million dollars."

Jeremy whistled, and then there was a long pause before he spoke. "This isn't a joke, right? That's awesome, Rebekah! So, have you already gone to claim it?"

"No, I wanted to talk to you first. I looked at the lottery website, but I'm just a little overwhelmed and needed to talk with someone who maybe could help me do this the right way. Just so you know, I'm living in Milwaukee for the time being and not sure if I'll ever come back to live near Rhinelander." She was sure he had heard about Ethan.

"I'm glad you called me. Give me a second. I'm going to pull up the lottery site on my computer too, and we can talk about it. Let's see …." Jeremy was silent while he looked everything over. "It looks like you have to go in to the lottery office in Madison, which is what I would expect."

"Yes, that's what the guy who ran the ticket through at the gas station told me," Rebekah said.

"Yeah, all it gives is a number to call. I'm sure you have to make an appointment. When you go, I would take with you your driver's license, passport if you have one, social security card, and your bank information for the account you want it wired to. Much safer than a check in the mail. Make sure you sign the back of the ticket right now. Let me know when the money might be coming so I can watch for the deposit and call you after it comes in. Then we can talk about what you want to do with it. I'm so excited for you."

"I'm in shock," Rebekah said. "I know they'll take taxes out, but what do you think I'll end up with?"

"Oh, I would say minimum of one-and-a-half million, probably a little more. A nice chunk of money. You know, with the money you already have, you're a well-off woman, Rebekah. Anything special you think you might want to do with it?" Jeremy asked.

Rebekah had been keeping her desire to open her own bakery a secret for a long time and wasn't ready to share it just yet. The thought of doing so made her feel like she was giving a piece of her dream away, and she couldn't bare it if someone shot her down.

"No, not yet. I'll get the money first and then decide if I'm going to spend some of it."

This answer seemed to appease Jeremy. "Smart move, Rebekah. Too many people go crazy when they win or inherit a lot of money, and before they know it, the money's gone. You know I'm here to help you. I'll wait for your call to tell me what's going on after you visit the lottery office. I tell you—you have to be one of the luckiest people I know."

"Thanks. I'll call when I know something."

Rebekah was relieved to have his help. The next step was to dial the lottery number.

"Hello, Wisconsin Lottery, this is Kami. How may I help you?" said the pleasant-sounding woman who answered.

"Um, yes, ah, I have a winning ticket." Rebekah stumbled as she tried to find the right words. "What do I do?"

"Well first, congratulations. Now, please give me the name of the drawing and the numbers."

Rebekah obliged.

"Yes, you do have the winning numbers!"

Rebekah felt like her chest was going to explode she was breathing so hard.

"Let's make an appointment for you to come in so we can confirm it. We have to check the ticket, and there's paperwork for you to fill out before you can get the money. Also, bring your bank account information where you want the funds wired and identification. Makes it much easier."

"Okay," Rebekah said. "Tell me when to come, and I'll be there."

"Can you come next week on Thursday? Where do you live?"

"I live in Milwaukee right now."

"How about eleven thirty in the morning next Thursday then? I think you should have no problem getting here by that time."

Rebekah considered it a moment. Nobody would even know she was gone. She thought it best to keep it that way until she knew for sure she had won and the particulars. She would be back in plenty of time before anyone came home, and if they did come home and she was still gone, she could make something up.

"Yes," Rebekah said. "Sounds good. I'll be there."

She hung up and let out a long, slow breath. Next Thursday was a week away. How was she going to make it through a week?

Chapter 20

"Hey, Mom."

It was Andrew but Rebekah didn't hear him. Her mind was on her appointment in Madison on Thursday.

"Mom? *Hello.* Mom!" Andrew said, and he put his face in front of Rebekah's to get her attention.

"Oh, I'm sorry, son. I was just thinking about something. What can I do for you?" Rebekah responded.

"Are you sure you're happy you came down here? You've seemed, I don't know, just not yourself the past few days. What are you thinking about?" he quizzed.

"Nothing," Rebekah said quickly and smiled. "Is that all you wanted to ask me?" she quizzed back.

"No. I wanted to know if you could meet me on campus for lunch Thursday so I could show you around. I have a long break between classes that day. So … ?"

Thursday. She had her lottery appointment that day. How was she going to get out of this? The words spilled from her mouth. "I saw it was going to be a nice day Thursday, so I planned to explore a little outside the city. You know I'm going to have to get a job, and the more informed I am about the area, the better things will be for me. I'm thinking I'll rent a place first and then buy a house." *Phew.*

"Well, okay, I guess. You know you can live with us as long as you want," Andrew said.

"I figure James is going to want a place with Violet after you graduate, and you'll get a job and want your own also. Nobody wants their mom hanging around. Right?"

"True," he said. "Well, okay. Just wanting to take care of you, that's all. Maybe you can have lunch with me another day. I sound like I'm in elementary school, don't I?" he said and laughed, turning slightly red.

"Not at all." Rebekah laughed as well, thinking he kind of did.

***

Thursday morning came, and as soon as everyone was out of the house, Rebekah got ready for her trip to Madison. She had already looked up the trip online and saw it was a straight shot from Milwaukee to Madison, roughly ninety minutes. She planned to arrive at least thirty minutes or more before her appointment, so she would need to leave by nine just to be on the safe side.

Happy the weather report had been correct about a sunny day, she headed out, feeling both excited and nervous. What if she got there and they said there was a mistake and she didn't win anything? She needed a distraction and instead shifted her focus to finding Dee.

The first thing she was going to do—after she confirmed she had won the money and saw it in her bank account—was search for Dee. It didn't matter what it cost, especially now. If Emily could have an investigator from Canada trace Ethan to Northern Wisconsin, surely one in Milwaukee could find Dee.

The long drive soon had her mind drifting as she stared at the continuous, straight road to Madison. With her guard down, she began to think about the turn of events in her life, taking her down the one path she was trying to block forever from her memory: *Ethan*.

How could she have lived with a man that long and never suspected a thing? She guessed that because he was a minister, no one would ever have doubted who he was—not even her—and decided she shouldn't beat herself up over it.

It surprised her how James and Andrew didn't seem angry or upset about their father's absence, though in reality, Ethan had never been an involved dad who did things with his sons. Her brothers and her own dad had served as the male role models in their lives, taking them hunting and fishing, showing them how to ride their bikes and drive, playing sports with them, and teaching other life lessons. She was grateful for that. Ethan never interacted with them, and their unconcern about him in their lives reflected that.

And then there was her relationship with them. She couldn't have loved any humans more than those two boys. And they loved her. This was more apparent than ever given how they had taken care of her ever since they found out the truth of their parentage. Yes, *she* was their mother.

She spent the rest of the trip overthinking all this until her phone's GPS startled her back to reality by announcing the exit. She navigated through heavy traffic as she wound around unfamiliar roads. At last, with her heart pounding, she arrived at the Wisconsin Department of Revenue building, where the lottery office was located. She pulled into a parking spot out front and stared up at the building in front of her. She wasn't sure what she had expected, but the building was a large, plain, rectangular structure, sitting by itself with no other buildings around. She double-checked her phone to make sure she was indeed at the right place and then saw the sign that said Wisconsin Department of Revenue. This was it.

Arriving a little earlier than planned, she sat in the car for several minutes in order to compose herself. She was nervous and felt like she was going to jump out of her skin. *Might as well go in,* she thought, put her purse on her arm, climbed out, and locked the car. Then, with a deep breath or two to calm her nerves, she entered the building to claim her money.

***

By 1:10 p.m., Rebekah was on her way back to Milwaukee. Her visit to the lottery office complete, she was now well over a million dollars richer. She felt as if she were in a dream, recounting in her head what had just taken place.

She had arrived early, and since no one else was waiting, they took her right away. She was greeted by Kami Butler, the woman she had spoken to on the phone earlier in the week, who made the whole process easy. After Rebekah had filled out several forms and provided her personal information, Kami informed her that it would take up to two hours to process the ticket, though it could be less. She suggested Rebekah grab a bite to eat and then come back.

Grab a bite to eat? Rebekah didn't know how she could keep anything down until she knew all was okay. She found a place close by and bought a sandwich that she only managed to eat half of before she went back an hour later to sit and wait some more.

"Everything is all set," Kami told Rebekah after a while and handed her a packet filled with information explaining the redemption process and taxes. Just as Jeremy had predicted, she would have a little over $1.5 million wired into her checking account sometime in the next few days.

And that was it.

She spent the rest of the trip back to Milwaukee daydreaming about what she would do with the money. One thing she also wanted to do was pay off both James's and Andrew's student loans. She and Ethan had only been able to support the boys by renting the house they were living in. The rest was on the boys to manage—scholarship money, student loans, and spending money from any jobs they worked. Now she could pay the boys' loans off, giving them a better start in life.

Although she wanted to buy a house and open a business, she was going to let the money sit for a while until she figured out the details. This money was her future and didn't need to be frittered away on foolish purchases and bad investments. Before anything else, however, she'd hire Violet's uncle to find Dee. Now more than ever, she wanted her sister by her side.

Her mind next went to how and when to tell Andrew and James. She would never tell the rest of her family but wanted her sons to know. Although she liked Violet and had a feeling James would eventually marry her, Rebekah wanted to keep this, and any other future plans, between her and her children.

Tonight she wanted to cook something she knew the kids would like, so she stopped by a grocery store on the way home and picked up what was needed to make a roast with carrots and potatoes and put it in the oven as soon as she arrived home. She also whipped up a lemon meringue pie—from scratch, of course—for dessert. The kitchen was definitely her happy place and where she wanted to be at that moment.

At about five thirty, she heard a car pull in the driveway and Andrew's voice as he came through the door.

"Oh my God. Do I smell a roast cooking? I'm in heaven. Where are you, Mom, so I can hug you?"

Laughing, Rebekah came into the kitchen, where Andrew immediately wrapped his arms around her in a smothering bear hug before she could respond.

"And I have a lemon meringue pie for dessert."

"I want you to live with me forever," Andrew said just as James walked in.

"Do I smell a roast cooking?" James asked, echoing his brother.

"And she made us one of her lemon meringue pies," Andrew said, clasping his hands together.

"When do we eat?" James asked.

"Oh, maybe about forty-five minutes. When does Violet usually get home?"

"Oh, I didn't tell you. She's having supper with her parents tonight. It's just us," James said.

"Okay," Rebekah said. *Couldn't be more perfect.* "You two go get changed then come set the table." She laughed. "Just like when you were little boys."

"If you keep cooking us stuff like this, I'll even do the dishes every night without being asked," James said.

Rebekah shooed them out of the kitchen.

They ate about half of the roast, talking between mouthfuls. After they finished, Andrew volunteered to serve up the pie.

"I'm kind of happy Violet is with her family tonight so I can have you both to myself," Rebekah said. "I've something important to share with you."

She had their attention as they both sat quietly, waiting for her to continue.

"I'm finding out more and more how we all keep some kinds of secrets to ourselves. Some are good, some are bad, some don't really matter, and then others can destroy. I have a secret myself that I think is good."

Rebekah took a deep breath before she continued.

"Early on, when your dad and I were first … well, when I thought we were married, I started buying lottery and scratch-off tickets. All the people I worked with—especially my friend, Tammy—bought them, so eventually I did too. And I won. Well, I knew your dad would have damned me to hell," she said, laughing and shaking her head, "so I figured the best place to keep the money was at work and decided to buy some more tickets. I started winning regularly and then started to win bigger jackpots, so I opened a savings account. Then I met an investment advisor at the bank, and he helped me make the money grow. Now I've been doing this for years, mind you, and I've never touched the money … with the exception of buying more tickets." She laughed again. "I've amassed a good amount of money—around five hundred thousand dollars"

Both boys' eyes were now huge as she continued.

"Now, you know I had a little spell where we weren't sure if I was going to have a mental breakdown or come out of the fog after your dad's … revelation."

"But you're doing fine now, right, Mom? We were so worried about you," Andrew said with concern in his voice.

"Yes, Andrew, I'm fine. I told you about the letters Dee wrote to your grandma. Well, it seems finding the letters about Dee was just what I needed to snap me out of the hopelessness I was feeling. Those letters gave me a new purpose. They brought me back to life. I hadn't bought any lottery tickets during that time, so the day after I found the letters, I went into a gas station and bought ten tickets for the state lottery, put them in my purse, and forgot about them until the other day, when I used that same purse. I decided to take the tickets into a gas station to run them through and buy a few more, and it turned out one of the tickets won me three million dollars."

After a very long silence, James spoke. "Are you sure, Mom?"

"Well, yes I am." She turned to Andrew. "I know you wanted me to have lunch with you today, and I fibbed a bit. I actually went to the Wisconsin Department of Revenue in Madison, where you have to go to redeem the big tickets and start the process to have the money direct deposited into my checking account. I'm a winner."

James stood up with a big smile on his face and hugged his mother. "Well, hot damn, Mom! You're full of surprises. Who's this advisor? Can you really trust this person?"

"Yes, son. I've been working with him for years. He's made me a lot of money."

With a puzzled look, Andrew spoke. "But you have to pay taxes on all this money you've won. How did you hide it from Dad? Sorry for the language, Mom, but he would have had a shit fit if he found out."

"Your dad told me we had to file taxes separately. I assumed it was because he was a minister and it was more profitable for us. I know nothing about taxes, not like you two do. Now I think he wanted to do it that way to hide his secret, you know just in case he could be linked to his previous identity."

James and Andrew looked at each other and laughed and then hugged each other.

"I've got to have a beer, brother, how about you?" James said.

"A beer? How about a few," Andrew replied, laughing.

Rebekah had no idea they drank.

"Mom, how about you? Can I get you a cold one from the garage fridge?" James said.

"Um, no, son," Rebekah said before James took his leave to the garage and came back with two beers, tossing one to Andrew. Nothing ceased to amaze her anymore. She'd definitely lived a sheltered life, but not anymore. They popped the tops and laughed before taking their first big gulps.

"I'm guessing you get to keep a little over half, right? So that means with what you already have, plus this, there's about two million dollars or more, Mom. Damn!" James said, shaking his head and laughing before turning to Andrew.

The boys looked at each other, clinked their cans together, and took another big swig of beer.

"Now don't go thinking about how *we're* going to spend this money," Rebekah said. "I want to make it clear—it's *my* money, and I have plans. First, I'm going to pay off your student loans, then I'm going to find Dee, and then …." She sighed and paused. "I'm opening my own bakery. It's been a dream my whole life."

"Well, I think that sounds great. Thank you for wanting to pay our loans," James said.

"It's so sweet that you'd think of doing that for us. We lucked out when we got you for a mom," Andrew said.

Rebekah smiled as she started to tear up.

"Aww, now don't go doing that, Mom, because you'll get us going next," James said and hugged his mom once more, Andrew following his lead.

They sat at the table a good while, talking. Rebekah told them about the time Mère had shared that she had wanted to open a bakery and Père had said no because women just didn't do things like that.

"I knew at that moment I wanted to open a bakery, not only because it was my desire but also because I knew Mère had wanted to. I've never shared this with anyone until now."

Rebekah felt a warm sense of well-being come over her, like a hug from the inside out. Was this Mère letting her know she was with her? A single happy tear rolled down Rebekah's cheek. She turned and brushed it away before the boys could see.

"Mom, we're behind you one hundred percent," James said.

"Yeah, all the way," Andrew added.

Just then, they heard the front door open and close before Violet entered the kitchen.

"Wow, it smells great in here. I mean, I just had a sandwich at my parents', but if that's a roast I smell … are there any leftovers?"

James got up to hug and kiss the always exuberant Violet.

"Yeah, Mom made one of her fabulous roasts, and yes there are leftovers we can divvy up between the three of us for tomorrow. And see this?" he said, gesturing toward the half-devoured pie. "I doubt there will be any leftover pie, so you better get a piece now."

He got a plate to serve her a slice, after which he and Andrew each had another, leaving behind only crumbs.

"Oh yeah, Rebekah, I got my uncle's phone number from my mom. Mom said he's been busy and is going on vacation up north to his cottage the next two weeks, but maybe when he comes back, you can give him a call." She handed Rebekah a piece of paper with a name and address.

"Thanks, Violet. I'll do that. I keep thinking my sister is somewhere here in Milwaukee. Maybe I'll even bump into her. I've heard stories where people have had things happen like that, so it's not impossible."

"I have too," Violet said. "I heard about siblings who were separated by adoption and then ended up living right around the corner from each other or even working at the same place. I think it would be so cool if you found her like that. I bet you could get on one of those talk shows then. Now that would be really cool." Violet's eyes opened wide in exaggerated excitement. "I actually know a guy named Bryan Krampton who works at one of the local stations here. He's on the news every day. I could hook you up with him if you want. It's a cool story no matter what."

"I'm fine keeping it to myself." Rebekah laughed. James had his hands full with this one. "I want to live a quiet, simple life."

"Yeah, me too," said Violet, and they all laughed—except Violet. "What's so funny? I'm just a simple girl."

"You are far from simple," said James, standing behind the chair where she sat. He kissed the top of her head. "Just the way I like 'em."

Violet smiled and took his hands in hers.

"So Mom, you know I think you should take some time for yourself and not look for a job right now," James suggested. "You've worked as long as I can remember. I think you deserve some time off. There's a lot to see here in Milwaukee—museums, the Horticultural Conservatory, the zoo, a bunch of theaters, nice parks, and festivals all summer long."

Rebekah was thinking the same thing. She really didn't have to work and was in the process of dealing with the most stressful thing that had ever happened to her, so why not take it easy? "I agree, son. A little down time would be good for me."

"The rest of the summer school classes I'm taking are online. I'll be working three days a week at my internship, so if you want company, I'm available," Andrew shared.

"I think it was meant to be," Rebekah said, thinking, *What a turn of events*. "You kids run along and do what you have to. I'm cleaning up the kitchen."

"No, Mom. We insist on doing the cleanup," James said.

Andrew and Violet nodded.

Rebekah took in a deep breath before she spoke. "No, it's okay. I need some time alone to think. The kitchen is a good place for me to do that."

The boys exchanged glances. They understood.

"Okay, but we're going to pick out a movie to watch when you're done," Andrew said.

"Sounds good—but not scary or violent or full of sex," Rebekah dictated.

"Yeah, yeah, we know, Mom," James said, and both boys laughed.

"Hey, James," Andrew said as the three of them walked out of the room, "see if Mary Poppins is on."

Rebekah chuckled as she started to rinse the plates and put them in the dishwasher, but her thoughts quickly became serious. What was her future going to be like? She wasn't going to live with the boys forever. If she found her sister, would Dee want Rebekah in her life? And would Rebekah ever find someone to love and trust again?

Going over and over the same things was not helping. She needed to focus on the more positive aspects of her life, which obviously included the boys and the two million dollars she'd soon have in her bank account. Money wasn't everything, but it sure did help. She could go anywhere and do anything. She thought of her bakery. She was going to do some thoughtful planning and then go on a trip somewhere. But who could she go with? She had no friends other than Tammy, and she was four hours away. Rebekah missed her friend so much at that moment and wondered if Tammy might come to visit this summer. Rebekah's eyes began to water. *Stop it!* she told herself. She was going to call Tammy this weekend.

She put the last pot in the dish rack, let the water drain from the sink, and dried her hands. The kids were laughing in the other room. She stopped in the bathroom and wiped her eyes before she joined them. She knew being here with them was the best place for her.

"So what movie did you find?" she asked with a big smile on her face as she walked into the living room, knowing that any movie they picked would be just fine with her.

Chapter 21

After her visit to the lottery office, Rebekah monitored her bank account online several times a day until the prize money showed up. Kami had told her it would take three business days, so it was Tuesday morning before the money was finally deposited. Jeremy must have been keeping a close eye on her account also because thirty minutes after she saw the money in her account, he called.

"Rebekah, wonderful news! I just checked, and the money's in your account. I have some great ideas for you. Since you're down in Milwaukee, I might come visit you in a couple of weeks, and we can go over some opportunities," he said, very hopeful.

Rebekah knew he could benefit from her money as well, so she chose her words carefully. "You don't need to do that. I want the money to just sit for a while, separate from the rest of my money, so let's open an account to transfer it into for the moment. I have several uncertainties in my life and don't want to do something I'll regret. I know it's a lot of money, but as long as it's in something safe, I'm good. I need to know that I can get to it if I want to."

This was what James had told her to say.

"Okay, Rebekah, if that's what you want," Jeremy said, sounding rather reluctant. "You know you're losing money if you don't have it invested well. I just don't want anyone taking advantage of you."

"I don't either, but I also don't want to make any mistakes. This was unexpected, and I feel it's all moving too fast. I need time to think," she told him.

"Got it. I'll be in touch."

Oh, I'm sure you will be, Rebekah thought as they said goodbye and hung up.

***

Two weeks had passed since Rebekah had become a millionaire, and surprisingly, she felt no different. *A millionaire.* She did like the sound of that, though.

Today was the Fourth of July, and all three kids had the day off. They were going to have a little cookout with hamburgers, brats, and all the fixings, Rebekah's German potato salad, baked beans, corn on the cob, homemade pickles and pickled beets that Violet had made, and homemade ice cream. Rebekah had picked up an ice cream maker, thinking it would be fun for them to make some. An all-American Fourth of July.

"Hey, Mom," said Andrew while they were enjoying the ice cream on their patio, "we can take some folding lawn chairs and a cooler with drinks over to Lake Park and watch the fireworks tonight if you want. You can get a pretty good view of all the areas around Lake Michigan that shoot them off. Kind of cool. We can just walk down there."

"That sounds like a great idea, son," Rebekah said. "I'm used to the little display over Lake Metonga we always have at home. This should really be something."

"Oh, it is Mom," Andrew continued. "It's an amazing display over the water."

Rebekah felt like a kid again with all the different things she'd experienced since she came to Milwaukee—a world she never knew existed. If someone had told her a year ago where she would be now and what she would've gone through to get there, she'd have thought them crazy. And to think there was even more world out there. She wondered if Dee had felt the same when she came to Milwaukee.

The world was a place of never-ending new experiences—at least her world seemed to be.

"Hey," said Violet, interrupting her thoughts, "my uncle Bobby will be back this weekend from his vacation. Do you still have his number? You should give him a call Monday morning and get an appointment to see him before he gets too busy. He works out of his house, so he'll meet with you in his office above the garage."

"Great," Rebekah said. "I can't wait to get started. I know this sounds silly, but I keep looking at people here to see if I recognize Dee."

Andrew put his arm around his mom. "It doesn't sound silly at all, Mom. I wish it could be that easy, but I want to make a suggestion: don't go walking up to strangers you think might look like her. Bailing you out of jail is not something James and I want to do."

Rebekah turned and playfully slapped him on the arm. "I would never do something like that."

Both boys looked at each other and then at Rebekah.

"Okay, if you say so, but I better not get that call from the jail," Andrew said.

"Just give me a call, Rebekah," Violet said. "It'll be our secret." Violet winked, and they all laughed.

***

The fireworks that evening were awesome, like nothing Rebekah had seen before. She loved the way she could look up and down the shoreline of Lake Michigan and see a dozen or more displays shooting off all at the same time.

"Do they do this every year?" she asked as they were walking back home.

"Every year," James replied.

"It makes me wonder what else I've been missing out on. Do you all think me," she hesitated, trying to find the right words, "backward or like a country bumpkin?"

There was silence.

"Not at all, Mom," James said. "I think you've been sheltered, not only by living where you did but also because of how you were raised. You were the youngest child with four older brothers, but of course if Dee hadn't left, that might have been different. You would have had someone to do things and go places with. We think you're perfect the way you are."

Violet put her arm through Rebekah's. "I think you're just about the sweetest person I've ever met. Now I know why James is the way he is. It's because you're his mother."

Rebekah felt a little flip-flop in her heart.

"Listen, Mom, when we get back, I'm making you a good old Wisconsin brandy old-fashioned," James said, putting his hand up in anticipation of her objection. "I'll make it weak."

"You know, I've never had an alcoholic drink before in my life," Rebekah said, remembering Ethan and the whiff she'd taken of the bottle of whatever it was he had. It didn't smell good.

"Well, I say it's about time then. We're taking you to the dark side, Mom," Andrew said, and he and his brother both snickered.

"Just ignore them, Rebekah. We girls will stick together," said Violet, patting her on the arm.

When they got home, Rebekah did indeed have a brandy old-fashioned and kind of liked it. Another new surprise. What a fun Fourth of July. Monday she would call Violet's uncle and begin her search for Dee. She would pay whatever it took for her to be with her sister again.

***

"Hello, Becker Investigators, Bobby Becker speaking."

"Hi, Bobby, this is Rebekah Hayward. Your niece, Violet, gave me your name."

"Oh ya, my sister told me you might be calling. Violet's dating your son or something," Bobby said.

"Yes, she is. So happy my son met her. It's nice having some female influence around for a change. I have another son and four brothers also."

"You don't say." Bobby laughed. "Can make life rough for a girl."

"I do have an older sister, but it's been about twenty years since I last saw her, and that's why I'm calling you. Violet said you might be able to find her for me. I know she came to Milwaukee at one point. For all I know she could still be here … but then again, maybe not. Do you think you can help me?"

"Well, every case is unique, so it's hard for me to say till I get into the evidence. I'll have you come in to talk and give me anything you have that might help. Driver's license info, social security number, passport info, any alias or married names she may have used, pictures you might have, friends she may have had at the time or boyfriends, you get the idea."

Rebekah felt discouraged. "I don't have any of that stuff, but I can talk to my older brothers; they may be able to help. I was only fifteen when she left, and no one in my family will talk about it."

"Well, since I just got back from vacation, I'm booked up for the next two weeks, so let me see." There was a long pause as Rebekah listened to Bobby's computer keyboard clicking away. "Looks like I can squeeze you in two weeks from today. Ah, let's see, yep, ten in the morning. Does that work?"

"Yes, it will work. I just thought I might see you before then. If anyone cancels, can you call me?" she asked, hopeful.

"Yep, I can, but don't hold your breath. I don't have enough hours in the day to handle all the work I get. I turn a lot of folks away, but you're like family since your son's dating Violet. She asked me to take good care of you. I'll keep you in mind if anything comes up but, in the meantime, it gives you a chance to get some of that info I mentioned together," Bobby recommended.

"Right," Rebekah said.

"So I'll see you in a couple of weeks."

"Yeah, thanks," Rebekah said and hung up.

Two weeks. Bobby was right about her needing some time to gather the information. She would see what she could get. She'd ask her brothers.

***

The next day, she called Steve.

"Rebekah, so good to hear your voice. We miss you. I hope you're calling to tell me you're coming to visit," Steve said.

"No, I think it's too soon. I want people to forget about me and not reignite their interest. Maybe someone else will have a tragedy in their life, and I can pass the baton," Rebekah laughed.

After a little chuckle, Steve said, "Faithful Shepherd Church has started interviewing new ministers. We've all decided we're not going back after the way they gossiped about you. Mom is still in another world, so she doesn't even notice we haven't gone."

"I didn't tell you before I left," Rebekah said, "but Mom shared with me what happened to Dee. Dee was pregnant, and Dad threw her out. I also found out Dee went to Milwaukee, and her baby girl, Rose, was born there."

"Wow. I'm impressed you found all this out. Mom told you this? I can't believe she kept it a secret all these years."

"Well ... I had to do a little coaxing to get the information, but she asked me to find Dee and bring her home. Now that I'm living in Milwaukee, I decided I'm going to try to do just that. In a couple of weeks, I have a meeting with a private investigator. I need your help, though. The investigator asked for any information I can give him about Dee. She was only eighteen, so there's probably not much to go on as far as records. A social security number or a picture of her around the time she left is all I think you might find from the list he gave me. My appointment is in two weeks, so see what you can find before then. Go through Dad's desk and some of those boxes of papers in the office if you have time. I don't think he threw away anything," she said with a slight chuckle.

"No, he sure didn't. Tom is going crazy looking for stuff he needs for running the business. He used to just ask, and Dad knew where it was since Dad had his own filing system. Oh, hey, talking about Dad made me think of this. It sure was lucky for us the lawyers were able to handle the claim made by Dad's brothers, wasn't it?" Steve said.

"Yes, it sure was," Rebekah said, quickly changing the subject back to Dee before Steve mentioned anything else about the money. "So just find whatever you can that might help find Dee. You can text or email me a picture. I'm sure you'll find one."

"I will, and I'll tell our brothers what you're doing and see if they can help. They might know more, since they're older and have just kept their mouths shut."

"That's true. Well, I'll stay in touch. Say hi to everyone and give them my love. Bye," Rebekah said.

"Okay, tell your boys tell your boys hello. Bye."

***

Steve called back a week later. All he could send Rebekah was Dee's high school graduation picture and a copy of her birth certificate. It was better than nothing, she decided.

Now all she had to do was wait for her appointment with Bobby Becker.

Chapter 22

The two weeks Rebekah had to wait for her appointment with Bobby went by fast. She stayed busy, exploring Milwaukee and cooking and cleaning for the kids. It was almost just like old times.

She was so excited about her appointment with Bobby, she couldn't sleep the night before. In the morning, she typed his address into her phone's GPS and discovered it was only fifteen minutes away. Bobby had sounded like an interesting guy on the phone, and she was curious to see if he fit the image she had in her head.

Turned out he did—and more.

Bobby was about as casual as they come. In addition to his scruffy beard, huge beer belly, and wild hair, he had on jeans, tennis shoes, and a Green Bay Packers shirt that said, "On a Quiet Night in Wisconsin You Can Hear the Bears Cry." This gave Rebekah a little chuckle.

"Rebekah, come on in and sit down. Can I get you something to drink? I got pop, bottles of water, and even some beer if you want one. Whatcha say?"

"I'm good Bobby, but thanks for asking." *Beer?* It was ten o'clock in the morning.

"So your son dates our little Violet. She's a cute kid now, but I'll tell you when she was a baby, I wasn't sure, if you know what I mean. Smart as can be, I hear. Not really sure where that gene came from," Bobby said and laughed so hard he fell into a coughing fit Rebekah wasn't sure he would recover from.

"So let's talk," Bobby said as his tone shifted and he got down to business. "You say you want to find your sister. Start at the beginning, and I'm going to take notes." He pulled a yellow-lined legal pad out of his top desk drawer along with a pencil; he licked the tip, then looked up at her and said, "I'm ready."

"Okay," Rebekah said, raising her eyebrows. "Twenty years ago, after a terrible argument with my parents, my sister, Dee, left home, never to be seen again. I—"

"Do you think she could have been murdered?" Bobby asked, seeming completely serious.

"Well, no. I don't have any information that would lead me to believe she was."

Bobby nodded, made some notes, and then looked up.

"As I said, my sister left home, and I never saw her again. My parents never spoke about it and acted as if she never existed. I'd wondered all this time what had happened to her. Then, just recently, I found three letters—written by my sister to our mom—that answered my questions. Dee was pregnant, and my parents, mostly my dad, were so furious, they threw her out. I have copies of the letters for you," she said, pulling the letters from a folder and handing them to him.

"Turns out she came to Milwaukee. I have the address for where she was staying when she first came here; it was with a friend named Jen. My sons and I looked it up, and it appears the place has since been torn down, and a parking lot's there now. She had a baby girl named Rose. The father deserted them, so my sister was alone. The last letter tells of her getting a job at an attorney's office along with her own apartment, but there's no address or name of the attorney."

Bobby scribbled fast and furiously on his notepad. Rebekah waited to let him get it all down. At last, he looked up at her.

"What else?" he asked.

"Her full name is Dorcas Ruth Boulanger."

Bobby looked up and tilted his head to the side. "Wow. Don't think we have to worry about another woman out there with the same name. That's going to help a lot. Dang, no wonder you called her Dee."

"Yes," Rebekah said, raising her eyebrows once more. "Anyway, my mother told me a few weeks ago that she secretly met with Dee once after the baby was born, but she had no information about where they lived or anything. The only things from your list of documents I can give you are Dee's high school graduation picture and birth certificate. No social security number, driver's license—nothing else. I wish I had more." Rebekah sighed.

Bobby finished writing and then looked at her for a long moment, tapping his pencil on the table.

"It's okay," he said. "I'll get started and see what pops up. Hey, wouldn't it be amazing if all I had to do is plug her name in and there she is? It's happened before."

"I would love that," Rebekah said. "So how much do you charge, Bobby?" Rebekah had no idea what to expect.

"I'm charging you the friends and family discount. Let's say," he paused for a bit while he thought, "a hundred dollars an hour. I'll need two hundred dollars up front today. It usually takes at least two hours or more to do something like this you know, to get started, just to give you an idea. It may turn out to be more if I have to do more research."

"Great. I appreciate it," Rebekah said, and she gave him her credit card to run through his machine.

"Don't expect to hear from me for about a week or longer," Bobby informed her. "Got to put the feelers out and give it a little time, ya know."

"Sure, okay," Rebekah said.

They shook hands, and Rebekah was on her way home, excited, nervous, and hopeful as to what Bobby was going to find.

***

Later in the day, Rebekah decided she would call Tammy. She missed her friend so much and needed a little bolstering. Rebekah had only briefly talked to her once since moving to Milwaukee.

"Oh my God, I was just thinking about you," Tammy said after she answered on the first ring. "It's that psychic bond we have, I'm sure. You know, I've thought many times we must have met in another life. So what's up?"

Rebekah wanted to cry but contained herself. "I miss you so much, Tammy."

"I knew you would, but life had other plans for your journey. Do you have a job yet?"

"No, not yet. I'm just not sure what I want to do. I'm busy enough, learning my way around and spending time with my

guys. Oh, and James is dating the cutest girl named Violet."
Rebekah paused. "She lives with us."

"Really? So how you taking that? It's the way it is today,
hon." Tammy knew her so well.

"I love her, actually. I see how happy she and James
are together."

"Sounds good. I figured you'd be running some bakery
down there by now, but I'm glad you get to take some time
with your kids and for yourself."

"I know. Hey, so guess what? Today I met with a private
investigator and hired him to look for Dee. I just know I'm
going to find her. I didn't have much information for him
to go on, but I think if he can find any little thing, it'll be
more than I know right now. When I find her, then my life
will be complete."

Tammy hesitated then drew in a quick breath before she
responded. "Rebekah, sweetheart, you're already complete.
Please don't put so much pressure on this one thing. Take
a look at all you have right now. I repeat: you are complete;
think of this as adding a little icing on the cake."

No, thought Rebekah. *I need Dee*. How could she expect
anyone to understand? But instead, she said, "I guess so."
Then, eager to change the subject, she asked, "Any chance
of you planning a visit here to see your family?"

"As a matter of fact, Spencer and I were talking about
that very subject last night. I told him I wanted to visit my
mom and you, wondering if he wanted to come also. He said
no and to just go myself. Before I decide anything, I have
to look at the vacation schedule at work to see who will be
on and off, just so I know everything is covered. I think I'm
doing a pretty good job with the bakery. You know there's

no one like you, but I'm a pretty close second, and I'm proud of myself. Now I'm even making enough money that I don't have to bartend anymore."

"That's great. I knew you would do good. Oh, that reminds me! The boys have been making me a brandy old-fashioned every so often. I like them—mind you, they make them weak for me."

"Ha ha, I love it!"

Rebekah heard a voice in the background.

"Oh, I forgot. Gotta run right now and pick up one of the kids, Rebekah. Listen, as soon as I know when I'm coming, I'll call you or send a text. Talk again soon."

"Can't wait," Rebekah said and hung up.

She sat for a moment, thinking. Nobody could understand how incomplete she would continue to feel until she found Dee. Waiting for Bobby to call her with some answers would be excruciating. She knew Dee must be somewhere in Wisconsin, and it could possibly be a matter of days or weeks until the sisters were reunited again.

***

"Hey, Mom. James and I were talking about how you've had the same car for ten years. Have you thought much about getting a new one?" Andrew inquired one morning on his way out the door for school.

"Well, no, I hadn't, son. Do you think I need one? The reason this one has lasted so long is because your grandfather and uncles have done maintenance on it regularly. A fringe benefit of having a family-run auto repair shop."

"I'm guessing you have over a hundred thousand miles on it from your driving back and forth to Rhinelander, am I right?"

Andrew was, and she knew where he was going with his questions. Because she had all this money, he wanted her to buy a new car. She heard her father's voice in her head, *Why would you get rid of a perfectly good, running car?* In their family, they'd never bought anything brand new. Her dad always had a good line on cars that were a year or two old, letting someone else take that new-car depreciation. And when anyone got a car, they ran it until it didn't run anymore. That was how she was raised.

"So … your point?" Rebekah was enjoying this.

"The point is you don't have to be driving around in a ten-year-old car, Mom. You should get the car of your dreams," he said.

"But I don't have a car of my dreams."

"Geez, Mom, everyone has that car they've always wanted. Come on. What's yours?" he asked.

She thought for a few seconds. Nope, she didn't have one. "Even with the family auto garage, I know very little about cars. Whenever I got a car, your grandpa brought it to me and said, 'Here's your new car,' and gave me the keys. Then he would come get it regularly to do whatever, and I'd just keep driving it until he gave me another new one. End of story." She shrugged.

"Well, Grandpa's not here, and I'm telling you it's time to buy a new one. You can afford it, and James and I are going to help you get a good deal."

Why not? Rebekah thought. It actually was a good idea.

"Okay," she agreed. She didn't need for her car to break down in Milwaukee and have to deal with finding someone to do repairs, so she and the boys spent the next several evenings visiting car dealers until she found an SUV she liked in the prettiest shade of blue. She discovered she loved that new car smell and felt good about her decision and happy the boys had suggested it.

***

Three weeks had passed and Rebekah had still heard nothing from Bobby Becker. She wondered if he'd had any luck finding anything about Dee, so she gave him a call. The call went straight to voicemail, so she left him a message and hoped he would call back. If she didn't hear from him soon, she would go to his office and wait for him to see her. She wanted to know what was going on, no matter what he found.

The next day, Tammy called with the best news. She was coming the following week to visit her mom and wanted to make sure Rebekah had time for her. Rebekah told her that was no problem, and Tammy said she would call when she got into town.

Bobby called on Friday and told Rebekah he was sorry for the delay and was available to talk with her on the following Tuesday at two in the afternoon. She asked if he had any information and he said yes, but she would have to wait until Tuesday. She was beside herself wondering what Bobby had found out and couldn't get the thought out of her mind.

Tammy called Sunday morning. "I'm here and can't wait to see you. Mom says to have you come for lunch at noon. Is that good?" Tammy's voice was like music to Rebekah's ears.

"You couldn't stop me," Rebekah replied.

The street where Tammy's mom lived was like many of the streets in Milwaukee—a long, straight road with little square houses lined up like soldiers, all of them built probably sometime in the 1950s and painted different colors. Towns all over Wisconsin had streets just like this. The light blue, two-story house Tammy's mom lived in had a front porch that, just like James and Andrew's, had been converted into a bedroom. Between each of the houses was a narrow driveway that led to the back of the house where, from the street, Rebekah could see part of a garage door adjacent to the home. She parked on the street in front of the house, took the walkway to the front door, and rang the bell.

"Rebekah!" Tammy threw her arms open and hugged her friend so tight Rebekah couldn't breathe for a few seconds. "I've missed you so much."

Soon, an older woman Tammy favored approached.

"Well, I finally get to meet you. This daughter of mine talks about you constantly. Come here and let me hug you!" said the older woman, and again, Rebekah lost a few seconds of breath. She didn't mind, however; it made her feel loved and wanted.

"Thank you …." Rebekah hesitated, unsure what to call Tammy's mom, who must have sensed as much.

"I'm Flo. Now, come in and let's visit."

Flo led her to the living room, which looked as if it were caught in a time warp and reminded Rebekah of her own parents' living room.

"You two girls just visit while I get lunch on the table. Oh, and I never thought to ask Tammy about this, but you're not one of those vegetarians, are you? I made my chili, and there's meat in it."

"No, I love meat," Rebekah replied, smiling.

"Well, good then," Flo said and left them alone.

"I love her to death," Tammy said, throwing her head toward the door her mom had just exited through. "She's done really good since my dad died. Even has a boyfriend of sorts named Fritz. They go out to eat and play bingo once a week. Kind of cute together. How's your mom doing since your dad died?"

"Not well. It's like she's had a breakdown and has a hard time functioning day by day. I think she must be heavily medicated because she's pleasant and seems to like me," Rebekah said with a laugh.

"Oh, come on. That can't be true. You're one of the kindest, sweetest people I know."

"For some reason, my mom has never liked me. I think it may have a little to do with Dee. Mom had always been a little stern and no-nonsense, but when Dee left, she no longer had any interest in me—except when I did something wrong. She was all over that."

Both women laughed.

"So have you done anything to find your sister since you got here?" Tammy asked.

"As a matter of fact, I have."

Rebekah proceeded to tell Tammy about Bobby Becker and how she had an appointment on Tuesday.

"Well, guess what? How about I go with you?" Tammy said.

Actually, Rebekah thought, *that's not a bad idea.* "I would love it," Rebekah said, patting her friend's hand.

Just then, a skinny guy wearing shorts and a Green Bay Packers T-shirt and sporting an out-of-control beard appeared in the doorway, looking like he had just rolled out of bed.

"Tammy, who's your cute friend here?" He turned to Rebekah. "Hi, my name is Johnny." He extended his hand to Rebekah.

What could she do but extend hers also?

"Rebekah, this is Johnny, my brother. I guess you must have smelled lunch, Johnny?" Tammy said, looking him up and down and shaking her head as he went to the kitchen.

When he was out of sight, Tammy said, "The lazy son-of-a-buck lives here, mooching off Mom. I guess every large family has one like that. He's forty years old and hasn't had a job in five years. That's one reason I came down here—to see what's going on and motivate him to start looking for a job. You've got a big family. Any of your brothers like that?"

"No, but we've always had the family auto repair business, so no one ever had to look for a job. It was just assumed the family would work there. If I hadn't found the job at Fred's, I probably would have also. So happy I didn't have to."

"Me too. I wouldn't have such a great friend."

As Tammy said this, Flo entered the room. "Lunch is ready."

Tammy's mom was just as entertaining as Tammy. Rebekah loved hearing the stories Flo told about the shenanigans Tammy had pulled as a kid and at times was laughing so hard, she had tears in her eyes. At one point, Johnny came back through the small dining room, once again smiling at Rebekah before going back upstairs. He was odd, for sure.

When lunch was finished, Flo insisted on cleaning up by herself, so Tammy took Rebekah to the back patio.

"Tomorrow Mom and I are going shopping at the mall, and Tuesday I'm going to spend the day with you. How about I come by, say around ten, and we hit a couple of bakeries. I want to see what's going on in the big city that I might capitalize on in my little corner of the world. We'll grab lunch and then see your Bobby Becker. How's that?" Tammy had it all planned out as usual.

"Sounds great." Rebekah felt good leaving things in Tammy's hands.

Tammy walked Rebekah to her car when it was time to go. "Wow. Is this yours?" she asked "Did you get some money out of that preacher? That's a beautiful car."

Rebekah didn't know what to say, wondering for a second if she should tell Tammy about her good fortune with the lottery. No, she decided. It was best she kept it to herself. "No. I've been saving for a long time, and my boys insisted I get a new car. The other had over a hundred thousand miles. It was time," Rebekah said as she got behind the wheel.

"I guess so. One thing's for sure. You look good in it," Tammy said and chuckled. "See you Tuesday."

"Bye, Tammy." Rebekah closed the door and waved as she pulled away to head home.

She was happy Tammy was coming with her on Tuesday and wondered about what kind of news Bobby would give her.

Chapter 23

On Tuesday, Tammy showed up at Rebekah's front door a little before ten in the morning. Andrew answered the door. The only time Tammy had seen Rebekah's boys was when they were young, never having glimpsed the full-grown versions. She *ooooed* and *ahhhed* over Andrew, causing him to turn a bright shade of red.

"That boy is as cute as can be and so polite. He's got to have a girlfriend," Tammy said as Andrew left the room.

"I think he's had girlfriends, but you know boys never want to tell their moms about their love life, and he never would have told Ethan. James, though, has been going out with Violet for some time. Since I'm living with the boys now, he had to tell me she lives here with him. Good thing Ethan doesn't know because I could see him disowning James—not unlike my parents did to Dee. Honestly, I think Violet is the girl for James. A mother can tell."

The two friends got into Tammy's car, and Tammy impressed Rebekah with how much she knew her way around the Milwaukee area. They went to areas Rebekah hadn't ventured into—like Wauwatosa and West Allis, little suburbs of Milwaukee. Everyone knew Tammy by name as she walked through the door. Soon, they had both collected several boxes and bags of goodies from various bakeries to take home with them.

Before they went to the appointment with Bobby, they stopped at a diner for lunch that looked like nothing had changed inside since the 1950s; it even had an old, manual cash register. Again, Tammy was known by name by the servers and cooks. Their lunch conversation centered around all the goings-on at Fred's. Rebekah missed the store more than she ever would have imagined, particularly as she heard about all the usual day-to-day drama that had unfolded in her absence.

Tammy also threw in that Michael had said hi.

They arrived at Bobby's place, and he welcomed them to his office with a rather businesslike manner—not reminiscent of the man she had met several weeks ago—as he asked them to take a seat.

"Since you brought your friend with you, I'm assuming I have the liberty to discuss my findings in front of her?" Bobby asked before he started. "I have to ask that."

"Yes," Rebekah replied, "she knows all about it."

"Okay then, great." Bobby put on some reading glasses and shuffled through some papers until he found what he was looking for. "Okay, yep. Well, here it is," he said and looked up at Rebekah. "You see, I was able to track down your sister's whereabouts from state to state for the first ten years after she left home. Turns out she became a paralegal and lived here in Milwaukee for a good three years before moving to Missouri, Texas, Colorado, Arizona, and California over a ten-year period of time. I was excited by how easily I was able to follow her. Then, somewhere in California, she disappeared. Can't find her anywhere. Even tried the child's name. I was able to find out several of the places where she may have worked during that time, but many of them don't know where she went, and the rest say they don't remember her at all. I'll keep searching. It's just strange."

Rebekah felt a tightness in her chest as Bobby talked. "How can someone just disappear like that? Are you trying to tell me she's dead?"

"No, no. Not at all. I haven't uncovered any death certificates. I'm not suggesting anything other than what I've found, which is that the trail stopped in California. I'm wondering if she took on a new identity and changed her name or left the country. It's the only thing I can think of. Sometimes the records of a name change can be held in secrecy for whatever reason. You say you or your family never had any contact with her after she left?"

"No, none of us. The only contact was the three letters I showed you that were sent to my mom, and there was the one time Mom met with Dee at a park," Rebekah replied, increasingly upset by the information Bobby had given her. This was not what she expected to hear, and she wanted to cry.

"How about other family members—say aunts or uncles— maybe a cousin she was close with? What about her friend that she lived with here in Milwaukee?"

"No, the only family was our immediate one. I know the friend's name is Jen, but unfortunately I have no last name. Maybe you can help me, Tammy?" Rebekah turned to her friend, who was uncharacteristically silent. "You seem to know everybody around Rhinelander. Dee worked with Jen at a restaurant up there. And Spencer would be close to Dee's age. He might know who Jen is. You could ask around when you get back home—maybe some of the people you know are around Dee's age as well. That might help."

"Well of course, sweetheart. That's a great idea. My husband, Spencer, has lived his whole life up there," she explained to Bobby. "I can go through his old year books and look for someone named Jen and ask him. Do you think that might help, Bobby?"

"It could." Bobby shrugged his shoulders. "I can't give any guarantee, but it could give me a new direction to go in."

"All right then. I'll see what I can find," Rebekah said and stood up to leave. "I'll be in touch."

***

The next day, Rebekah called Steve.

"Good to hear from you. How are things going?" he asked.

"Things are okay. It's been a big change for me. I'm enjoying James and Andrew and finding my way around the area. My friend Tammy, who I worked with at Fred's, grew up in Milwaukee and is visiting her mom this week. Got to spend some time with her."

"That's great. Hey, how's your search for Dee going? We're all hoping you might have found out something by now."

"As a matter of fact, I met with the private investigator yesterday. That's why I'm calling. He says he can follow Dee to a certain point, and then it's as if she disappeared. She got all the way to California, Steve," Rebekah said.

"Ya gotta be kidding! California? How the heck did she get there?"

"Not really sure. She went from Milwaukee to Missouri, Texas, Colorado, Arizona, and then California during the first ten years. After that, there's no records. The investigator suggested she maybe had a name change or left the country."

"Like a name change from getting married? I would think that wouldn't have been hard to find out. If she left the country, she would have a passport that might be traced," Steve said.

"That's true. I don't know, Steve. But maybe you can help me. I wonder if you knew a girl by the name of Jen? She worked with Dee at that restaurant up there." Rebekah so hoped he did.

"I remember some girl she was friends with that Mom and Dad didn't like, so I'm guessing that it might have been Jen. Sorry, but I just didn't pay much attention to what she did at that time. I was older and doing my thing. You know how it is."

"Yeah, I understand," she said. "Dee actually lived with Jen in Milwaukee till after the baby was born. Could you ask around and see if any of your friends remember? It might be the only lead we have."

"Sure. Hey, let me know if I can help pay for this private investigator. That's got to be expensive," Steve offered.

"Don't worry about it. I'm getting a deal because he's James's girlfriend's uncle." It was sweet of him to offer.

"Girlfriend? Well that son of a gun never said anything about a girlfriend. Did you know about her?" Steve asked.

"Nope, but he kind of had to tell me; she lives with us. I like her—and I'm okay with their living arrangement before you ask. It's a different time, and he's an adult making his own decisions. Her name is Violet, and she's perfect for James."

"Well, I hope you know Dad is spinning in his grave right now as we speak."

They both laughed.

"I don't care if you tell the rest of our family, just keep it from Mom, okay?" she pleaded.

"Oh, you don't have to worry about that," he said, and they shared another laugh.

During the rest of the conversation, Steve told her about the family and how Ruth had stayed about the same. The lady who came in several times a week to help their mom was working out great. The auto repair shop was doing as well as ever. Steve said he might just come and visit and promised to get back to her soon.

Sure enough, two weeks later, Steve called with great news. Turns out Jake had been friends with Jen's brother Wesley. Jake was going to get in touch with him and find out where Jen was and how Rebekah could get in touch with her. This is just what Rebekah needed. Surely Jen would have some answers.

***

"Rebekah, for cripes' sake, I miss you, little sister."

It was Rebekah's brother, Jake, and she hoped he had some good news. He was the most outgoing of her brothers and, like Tammy, seemed to know everyone.

"I miss you too. You can always come visit here, you know," she said. "I'm afraid you might forget about me."

"Ya, ya, I know I can. I just might do it, so don't be surprised."

"Well, I'm so glad to finally hear from you. It's been two weeks since I called Steve!" What had been life altering for Rebekah was obviously no big deal to them. *Brothers.*

"Oh ya, really? Well, hey, listen—I think it's great that you're looking for Dee, and I want to do anything I can to help you. It always bothered me the way Mom and Dad threw her out of the house. Up till now, I didn't know what had happened, but I figured it had to do with a guy, you know? 'Cause Dad sure didn't like us fraternizing with just anyone. He had to have the stamp of approval on anyone we wanted to date in case they were undesirable. Glad he wasn't alive to see the whole thing that went down with Ethan and you. Whew! Don't you know what that would have been like?" Jake said. "Actually, I don't even wanna imagine."

"I know," Rebekah said with a sigh. "I'm just trying to put it behind me and look to the future. That's why I want to find Dee. How nice would it be to have her back as part of our family?"

"It sure would be. Dad would never have had it, but it doesn't matter now. And Mom is so out of it, she'll go along with anything. Kinda surprised me how she's taken Dad's death. I never thought they were that crazy about each other," he said and shook his head. "I guess she was more dependent on him than it looked like."

"I guess. So did Steve explain what I was looking for?" She wanted to catch up with her brother but wanted to know about Jen even more.

"Yep, I knew Jen's brother Wesley pretty well. Still see him once in a while, and I knew Jen when we were young. She worked with Dee at a restaurant in Rhinelander that's closed now. I remember him telling me Jen still lives in the

Milwaukee area—in Wauwatosa. She's married and has a family. I can get him to give me her phone number and address if that's what you want."

"That's great, Jake. Make sure he tells her I'll be calling though," Rebekah suggested.

"Why? Just call her and tell her Wes gave you the information," Jake said.

"I'd feel better if she knew I was calling. I want her to know I'm Dee's sister so she doesn't think I'm some random stranger. If anyone called me about any of you guys, I wouldn't feel comfortable telling them anything till I had checked with you first. Please ask him to tell her and get back to me. Can you do it right away? This search for Dee has been dragging on since July, and it's already September. I want to get some answers, Jake. Do you think he can call her today and you can get back to me by tomorrow?"

Rebekah knew she sometimes had to put a deadline on her brothers to get results.

"Sure. I think he works days, so I'll catch him tonight and call you tomorrow or maybe the next day, okay?"

"I'll call tomorrow afternoon if I haven't heard from you. When you find out, just text me her name, address, and phone number," Rebekah instructed.

"Sure, sure, will do as soon as I find out," he said. "Okay then. I'll talk with you tomorrow."

"Okay. And Jake?"

"Yep?" Jake replied.

"Thank you for your help. I really appreciate it."

"Well, of course, Rebekah. She's my sister too, and I would love to know how she is and see her again. Anything I can do, you let me know. Talk with you tomorrow."

***

Jake got back to her late the next day.

"When Wes talked to Jen, she wanted to know who was asking. He told her it was Dee's sister. Jen wanted to know why someone was wanting information. He said 'For Pete's sake. It's her sister, and she's trying to find her!' And then Jen said she didn't really know anything. Kind of weird if you ask me," Jake said.

Yes, very weird, Rebekah thought. *Jen must know something, but how can we know for sure?*

"I'm not sure what to think, Jake, other than she knows more about Dee than she's willing to admit," Rebekah said. Then an idea came to her. "Why don't you just give Wes my number and ask him to share it with his sister. Have him tell her I'm living in Milwaukee and want to meet her anywhere she chooses, just to talk about Dee. Tell him I recently found out about the baby and only want to hear about what happened during Dee's time in Milwaukee. Can you do that?"

"Sure. I'm guessing you have another plan in that head of yours." Jake knew his sister.

"Yes, I'm going to win her over. I think she may have information that might help me. I respect her wanting to protect Dee, but it's all about finding Dee and Rose for me. If I can just meet with her, I'll make her understand. Thanks for your help. Oh, and please ask Wes to tell Jen that I love Dee and only want to know she's safe. If for some reason she doesn't want to meet with me, I'll tell her I only want to know Dee's all right."

"Sounds fair enough," Jake said. "Let's hope it works."

***

Late on the last Wednesday in September, Rebekah's phone rang with a number she didn't recognize. She could tell it was local by the area code and decided to answer.

"Hello?"

"Hi, is this Rebekah Hayward? I think your name at one time was Rebekah Boulanger, am I right?" the woman asked.

"Yes, you're right. Is this Jen?" Rebekah hoped to heaven and back again that it was. She had almost started to give up on ever hearing from Jen. When she had talked to Jake again, he said he hadn't seen her brother since he talked to him before but would ask again if she wanted.

"Yes, it is," Jen said. Then, after a long pause, she continued. "I've thought about it and wonder … How about we get together on this upcoming Monday at one in the afternoon?"

"Sounds good," Rebekah responded. "I really appreciate you meeting with me. I only want to find out more about my sister. I was fifteen when she left, and until just recently, no one in the family would talk about it. My dad died this spring, and I finally got my mom to tell me some of the story."

"Well, I know the whole story," Jen said and paused once more. "See you on Monday. I'll text you where we can meet, okay?"

"Sounds good. See you Monday. Bye."

Rebekah couldn't believe it. In five days, she was going to find out what she had been wondering for over twenty years: exactly what had happened to her sister after that fateful night. She was so excited her heart felt like it would beat out of her chest, and a few spontaneous tears found their way onto her cheeks. But then she was also a little afraid of what Jen would tell her. Jen didn't seem excited about the meeting. Rebekah needed to calm down and think positively. This was the closest she had been to getting some answers. In five days, she would know where to find her sister at last.

Chapter 24

The restaurant Jen chose to meet was on West North Avenue in Wauwatosa, not far from where Rebekah and Tammy had gone to lunch several weeks prior. Rebekah arrived about ten minutes early, got a table, and waited.

She so hoped Jen would be able to tell her where Dee was or at least where her sister had headed after California. Any new information might be enough to lead Bobby in a new direction. First, Rebekah had to make sure Jen trusted her.

A little after one, a woman in a red, lightweight sweater walked in and began to look around. *That must be Jen,* Rebekah thought. Rebekah put her hand up to get Jen's attention, and she walked over.

"Rebekah?" the woman inquired.

"Yes, hi. You must be Jen."

"Yes. Well, it's nice to meet you. I heard so much about you from Dee. You favor her—that's for sure. I knew you were her sister at first glance," she said.

Jen was about five feet, ten inches tall with black hair in a short cut, and she wore no makeup. She set her purse down on the chair next to Rebekah's.

"So you've lived in this area a long time?" Rebekah asked. "I just moved here in June, and I love it. My two sons have gone to college at UWM. In fact, my youngest is graduating in December. The other graduated several years ago. Both have majored in business."

Then, a thought occurred to her: Dee had been kicked out for getting pregnant out of wedlock. She decided to explain herself. "I know the numbers don't add up agewise. They're not my biological children and were older when I became their mother. They weren't … I mean, I wasn't … it was a second marriage for their dad."

Rebekah wasn't about to go into the details of her current situation. "I'm living with them right now but plan on buying a house soon, I hope. Just not sure where I want to live yet. So tell me about yourself?" Rebekah asked, realizing she had been rambling.

"Well," Jen lifted her shoulders a bit, "not too much to tell. I moved down here to get away from up north. Wanted more of the big-city life, which I found in Milwaukee. Met my husband, got married, and had three kids—a girl and two boys. The girl and my oldest boy are in high school, and my youngest is in middle school."

Just then, the waitress walked up, and they placed their order. They chitchatted a bit more, and then Jen got to the point.

"You didn't come here to find out about me, though," Jen said. "Where do I start with Dee? It's a long story."

The waitress came again and brought them both a glass of water. Jen waited until the waitress had stepped away from the table, then began.

"Dee got mixed up with this guy in Rhinelander who was not what he seemed to be. Turned out he was married, but by the time she found that out, she was pregnant. She was beside herself. I'm a year older than Dee and had moved to Milwaukee six months earlier, so I wasn't around when this all happened. We had been best friends at work, though, and kept in touch. After she told the guy she was pregnant and found out he had lied to her about being married, she called me crying from a phone booth; she didn't want anyone at home to hear or ask questions. I managed to finally get her to calm down and tell me what happened. She was so afraid of what your parents would do if they found out. I told her to just tell them—at first, they'd be mad but surely, they'd support her, right? She told me I had no idea how angry your dad would be."

The waitress came by with the food, providing Rebekah with a moment to take in what Jen had just told her. She wished Dee would've confided in her. But then again, Rebekah was a grown woman now; a fifteen-year-old girl living a sheltered life might not have handled the news the same way when this all had happened.

Once the waitress was gone, Rebekah spoke. "My parents were very strict—mostly my dad—and had certain opinions about the way things should be. You can't even imagine. But please, continue."

"So," Jen said, "Dee ended up telling your parents, and they threw her out of the house with just a suitcase. She had no money. Now what did they expect her to do? They could have given her *something*. I mean, she was carrying their grandchild.

"She went to my parents' house that night, and they took her in. Somehow, your mom found out where she was and knocked on my parents' door a few days later. She handed them an envelope and told them to give it to Dee—never asking to see her. The envelope had five hundred dollars in it. I convinced Dee to come live with me till the baby was born. So my parents took her to the bus station with her suitcase, and she bought a one-way ticket to Milwaukee."

"You were such a kind friend to do that. I shudder to think of where Dee would have gone otherwise," Rebekah said.

"I loved your sister," Jen said, smiling. "We were best friends back then. She was kind to a fault, so I guess that's how she got herself in the situation in the first place."

"I guess you're right," Rebekah agreed.

"She arrived in Milwaukee. The place I was renting was a two-bedroom house, so that worked out. She was going to need a job to support herself and the coming baby, but who was going to hire a pregnant woman? I was working for a lawyer as a paralegal and found out he had a friend who was looking for someone to do the same type position I had, so I suggested her, and they took a chance.

"It worked out perfectly. Dee was so smart, she picked up on the job quickly and worked right up to the day the baby was born. I was with her the whole way, even as her coach in the labor room. They liked her so much at the attorney's office, they gave her work she could do from home till she felt ready to come back.

"That baby was so sweet and good. It was as if she knew she had to be. Dee named her Rose because she was as pretty as a flower."

Rebekah smiled. Her little niece.

"Then, one day, Dee got her own place. It was sad, but it was time for us to each have our own spaces. The older woman next door took care of Rose while Dee was at work, though, so I still saw them almost every day."

Rebekah loved hearing this about her sister. It was no surprise to her that Dee had taken an unpleasant situation and made it work for her.

"Did Dee date anyone?" Rebekah asked.

"Not here she didn't. But let me continue. That will come later," Jen said.

Rebekah nodded and gestured for her to keep speaking.

"The law firm Dee worked for bought some other firms in other states. Dee was promoted to an assistant and became valuable to the firm since she understood many aspects of the business. They then decided to make her the troubleshooter for the new offices they had acquired and sent her to each one for a period of time to get them all working smoothly."

"I did find out she had lived in several other states," Rebekah shared. "I didn't mention this earlier, but I hired a private investigator when I first got here, thinking Dee was probably still in the Milwaukee area. He found evidence of her in several states, but he's hit a dead end and couldn't find anything after about ten years ago."

"Yes. I'm getting to that," Jen said.

Rebekah felt puzzled. *What could be next?*

"The firm sent her to several states until Dee ended up in California. They kept her there, and she became involved with Keith, a wealthy client of the law firm. The two of them hid their relationship for a while—until they became engaged. At that point, Dee gave up her job; she couldn't continue working there and be involved with a client. But she was so happy; she was getting married and would be able to stay home with her sweet Rose. Now Dee could give Rose the family life she had always wanted her to have."

Rebekah had never dreamed Dee's life would have gone on all these twists and turns and was attempting to process all she was being told.

"We talked at least once a week on the phone and emailed all the time. Then ... something changed. Dee didn't seem like herself, and I pressed her about it. Turns out that bastard had started getting rough with her—you know, shoving her around and telling her how stupid and unattractive she was. Then he would come back and apologize, giving her gifts of jewelry, clothes, and, one time, even a new car. I told her, 'I don't care what he gives you or how bad he feels after, you need to get out.' "

Rebekah felt sick to her stomach. Poor Dee. She had to ask the obvious, praying Jen would say no. "What about Rose? Please tell me he didn't hurt her."

"No, he never hurt her, but it made you wonder if it was only a matter of time. The worst part was that Dee didn't have a job. Even though she and Keith were married, I knew the firm would take her back. And I told her as much.

"Then one day he hit her—hard. Something hurt inside, and she needed medical attention. She didn't say anything, waited till he left, and took the car, herself, and Rose to a battered women's shelter. Dee figured they would know what to do and protect her."

By this time, they had finished their lunch, and Jen paused as the waitress came by with the check and asked if they needed anything else.

"I'll take care of this," Rebekah told Jen, then addressed the waitress. "Here's my credit card. Do you mind if we stay here a while and talk?"

"Sure, that's fine. We won't have another crowd till closer to supper time. Let me know if you need anything. I'll be right back with your receipt." She left with Rebekah's card.

"You know, I really need to run to the ladies' room while she's gone if you don't mind," Jen said and left.

The waitress came back, and Rebekah added the tip, signed the receipt, and handed it back to her. This was beyond anything Rebekah could have dreamed of happening to her dear sister. She was deep in thought when Jen spoke, returning her to the present.

"Before I forget, thanks for lunch," Jen said as she took her seat.

"Well, it's the least I can do to thank you for taking the time to meet with me," Rebekah replied.

"Okay," Jen said and jumped right back in where she'd left off. "So Dee and Rose went to the shelter, and Keith went crazy looking for her. He called the law firm where she had worked, wanting to know where she was, and flipped out. He even threatened to put them out of business and kill Dee when he found her.

"The senior partner of the firm filed a police report and then, with further help from the police, found Dee at the shelter. Turned out, she had broken ribs. Said she wasn't going back because she knew he would kill her."

"Please don't tell me she went back," Rebekah said, leaning forward with her elbows on the table. The thought of Dee returning to the animal she was married to enraged Rebekah. Poor Dee all alone. If she had just taken the chance to reach out, Rebekah would have somehow made sure Dee and Rose were protected.

"No, she didn't."

"Thank God," said Rebekah, sighing heavily and easing back into the chair. Her head was spinning by this point.

"But she knew he had enough money to find her," Jen continued, "even pay someone to kill her and Rose. Larry McMillan—one of the partners at the office where she had worked—offered to help Dee and Rose create new identities and begin a new life where they couldn't be found. He'd had to help a few clients do this over the years and knew people who could get it done in secret. She talked to me about it, and I encouraged her."

Rebekah knew all too well how someone could start a new identity. Ethan had pulled it off flawlessly.

"So do you know where she is?" Rebekah asked, hopeful.

"No. Only Larry does. It had to be that way for her own safety. I talked to Dee right before she left and received a couple of letters off and on for a few years, letting me know she was settled and doing well. Of course, the letters came through Larry, but I haven't heard anything for years. None of the letters I received included any details of where she was."

Jen took a sip of water and shook her head.

"That's all I know. Like I said, it's been a while since I've heard from Dee. I sent a couple of letters through Larry over the past several years, but a response never came, so I stopped pursuing it. I gave Larry a call before I came today to see if he could help, and he was out of town on business. So I left a message and asked for him to call me back."

Rebekah felt the excitement well up inside of her. She was overwhelmed and had to fight back some tears she could feel stinging her eyes. This was finally the break she was waiting for. If this Larry knew where Dee was, he could send her a message from Rebekah. Surely Dee would want to see her. Rebekah was another few steps closer. She had waited this long, what were several more days if they would bring her to Dee?

"Jen, you've been most helpful," she said as she lost control of her tears. "This is just the best news I've had since Dee left. As soon as Larry talks to Dee, I'm sure she'll want to see me. Please let me know as soon as you hear from Larry."

"Oh, I will. I think of Dee and Rose frequently. Rose would be about twenty by now, I believe. Who knows, she may even be married and have her own child."

"That's true." Rebekah had an image of Rose as a little girl in her mind. She gave a small laugh at the thought. "I hadn't really thought about how she would be a young woman by now. Who knows, Dee may have married and had other children as well." It was amazing to think about.

Both women rose to their feet.

"It was so nice to meet you," Rebekah said and gave Jen a big hug. She liked the woman. "Maybe we can do this again, and when I find Dee the three of us can get together. I can see why you and Dee were close friends. Thank you so much for meeting with me. I look forward to hearing from you after Larry calls. You have no idea the gift you have given me today."

With that, the two women chatted a bit more and hugged one more time before they said goodbye.

***

Rebekah wasn't ready to go home, preferring to be outside so she could think over what Jen had told her. It was the last day in September and pretty out, so she decided to stop at Lake Park, where she and the boys had seen fireworks on the Fourth of July. Since discovering the park, Rebekah had visited many times to walk or just enjoy the outdoors.

Being a Monday, it wasn't very busy. A few runners and moms with kids in strollers passed by as she sat on a bench and stared across the water. A little laugh escaped as she thought about how, if she were back home, her first move after seeing Jen would have been to go to the pond on her family's property. She was doing the same thing now, she supposed, except Lake Michigan was a much bigger pond.

As she looked out over the lake's endless horizon, she thought about what she would do with Dee after they got together. Surely once Dee knew Rebekah was looking for her, they would become a part of each other's lives. Maybe they could travel together. They might have to pretend they were friends and not sisters because of Dee's identity, but it would be a good start to make up for lost time.

After a while, Rebekah looked at her phone and saw it was already after four thirty, so she figured she better head on home.

At supper, she told the kids what had happened, and they were nothing but encouraging.

"Mom, you never know. Dee may have been wanting to reconnect with her family. It's been a long time, and she might feel safe now," James suggested, and the other two agreed.

"Yes, Rebekah," Violet said. "And if not, Dee will surely want to see you."

"Yeah, hang in there, Mom," Andrew said.

"You all make me feel that everything is going to work out just fine," she said, fanning her face to keep from crying. "I'm so happy to be here with all of you."

"Aww, stop Rebekah, or you'll have the rest of us going," Violet said.

"So on another subject," Rebekah said, using a knuckle to wipe tears from the corners of her eyes. "I've made a decision. I've decided I'm going to start looking for a house next month. I like what I've seen in Wauwatosa, so I'm going to start looking there. That way, wherever Dee is, I'll have a house so she and Rose can come visit me."

"That's great, Mom," Andrew said. "I have a friend who's a realtor. I know he'll take good care of you, so maybe you can let him help you out."

"Thanks, son. Now let's clean up here and watch a movie. Something that will make me laugh," Rebekah said and started clearing the table.

**

Several weeks later, Rebekah did meet with Andrew's realtor friend and gave him an idea of the kind of house she was looking for—newer and not a fixer-upper. She figured she could afford move-in ready, after all.

Later in the same week, she noticed a missed phone call and message from Jen, so she called her back, eager to hear any news she may have received from Larry.

"Hi, Jen. This is Rebekah Hayward. I got your message."

"I have some great news," Jen said. "I finally got a call from Larry McMillan. I was afraid that since I haven't had any contact with him for years, he might have forgotten who I was, but he remembered. He said since I'm able to identify you as her next of kin, he'll talk with you. I'll text you his name and number. He said to call on Monday. Their office opens at ten, and there's a two-hour time difference, so take that into consideration when you call."

Rebekah couldn't believe it. Larry could lead her to Dee. "I can't thank you enough, Jen. You've been a kind friend to Dee and now to me. I'll never forget this," Rebekah told her.

"I want to do what I can to bring you and Dee back together. Good luck and let me know what you find out if you can."

They said goodbye, and Jen hung up.

Rebekah put her phone in her lap and clasped her hands over her mouth. Her dream was going to come true. She couldn't wait to tell the boys and Violet tonight.

Monday was just a few days away, but it seemed like forever.

Chapter 25

Monday morning had arrived, and Rebekah looked at her watch. It was nine o'clock, so that meant it was only seven o'clock in California—too early to call Larry McMillan. She would wait until it was twelve thirty her time, giving him an opportunity to settle into his office before she called him. Now that she was only a few hours away from knowing where Dee was, the wait was going to drive her crazy. Wouldn't it be something if her sister were somewhere in Wisconsin after all?

The best thing for Rebekah to do was take to the kitchen and bake. *A batch of snickerdoodle cookies should do the trick,* she thought as she uncovered her mixer and plugged it in before gathering up the ingredients she needed. She sighed as she discovered she didn't have cream of tartar, so she decided on chocolate chip cookies ... except there were no chocolate chips. Finally, after looking through the pantry, she found cocoa powder, so it would have to be brownies. It didn't matter what she made because the kids would be excited and gobble it up anyway. Rebekah would make sure that when she bought her new house, her pantry would be full of all the essential ingredients she needed to bake.

After she had cleaned up the kitchen and the brownies were in the oven, she threw in a load of wash and vacuumed. By the time she finished all this, it was close to noon, so she made a sandwich, then figured it was necessary to test her brownies, just to make sure they were okay.

Yum. I'm pretty good at this baking thing, she thought and chuckled as she took her time to eat the good-sized brownie she had cut from the pan. It was still just barely warm and made her mouth happy with every chewy, chocolaty bite.

The next time she looked at the clock on the stove, it said 12:20 p.m. She wasn't going to wait another moment, so she found her phone and dialed the number Jen had given her.

Her heart leapt as it began to ring.

"Good morning, McMillan and Partners, how may I help you?" said the friendly woman who answered.

"Hi, my name is Rebekah Hayward. I'm calling to talk with Larry McMillan. I believe he's expecting my call," Rebekah said.

"Yes, he did mention you may be calling this morning. Please hold."

After several minutes, a man's voice came on the line. "Hello, this is Larry McMillan," he said, his voice strong and even in tone. "So happy to be able to talk to you, Ms. Hayward."

"I'm happy to talk with you also, but please call me Rebekah," she said.

"Well then, you call me Larry," he said.

"I appreciate you agreeing to talk with me about Dee," Rebekah started. "I was fifteen when she left home, and I've wanted to find her ever since. It was only recently that I found out why she left, and I've been trying to trace her steps without much luck. Jen was kind enough to call you to help me out."

Larry was quiet for a good while before he next spoke. "Your sister was an important part of our team here. Smart and a hard worker. I know Jen told you about her situation with Keith. I'm not going to lie—between you and me, I wanted to go break a couple of *his* ribs. I truly believe he would've killed her, so that's why I suggested she take on a new identity. We worked quickly and were able to have her safely established in a new life, in another city, before Keith knew what was happening. I had to deal with him coming into the office several times looking for her and ultimately got a restraining order. Excuse my language, but he was an ass."

"I gathered that," Rebekah said and rubbed her forehead. "Jen told me how you were instrumental in helping Dee with her new identity, and I want to say thank you."

"It was my pleasure to help such a wonderful person," he responded.

"So I was hoping you'd be able to tell me where I'll find my sister ... and perhaps my niece, Rose," Rebekah said, her voice shaking.

"Yes, well. I've been the only person to know your sister's whereabouts. She changed her name to Sarah, and Rose changed to Anna. Their last name was Tucker." Larry cleared his throat, paused for a moment, and then continued. "It's with a heavy heart that I have to give you some sad news, though."

"What do you mean? You're going to tell me where she is, right?" Rebekah felt panic rising inside her chest.

"I'm sorry to have to tell you … your sister, Dee, died four years ago of a brain aneurysm. She died in her sleep."

Rebekah felt physically ill; her head was buzzing, and the pressure inside her chest grew, as if somebody were slowly squeezing it in a vice. This couldn't be happening. "How can that be? Had she been unhealthy?" Rebekah asked.

"No. Brain aneurysms can happen to anyone. From what I understand, sometimes they cause symptoms, and other times, they don't. Again, I'm so sorry to have to tell you this."

"I'm not sure what to do now," she said slowly. "In your line of business, I'm sure you've heard many interesting stories. I just recently found out that the man I was married to for eighteen years had another wife who was still living. He'd told me she was dead. Looking for Dee is what has kept me going. And now …." How could she find the words?

"That's one story I've never heard. I hope you have a good attorney." Larry replied.

Rebekah wasn't going to go into it any further. "Yes, I'm fine."

"Dee relocated to Asheville, North Carolina. A beautiful place. She ended up getting a job at a clothing store. Rose was twelve when they moved. I talked with Dee occasionally and found she was happy and led a simple life."

"I'm sorry. I'm so overwhelmed by what you told me. What about Rose? She would have been sixteen when Dee died then, right? Please don't tell me she went into foster care when she had family who would have wanted her. You should have let us know." Rebekah was now concerned about her niece. Rose had no family to support her.

"No, Dee made a will, which I put together, and designated a guardian for Rose. Dee had become very close to Lois Bender, the woman who owned the clothing store she worked for, and appointed her as guardian. Now that Rose is no longer a minor, I haven't heard anything about her for several years. Probably still lives in Asheville, though."

Now what?

Larry remained silent once more, giving Rebekah time to process.

"Would you be able to find out where Rose might be now?" she asked after a minute.

"I can't promise for sure, but I have a number for Lois and an email, so I can try. Does that sound good?"

"Yes, Larry. I've been waiting for over twenty years to find Dee." She hesitated to keep her tears back. "I feel … I'm in shock. This isn't the way I had it planned." The tears came, and there was no fighting them. She swallowed and then spoke, her voice trembling. "Let's find Rose then. Thank you so much for all you've done today."

"You have a great attitude, Rebekah—just like your sister. I can tell by our conversation today that you're very similar. Kind of like talking to Dee."

"Thanks for the compliment, Larry." She was touched and on the verge of sobbing. "Please call me anytime, day or night, okay?"

"Sure, Rebekah. I understand," Larry responded, and they said goodbye.

***

Of course, the first thing James and Violet asked Rebekah when they got home from work at five thirty was what had happened when she talked with the lawyer. She told James and Violet she only wanted to say it once, so they would have to wait for Andrew to come home. Rebekah was sure James and Violet could tell by her lack of enthusiasm that the phone call hadn't turned out the way she wanted. She was grateful they didn't press her any further.

Tonight was a leftover night, so they all picked what they wanted out of the fridge. Rebekah had no appetite herself. As they sat down at the kitchen table, Andrew arrived, his disposition cheery until he noticed the look James gave him; he knew immediately that something was up. Andrew had eaten a late lunch but said he could go for a brownie. Rebekah put the pan in the middle of the table, and as the kids all grabbed a piece, she decided to begin, unsure she could keep it together for much longer.

"I did talk to the lawyer today, a very nice man named Larry who had been helpful to Dee." Rebekah took a deep breath. "He told me that after she left California, Dee started a new life in Asheville, North Carolina—she and Rose. Long story short, Dee had changed her name to Sarah and Rose to Anna, both using the last name Tucker. Dee worked for a woman who had a clothing store in Asheville, and according to Larry, they were very close ...." Rebekah couldn't continue, her words failing her as she stared at her hands that were clasped together.

"What is it?" Andrew asked, pulling her close. "We're here for you," he said.

Rebekah shook her head as her eyes flooded with tears. "Dee died four years ago," she managed to say before burying her head in Andrew's chest. She felt protected with his arms around her and allowed the tears she'd had under control to break free. James and Violet took turns hugging Rebekah and telling her how much they loved her. After several minutes, her crying began to subside.

James asked a question. "Okay, Mom. Do you think you can tell us some more? Like what happened and where Rose is? Or we can wait if you want." He quickly added, "Rose is still alive ... right?"

"Yes, she is," Rebekah said, wiping her face. "Dee had a brain aneurysm and died in her sleep. It was nothing that could have been predicted. She was close to a woman, Lois, who owned the clothing store where she worked. Dee left a will, making Lois Rose's guardian."

Her voice began to quiver. "It's such a letdown for me. But I'm happy to know what became of Rose. I don't feel like talking about it more tonight, but I'll tell you the whole story of what led her to Asheville after I've had more time to process all of this," she said, brushing a few brownie crumbs across the table. "So now I don't know what I'll do."

"Well, you're going to find Rose—or Anna—aren't you?" asked Andrew. He raised his eyebrows. "Have you noticed a trend here? New identities and name changes in our family? I feel like we all need to change our names to fit in. I want to be Ralph. How about you, James? Maybe Cornelius?"

They all had a much-needed laugh to break the sadness.

"Yeah, Mom," James said. "I think you need to go find Rose. She should know she has a family that would like to be part of her life. Dee would want you to do that."

"Larry said he's going to see what he can find out for me."

"Listen, let's you and I go to Asheville, or wherever this Larry tells you she is," Andrew suggested. "I graduate in December and don't have a job yet, so I'm free to go with you. I wouldn't let you go alone anyway. This is way too important—your first trip out of Wisconsin." He chuckled. "How about after the first of the year? We can test out that new car of yours and get out of the snow for a while. What do you say?"

"Well, I don't know. I'll have to get back with Larry to see what he's found out and where we can even find her. Besides, she may not want to see us."

"Sure, Mom, but I really think she's going to want to see you," Andrew said.

"I think you should go for it and find her. She's our family, and we want her to know we're here," James said.

"I agree, Rebekah," Violet said to share her two cents.

"Like I said, I'll think about it." But inside, Rebekah already knew she was going to find Rose.

She had to.

***

Rebekah called Larry back at the end of the week.

"Hi, Larry," she said. "I wanted to say thank you again for your help. At least I now have an answer to where Dee was—as sad as it makes me—and even though I didn't get to see and talk to her, you and Jen helped me fill in the missing pieces. I feel like I know her a little better now. I'm grateful for that."

"You're welcome, Rebekah," Larry said. "I was happy to help. How did your family take the news?"

"I haven't told my brothers yet, and my mom is really not in a condition to adjust to hearing the information. My dad died a little over six months ago, and she hasn't been handling it well. I did tell my children that night after you and I spoke. They've helped me begin to come to terms with the news. I think I'll call my brothers today, though. They're all older than Dee and I were, so they remember more than I do."

"If you like, I can probably find out where she might be buried." Larry said.

"Yes, thank you. That would be nice. But what I really want to do now is find Rose. Were you able to get in touch with Lois? I would like to meet Rose and maybe become part of her life in some way. My son suggested that he and I could maybe go down to Asheville, or wherever Rose might be, after the first of the year to meet her."

"I tried calling Lois Bender, but the phone number was no longer a good one, so I sent an email and haven't heard back yet. And you're going to have to get used to calling her Anna, you know. She's been Anna for almost half her life now."

"I guess you're right," Rebekah said. But to her, she'd always be Rose.

"Let me see what I can do," Larry said. "I'm going out of town for two weeks in November, but since you're not going until next year, that should give us some time to find Anna. I hope to hear from Lois soon and get the ball rolling."

"Larry, I can't thank you enough for everything."

"You're welcome," Larry replied, and they said goodbye.

***

"Well, hey, Rebekah!" It was Tom, sounding happy to hear her voice as he answered her call.

Rebekah finally had it together enough to call him. She had decided to tell Tom everything and make it easy on herself by letting him inform the rest of the family. "Hi, Tom. Do you have some time? I have a lot to tell you."

"I'll make the time. I'm guessing it has to do with Dee?" he inquired.

"Yes, it does," she responded flatly.

Rebekah started with all that Jen had told her: Dee's move to Milwaukee; Rose's birth; their journey to California; and Dee's involvement with Keith, followed by his abuse and her escape.

"All she had to do was call us, Rebekah, and I would have been on the next plane with Jake, Ben, and Steve to beat the crap out of this guy. I don't understand people who can do stuff like that to another human being—or an animal, for that matter. Those people are sick," Tom said.

"I feel the same, Tom." Rebekah was dreading having to share the last bit of the story.

"So when do we get to see Dee?" Tom asked. "Have you talked to her?"

She couldn't help it—she sniffled and Tom heard.

"Rebekah," Tom said. "I know you must be excited. Get it together. Is she going to come up here to see us? Or can we go there? It might be just the thing to get Mom back to her old self."

Rebekah collected herself and responded. "It's not good news, Tom."

Just say it.

"Dee died four years ago."

Tom gasped. "No! That can't be. There must be a mistake. Are you sure?"

"Yes, I'm sure," Rebekah confirmed, placing a hand to her forehead.

It was hard, but she continued telling Tom the story— Dee's new identity as Sarah Tucker, her and Anna's move to

Asheville, and how, after Dee had died, Lois was appointed Rose's guardian.

"I wonder why she didn't name one of us as guardian?" Tom questioned.

"Because Dad and Mom ostracized her from our family. She had been shunned by them. None of us would have come back if they'd done the same to us," Rebekah said with anger in her voice, which felt better than the sorrow that had occupied her heart for days.

"Yeah, I guess you're right," he agreed.

"I've decided to find Rose and see if I can develop a relationship with her. I want her to know she has a family and that we want her to be a part of it. That's my goal."

"I think that's great, sis. There's no one better than you to do it either. You're one of the kindest, most loving people I've ever known," Tom said.

"Stop it, Tom, or you're going to have me crying again," Rebekah scolded him, and they shared a laugh.

"So how soon are you going?" he asked.

"Not till after the first of the year—if we can find her, that is. Andrew is going with me. It'll be fun for us to go together, I think. Oh, and by the way, I bought a new car! Brand new in fact. Dad wouldn't approve, I know, but it's what I want. I really like it."

"That's great news. We all miss you," Tom said, and she knew he meant it.

They talked a little more about Dee, and Tom filled Rebekah in on the latest about Ruth, who was the same, and their brothers. Ben was doing great in Green Bay and came home to see them every three or four weeks to help out with their mom. Tom missed him at the repair shop, but Tom understood that they all needed to be happy.

When they were off the phone, Rebekah thought about all that had happened in the past year and where she was now; she could hardly believe it. Despite the chaos and grief, she felt herself emerging from the fog and—slowly—making a new way. Of course, the lottery money helped. It made her feel secure and gave her the means to live any kind of life she wanted.

She couldn't believe the path she'd been led down and how now that path had her looking forward to her first road trip out of the state of Wisconsin. Who knew what she'd do or where she'd go next? And her dream of opening a bakery felt more real every day.

Chapter 26

The sign in front of her said: WELCOME TO ILLINOIS. It was January 15, and Rebekah had just crossed the Wisconsin border. For her, it was an important day. Andrew turned to look at her briefly as he drove her car steadily down the highway.

"You're on the verge of becoming a woman of the world, Mom," he laughed. "Next it'll be Europe! Would you like to go there? Maybe France or England? You can afford it. Let's get you a passport so you can go anywhere you want if you get the urge. It's good to have one as a second ID also."

"Son, I'm going to stick with this trip right now and not make any more plans for the time being. In the past year, I've learned to live in the moment and no further. That's my story, and I'm sticking to it. But I'll think about the passport and let you know," Rebekah responded and smiled as she looked once more at the road ahead of her.

This was going to be a nice trip with Andrew. He wasn't sure exactly what he wanted to do with the business degree he'd just received, and she hoped getting away might give him some time and space to decide. At the moment, though, she wanted to hear about his and James's trip to visit their dad in Canada.

Ethan had insisted the boys come for Christmas. Rebekah figured it was more likely that Emily wanted them there. The boys both said they needed to stay in Milwaukee, especially since Rebekah had decided she wasn't going back up north to spend the holiday with her siblings and mom. Finally, to appease their dad, they'd agreed to head up to Canada after the first of the year. They had just gotten home two days before the planned trip to Asheville, so Rebekah hadn't yet gotten the scoop. This was her chance.

"Hey, tell me more about your visit to see your dad. We've been so busy getting ready for our trip, and you haven't said much," she said, both eager and nervous about what he may tell her.

"Well," he hesitated, "it was … different. I know Emily is my birth mother, but I just can't connect with her. I feel kind of guilty about that and so does James. She's nice enough but a little on the odd side. Dad sure has a different personality around her than he did with us growing up. He used to love telling us what we should be doing and passing judgment. Now Emily does that to him, and he doesn't say a word. It's not like him at all."

Rebekah turned her head to look out the window. She felt a little guilty because she didn't sympathize at all with Ethan. That normally was not in her nature, but he was getting what he deserved. Andrew continued, and she turned back.

"We were very uncomfortable and couldn't wait to come home. Let's just say we did our duty. It's not that I don't love Dad—I do, but I don't feel I have any connection with him. Never really had one, I guess. Don't get me wrong—I appreciate him providing a good life for us. He was just always busy with his church stuff. But I'm happy we have you, Mom," Andrew said and squeezed her hand briefly.

Rebekah was happy to have the boys also. They warmed her heart and gave her a reason to keep going. She was glad they'd been able to see their dad, though by no means would she go out of her way to encourage them to see him again, nor would she make them feel it was their "duty." They were old enough to know what they wanted.

She rested her head as she looked out the window. They would be going through five states, including their final destination. Andrew had suggested they do the trip in two days—or three if she had somewhere she'd like to stop along the way.

Rebekah just wanted to get to Asheville and meet Rose. She'd read up on the state and found it had not only mountains to offer but also beaches—and everything in between. She would love to go to the beach. She'd noted that Asheville was nestled within the Blue Ridge Mountains. After having spent her whole life in the flatlands of Wisconsin, Rebekah couldn't imagine what it would be like in the mountains. She knew Asheville still received snow in the winter, so how did people drive on the hills without sliding everywhere? Since it was January, Rebekah guessed she and Andrew might find out. They hadn't decided exactly how long they were going to stay because they didn't really know what to expect, but they figured they'd be there at least a week.

Larry hadn't found any information about Rose until almost the end of November. He'd had a hard time getting in touch with Lois Bender, Rose's guardian. When he had finally reached her, Lois felt she needed to talk to Rose first and see if she even wanted to meet with Rebekah. Finally, she'd called Larry back to say she thought it was a good idea, and so it was set.

Surprisingly, Rose had decided to go back to her birth name after Dee died but kept the last name Tucker because it was easier to pronounce than Boulanger. Rebekah could relate; it was the same reason she was still a Hayward.

Lois had called Rebekah to see when she planned to come to Asheville and invited her to dinner at her home with Rose. They eagerly accepted, and Andrew found a house to rent for the week. Rebekah liked that idea better than a hotel because then, perhaps, they could have Rose and Lois over as well.

She wondered why Rose hadn't called them herself. *Well,* thought Rebekah, *she is twenty years old and probably consumed with her life.* Still, Rebekah would have felt better about the meeting had Lois mentioned any excitement on Rose's part, but she hadn't heard as much. Time would tell, she supposed.

"Whatcha thinking about, Mom?" Andrew broke her train of thought.

"What? Oh, I was just thinking about how happy I'll be when we meet Rose. Grandma said Rose looked like me as a baby, but babies grow up, of course. The whole thing's making me nervous, though."

"Yeah, me too. Do you know if she's in college or has a job?" Andrew asked.

"No, I haven't any idea. Larry said Lois didn't volunteer much. Might be better that way because then there's not much expectation on how she should be," Rebekah said, wanting to convince herself.

"I guess," Andrew said.

She wanted to change the subject. "So how long do you think before your brother asks Violet to marry him?" Rebekah asked Andrew.

"I've got my money on by the end of this year. How about you?" he asked her.

"I think the same. I wonder if your dad and Emily will come to the wedding. They'll have to be invited. It's going to be awkward, for sure. At least the wedding will probably be in Milwaukee. Or maybe they'll decide to have a destination wedding, and then the people attending will be fewer, probably just family."

"Mom, you women are all the same. A lot can happen in a year. Why do you overthink everything?" he said, shaking his head.

"And you think you know so much about women," she countered, poking him in the ribs.

They both laughed.

The two shared a quiet companionship for the day's ride, occasionally pointing out interesting sites and signs along the interstate, and finally decided to stop for the evening south of Lexington, Kentucky. The next morning, their plan was to arrive in Asheville sometime in the afternoon, settle in at the rental house, and go that night to meet Rose and Lois for dinner.

Rebekah's stomach churned each time she thought about it. She felt like she was in another world the closer they came to Asheville. *People even talk funny down here,* she thought. *What if I can't understand Lois and Rose?* There she went again—overthinking. *No, no,* she reassured herself. *It's all going to work out fine.*

***

"So what do you think of the place we're staying at?" Andrew asked as they were driving to Lois's home for dinner. "Not bad, is it?"

"No, I had no idea you could just stay at places like that. And you know last night was the first time I've ever stayed in a hotel," Rebekah said, a little embarrassed to admit that fact, even to her son.

"I know, but we're going to change that. It's like you're coming into your own like James and I are, except you're in your midthirties. We're going to do it all together. You're just a *late bloomer*."

Rebekah gave him a sideways look. "I guess you're right, Andrew. I appreciate you reminding me." *A "late bloomer,"* she thought. Well, that was a nice way of putting it.

***

Lois lived in an established neighborhood that looked like it had been built in the late 1970s or early 1980s, given the architectural style of the homes. Her brick, one-story house had black shutters, white trim, and a lovely yard. "Well, here we are," Andrew said as he stopped in the driveway and put the car in park. "The anticipation is almost over, Mom."

"Hush," Rebekah said. "You're making me more nervous."

They got out of the car, and Rebekah led the way to the door and then rang the bell. She was looking at the cute brass pineapple door knocker that read WELCOME when an older woman—most likely Lois—opened the door. She was petite, twenty to twenty-five years older than Rebekah, and had an unusual shade of auburn-colored hair. She was dressed in a multicolored sweater with slacks to match, and around her neck hung a pair of reading glasses on a colorful beaded chain that coordinated with her outfit.

"You must be Rebekah," she said with a thick Southern accent. "I'm Lois. Y'all come on in." She opened the door wide so they could enter.

"And who is this handsome young man?" Lois asked as they stepped inside.

"Thank you, Lois. This is my son Andrew," Rebekah responded.

"Let's go in here so we can visit." Lois led the way to a formal living room, where they took a seat. "Can I get you a glass of wine, Rebekah? I'm going to have one. Red or white?" she asked from the doorway as she headed toward the kitchen.

Rebekah had never had wine before, but Lois had offered no other choice. "I'll take whatever you have, Lois." *Good answer,* Rebekah thought.

"Great. How about you, young man? I'm guessing a beer," Lois said.

"Sounds good to me," Andrew answered.

"I'll be right back," she said and shuffled out of the room.

"Nice place," Andrew said, taking it in.

Rebekah nodded her head.

Lois was back in a few minutes, carrying a tray with two glasses of white wine, a bottle of beer, and a pint glass.

"Hope you like this beer, Andrew. It's from one of the breweries we have in Asheville. It's become a popular business here that attracts a lot of tourists. Most of them have public tours you can go on. Check one out before you go home."

"I will, thank you. We have quite a few small craft breweries in Milwaukee as well as some major companies," Andrew shared as he poured the beer into the glass.

"I've heard that you folks from Wisconsin are partial to beer and the Green Bay Packers. Is that true for you?" Lois smiled at Andrew and took a drink of her wine.

"Does the sun shine?" Andrew asked, smiled and took a big swig of beer. "This is good," he said, his eyes widening as he lifted the glass to look at it.

They all laughed. Rebekah knew she was going to like Lois Bender.

They visited for a while longer. Rose still hadn't made an appearance. Rebekah wasn't sure how to ask, so she decided to broach the subject.

"I was wondering if Rose was going to be joining us tonight?" Rebekah asked, feeling awkward.

"Well, one never knows with her. A little unpredictable. Let me go call her and see. I'll be right back," Lois said and left the room.

"I thought Rose would be here tonight, didn't you, Mom?" Andrew whispered.

"That was what I understood," Rebekah answered. "Oh, here comes Lois."

"She didn't answer, so we'll eat without her, I guess," Lois said, seemingly unconcerned.

Lois led the way to her formal dining room that had been beautifully set for four people. They sat down, and Lois brought in a big bowl of salad, some kind of grilled, marinated chicken breasts, and a basket of bread.

"I like to bless my food, so if y'all will bow your heads." She waited a moment as they obliged. "Heavenly Father, please bless this food we are about to partake in. Amen. I like it short and to the point." Lois winked as she passed the salad. "So where do y'all go to church up there in Wisconsin? Sarah—or *Dee*—told me your parents were Fundamentalist, but I wonder if you followed them on that path," Lois inquired as she opened her napkin and placed it in her lap before looking up.

"My dad actually was the minister at the church Dee grew up in ..." Andrew shared, catching a look from his mother, "... but not anymore."

Rebekah wanted to kick him under the table.

Lois looked at Rebekah. "So you're married to a minister, but he's not a minister there anymore?" she said and took a long sip of her wine, waiting for a good story.

How should Rebekah respond to this? "It's a long story, but no. We're not married anymore."

"So you're divorced then?"

Lois wasn't going to stop.

"Like I said, it's a long story. And not one for tonight," Rebekah said as politely but firmly as she could.

"I see," Lois said, raising her eyebrows and giving Rebekah a smile. "Maybe you can tell me about it another time."

This woman is shrewd, Rebekah thought. "Yes, another time," she said before changing the subject. "So tell me about yourself and how you met my sister." Rebekah figured this would take some time, and Lois wouldn't come back to her marriage.

"I've lived in Asheville a good part of my adult life," she said as she tore off a piece of bread. "My husband opened a clothing store in downtown Asheville about thirty years or so ago; it sold men's suits and casual clothes, then eventually expanded over the years to carry women's clothing also.

"We bought the building our store was in ten years after we opened, which was a smart move on our part. Like many of the old buildings around here, it had an apartment above the store that we remodeled and rented out. A nice little extra income. I helped out in the store when I could. We have two children—a boy and a girl—who are grown and living in other parts of the country, building their careers with no interest in retail *or* starting families," she said, raising her brows and waving her hand.

"My husband died about six months before your sister showed up one day, interested in renting the apartment. I found out she also needed a job, so I hired her. Worked out well for Dee because she was just downstairs if Rose needed her." Lois leaned back and took a few sips of wine.

"It sounds like it was meant to be," Rebekah interjected.

"It sure was in so many ways. Sarah—sorry, *Dee*—was a hard worker. Over time, we became close, and she confided in me what had happened to her from when your parents turned her out up until she acquired her new identity. That girl was strong. She and Rose, who we called Anna at that time, were a team." Lois looked at Rebekah with a softness in her eyes before continuing. "They only had each other."

She took another long, slow drink of wine, finishing the glass and pouring herself some more. "Then I got an early phone call one morning from Rose. Her mom wasn't breathing. I immediately called 911 and flew over to the store. The paramedics were there when I arrived and had already pronounced her dead. They told us there would be an autopsy. That's when we found out she had a brain aneurysm."

Rebekah lowered her head, focusing her eyes on her plate.

"After that, Rose took her real name back, saying that's who she really was—not Anna. Then, to my surprise, we learned your sister had named me as Rose's guardian. I wasn't prepared for that, but it was only for two years. And now, as you know, it's been four years since your sister left us. I don't believe Rose will ever get past her mom's death.

Rebekah looked back up at Lois and just happened to see a lone tear in the corner of her eye before it was quickly wiped away.

"When I found out about you coming here, I thought it might help Rose. You know, so she can find her people and know she belongs somewhere. We all want to belong, especially a twenty-year-old girl."

That's so true, Rebekah thought. She had been in the same position herself ever since Ethan's deception was revealed, but poor Rose had been there for years.

"Does Rose go to school or have a job?" Andrew asked.

"No school," Lois shook her head, "but she does work part-time for me and at the Biltmore Estate in one of the shops there. Have you heard of it? Y'all just have to go while you're here. I insist. Rose still lives with me. She's been back to that apartment above the store only a few times since her mom died but not in years. I haven't rented it out since. I don't want to hassle with it after having such an easy tenant as your sister," Lois said, somewhat thoughtful.

"I can understand that," Rebekah said, remembering her reluctance to go back to the parsonage for her belongings. Good memories turned bad.

"Can you?" Lois asked. This caught Rebekah's attention, and Lois looked deep into her eyes over the rim of her wine glass as if she were reading Rebekah's mind. "Yes, I see you can."

Lois looked away quickly then stood up. "Now ... I have some pound cake with strawberries and whipped cream for dessert. Andrew, I could use some help. Come with me," she said, and Andrew followed Lois out of the room.

Rebekah got the impression that Rose was a troubled young woman.

Andrew came back with one of the most beautiful pound cakes Rebekah had ever seen; Lois walked behind him, holding bowls of sliced strawberries and real whipped cream.

"This looks beautiful, Lois. Do you enjoy baking?" Rebekah asked.

"I do, but I don't have anyone to share it with anymore. How about yourself?" Lois asked.

Before Rebekah could answer, Andrew did. "She not only enjoys it, she's an artist when it comes to baking and ran a bakery until last year. Her cakes, baked goods, and pastries could win prizes. Trust me—I've had them all."

Lois turned to Rebekah. "Really? I'm so impressed. Have you been trained at a French culinary school or something?"

Not sure what to say, Rebekah told her the truth. "Well, kind of. When I was a child, I learned at the hand of my French-Canadian grandmother, Mère. Before our family came to Canada from France, they had been bakers, so Mère taught me all she knew. The experience was better than any school I could have gone to. In fact, Boulanger means 'baker' in French. My great-grandparents came to the US to live, but their children wanted to do other things, so the family tradition ended. My grandmother's dream was that baking would live on through me," Rebekah said and smiled.

"That's beautiful," Lois said. "I hope I get to try something of yours while you're here. Do you specialize in anything?"

"I enjoy decorated cakes, but I love baking anything, really."

"I tell you, my favorite thing in the whole world is her lemon meringue pie, and then there's her salted caramel cupcakes, surprise cookies, and macarons … it's hard to pick, I guess is what I'm saying," Andrew expounded, obviously a fan.

"Well, you're going to have to check out some of our local bakeries while you're here and maybe make us that lemon meringue pie, which just happens to be one of my favorite things also," Lois said with great excitement and sent a glance and a wink Andrew's way.

"Well, sure, okay," Rebekah said and laughed.

Just then they heard a door close, and a young, slender woman about five feet or so with shoulder-length brown hair walked through the door.

Rose.

Rebekah's heart leapt into her throat.

"I'm happy you made it, sweetheart," said Lois. "This is your mom's sister, Rebekah, and her son Andrew."

Rose looked first at Andrew and then Rebekah. Anger shone in her eyes.

"You look just like her," she said and extended her arms at her sides. "So you've gotten your curiosity satisfied, I guess. I'm alive, see? You can go back to the north woods of Wisconsin and tell my grandparents—who threw my mother out—that I'm doing okay so they can sleep at night."

"It's not like that, Rose," Rebekah said, her jaw quivering. "We didn't know where you were."

"Whatever," Rose said and left the room.

They heard a door slam.

Lois had stayed seated the whole time. "I so wanted this to go better," she said and gulped down the rest of her wine.

"I wish you would have given me a warning, Lois," Rebekah said. She couldn't sugarcoat this. "I had no idea she was this angry. I've spent my entire life, from the day Dee left, wanting to find her. I only found out anything when I discovered some old letters of Dee's at my parent's house. I then hired a private investigator because I was so desperate to find them. I want Rose to know this."

"Not tonight, Rebekah," Lois said, raising a hand to signal that she was done listening. "I'll talk with her. Why don't you come by my store tomorrow? I'll be there in the morning to open at nine thirty and stay till noon. I'd love to show you my store and the apartment where Dee lived. Does that sound okay?"

"Okay." Rebekah stood up. "Dinner was delicious, Lois. Thank you so much, but I think it's time for us to leave." She looked at Andrew.

"Right," Andrew said and got up from the table. "Maybe we should help clean up first?" he suggested.

Lois waved her hand. "I've got it, but thank you, young man. You're a good one."

"Thanks," Andrew said. "And we'll see you tomorrow. Can you give me the store address so I can put it into my phone?"

Lois did, fetched their coats, and then walked them to the door.

"See you tomorrow and thank you, Lois. For everything," Rebekah said and the two women hugged.

When they were getting into the car, Andrew said, "Lois told me I could take home a piece of cake for a snack later. I'll be right back."

Rebekah shook her head and let out an exasperated chuckle as he took off for the house; he returned after a minute with a piece for each of them.

Rebekah didn't speak the whole way back to the rental house, and Andrew knew enough to not engage her. This was not at all the way she'd thought it would turn out. She was determined that if she had to, she would stay several weeks, if only to show Rose that she was loved and wanted.

She wasn't giving up yet.

Chapter 27

The house Rebekah and Andrew had rented wasn't too far from Downtown Asheville. Rebekah felt the area was reminiscent of a small Wisconsin town with its retro buildings—except on a larger scale and set into a hilly area. They spotted Lois's store, found a place to park, and walked up to the front of the building. Across the front of the store was a large sign in simple black lettering: BENDER'S CLOTHIER.

By all appearances from the outside, the store looked like it had stepped out of the 1970s due to the worn look of its block-lettered sign and the striped awning adorning a large glass window that showcased mannequins from another era. This sentiment was reinforced by the store's interior. Its brass fixtures were tarnished, and the clothing hung limply on headless plastic torsos scattered around the sales area. A bright yellow paint instead of the mustard yellow that greeted them would have been a better choice for the walls. Rebekah didn't doubt Lois was struggling.

"Hello, welcome!" Lois greeted them. "Hope y'all slept good last night. I sure did enjoy having you over. Oh, where are my manners," she said, turning to a petite, brown-haired, brown-eyed young woman with a friendly smile who was around Andrew's age. "This is Mary Sue."

"Hey, pleasure to meet y'all," Mary Sue said as she took a break from folding shirts on the table in front of her. "Lois has had nothing but kind things to say about you. And you're here all the way from Wisconsin. I've never been there."

"If you ever visit, I would suggest doing so in the summer," Andrew told her. "Right now, I don't think you could imagine how much snow we have."

"We get some here, but it never lasts long," Mary Sue replied. "Well, nice meeting you," she said, batting her big brown eyes in Andrew's direction and giving him a wide, lingering smile before going back to her folding.

Rebekah noticed how when Andrew smiled back, his face flushed a little.

"Mary Sue," Lois said, interrupting the moment, "I'm going to show them the apartment upstairs. Hold down the fort."

"Yes, ma'am," she replied.

"Nice girl, that Mary Sue. I saw her looking at you, Andrew. You got a girlfriend up there in Wisconsin?" Lois asked with a little smirk on her face when they reached the top of the stairs that led to the apartment.

"Um, no. I'm focusing on my career right now, Lois. Someday though," Andrew said, his face becoming slightly flushed again. He looked to Rebekah for help, but she just smiled.

"Well, here it is," Lois said as she unlocked and pushed open the door. "It's much bigger than you would think. The space is utilized well. Like I said, no one has lived here for four years. It needs some updating, but it's not bad. Three bedrooms, two baths, nice kitchen with eating area. Here's the sitting area, and there are the stairs that go to a patio on the roof. The way business is going, I may end up selling my house and moving in here," she said and laughed.

"So business isn't good?" Rebekah asked.

"No. I'm not the retailer my husband was. I learned a lot from him, but I'm just not feeling it anymore. Now," she paused, looked side to side, and pointed a finger at them before she continued, "this better not leave the room. I just turned sixty, and I want to retire someday. Tomorrow would be ideal, actually," she said, laughing at herself again. "So I have to look at my options and figure out my next move. Don't mean to bore you with my stuff, but that's the way it is. So what do you think of the place?" She extended her hand around the room as if she were Vanna White on *Wheel of Fortune*.

"Not bad," Rebekah said. The space was nice and indeed larger than what she had expected but was not kept up well. You could tell no one had lived there for a while, though most of the issues were cosmetic. They walked through all the rooms.

Dee's home, Rebekah thought as she scanned the room, hoping to find something that might connect them.

"Want to see the roof?" Lois asked. "Might be a little windy and cold this time of year, but I guess you folks are used to that. The door's over here," she said and led the way up.

It was nice. *You could even have a little garden up here*, Rebekah thought.

"Did Dee grow things when she lived here?" she asked.

"As a matter of fact, she did. Had some big containers where she grew tomatoes, lettuce, carrots, and some strawberries. Seemed to make her happy. She spent as much time up here as she could, or so I remember," Lois said.

"We always had a good-size garden at home that us kids helped with. I remember my mom often gave me a colander to go out and pick green beans or ears of corn for supper. We grew our own Halloween pumpkins too. After the blossoms faded away, we would all stake out the pumpkin we wanted and had a contest to see whose was the biggest by Halloween. My mom also canned a lot from the garden and made pickles. There was a farm down the road from us where we would go to pick strawberries so we could make jam, and we would even make applesauce from the apple trees in our backyard," Rebekah shared.

"Sounds charming," Lois said, "like a Norman Rockwell painting. I can see it as if I were there. No wonder Dee enjoyed it up here so much."

Rebekah smiled to squelch the emotions that were creeping up from the memory.

Andrew stepped in. "This is nice, Lois. I think it would be cool to live here. From what I see, the downtown area is thriving. They've done a good job revitalizing it. Lots of nice restaurants and stores. I just got my degree in business and could come up with some suggestions for you that might help in the store if you'd like." he offered.

"If only you had come around after my husband passed away. I'm sorry, young man, but I'm not interested anymore. I'll probably look at selling the building next year, but thank you," she said and patted his shoulder. "You did a good job with this one, Rebekah."

Rebekah smiled at Andrew. "I think I did also."

They went back down to the store and to Mary Sue, who kept smiling at Andrew.

She does *like him*, Rebekah thought.

"Andrew, I was wondering if I could impose on you to get some boxes down from a shelf in the back. It's just a few, but they're a little heavy for me. Would you mind, dear?" Lois asked.

"Not at all. Show me the way," he said and followed Lois to the back room.

Rebekah walked to the front of the store and looked out to the road. This sure was different than the small-town life she was familiar with. Cars continually parked in front of the store, then pulled out into the never-ending traffic that passed in front of her. She wondered where they were all going. On the other side of the street was a quaint gift shop, a pizza place, an olive oil store, and an antique shop. She stood, almost motionless, as she observed the people who streamed in and out.

It seems like a pretty good location for a business, Rebekah thought. She was imagining Dee running across the street into one of the shops, maybe to get pizza for herself and Rose, when Rebekah's mind switched to the present and the Rose she had met last night. Rebekah was at a loss. What was she going to do to win Rose over? She didn't blame the girl; Rose had moved all over due to her mom's job, watched her stepdad abuse her mom, took on a new name and life, and lost her mother when she was still a kid. Not many adults could handle that, let alone children.

Rebekah wished she could convince Rose to come back to Wisconsin and live with her. She had the money to pay for college or to support her niece in anything she wanted to do, though doing so would uproot the poor girl again. It was fortunate Rose had Lois, but Lois was at a place in her life where she wasn't prepared to deal with a troubled twenty-year-old—and Rebekah didn't blame her. Rebekah had to come up with something.

Feeling restless, she turned and walked back to Mary Sue.

"There must have been a lot of boxes," Rebekah said. "They've been back there a while."

"Let me go check," Mary Sue responded eagerly, but as she turned to go, Andrew and Lois walked out together, laughing.

"Everything okay?" Rebekah asked.

"Oh, it's fine, my dear. Your son was charming me," Lois said as she patted him on the arm. Then she asked, "How about you and I go to lunch today, Rebekah? Just the two of us? I have to be here till noon, so Andrew gave me the address of where you're staying. I'll come by and pick you up, say around twelve thirty. Andrew has volunteered to do a little handyman work at my house this afternoon. It would give us a chance to get to know each other better, don't you think?"

"I would enjoy that. Thank you, Lois. I'll be ready."

***

"I love this little restaurant," Lois said as the waitress seated them. "It's on a side road, so mostly just the locals know about it. Southern food, salads, soups, sandwiches, and only open till three," Lois told Rebekah.

"Sounds good to me," Rebekah told her.

Rebekah looked around the restaurant. By the looks of the old brick and the placement of the windows and door, it appeared that the building had been repurposed from some type of manufacturing facility. Maybe she could find an old building like this when she got back to Milwaukee for the bakery she wanted to open. That could be a good idea. When she opened her menu, she found some items she had never heard of before, like fried green tomatoes and shrimp and grits. She decided she would stick to something she was sure of—a club sandwich. That was more like it for today.

"Tell me about the bakery you managed," Lois asked after they had ordered.

"It was in Rhinelander—the closest big town to where I lived, which still is considerably smaller than Asheville—and was part of a gourmet grocery store. In addition to a full bakery, the store also had a deli, where you could buy meat sliced to order or grab a sandwich. There was a little café between the deli and the bakery. A lot of people would then get dessert from the bakery after their sandwich. I started working there as a grocery store cashier when I was sixteen and moved up to the bakery when I got married—" The words were out of her mouth before she could think. Lois would probably ask about her marriage now. *What should I say?* she wondered.

"Andrew mentioned you managed it."

"After a few years, I did. They gave me free rein in the bakery, so I came up with new and different things to sell and built a reputation for the store. I then got into cakes and was making wedding and special occasion cakes," Rebekah said proudly.

"And you learned all this from your grandmother you told me about last night? What a wonderful legacy. Dee baked occasionally, I remember, and it was always wonderful. Did your grandmother teach her also?"

"Yes, she did teach both of us, but I was more interested in it. Dee liked eating what we made more than actually baking it," Rebekah said and laughed.

They continued getting to know each other for a while and then, after a few minutes, Lois asked the question.

"So how long have you been single? Your ex-husband is a minister. That must have been hard going through a divorce from someone in the clergy," Lois inquired.

"Well, like I said last night, it's a long story," Rebekah answered.

"You also said last night you would tell me about it another time. Now's as good as any." Lois sat up straight in her chair and leaned forward to look Rebekah in the eyes before she spoke again. "Rose means a lot to me, Rebekah. After all, Dee appointed me to be her guardian, and I take that job seriously, even if she is twenty years old now. I want to know everything about you before you become an integral part of her life," Lois explained.

"Well, I guess that's fair enough," Rebekah said, knowing she would feel the same way if their roles were reversed. Last spring, after eighteen years of marriage, I found out that my husband was actually already married. He had a wife who he didn't know was dead or alive, and never took the care to find out for sure before marrying me. Andrew and James are his sons, not mine biologically, but they consider me to be their mother. I did raise them, after all.

"We learned their dad's secret last year when their biological mom showed up—that's a whole other story—looking for her husband and sons. Right now, the boys have distanced themselves from their dad. It's been a lot for them to take in. Maybe in time they will feel different. They're adults now and can do what they want. I love them as if they were my own and enjoy being a part of their lives.

"Now personally, I hope to never see their father again. I'm looking forward to a new start in life. That's why I moved to Milwaukee last summer—to get away from all the gossip." She took a deep breath, then looked Lois straight in the eyes. "I'm a good woman, Lois, and want more than anything to be in my niece's life."

Lois looked at her for a while before speaking. "Yes, I think you're a good woman, Rebekah. You understand I had to know."

"Yes, and I appreciate your dedication to Rose. I would do the same if the tables were turned."

After that topic was out of the way, the rest of the lunch was very enjoyable, and Rebekah hoped they would do it again before she went back to Wisconsin.

Later, as Lois pulled up in front of the house Rebekah and Andrew had rented, she asked, "Hey, how about I come in and see this place you're staying in? Looks kind of cute."

"Oh, it is. I feel right at home. My hope was to have you and Rose over one night for dinner," Rebekah said with a smile. Then, noticing her car in the driveway, she added, "Great. Looks like Andrew's back from your house."

They walked through the door and were surprised to see Rose with Andrew.

"Hi, Mom," Andrew said. "Look who decided to come back here with me."

Rebekah didn't know what to say. "I'm so happy you did, Rose," she said fully and turned to Lois who looked as surprised as she did. "Lois, and I had the nicest lunch and then to come back here and find you—well—makes my day," Rebekah said as calmly as she could without showing *too* much excitement for fear of scaring Rose off.

"Well, I changed my mind," Rose said, looking Andrew's way.

Andrew lifted his shoulders briefly and smiled at his mom.

"I realized how important it was for you to find my mom and me." Rose looked down at the floor and then up again before she continued. "Truth is, my mom talked constantly about you, Rebekah. I know it would make her happy if I got to know you better. I mean, after all, you and Andrew are the only relatives of mine I've ever met. It had always been just mom and me, so it's something I'll have to get used to."

Rebekah wanted to hug the girl but kept her distance. "And there's even more people you're related to who would love to know you as much as I do, but we'll take it a little at a time."

"Okay," Rose said and smiled slightly.

To Rebekah, that was as good as a hug. *Now what should I do?* she wondered. She hadn't thought that part through.

Fortunately, Andrew stepped in. "Mom, I noticed there's a gas grill on the patio out back. Rose and I are going to run to the grocery store down the road and see if we can find some bratwurst. I was telling her about how we love them in Wisconsin and thought we could do a cookout and have her and Lois over for supper. What do you think about that?"

What did she *think*? "I think it's a great idea. Let's make a list," she said and rummaged through her purse for a pen and scrap paper. "I want you to get what I need to make a lemon meringue pie also."

"I love lemon meringue pie," Rose said, eyebrows raised. "It's one of my favorites. Mom used to make it for special occasions—in fact I used to ask for it instead of a birthday cake. She would even stick candles in it for me. I haven't had a piece in years." Rose clasped her hands together, visibly excited.

"You're in for a treat. My mom makes the best one in the world," Andrew said and gave his mom a wink.

"What do you say he also picks up a bottle of wine for us, Rebekah?" Lois said with a Cheshire cat grin.

Rebekah looked up from the list and returned the smile. "Excellent idea Lois, but what kind?"

"Oh, we'll let Andrew surprise us." Lois turned and winked at him.

"Yes, ma'am," Andrew responded and left for the store.

***

The cookout was a great success. Much to Rebekah's surprise, Andrew had quite the talent for talking to people. She guessed she'd never noticed this before because usually James was around, running the show as the big brother and not giving Andrew much space. She was seeing a side of Andrew she'd never known he had and was grateful they'd taken this trip together.

It seemed the more she was around Lois, the more she liked the woman. It was kind of the same way she'd felt about Tammy; both of the women had strong-but-caring personalities and the ability to make Rebekah feel at ease and want to be their friend. *You can never have too many people like that in your life*, she thought.

And then there was Rose. All this time, Rebekah's dreams had included only Dee, the two of them reuniting and picking up right where they'd left off. The dream Rebekah had carried all this time in her heart was that of a young girl, one who never imagined, even as she became an adult, that it could have turned out any other way. Now she realized how her expectations had been unrealistic. She had to rethink and change gears—come up with a new dream, one that focused on Rose instead. One thing she knew for certain was she wanted be a part of Rose's life. After all, Rose was half Dee, and Rebekah would take any part she could get of her beloved sister.

Over the years, Rebekah had never thought much about Rose growing up into a young woman. But young woman she was—and a spirited one at that. The change in Rose's disposition made Rebekah feel that maybe, deep down inside, the girl had secretly been curious and longed to be part of her mother's family. Rebekah could only wonder and hope that Rose would want to get to know them better.

Tonight, Rose was an entirely different person than Rebekah and Andrew had witnessed previously. And who could blame the poor girl for being on edge? After all, she didn't know them from Adam. But Rebekah just wanted to protect her and be like a mother to Rose—if Rose would only let her. Rebekah was coming to understand that it would take time.

Then she had an idea.

Maybe she could get Rose to come back to Wisconsin and live with them in Milwaukee. She was sure Rose would like Milwaukee. Why wouldn't she? In fact, Rebekah could see Rose and Violet becoming friends. Named after two beautiful flowers, the both of them.

Rebekah hated that the evening was coming to an end. She and Rose were alone, carrying some dishes into the kitchen, when Rose spoke.

"This was really nice, Rebekah. I'm sorry about how I acted last night," Rose said, looking down at the floor and up again. "You have to understand my mom never spoke fondly about your parents. She felt deserted, and I guess that rubbed off on me. When I first saw you last night, all that anger came out. I felt bad after because it wasn't your fault and then—well I realized I was just projecting my anger onto you."

Rebekah could have cried. She wanted to wrap her arms around the girl but knew she still needed to give Rose some space.

Just then Lois entered the kitchen and broke the mood. "Thank you for a lovely evening," Lois said. "I never had a bratwurst before, but I'm looking forward to the next one. And Andrew wasn't lying about the pie! I'll dream about it tonight."

"Thank you, Lois. I'll be happy to write down the recipe for you. We're planning on doing some sightseeing while we're here but want to spend as much time as possible with both of you, so let us know," Rebekah said and looked at Rose as she placed a light hand on the girl's back.

"Just so you know," Lois said, "I spend most mornings in the store, so you can always find me there. Let's just plan on you coming to my home tomorrow night, okay? Go to Biltmore tomorrow. It's a Saturday, but the city's not that busy this time of year. You can't come to Asheville without going there," Lois told them.

"That sounds good. Will you be working there tomorrow, Rose? We'll stop and say hi if you are," Rebekah wondered.

"No, I work at Bender's on Saturdays," she said and turned a big, toothy smile at Lois.

Lois hesitated, then sighed. "Okay, you can go with them to Biltmore. But next time I need you to fill in—no excuses."

"Yes, ma'am. I promise. Thanks, Lois," Rose said.

"Wonderful!" Rebekah said. There was no containing her excitement this time.

They said their final goodbyes, and after she saw Lois's car pull out of the driveway, Rebekah looked up to the night sky, its canvas dusted with stars, and said in her heart, *I'm so happy there's a God in this world looking out for me.*

"I think everything turned out pretty good, don't you?" Andrew broke her thought.

She didn't answer right away but closed the door and walked to the living room, where she and Andrew sat down.

"So what did you do to get Rose over here?" Rebekah asked. "I know you did this. How were you able to change her mind?"

"When I went to the back of the store to help Lois with the boxes, she had the idea. She said since Rose and I are close in age, it might be good for me to befriend her. So when I went over to their house today. It wasn't for any handy man stuff, but just to talk to Rose. I was honest. I told her the whole story, but I didn't tell her about the lottery. Don't worry." He laughed. "I told her I couldn't have asked for a kinder, more loving mother. I did good, didn't I?"

"Yes, you did, Andrew. Rose truly has a different opinion of me now," she said, tearing up a little.

"Aww, don't do that, Mom. Hey, stop it. It's all going to be okay." He leaned over and held her as they sat a while in silence.

Rebekah couldn't even begin to explain the emotion she felt. For that matter, she couldn't explain it to herself. There were no words, only feelings going through her. *It's all going to be okay*, she repeated to herself. She knew there was an inner part that was guiding her; now she needed only to listen.

She pulled away from Andrew and wiped her eyes before she spoke. "Sweetheart, I know that I somehow need to be a part of this girl's life." She placed her right hand in the center of her chest. "I feel it right here. I'm going to have to figure out how to do that before we go home."

"I know, Mom. We'll do it together," Andrew said and held his mother tight.

Chapter 28

The more Rebekah saw of Asheville, the more she fell in love with it. It reminded her of back home, except it wasn't as isolated—or flat. She liked the fact that if you wanted to go off somewhere and be alone in the woods you could, but the stores, restaurants, and other conveniences were still at your fingertips.

The Biltmore estate was a massive, elegant residence of the George Vanderbilt family built in 1889. *This was the family's country house? What did their city house look like?* Rebekah couldn't even imagine. According to Rose, they held events all year on the estate, but the best was Christmastime at Biltmore.

"People get tickets for the candlelight Christmas evenings months ahead of time. Do you think you might like to come back here at that time of year?" Rose asked as they walked up the winding staircase to the second of four floors in the house.

"I would love to," Rebekah said, thrilled to hear Rose propose plans for the future that included her.

Andrew had decided not to go with them to Biltmore, saying it was "girl stuff." He was going to check out a couple of the breweries instead. This gave Rebekah alone time with Rose, and she was grateful for it.

"Maybe we could bring my other son, James, and his girlfriend, Violet, down here sometime. I think you and Violet would hit it off well. She's a few years older than you and just about one of the sweetest girls I've ever met. I don't want to jinx it by saying this, but I hope she and James will get married. Andrew thinks he may ask her by the end of the year."

"Well, they also do weddings here." Rose laughed. "Just about any kind of event you want actually. That's why I love working in the shops. Always something different going on," she said. Then her eyes lit up as she remembered something. "You know what you'd really love? The Grove Park Inn has a national gingerbread house competition every year around the same time. The place is fabulous. Keep it in mind also."

"That sounds great," Rebekah said and decided it would be a good time to find out how Rose felt about Asheville. "And what about the clothing store? How do you like working there?"

"Well." Rose bit her lip and cocked her head to the side, the same way Dee always had when she was reluctant to say something. "Lois has been so good to me and Mom. I work there mostly to help her out. Business isn't very good. I've told her she just needs a fresh new look and different merchandise; she sells clothing people coming to downtown Asheville are just not interested in. People go to the malls or outlet stores to shop for the type of high-end clothing she sells because they can get lower prices there. Truth is, she feels obligated to keep it going because of her husband. I've told her several times she shouldn't feel guilty about getting out of the business. I think she needs to sell her building, move on, and enjoy life. Her kids never come visit—I think because they're afraid of getting stuck with the store. They're actually very odd. I'm really all she's got."

Lois needed a sense of purpose. Rebekah understood that. What would Lois do if she didn't have the store to go to every day? Rebekah would have to deal with the same thing when she got back to Milwaukee; she'd spent her whole adult life trying to find Dee, and now she'd done it. What was next?

Rebekah and Rose enjoyed a nice lunch in the Biltmore Antler Hill Village and then visited the winery, which had been the estate's dairy farm when the Vanderbilts lived there. Rebekah had liked the wine she had with Lois, so she bought a bottle of wine for herself and one for Lois as well. She had never bought alcohol before and knew her brothers would get a kick out of this. Before they knew it, it was four o'clock and time to head home.

"I really enjoyed this today," Rebekah said as they walked back to Rose's car. "It was nice spending time together and getting to know you better." Then she took a chance. "Would you ever consider coming to Wisconsin to meet the rest of the family? Your mom has four older brothers who would love to meet you. Our dad, your grandfather, passed away this spring, but your grandmother is still alive, and I know she would love to see you too. You probably don't know this, but she got to hold you once, not long after you were born. Your mom met her somewhere far from home where they wouldn't be recognized. My mom only told me about it recently; at that time, she gave your mom some money to help out. You don't have to give me an answer right now. Just think about it, okay?"

Rebekah was hopeful.

"I will," Rose said. Then, her face puzzled, she asked, "Do you really think they want to meet me?"

"Oh, Rose. More than you can imagine."

"I have a question for you too, Rebekah. Why don't you move here? You seem to like it."

Rose had taken Rebekah totally off guard. "I do, but my home is Wisconsin. Believe it or not, this is the first time in my life I have left the state," Rebekah shared.

"Seriously? You'd never been out of Wisconsin before?"

"Never."

"You know, Andrew told me about your husband. That really sucks. I mean, how can someone mess with someone else's life like that? I think he should be in jail," Rose said and exhaled loudly.

"As long as he stays in Canada and away from me, I'll be fine," Rebekah said and knew now that she meant it.

"It's crazy that Andrew's real parents live in Canada, but he considers you his mom. Did you adopt him and his brother?"

"Well, no. Since their mother is alive, she would have had to give permission," Rebekah replied, a little taken aback.

"I guess that means he and I then aren't really cousins or related at all."

"No, not by blood. But you can think of him and James that way. After all, they are my sons, even though we aren't related by blood. We are your family." Rebekah turned to Rose and wrapped her arms around her, like she had been wanting to since she first saw the girl.

Then after a moment, she pulled away and said, "Don't forget, your mom and I have four older brothers with quite a few cousins who are related by blood to you."

Rose was thoughtful for a moment before she spoke. "That's kind of cool since I've always thought of myself as being alone."

"You're just going to have to come visit then, I guess, so you can meet them. I think you'd enjoy where I live now; Milwaukee has a lot to offer," she said, trying to stay on subject. "It would give you a fresh start. You could live with me and go to school if you came back with us. Is there anything you would like to do or learn about? I would pay for school if you decided to go."

"Why don't you just move here?" Rose said again. "I could still go to school. It would give *you* a fresh start," Rose said and flashed the same cheesy grin she'd used to convince Lois the night before.

"Moving to Milwaukee *is* my fresh start." Rebekah was not going to give in. "I'm not sure what I would do here."

"You could do whatever you were going to do in Milwaukee just as easily here. Maybe even better," Rose replied and laughed.

Rebekah knew she wanted to open a bakery—in Milwaukee. She had to change the subject. "Tell me more about North Carolina," Rebekah said. "I would love to visit the beach if we come back in the summer."

Rose went into detail about the coastal area, including the Outer Banks and the Carolina beaches. Rebekah was relieved to get off the subject of moving. She would have to find another approach.

***

The next few days were split between sightseeing and their visits with Rose and Lois, the time was going fast. The weather was cold but enjoyable compared to what was waiting for them back in Wisconsin.

Rebekah was at Lois's house one afternoon, enjoying a cup of tea, and inquired as to how warm the summers could get.

"Oh, they're generally pleasant but can get hot. Of course, we need air conditioning here in Asheville, but many places up higher in the mountains really don't need it at all. You'll just have to come back in the summer ... and for sure in the fall to see the leaves turn and, well ... the spring is beautiful also," Lois said and laughed. "You can tell every season is my favorite. I don't know how a person couldn't love living here, honestly."

Rebekah was beginning to agree with her. The area was like nothing she had ever imagined.

The next day, when Rebekah went to the kitchen to make her cup of morning coffee, she saw it: snow was drifting down lazily, creating a light dusting across the backyard. She had begun to think there was no snow in Asheville. After she poured herself a cup of coffee, she sat at the table next to the window so she could watch the snow as it floated down. This made her visit even more special.

"Whoa, look at that snow," Andrew said as he sleepily sauntered into the kitchen a few minutes later. "I was beginning to think they were lying about it snowing here. How about you?"

"I also had my doubts, but this is beautiful," she said, not looking away from the window. "So much prettier than our snow right now at home." Rebekah laughed. Their snow was dirty and icy and not nearly this pristine by this time of the year.

Rebekah yawned and stretched her arms. "Anyway, I don't want to just sit around all day. Lois said she and Rose will be working at the store till six, so I've got a great idea. Let's go for a drive and see what the snow's like here. I'm sure it's no big deal. After all, we're from Wisconsin—we can handle any kind of snow. And Rose told me about this Grove Park Inn I'd like to visit. Let's stop there for lunch," she said, unable to contain her excitement.

"Okay, sounds good to me." Andrew didn't need much convincing about lunch.

They had the best time riding around in Asheville's winter wonderland. The ground was warm enough that the roads were fine to drive on. They even went on the Blue Ridge Parkway so they could see the mountains and take some pictures to show James and Violet. The fresh snowfall was beautiful as it blanketed the mountains and weighed down the boughs of the trees that spotted the ridge lines. It was like nothing they had ever seen before. The pictures they took would never do the place justice.

The Inn was perfect as far as Rebekah was concerned. The brown, chunky, stone exterior and reddish, tiled roof that peeked through the snow made it look like a place one would find in Germany. The massive building's interior was like a little city with shops, restaurants, and the two biggest fireplaces Rebekah had ever seen; she figured they could each accommodate a full-grown tree. They ate lunch in one of the restaurants that overlooked the mountain view and then walked around the hotel.

"Let's stay here next time we come," Andrew said, reading Rebekah's mind and smiling as they pulled out of the parking deck.

"I could get into that," Rebekah said, knowing she could afford it, when her phone rang. "Hi, Lois. Sure. I'm in the car right now. I'll have Andrew drop me off. No, of course not, it's no bother. Sure, I understand."

She hung up and looked at Andrew. "Lois says she needs a friend right now. Can you drop me off at her house? She wants me to come by myself" Rebekah said, hoping everything was okay.

"Sure, Mom. Just give me a call when you want to be picked up," Andrew said and turned in the direction of Lois's house.

Lois must have been watching for her because when Rebekah arrived, she opened the door before Rebekah could ring the bell.

"Thank you so much, Rebekah. I appreciate you coming over so quickly. I have to talk to somebody. I have nobody I'm really close to that I can talk to about this." Lois looked as if she were on the verge of tears. "Come in my family room and have a seat. I've already opened a bottle of wine for us—here," she said and poured Rebekah a glass.

It's only two in the afternoon, but why not? Rebecca thought and took a sip.

"This morning I met a man at the store who said he needed to talk to me. He told me he wanted to buy my building. I told him it wasn't for sale. He suggested I take his offer now, because he knows my business is failing and thought he would give me a break. Said he figures it will sell for a lower price if I wait too long. He said it was 'just a matter of time.' The nerve of that son of a—" She stopped, her chin quivering, and broke down crying before she could finish the sentence.

Rebekah moved over to the sofa where Lois was sitting and put her arm around her. "It's going to be okay. I understand why you're upset. I would be also."

Rebekah looked at the wine bottle where it sat, nearly empty, on the hand-carved antique coffee table in front of them. She guessed Lois had been soothing herself before she got there.

After a few minutes had passed, Lois began to calm down.

"So, who is this man? Do you know him?" Rebekah asked.

"He's come by before, wanting to buy, and I always say no. He's usually very nice, but today he was pushy. Kind of mean. Maybe it *is* time to sell—but not to him. He gives me the creeps."

Something came over Rebekah. "How much did he offer you?"

"He said $300,000. I think it's a good price. We paid $65,000 for it back in the dark ages. I just don't know."

And then Rebekah heard Rose's voice in her head as if she were right next to her. *You could do whatever you were going to do in Milwaukee just as easily here. Maybe even better.*

The words were out before she knew what she was saying. "I'll buy your building."

Lois turned to her and stared, her mouth hanging open for several seconds. "Did you just say you'd buy my building? Is that a joke? You're just trying to make me feel better, right?"

"No, I mean it. I'll pay you three hundred fifty thousand dollars. Cash. I think it's worth it."

"Do you have that kind of money? What kind of bakery was that you ran in Wisconsin?" she said and let out a laugh.

"Will you sell it to me?"

"Well, if you really want it, yes. But let's say three hundred twenty-five thousand dollars."

"I want it," Rebekah said.

"Wait. No. This is too crazy, Rebekah!" Lois said. "What do you want to do with it? You must have an idea to make an offer so quickly."

"I told you about my grandmother Mère. She had always wanted to open a bakery, but my grandfather told her no. She told me she hoped I would do it for her one day. I told her I would, and I've thought about it my whole life. Since Andrew and I got here, I've begun to realize this is all more than a coincidence. Dee brought me here. It's my destiny."

"So you want to open a bakery in my building?" Lois asked, clearly impressed.

"No, actually, I want to open a tea house and bakery combination. I know everything about baking and will learn what I need to about tea," she said and smiled.

Lois's eyes widened as she spoke. "That's very interesting. My mother was English, an expert in tea, and she taught me everything she knew. Tea was part of every day, and in fact, we had high tea every Sunday at four o'clock. I'm believing your theory about no coincidences," she said, her whole mood having changed. "What's your family going to say?"

"I only really care about what the boys think, and they'll be happy for me." At least she thought they would.

"I want you to talk with your boys first and think about it a few days. You haven't been in Asheville long enough to know if you'll really like it here. People who open businesses these days research things for months and years. They don't just open one on a whim," she said, waving a hand around.

"I know it's crazy. But this is where I need to be," Rebekah said with confidence.

"Well, okay then," Lois said, and they both laughed.

A few minutes later, Rebekah called Andrew to come get her and told him the news as they rode back to the house.

"You did *what?*"

"I'm buying Lois's building. It's perfect, Andrew. I want to open a bakery, Lois has a building she wants to sell, and Rose needs some family in her life. I've tried talking to Rose about coming to Wisconsin, and she won't hear it. So I'm going to stay here. I have the money, and I wanted a new start; this is it." Rebekah was determined.

"You're going to have to let me sleep on it," he said.

"That's fine, but I've made my decision."

The next morning, Andrew told Rebekah he was behind her—under one condition: that he move to Asheville as well so he could help run the business. Rebekah agreed wholeheartedly. She was going to need someone with business sense to help her and who better than Andrew?

Rebekah spent three days "thinking about it" and told Lois she hadn't changed her mind.

Rebekah's emotions vacillated from anxious to calm, sometimes five minutes apart, but what finally assured her was Rose's excitement when she told her the news. The girl was so happy. At first her face had been one of disbelief—until it sunk in. After a minute, she threw her arms around Rebekah and hugged her like she would never let go.

The rest of the week consisted of making plans.

Since Rebekah was paying cash for the building, Lois told her attorney what was happening, and he started preparing papers for the store purchase. Then Lois went to work on a closing sale for Bender's Clothier.

Rebekah had decided to renovate the apartment above the store. When or if she eventually bought a house, she could rent it out like Lois had. For now, she liked the thought of living where Dee had. She needed that connection.

But where to begin? She could start the apartment renovation while Lois was closing down the business, then begin work on the store. Lois offered for Rebekah to live with her until the apartment was done, and Rebekah quickly took her up on it, figuring it would let her be closer to Rose. Rebekah wouldn't suggest Rose come to live with her; she knew it would be hard for her to go back to the apartment after all that had happened there. But perhaps time would begin to heal some of those wounds.

Andrew would fly back to Milwaukee on Sunday and stay there until the apartment was ready. So Saturday night, Lois made dinner for everyone. Rebekah looked around the table. It was hard to believe they had only been there a little over a week, and now this city was going to be her home. It hadn't sunken in yet.

"Mom, you need to start looking at contractors. Maybe ask some of the other store owners around you if they can recommend someone they have used," Andrew suggested.

"Oh, no need to worry about that," Lois said. "There's only one guy to do the job. I've known him since he was a boy, and my husband was best friends with his dad. He'll give you the best deal and excellent work. I'll have him come by and look at the apartment and store space, then get in touch with you, Rebekah. I would trust no one else."

Lois was convincing.

"Well, that sounds good. Thank you," Rebekah said.

Things were coming together nicely.

***

Rebekah had just dropped Andrew at the airport to fly back to Milwaukee. She knew she might have to go back to get some of her things, but then again, Andrew could always bring them when he came. The past eleven days had been a whirlwind. Her head was spinning, and she felt like maybe this was a dream she would soon wake up from.

Lois had given Rebekah a key to the apartment above the store in case she needed to check on things or meet with someone about the remodel. Since it was Sunday morning, the traffic was minimal, so she decided to go back and look at the place by herself.

She parked behind the store, where the outside stairs and entrance to the apartment were located. She climbed to the top and put the key in the lock.

This is the first place I will live in that's actually mine, she thought.

A peace came over her, and she felt a little emotional as she walked through the door, thinking about how many times Dee must have crossed that same threshold. Her sister had been here and now Rebekah would be.

It was so silent inside.

Rebekah walked from room to room, imagining first how it must have looked while Dee was there and then, how it would look after she made it her home. She came back to an old, dusty chair in the living room and sat down as she began to sob. What had she done? Everything seemed to hit her at once, and she felt herself let it go.

Forgive.

Forget.

That's what she hoped this place would do for her.

She had just begun to feel better when she heard a toilet flush. Had she imagined it? No, she heard the water running. Then the door opened, and a man appeared, tucking his shirt into his pants and proceeding to buckle his belt.

She froze in place. What was going on?

"Hey," the man said with a surprised look on his face. His voice was friendly as he pointed back to the bathroom. "I wouldn't go in there if I were you." He chuckled and fanned his hand in the air as he walked toward her.

Rebekah was so afraid, she couldn't speak or move. *"STOP,"* she finally blurted.

"Okay," he said and stopped dramatically. It would have been comical in any other situation.

Rebekah stared at him as several awkward moments passed.

"What?" he asked.

Rebekah stood up and slowly backed to the door. "I don't know who you are or why you're here, but I'm calling 911."

The guy looked at her and scrunched his face. "Are you Rebekah?"

"Yes, how do you know my name?" she asked and stopped before pushing the last number.

"Geez, Lois said she told you all about me. I'm Harrison," he said with his hands lifted at his sides, "The contractor? I do all the stuff around here for her."

Lois had never told Rebekah his name. She looked him over from head to toe. He did look like a contractor; he sported a navy-blue hat—worn backward—a red-and-navy plaid shirt, painter's pants, heavy work boots, and, behind one ear, a flat pencil contractors use.

"Oh, just a minute," he said and rushed back to the bathroom, returning with a tool belt. "Had to take this off back there, and I forgot it," he said as he buckled it around his waist. "Came to take some measurements and look at the wiring, HVAC, plumbing, you know. It's an old building, and I figured if you're going to remodel, you might want to update some of that stuff." Harrison paused for a second and laughed. "Plumbing seems to be okay," he said and laughed again. Rebekah didn't, so he became serious. "Okay, since you're here, do want to talk about anything?"

"Not at the moment. I was just looking around."

"Well, I got all the looking around done I needed to do. Here's my card, and let's say, when you're ready to get down to business, call me. Sound good?"

"Yes, let's do that," she responded, still a little shaken.

"Well, okay then," he said and headed toward the door, then turned around. "Oh yeah, I heard you're from Wisconsin. Don't tell me you're a Packers fan."

"Ah yes. It's a requirement for living in the state." Now she was getting annoyed.

Harrison opened the door and was halfway out before he said with a wink, "I'm a Bears fan," and then disappeared down the stairs.

Rebekah sat in the chair again. *What just happened?* she thought and scoffed. This guy was unbelievable. If it weren't for Lois giving this *Harrison* a glowing endorsement, their awkward encounter might have been enough to make her find someone else.

Rebekah walked over to the window; watched Harrison get into his truck. He looked up at the window; before she could get away, he saw her and waved. *Darn*. What else could she do now but wave back? She watched the truck pull out and followed it until it disappeared down the street.

She plopped herself back down in the dusty chair and looked around the room as she felt a momentary flutter in her chest. What had she gotten herself into?

LEMON MERINGUE PIE
Recipe courtesy of Claudia Leeflang

LEMON CURD
1 1/2 cup sugar
1/3 cup cornstarch
1/8 tsp. salt
1 3/4 cup milk
4 egg yolks
1/2 cup fresh lemon juice
2 tsp. grated lemon zest
3 Tbs. unsalted butter

1. In a pot, whisk together the first 3 dry ingredients.
2. Mix the milk and egg yolks into the dry ingredients then place over medium heat, stirring constantly.
3. When mixed well, add the fresh lemon juice and continue to stir until mixture is thick and bubbly. *Do not stop stirring.* The curd should coat the back of a spoon when it's done.
4. While still on the stove, add lemon zest and butter to hot mixture and stir until smooth.
5. Remove from heat.

MERINGUE
6 egg whites
1/2 tsp. crème of tartar
1/2 cup sugar
1 tsp. vanilla

1. Beat egg whites and cream of tartar at high speed with an electric mixer until just foamy.
2. Gradually add sugar 1 tablespoon at a time, beating until stiff peaks form and sugar dissolves (about 2–4 minutes).
3. Add vanilla, beating well.

PIE
1. Fill your pre-baked pie crust with the hot lemon curd.
2. Spoon the meringue on top of the lemon curd, making sure to seal it around the pie crust. The meringue should be mounded in the center.
3. With a spoon, fluff the meringue to make peaks.
4. Bake at 325 degrees for 20–25 minutes or until meringue peaks are lightly browned.
5. Let cool completely on a wire rack. Store in refrigerator until ready to serve.

CPSIA information can be obtained
at www.ICGtesting.com
Printed in the USA
BVHW031331270223
659294BV00004B/177

9 781954 614925